we don't lie anymore

USA TODAY BESTSELLING AUTHOR

JULIE JOHNSON

Cover design by: ONE CLICK COVERS

www.oneclickcovers.com

Subscribe to Julie's newsletter:

http://eepurl.com/bnWtHH

———

You should've known better.

———

*I have blisters on my feet from
dancing alone with your ghost.*

Tyler Knott Gregson

ONE

josephine

THE SPRAWLING STONE estate looms before me, a foreboding shadow growing ever-larger as the town car rolls slowly up the circular driveway. I close my eyes and focus on the sound — tires crunching against imported pea stone — trying to breathe around the sudden lump lodged in my throat.

I'm home.

A year away should've been enough to fade the painful memories stitched into the fabric of this place. But as the chauffeur helps me out of the back seat and carries my bags up the steps to the imposing front entrance of Cormorant House, I realize no amount of time will ever be enough. Not a year, not a decade, not a lifespan.

The scars here run far too deep.

"Will you be okay all alone in this drafty old place, miss?" my driver asks, a crease of fatherly concern marring his brow as he glances around.

My gaze follows his, taking in the familiar grounds. Weeping willows stir in the breeze, their branches heavy with early summer leaves. impeccably trimmed topiaries stand guard along the driveway perimeter, verdant sentinels in the night. The lawn is bathed in pale silver moonlight as it slopes downward toward the sea. Even from this distance, I can hear the waves crashing against the rocks, a melancholy metronome.

It's beautiful, but cold.

Colorless.

Like the dark wood of a grim fairy tale.

I take a bracing breath and turn back to the driver. "I'll be fine."

"If you say so." He whistles lowly. "Awful dark out here on the cliffside, that's all. Though I guess you're used to it, if you grew up here..." His cheeks redden slightly. "Sorry. Listen to me, prattling on like a fool. You must be exhausted after that long flight. I'll get going, now. Unless you want me to carry your bags inside for you..."

"No, I'll manage just fine."

"You sure? On the phone, Mr. Beaufort was rather insistent that I get you settled in safely—"

"And so you have." Smiling through pressed lips, I reach into my black leather YSL clutch and extract a crisp fifty-dollar bill. "Thank you."

His head incants in a respectful nod before he pockets the tip and walks back down the steps to the town car. I wait until his taillights disappear at the far end of the driveway before I punch in the front door access code and step into the vaulted foyer. My footsteps rap a sharp staccato against the marble floors. The wheels of my suitcase sing an ominous refrain in the darkness.

This house has always felt haunted to me, though rarely more so than in this moment, surrounded by furniture draped in white sheets, shadows pressing close at every window pane. Ghosts seem to linger around each corner — not the result of paranormal activity, but fragments of my own painful memories, hiding in plain sight.

A life I once lived.

A girl I used to be.

Leaving my luggage by the door, I move from room to room flipping switches, flooding the vacant mansion with light. Dust plumes in the air as I yank the coverings off the furniture, exposing a collection of fine-crafted antiques. Form has always taken priority over function here at Cormorant House — a sofa you admire from afar but rarely feel comfortable actually sitting on, a Persian rug so ornate you tread across with self-conscious lightness, porcelain teacups far too fragile to sip absentmindedly. There is no homey atmosphere, no comforting ambiance. Just a pervasive emptiness, creeping over your skin with clammy fingers.

The only warmth this place ever possessed was borrowed from the caretaker couple that lived in the small cottage at the edge of the property. Flora and Miguel Reyes — my personal space heater in the corner of an ice castle. In retrospect, I probably should've known better than to pin my survival on something so easily unplugged and relocated. I should've realized the people I once saw as surrogate parents were under no obligation to stay with me forever.

Still...

They could've at least said goodbye.

I'd be lying if I said it didn't sting, even after all these months. The glossed-over explanation my mother gave last summer did little to assuage my curiosity — or soothe my hurt feelings.

Miguel took a job opportunity back in Puerto Rico, Blair informed me blithely, barely looking up from her newspaper. *They're already gone. Packed up and left Cormorant House last month. Oh, don't look so sour, darling. It's all for the best. Now, eat your frittata before it gets cold. We have a meeting with the VALENT marketing team in twenty minutes.*

I knew coming back here wouldn't be the same without the Reyeses. I thought I could handle it. But standing in the empty kitchen without Flora's gentle humming to fill the void, without a quick wink from Miguel to spur a laugh... I realize the severity of my miscalculations. The gloom is all-encompassing; my solitude razor-sharp. It seems to cut at my ribcage with each breath.

Turning on the sink faucet, I gather my long fall of blonde hair out of my face, lean forward, and chug water straight from the tap, quenching my thirst in desperate gulps. If my mother were here, she'd be positively scandalized by my lack of decorum. Though, likely not as scandalized as she'll be when she learns I've left Switzerland — and my internship — without warning.

I didn't have much choice in the matter. If I'd informed my parents of my plan to return to Manchester-by-the-Sea, they would've done everything in their power to talk me out of it. To keep me in Geneva for another summer, working beside them at their organization, VALENT. I know exactly how persuasive they can be — given the chance, they might've successfully convinced me to push off my acceptance to Brown University yet again, in favor of a second gap year.

But I can't let that happen.

I won't.

It's not that the past twelve months haven't been good. Occasionally even *great*. Geneva is a gorgeous city full of history, culture, international business, art... and, most unexpectedly, love. Working with Vincent and Blair at VALENT, for the first time in my life I've actually felt like I'm earning their affection. They've paid me more attention in the past year than in the eighteen that came before. Combined.

But as good as things are, as happy as I tell myself I am... in the back of my mind, a stubborn little voice nags at me — wondering how I found myself so far from home, so far from everything I thought I wanted; whispering in the small hours of the night that this new life isn't one I would've chosen for myself, given the chance.

What about college?

What about fashion design?

What about your big dreams to start your own label someday?

Left unanswered, those questions have grown from a subdued buzz to a screaming roar that wakes me, gasping, out of sound sleep. The sudden claustrophobia of my circumstances has begun to weigh on me so heavily, some days it's difficult to breathe. To laugh. To do anything at all, except go through the motions like a robot on autopilot.

I need a break from it all — the board meetings and family dinners, the crushing weight of expectation on my shoulders. I need some space to sort out my own desires without thinking about what anyone else wants for me, and from me.

Not my parents.

Not the VALENT board of directors.

Not Oliver.

As if he's heard my thoughts, my cellphone begins to buzz in the depths of my clutch bag. I pull it out, staring at the name OLIVER BEAUFORT flashing over his picture on my screen — sandy blond hair, dark blue eyes, well-groomed beard. For a moment, I contemplate letting him ring through to voicemail.

He'll worry if you don't answer, I chide myself, connecting the call with a terse finger-tap. *Don't be selfish, Jo.*

"Hi."

"Hey, darlin.'" His warm, faintly accented voice blasts into my ear canal. "Home safe, then?"

"Standing in my kitchen as we speak."

"How was the flight?"

"Long. Uneventful." I lean back against the edge of the countertop. "I slept almost the entire way."

"I still wish you'd taken the jet. Absolute nonsense to fly commercial like a commoner when your parents own a Gulfstream, if you ask me."

I pinch the bridge of my nose. "I don't want to fight about this again, Ollie."

"Fine, fine." He sighs deeply, no doubt remembering the massive row we got into about this very topic before my departure. "I won't open a can of worms. I only want the best for you."

"I know you do."

"You sound tired, darlin.'" He pauses. "Are you sure you're all right?"

"Of course. It's just... being home after all this time away. It's an adjustment."

"I bet. Everything as you remember?"

"A bit dustier, but I'll manage."

"I thought you had staff on the property to deal with the upkeep?"

"We used to. They're..." I struggle to keep my voice steady as Flora and Miguel's faces flash inside my mind. "They're gone. They left."

"I didn't realize that. I don't like the thought of you being there all alone."

"I have a state-of-the-art security system, Ollie. That's all I need."

"Is that so? A security system won't keep you warm at night."

"Are you flirting with me, Mr. Beaufort?"

"Always." I can hear the smile in his voice. "You should get some rest. It must be late there."

I glance at the grandfather clock in the hall off the kitchen. Ornate gold hands inch slowly around its face, marking each passing second with an audible tick.

"Nearly two."

"Mmm." I hear the muffled sounds of keys jangling, a door swinging shut. I picture him locking the deadbolt of his luxurious apartment in Eaux-Vives, stepping out onto the quay that runs along the lake. Strands of his blonde hair catching the morning sunlight as he takes a sip of his coffee. "It's not quite eight here, but I'm already on my way into the office. I'm meeting with your father in twenty minutes. You know how he feels about tardiness."

"I do, unfortunately."

"He'll be in fine form today, seeing as his one and only daughter has effectively fled the country under the cover of darkness. I assume by now they know that you're gone?"

"I left a note."

He snorts. "Blair must be apoplectic. Should make for a lovely work atmosphere."

"I'm sorry."

"Don't be. I'm a big boy. I can handle whatever fallout your parents throw at me. You know I fully support you taking some time for yourself." He pauses. "Not that I'd object if you changed your mind and came back..."

I glance up at the ceiling, studying the decorative crown moulding. It, like the rest of the house, dates back nearly two hundred years. "I told you, I need a little time to figure out my next steps."

"How much time?"

"I'm driving down to Providence later this week to meet with an academic advisor at Brown and discuss my options. After that, I'll have a clearer picture of the future."

"A future that still involves me, I hope?"

I press my eyes closed. "Ollie..."

"Okay, okay, I'll stop pushing. I miss you, that's all."

"I've been gone less than a day."

He's silent for a long beat. So long, I think maybe our connection has cut out. Finally, in a quiet voice, he says, "I just... I want to make sure I didn't scare you away the other night... with the key thing..."

He trails off, clearly nervous. It's uncharacteristic of him. Oliver Beaufort is one of the most articulate men I've ever met. In the ten months I've known him, he's never once been at a loss for words — not the warm autumn afternoon we first met in a VALENT conference room, not the cloudy November evening he asked me to dinner after a late marketing meeting, not on New Year's Eve when he told me he'd fallen in love with me as fireworks exploded in a star-studded sky, the Swiss Alps providing a dramatic, snow-capped backdrop.

To hear him like this — fumbling for the right thing to say to me — stirs an uncomfortable amount of guilt inside my stomach. Silence blasts over the line, broken only by the background noise on his end — tourists laughing in the park, a tram screeching to a halt, the sharp beep of a taxi horn. I tell myself to say something, anything, to reassure him.

Of course my future involves you.

Of course I'm in love with you.

Of course I'll be back soon.

For whatever reason, my stubborn mouth refuses to form the words.

"Josephine," he murmurs into the receiver. His slight Southern twang, a remnant from his upbringing in North Carolina, tugs at each vowel. "Running away from your responsibilities for a little while is fine. I get it. So long as you're not running away from *me*."

"I told you, I just need some time." My teeth grind together. "This isn't about you — or *us*. It's about me."

"Okay, darlin.' Whatever you say." There's another long beat of silence. "Call me tomorrow, after you've gotten some rest."

"I will."

"I love you."

I force my teeth to unclench. "You too."

Only after I've disconnected the call do I realize my hands are curled into fists at my sides, so tight my knuckles have gone white.

archer

I CHASE the dawn out to sea, already well beyond the outer reaches of Gloucester Harbor by the time the sun makes an appearance on the eastern horizon. The ocean's surface is stained red as blood; the western sky still blanketed by a dense gray cloud cover. We chug northward along the craggy Cape Ann coast, headed toward Rockport and Ipswich. The steady hum of the boat engine buzzes between my ears.

Most people ashore are still sound asleep in their beds, but I've been awake for hours — loading barrels of fresh bait from the supply docks, refueling the diesel tank, repairing a few busted traps. The Ebenezer — the mustard yellow lobster boat rumbling beneath me — is older than I am, and her age is apparent in every fiberglass crack and paint-chipped plank. Even after all these months, I haven't fully sorted out her many idiosyncrasies.

"Put a little speed on, kid," a gruff voice orders from my left. "I'm not paying you to take me on a cocktail cruise."

"Wasn't aware you were paying me at all, seeing as my last two checks mysteriously got lost in the mail," I mutter under my breath. My left hand tightens its grip on the wooden steering wheel as my right punches the throttle into higher gear.

"What was that?" Tommy growls.

"Nothing."

"*Hmph*." He settles into the lofted seat on the port side of the wheelhouse, glaring through the salt-stained glass at the stretch of Atlantic ahead of us. "Got a big haul today. A hundred traps to check. No time to waste."

"I know."

"Glad to hear something permeates that thick skull of yours."

I mash my teeth together, trying not to snap at my boss. Not that he doesn't deserve it. Tommy Mahoney is as curmudgeonly as they come. A lifelong lobsterman, he's been catching sea-bugs longer than I've been on this earth. I wouldn't be surprised to learn his veins run with briny ocean water instead of blood. He's not quite sixty but after decades of grueling work, his body is that of a much older man — his back curved in a perpetual hunch, hands arthritic from overuse, hair white as salt.

You take from the sea, she takes back.

Tommy treats me like an imbecile half the time and ignores me completely the other half. I try not to take it personally. He's equally unpleasant to everyone who crosses his path. Most captains prefer to work with a stern-man — a grunt worker to order around, passing on the tricks of the trade in exchange for a menial wage. Hauling as a two-person team lightens the load; makes the backbreaking task of checking traps somewhat easier to bear.

Not Tommy Mahoney.

Word on the dock is that he's always toiled solo rather than subject himself to the pain of human company. He took me on last fall only out of pure necessity, when he finally found himself unable to keep up with the demands of the job. Most of the time we exist in grudging silence, carrying out our respective tasks without exchanging more than the most basic of words.

Slow up on the throttle.

Buoy off the port side.

This trap needs fresh bait.

Gulping from a warm thermos of coffee, my breath fogs the air. This early in the day, it's still cold out on the water — even in June. Lobstering does not favor night-owls. My alarm goes off at 4AM. I'm at the dock long before the sun has begun to creep over the horizon. Despite the dismal hour, Gloucester Harbor is a ceaseless hive of activity, especially in the summer months. As one of the busiest commercial fishing ports in Massachusetts, it's home base for hundreds of lobstermen.

Our comrades.

Our competition.

After all, lobsters are a limited commodity. There are only so many buyers willing to purchase at market price, and so many bib-wearing tourists willing to pay it. Some days the Atlantic coastline feels more like the Wild West — a lawless land of maritime desperados staking claims to tracts of sea.

Alongside us, a handful of familiar boats motor out the channel, each eventually branching off toward their favored fishing spots. A massive offshore trawler emits a foul cloud of exhaust as it chugs for the horizon, headed for deeper waters, its dragger-nets coiled at the ready on dual booms. Back at port, the first ferry of the day rumbles to life with a throaty roar, a lion shaking awake after a deep sleep.

We're circling the coast of Straistmouth Island when I spot one of the Ebenezer's buoys — solid black with a mustard yellow X on either side — bobbing off the starboard bow. Every working vessel uses a unique paint pattern to distinguish their buoys from others. A blue-collar coat-of-arms, so to speak.

I gradually ease up on our throttle and feel the boat slow in response. Wordlessly, Tommy takes my place behind the wheel. I pretend not to notice the stiffness in his hands as he adjusts his grip; the slight wince he looses as he settles his hunched frame into the captain's chair. Chugging the last sip of coffee from my thermos, I grab a pair of thick neoprene gloves from the gear box. Lobsters are feisty; you don't want to be caught on the wrong side of their crusher claws. And let's face it, after the accident last summer, my hands have enough damage already. The last thing I need is another broken bone.

Tommy steers us slowly beside the black and yellow buoy. Leaning over the rail, I use a long gaff hook to grab the submerged line and tug it aboard. My hands move on autopilot, feeding the saturated line into the electric pulley, flipping the switch to reel it in. The engine moans, straining to bring the string of traps up from the bottom. It doesn't take long — most of our traps are laid in the rocky shallows, about twenty or thirty feet down, where lobsters are plentiful.

When the yellow cage breaks the surface, I switch off the pulley and bend to drag it aboard. Inside my glove, my right hand spasms a bit at the effort. I power through the familiar pain with a grunt. Seawater streams onto my rubber boots, splashes onto the bib of my waterproof pants. Overhead, gulls circle the air with throaty cries, their beady marble eyes fixed on us, waiting for the right moment to swoop down and claim any tossed scraps of bait.

"How'd we do?" Tommy calls, dropping the boat into idle and walking back to join me at the stern. "Any keepers?"

"A handful."

Popping the top of the trap open, I lean forward to examine the contents. Several opportunistic crabs cling to the sides; I toss them back into the waves. Eight lobsters scurry along the bottom, serrated claws clicking at the air. An empty bait bag hangs limply at the back of the trap's parlor. With practiced ease, I check each lobster for size and sex, making sure they're legal. Keepers get their claws banded before being tossed into the aerator tank; shorts and shedders are released back to the wild, to live another day.

The last bug in the trap is a female — thousands of tiny black eggs coat her underside.

"Berries," Tommy barks gruffly, leaning over my shoulder. "Toss her back."

"I was planning on it," I say, annoyed. Even after months as his stern-man, he still treats me like I know nothing — just some dumb kid, reckless enough to scrub a pregnant female and get his license revoked.

Tommy scowls. "Don't back-talk me, boy."

"Don't micromanage me, old man."

"This is my boat. How 'bout you show a little respect?"

"How 'bout you earn it?"

His jaw tightens. "Watch yourself. Or I'll find myself another deck-hand to help."

"Good luck finding someone willing to put up with your crap."

We glare at each other as we trade barbs, but there's no heat behind the exchange. No emotion at all. It's almost perfunctory, as arguments go. Just another part of our daily routine.

Haul buoys.

Band claws.

Reload bait bags.

Bicker.

Despite our frequent clashes, deep down, I doubt either of us is capable of mustering the proper enthusiasm for a real fight. Frankly, mustering enthusiasm for anything these days seems an impossible feat. The apathy inside me is an unrelenting tide, strong enough to blot out everything else — joy, rage, fear, hope. Those emotions are the faintest of undercurrents, too weak to stir the ice water inside my chest cavity where a warm heart used to pound.

A loaded beat of silence stills the air. Tommy's dark gray eyes narrow on mine before he throws up his hands and turns away with a martyred sigh.

"Just reload the bait bag, will you? We've got more traps to pull and the day's wasting."

I turn to do as he says. The brief flicker of annoyance his words inspired has already slipped away like a stone beneath the ocean's surface. In its place, I feel nothing at all. Nothing but numb. But that's just fine, as far as I'm concerned.

Numb is better than broken.

———

I make eye contact with the bartender over the rim of my glass as I drain its contents, signaling for another. The whiskey barely burns going down.

"Slow down, kid," Harvey says, eyeing me sharply as he pours two fingers of Jack Daniels into my empty glass. "I don't want to have to cut you off again."

I grunt out an acknowledgment, already lifting the fresh pour to my lips. Harvey just shakes his head and walks away. He knows by now that any lecture will only fall on deaf ears. Not that he's wrong to judge me. It's my third refill. Deep down, somewhere beneath the buzz of Jack in my veins, I'm aware my drinking is probably a bit excessive for a Tuesday night — or any night — though I'd be lying if I said it was a rare occurrence. I'm one of Harvey's best customers. Almost every afternoon, as soon as I've finished my shift on The Ebenezer, I find my way to his bar.

Biddy's, a dark ramshackle dive on the fringes of the commercial docks, is the kind of place people go to disappear. Tourists don't come here. Hell, locals don't come here. The patrons are exclusively lobstermen and long-haul fisherman, reeking of mackerel, hands rough with calluses, half of them still wearing their rubber boots as they slug down cheap domestic beers and razz each other with the same jabs they've been trading for decades.

Tommy brought me here after my first shift. Sat me down on a weathered wooden stool, shoved a whiskey into my hands, then drained his own in one long sip. With no more than a nod to the barkeep, he slammed down a twenty-dollar bill to cover the tab and left me behind to drink alone. His version of bonding, I suppose.

Tommy never came back here after that first night, but that hasn't stopped me from showing up on my own. I'm certain the owner, Harvey, knows I'm underage, but Biddy's seems to operate on a strict don't-ask-don't-tell policy. In the six months I've been drinking at his bar, he's never asked for ID or hesitated to pour me a dram. To him, I'm just another dock-rat seeking liquid oblivion after a long day on the water.

"Hey," a beer-laced voice interjects from my left. Its owner is a ruddy-cheeked man in faded flannel. He's holding a Bud Lite that I very much doubt is his first. Or fifth. "You look familiar, kid. I know you from somewhere?"

Here we go.

"Doubtful," I say flatly.

"No, no, I'm sure of it." The man peers closer at my face, trying to get a better look at me. "Wait, I know! You're that hotshot pitcher, aren't you? From Exeter Academy."

"You're mistaken," I mutter around a mouthful of whiskey.

The man is undeterred. "My son plays for Gloucester High. He's total shit — boy can barely catch a ball — but I try to make it to all his games. Boring, mostly. Not that Exeter-Gloucester game last season, though. The way you threw... Never seen anything like it! Thought I was watching the next Roger Clemens."

Something is beginning to bubble up inside me, fierce enough to disturb the deep waters of indifference I've been drowning in for the past year. Something that makes my pulse pick up speed, the breath catch in my throat. It's been so long since I've felt anything at all, it takes me a moment to name the emotion.

Rage.

Pure, undiluted. It ripples outward from my chest into my limbs. My fingers tighten around my glass, clenching so hard I'm worried it might shatter as I lift it to my lips and drain the rest of its contents in one large gulp.

"So what happened, huh?" The man is still peering at me, oblivious to the sudden anger stirring my blood. "You playing college ball, now?"

I cough as the alcohol slams into my stomach, eyes stinging. Setting the empty glass on the bar, I push back my stool and lurch to my feet. With a farewell nod to Harvey, I toss down a few bills and turn for the door.

"Hey! Where are you going, kid?"

I ignore the man's slurred calls as I step outside, into the alley. Warm early evening air envelops me, thick with humidity. Squinting against the sudden brightness, I make my way down the docks toward town, trying to calm the storm inside me with each step. But the rage will not quiet — not as I climb the stairs to my crappy harborside apartment. Not as I flop down onto a creaky metal frame and listen to the sound of my neighbors screaming through the floorboards. Not as I stare at the ugly mess of my right wrist, angry red scars crisscrossing the flesh like the outlets of a river delta.

I press my eyes closed to shut out the sight. But the damage lingers even in the darkness. It swims beneath my skin, poison in my bloodstream. Some nights, I find myself wishing that poison was strong enough to put me out of my misery; to release me from the pathetic existence I eke out day after day after day.

I'm not suicidal.

I don't seek out death with any sort of real intention.

But that's not to say I wouldn't welcome it with open arms.

What use is living on when all your dreams have died?

THREE

josephine

THE BUZZ of the outer gate wakes me with a start.

Blinking, I groan as midday sunshine slants straight into my eyes through the window of my childhood bedroom. After a night of tossing and turning, I feel as if I slept only seconds before my rude awakening. Not nearly enough to stave off the jet-lag still infusing my limbs with lead. My bodily clock is six hours out of sync.

The gate alarm sounds again — an insistent buzz, demanding entry.

Who the hell is at my door? I can't help wondering as I push back my duvet with a frustrated shove. *No one even knows I'm back on this continent.*

Yawning wide, I slide out of bed and make my way downstairs. The dust is so thick on the floors, I leave a trail of footprints all the way to the atrium, like bare feet in fresh snow. I'll have to do something about the filthy state of this place once I'm thoroughly caffeinated.

When I reach the front door, I toggle on the exterior gate camera. An unfamiliar woman with gray hair pulled back in a neat bun is staring at me through the fisheye lens. I know she can't see me, but her shrewd gaze makes my spine straighten regardless. I tug the bottom hem of my oversized sleep shirt a bit more firmly over my exposed butt-cheeks before I activate the intercom.

"Um. Yes?"

Her throat clears. "Miss Valentine, I presume?"

"Can I help you with something?"

"My name is Mrs. Agatha Weatherby Granger. I've been hired on by your parents as the new housekeeper at Cormorant House."

I recoil.

Housekeeper?

Babysitter is more like it. I should've known Blair and Vincent wouldn't respect my need for independence. I wonder how long after they realized I'd left Geneva they started sending inquiries to potential staff. Mere seconds, probably.

"I've been waiting here for some time now," the woman informs me primly. "I was beginning to think the buzzer was broken."

"I'm sorry, I didn't hear it. I was still asleep."

"It's past *noon*." She sounds positively aghast at the thought.

"Right..." My lips press together. "I'm a bit jet-lagged. I didn't get in until late last night."

To this, she says nothing. She doesn't need to — her disapproval is so thick, it requires no words.

"Look," I say trying to keep my voice free of exasperation. "I appreciate you driving all the way out here, but it seems there's been a mistake. I'm not in need of a housekeeper at this time."

Mrs. Agatha Weatherby Granger's flat expression never so much as flickers. "With all due respect, I was not hired by *you*, Miss Valentine. Now, I would very much appreciate it if you would do me the dignity of admitting me inside, so we may discuss the particulars of this new arrangement in a more civilized manner."

I sigh.

God damn my parents and their insufferable need to manage every facet of my life.

Recognizing this is a fight I'm not likely to win, I jam my finger against the access button to allow Mrs. Granger's compact tan sedan through the outer gates. I rub my bleary eyes as I lean back against a nearby ceiling column. Only when the cool marble presses against my bare thighs do I remember that I'm not wearing pants — which is probably not the first impression I want to make on the frigidly proper housekeeper heading up the circular drive at alarming speed.

In a stroke of luck — or post-travel laziness — my suitcases are still sitting in the atrium where I left them. I quickly root through the topmost duffle, grabbing the first pair of jeans my hands land on. I barely have the waist buttoned when a knock sounds at the front door. Three sharp, no-nonsense raps in quick succession.

"Mrs. Granger," I say breathlessly, yanking the heavy oak door inward with one hand, brushing frizzy blonde flyaways out of my face with the other. "Please come in."

She steps inside — kitten heels clicking against the floor, purse held before her like a shield. Her lips are pursed in disapproval as her eyes sweep the space, lingering on the dusty piles of sheets I pulled off the furniture and summarily discarded last night. Her thin neck cranes to examine the crystal chandelier hanging overhead, its grandeur somewhat dimmed by millions of dust motes caught in sunbeams streaming through the overhead skylights.

After a heavy stretch of silence, those shrewd eyes make their way to me. My rumpled t-shirt, messy bed-head, and bare feet are all evaluated with the same stiff-upper-lip she showed the house.

"It seems you are, in fact, in need of a housekeeper, Miss Valentine," Mrs. Granger says slowly, as though speaking to a child. "Your former help left things in quite a state."

"No one has lived here in over a year. There was no need to keep full-time staff."

"Mmm. Thankfully the exterior grounds are in much better shape than inside. Your parents hired a landscaping company to care for the lawn and flowerbeds in your absence. As I understand it, the pool, tennis courts, and docks are being maintained once per week by a local man from the boating community — at least, until a more permanent arrangement can be made." The way she says *boating community* makes it sound like a backwater slum, unfit for association with Cormorant House.

"Great," I say tiredly. My head is beginning to pound. *Once again, Blair and Vincent have snapped their fingers and set my world to proper order.* My voice drops to a low grumble. "God forbid I ever do anything myself."

"What was that, Miss Valentine?"

"Nothing." I pinch the bridge of my nose with two fingers, trying to pull my thoughts into focus. "Do you have any luggage?"

"Luggage?"

"I assumed you'd be staying on the property, in Gull Cottage..." I manage to keep my voice remarkably steady, considering the mere thought of someone besides the Reyes family living in the small staff house on the edge of our lot makes my throat constrict. "I'm happy to show you the way there, help get you settled in..."

"Ah." Mrs. Granger makes to set her bag on a nearby table but, seeing the film of dust coating its surface, quickly reverses course. "The offer is appreciated but unnecessary, Miss Valentine. I will not be residing in the staff quarters during my tenure at Cormorant House — unless you are objectionable. My own home is only twenty minutes away, in Beverly Farms, should you ever need my assistance outside business hours."

Relief floods me. "No objections here."

"Excellent. I will be at your disposal from breakfast until dinnertime on weekdays. If you need me on weekends, you need merely inform me with three days' notice."

"I'm certain I won't need you on weekends. In fact, I won't need much help during the week, either."

"Yet you shall have it." Her eyes narrow — a pointed contradiction to her polite expression. "Given your proclivity for late-rising, I'm certain our paths will barely cross."

I bite back a less-than-polite response. My smile feels rigid on my face, more grimace than grin, but I maintain it anyway. Blair and Vincent drilled the importance of good manners into me from the time I could hold my head upright.

Mrs. Granger walks in a slow orbit around the atrium, mentally indexing every dirty surface and streaked pane. When her path crosses back to mine, she pauses only long enough to wrinkle her nose at my messy attire. "Will you be wanting coffee once you've dressed?"

"More than likely."

"I'll put on a pot. One would assume the kitchen is in as thorough a need of scrubbing as the foyer..."

"One can only assume."

"Then I won't dally. There's much to be done. But never fear, Miss Valentine, I will have Cormorant House restored to its former glory in no time at all."

This house holds no glory, I want to tell her. *Only pain.*

I don't bother. I merely smile my rigid smile as, gripping her purse tighter, she pivots on her kitten heels and walks out of the room with the confidence of someone who's been here a thousand times. Clearly, she doesn't need — or want — a tour of the house. I stand alone for a moment after her footsteps have faded out of range, as caught in my own thoughts as the dust motes suspended in sunbeams all around me.

Agatha Weatherby Granger is no Flora Reyes, that much is certain. Five minutes in her presence made it clear she's about as maternal as a feral cat from the Gloucester fish docks. She will not fold me in her arms after a long day, or hum Spanish lullabies under her breath while she goes about her work, or make me my favorite chicken stew when I'm under the weather. She will not take one look at me and know, without words, how I'm feeling, what I'm thinking, and exactly how to fix it.

She will not be the mother I never had.

This feels intentional — a calculated move on Blair and Vincent's part, overcorrecting for what I'm sure they perceive as a mistake. I can almost hear their conversation playing out inside my head.

Josephine was far too attached to our previous help. Make sure to get someone cold as ice this time around, dear. Proper decorum must be maintained at Cormorant House.

Blinking dust out of my eyes — not tears, surely, for I have no real reason to be crying — I turn and head upstairs to get dressed for the day.

———

Leaving Mrs. Granger to her tasks without interference, I meander down the lawn toward the ocean, my leather flip-flops smacking lightly against my soles with each step. My pace falters as I round the final bend and the boathouse comes into view. I stop dead in my tracks at the sight. It's beautiful as ever — an architectural feat of stone hanging out over the water, housing my father's Hinckley. But I can't see the beauty in it anymore. All I can see are the ghosts of my past.

Two ten-year-olds sitting side-by-side up in the rafters, legs swinging as they pick out starry constellations in the night sky.

Those three bright ones are Orion's Belt, Jo. Do you see them?

Two twelve-year-olds learning to tie bowline knots with frayed dock lines.

Pretend your rope is a rabbit, Archer. Through the hole, around the tree, back down the hole. Pull tight!

Two seventeen-year-olds fumbling for buttons and belt buckles in the darkness, limbs shaky with lust.

This might hurt, Jo, the boy warns softly. *If it does, just tell me to stop.*

I trust you, Archer, the girl whispers back.

God, what a lovestruck fool I was. I handed Archer Reyes everything on a silver platter — not just my body or my virginity, but my brimming, beating heart. And he happily took it all... only to disappear from my life the very next morning with no more than a halfhearted goodbye scrawled in a letter he wasn't even man enough to give me himself.

Before I left for Switzerland last summer, I tore that letter to shreds and dropped it into the ocean, piece by piece. Watched the waves swallow it whole, disintegrate it into pulp. I couldn't bear to keep it — I knew if I did, I'd just wind up reading it over and over again, tracing the lopsided letters of his penmanship, seeking hidden meanings amidst his bland rejections.

Unfortunately, destroying the note didn't make a damn bit of difference in the end. His words are burned forever in my brain, a painful brand I cannot erase. They play across my memory in a relentless stream.

Dear Jo, he wrote, with a stiff formality reserved for obligatory pen pals and awkward acquaintances. *I thought it would be easier to put everything down on paper, so there's no confusion.*

My pulse picks up speed, thudding dangerously fast as more words stream through my mind.

As soon as I woke up the next morning, I realized we'd made a terrible mistake.

I'm sure you realized it, too.

I shake my head vigorously, trying in vain to clear it. Trying to stop the words, but they keep coming.

I hope you know, I value our friendship so much.

Too much to risk it with something as meaningless as a hook up.

I close my eyes, trying to keep gathering tears at bay.

Have a nice summer.

My chest aches like I've been sucker-punched straight in the ribcage.

Best,

Archer

And that was it. I haven't heard from him since. Not a single word. No calls, no texts, no emails. Not even a damned snail-mail letter.

His silence speaks louder than any words ever could. His absence tells me everything I need to know.

He did not wake that morning in the aftermath of our love-making and feel joy. Those moments we shared in the darkness last June were not transcendent, effervescent, incandescent. To him, sleeping together was simply...

A mistake.

A regret.

An error in judgment.

I crane my head up toward the clear blue sky to keep from dissolving into a weepy mess. I told myself long ago I would waste no more grief on that boy. But, God, how can it still hurt like this? How can the pain of his absence feel as fresh as it did that morning when I woke alone in bloodied sheets, the scent of him lingering on my skin, my lips still swollen from the kisses he regretted in the cold light of day?

Deep down, I know the answer to these questions. Even after all this time... all this space... all this silence... my stupid, stubborn heart refuses to let go of the hurt it's harboring. Within me, Archer is a jagged scar that will not heal, a shard of glass straight through the fabric of my soul.

If he were someone else — anyone else — I might be able to forget anything ever happened between us. But I do not even have the luxury of forgetting him — not without erasing parts of myself. Until last summer, our lives were so thoroughly intertwined, it's difficult to separate the girl I was from the boy I loved; difficult to recall a single pivotal moment of my existence that did not also include him there, by my side.

There is no Josephine Valentine without Archer Reyes.

Bypassing the boathouse — and all the ghosts it contains — I jog down a short flight of stairs onto a private pier that extends out into a small rocky cove. My heart lightens as I catch sight of Cupid, my 20-foot red Alerion sailboat, bobbing happily at the end of the dock. It shouldn't surprise me to see she's been well cared for in my absence — the house may've fallen into dusty disrepair, but my father would never let the boats suffer a similar fate. I'm sure his Hinckley is ship-shape at its slip inside the boathouse.

Whoever's been caring for the boats seems to be doing a fine job — Mrs. Granger's snide comments aside. Cupid's dock lines are tied in neat coils. Her sails are perfectly rigged. Her wooden seats are freshly varnished. Her poppy-red paint is buffed to a lustrous shine.

Kicking off my flip flops, I climb aboard. The boat sways lightly under my weight as I move around the narrow cockpit. My sea-legs are out of practice — it's been a long time since I've been sailing — but the muscle memory of a million past days on the water eventually kicks in as I hoist the halyards and unwind the dock lines from their cleats. Taking hold of the tiller, I trim my sails until they catch the wind. Cupid picks up speed as I point her bow out of the small cove, toward open water.

It's a perfect summer day — steady breeze, minimal chop. I find my spirits soaring as I chart a southward course toward Salem Sound. The sun shimmers on the surface of the water, dazzling gold ripples so beautiful it takes my breath away. With the wind in my face and the sun warming my skin, I feel alive in a way I haven't for far too long. Alive and *free*. Switzerland, for all its alpine beauty, could never quite capture my heart the way the wild Atlantic manages with such ease.

My smile slips a bit at the thought of Geneva. I wonder how my parents are coping with my sudden departure. Likely better than Ollie, who's left two voicemails and sent six texts this morning alone, wondering how I'm settling in. I haven't yet dared check my email but there's no doubt when I do, I'll have at least one message from o.beaufort@VALENT.org in my inbox.

It's sweet of him, I tell myself, gripping the tiller tighter. *Not the least bit smothering.*

Most girls would be overjoyed to have a handsome boyfriend so invested in their wellbeing. Most girls wouldn't feel suffocated despite several thousand miles of distance. Most girls wouldn't look into the future and see two paths diverging in opposite directions — to the left, independence at

Brown University; to the right, an early engagement and familial acceptance at VALENT — neither of which she can picture walking down with any sort of confidence.

Turning into the breeze, I allow the fresh salt air to sweep those thoughts from my head. I focus on the present as I tack my way across the stretch of sea abutting Beverly. Soon enough, the Misery Islands come into view. Despite their rather unappealing name — credited to an unfortunate ship-builder who found himself stranded there for three miserable days during a storm back in the 1620s — Great Misery and Little Misery are both quite beautiful in a wild, uninhabited sort of way. Several other sailboats have dropped anchor in the cove on the northeastern side of the larger island and taken their dinghies ashore. Day-trippers, most likely, eager to explore the hiking trails and sweeping views of Massachusetts' craggy coast.

Rounding the islands takes up a good chunk of my after-noon. Before I know it, the sun is beginning to tilt toward the westward horizon. As tempting as it is to stay out another few hours, Cupid isn't equipped for overnight trips or rough seas.

There will be more sailing days, I console myself, steering begrudgingly northward. *As many as I can manage before I leave this place again.*

As I navigate past the tip of Little Misery, my eyes linger for a moment on a mustard yellow lobster boat puttering around the rocky shallows. The men aboard are too far away to see clearly — just two distant figures in orange rubber coveralls, one slightly hunched with age at the wheel, the other strong and broad-shouldered as he checks traps at the stern.

It's been ages since I had a lobster.

My stomach rumbles loudly at the thought. A full day of sunshine and salt air has left me borderline ravenous. Pulling the tiller toward my chest, I duck low as the boat executes a sharp gybe, the metal boom swinging from port to starboard over my head. With the bow knifing northward, I fix my eyes toward home, allowing the fair afternoon winds to sweep me along the coast. My mind is consumed by mouth-watering visions of a steaming lobster, fresh coleslaw, and a bucketload of melted butter on the side.

Focused as I am, I don't see the moment the young lobsterman turns from his task and catches sight of Cupid's poppy red hull cutting through the gentle swells. I don't see the way his face goes pale with recognition, or how his fingers fumble with the bait-bag he's holding. I don't hear the whoosh of air that leaves his lungs, or realize I've just set in motion a sequence of events that will change both our destines forever.

I'm far too focused on dinner.

FOUR

archer

SHE'S BACK.

The words replay on a constant loop, driving everything else from my head. Since I saw Jo out sailing last week, I've thought of nothing else. I can't eat, I barely sleep. Even whiskey can't drown her out. It's enough to drive a man mad.

The minute I saw the small red sailboat, I knew. Even before I read the name Cupid in golden letters on the hull. Even before my eyes moved up to take in the blond hair whipping in the wind, the slim shoulders wrapped in a thin cotton sweater, the small hand so confidently steering the tiller. Even before I felt my stomach hit the deck like a lump of lead.

She's finally back.

For a ludicrous moment, I wanted to go to her. To rip the wheel from Tommy's arthritic grip, blast the throttle into full gear, and chase her across the ocean before she vanished from my line of sight. But the cold reality of my situation soon slammed into me like a sucker punch.

If I went to her, what the fuck would I say?

There's no way to make up for what I did last summer. The

things I wrote in that note... the way I twisted the truth into an ugly lie designed to tear her apart...

I shudder at the memory.

With a few reckless words, I made her believe she meant nothing to me. That *we* meant nothing to me. A misguided hookup, better forgotten.

She must think I'm a monster.

Hell, I *am* a monster.

I shattered us worse than the bones in my wrist. No amount of time or space can heal that kind of damage. And if there's one thing I know about Josephine Valentine... the girl holds a grudge. She'll never forgive me. Even if I try to explain, to rationalize my thought process that fateful day when my world fell apart. Even if I tell her how Blair and Vincent backed me into a corner with their threats of jail time and family ruin.

Even if...

Even if...

Even if...

Evens and ifs are nothing but a fool's mirage, offering optimism where there is none. I find a shred of consolation in the knowledge that my parents are safe and financially secure thanks to the choices I made... but that does little to temper the agony of my own reality.

No scholarship.

No baseball.

No college.

No prospects.

Can you really picture Josephine in that future with you? Jo's mother Blair asked with such perfect bluntness, staring at me across a fluorescent-lit hospital room. *Do you really think she'd want you like this?*

You have nothing to offer, her father told me, staring at the cold metal handcuffs on my wrists. *You can't elevate her to the heights she deserves. You will only bring her down, into a life of misery and despair. And, eventually... she will hate you for it.*

Looking at myself now — the depths to which I have fallen — I can't help thinking they were right. The old Archer is dead and buried, his dreams with him.

Rest in Peace, you useless fuck.

I was once dumb enough to hope that if I simply worked hard enough, got good enough, pushed far enough... I'd finally be worthy of standing by Josephine Valentine's side. Not only as her friend, but as her equal. As a man she'd be proud to call her husband, one day.

That foolish hope evaporated the minute my truck flipped in that intersection.

There is no longer any possible outcome in which our orbits intersect. She is destined for a career as CEO at one of the world's largest global health organizations... and I'll spend the rest of my days hauling lobster traps, until my bones wear out.

She's back.

But she might as well still be halfway across the world, for all I can close the distance between us.

josephine

THE WIND WHIPS strands of my hair into my eyes as I race down the deserted road that cuts across the marshes. I press the gas pedal harder and shift into a higher gear, grinning as the convertible picks up speed. Though I'm a relatively cautious person by nature, there's no denying the thrill of fast driving — especially when I'm behind the wheel of my father's vintage 1965 Porsche Cabriolet.

The speedometer is inching past ninety when I hear the sound of sirens behind me. My eyes flicker up to the rearview mirror, widening as I see a police cruiser roll out of a camouflaging thicket of foxtails.

Shit.

I slam on the breaks and pull over, dust kicking up in a cloud behind me. The flashing blue and red lights never cease, even as the siren cuts off sharply and the officer steps out of his squad car. I flinch at the loud crunch of his approaching footsteps on the gravelly earth.

Come on, Jo.

Compose yourself.

Hands in the ten-and-two position.

Eyes downcast.

Deep breath.

And wipe that guilty look off your face.

The officer comes to a stop beside my door. "Young lady, do you have any idea how fast you were going?"

"Uhh..." I keep my gaze averted; I can't quite bring myself to look at him directly. "Too fast?"

"Damn straight." There's a long pause. "You privileged rich girls think you can rip down these roads in your fancy imported cars without any repercussions, huh? Putting community lives at risk for the sake of a cheap thrill?"

"No, officer! I promise that's not—"

"Save it." He cuts me off sternly. "License and registration."

"Of course," I murmur, fumbling for the proper documents in the convertible's tiny glove compartment. "I'm so sorry. I shouldn't have been going so fast. There's no excuse, I just—"

The sound of muffled laughter makes me go still. When my eyes fly up to the officer's face, I'm shocked to see it's a familiar one — my former Exeter Academy classmate Chris Tomlinson is grinning down at me, his eyes crinkled up with mirth. With the beginnings of a beard dotting his jawline, he looks older than the last time I saw him. More mature. Or maybe that's just a side-effect of the well-starched navy blue MBTS Police Department uniform he's wearing.

"God, Valentine, you should see your face!" He laughs hysterically. "I really had you going there, didn't I?"

"Just about gave me a heart attack," I confirm. "Thanks for that."

"Sorry. I couldn't resist." He plants a hand on his hip, above his gun holster. "You can put your license away, I'm not arresting you. Unless you'd like to head back to my place and test out my new cuffs..." His eyebrows waggle suggestively.

"Does that line ever work on the ladies, Chris?"

"You'd be surprised! There's something irresistible about a man in uniform. If you only knew how the women of this town swoon when I step up to their windows..."

"They're just trying to flirt their way out of a ticket."

"Don't ruin the fantasy, Valentine."

I tilt my head, contemplating him. "I didn't know you planned on joining the force after graduation."

"Dad's the Chief." He shrugs. "Police academy attendance was basically a birthright."

"Right. I forgot." My lips twist into a smile. "You always threw the rowdiest parties back in high school, but the cops mysteriously never busted them. I wonder why?"

He grins wider. "Those were the good old days. Been ages since I threw a good old fashioned Tomlinson rager. Speaking of — I'm planning a big BBQ and bonfire for the Fourth next weekend..." His eyes twinkle in the sunshine as he stares down at me. "You should come!"

"Oh. Um... I'm not sure I'll still be in town. But thanks."

"You never were big into the party scene, even back in our Exeter days. Haven't changed a bit, I see." He leans forward, still grinning. "I take that back. You're even prettier now."

"Are you flirting with me, Tomlinson?"

"Do you want me to?"

"No."

"Then of course I'm not flirting with you, Valentine. Gosh, can't a man do his job without being treated like a piece of meat?"

I roll my eyes. "My apologies, officer."

"Anyway, how the hell are you? Last I'd heard you were over in Europe somewhere, ruling the world with your folks at their nonprofit."

"I don't know about the *ruling the world* part." I scoff. "But you heard right, I've been living in Geneva since last summer.

Glad to know the Manchester rumor mill is still running at top speed."

"You know the drill, Valentine. Everyone talks. Town this small, it's shocking I didn't catch wind of it the minute your plane touched down."

"You're actually the first person I've bumped into."

"Well, in that case, let me be the first to welcome you home."

"Thanks."

"Must be weird to come back after so long away."

"Sort of." I drum the steering wheel lightly with my fingertips. "Nothing's the same."

His brows lift. "Seriously? Figured it'd be the opposite. Far as I can tell, nothing in this place has changed since the colonists came over on the freakin' Mayflower."

He's right.

The town itself isn't different.

It's me that's changed.

"So, what brought you back?" Chris asks, curiosity plain in his voice.

"Would you believe me if I told you I just missed driving this car?"

"Actually, I might." His eyes are crinkled in good humor. "Downright criminal to let her rot in a dusty garage. Though in my new, official capacity as an officer of the law, it's my duty to suggest you drive her at a slightly more reasonable speed from now on."

I salute him sharply. "Sir, yes, sir."

"Where were you speeding to so fast, anyway? I think I've got a right to know if I'm going to let you off without a ticket." He pauses. "Though if you say you have a hot date, I might have to reconsider..."

A laugh tumbles from my lips. "Nothing nearly so exciting.

I'm heading down to Providence. I have a meeting with my academic advisor at Brown. They want me to decide whether I'm attending in the fall or deferring my acceptance again."

"And?"

"Honestly? I have no idea what I'm going to do."

"Miss Josephine Valentine, Exeter Academy of Excellence Class Valedictorian, doesn't know what to do? I find that slightly alarming. You always seemed like you had your whole life figured out."

"Guess I fooled you then. I'm just as much of a mess as anyone, I assure you. Probably more of a mess, in fact. Everyone else in our graduating class is out there chasing their dreams, making names for themselves... and here I am, right back where I started, unsure of everything." A note of bitterness creeps into my tone as Archer's face flashes behind my eyes. "But I guess we can't all be star pitchers who skyrocket off into the sunset, huh?"

Chris doesn't respond to my — I must admit — rather cheap shot. That shouldn't surprise me. He and Archer were always friendly during their days on the varsity baseball team. For all I know, they're still friendly.

Just because Archer Reyes left me in the dust when he blew out of this town, doesn't necessarily mean he did the same to everyone else.

The silence between Chris and me drags on, broken only when he coughs uncomfortably. Shifting his weight from one foot to the other, suddenly he can't quite meet my eyes. I struggle to interpret the look on his face — a mix of skepticism and... Could it be sadness? Perhaps I was wrong about them keeping in touch.

"Look, Valentine," Chris says haltingly. "About Reyes—"

"I don't want to know."

His brows lift. "What?"

"I don't want to know how he's doing, Chris. I don't want

to hear how great his life is, or which MLB teams are recruiting him, or how high his star has risen. I don't want to hear any of it. I can't." My words come out in a choked voice that sounds nothing like my own. Behind my eyes, the pressure of impending tears is growing stronger by the second. I take a deep breath, desperately trying to keep it together. "Frankly, after last summer... let's just say, Archer made it crystal clear he doesn't consider me privy to the intimate details of his life. I think we should keep it that way."

Chris' eyes are rounder than the buggy headlights on the Porsche. His face has gone pale beneath the blazing midday sun.

Great job, Jo. You've gone and made the boy uncomfortable with your emotional meltdown.

"So, you..." The Adam's apple bobs in Chris' throat as he swallows sharply. His wide eyes are riveted on my face. "You don't know, then. About—"

I cut him off. "How would I know anything about him?" A cynical smile twists my lips — somewhat undermined by the tears now leaking down my face. "We don't talk anymore."

It's the truth.

The painful, excruciating, unfortunate truth.

It's not exclusively Archer's fault. Excommunication is a two-way street. He might've been the one to walk away, but I'm the one who bolted the door shut behind him. Not just him — everyone from Exeter Academy. It was easier that way. Easier to throw my whole former life out the window than risk seeing Archer's face in the background of some snapshot on Facebook, or tagged in a video on Instagram by a loose acquaintance I forgot to unfollow.

It was shockingly easy to erase all traces of Josephine Valentine from cyberspace. A few minutes, a few finger taps on a smartphone screen. By the time the VALENT jet wheels hit the tarmac in Switzerland last summer, I'd scrubbed my social media presence completely.

A drastic measure?

Perhaps.

But in my eyes, also a necessary one.

I know myself too well. Given the ability, it would only be a matter of time until I caved to the impulse to internet-stalk Archer via our mutual acquaintances, or poured pathetically over old posts featuring our once-smiling faces. It was better to remove the temptation; to stop all association cold-turkey, like an addict entering rehab. Sure, the detox was a painful one. But in a foreign country with a new phone and an unlisted number, there was zero possibility of reaching out to anyone for an update on the great Archer Reyes.

"Look, Valentine..." Chris rubs the back of his neck, looking deeply unsettled. "It's not really my place to say anything about this, but I think..."

"No, no! Seriously, don't worry about it. I'm fine. I swear." I brush the wetness from my cheeks. Mortification churns through my bloodstream. I can't believe I'm crying in front of him. "It's been great catching up with you, Chris. Really. But I need to get back on the road if I'm going to make it to Brown in time for my appointment."

"Right," he murmurs.

He's still staring at me with that strange look. It leaves me unsettled. I feel like I'm missing something. Confusion and curiosity rise up inside me in a swift tide. The urge to ask what's going on with Archer is so strong, it nearly knocks the wind out of my lungs. I bite my lip to physically contain the words as I reach for the ignition key.

"See you around, Chris."

"Sure..." He blinks a few times to clear the faraway look from his eyes. "See you, Valentine."

As my tires begin to roll from the shoulder back onto the roadway, I glance in the rearview when he calls out one last thing.

"Those big signs on the side of the road with the numbers on them? Those are called *speed limits*, Valentine. Pay attention to them, will ya?"

I smile through my tears as I hit the gas pedal.

———

"Miss Valentine, I presume? Right on time. Come in, come in."

A thin woman in a camel brown blazer, tweed slacks, and wire-framed glasses ushers me into her office. The space is cluttered but cozy, with books piled on almost every surface and a perilously tall stack of file folders balanced on the corner of her desk. She grabs the one on the very top. I spot my name stamped across the tab as she flips it open.

"Let's see here..." Her lips purse as she studies the pages before her. "So, you've already deferred your acceptance for one year..." Her eyes flicker up to mine. "I assume you've spent that time productively?"

"I've been interning at my parents' organization, in Switzerland."

"That sounds very impressive. Tell me a little about your work there."

I know this answer by heart; I think my parents sang their mission statement to me in lieu of lullabies when I was a newborn. "VALENT is the world's largest health nonprofit, dedicated to eradicating food insecurity in at-risk populations across the globe—"

"Spare me the corporate policy speech, Miss Valentine." Smiling with closed lips, she pushes her glasses higher on the bridge of her nose. "I want to know what you did there, what

41

you learned, what the experience taught you. How it changed you. Or how it didn't." Her eyes narrow a shade. "Because, while solving world hunger is surely a worthy endeavor, it is quite a leap from your intended course of study here at Brown's School of Design. Or is that no longer a career you are interested in pursuing?"

My mouth gapes. "Well—"

"I assure you, if you've changed your mind, there are thousands upon thousands of other applicants who would jump at the chance to attend an arts program as prestigious as ours."

"I'm still very much invested in studying design here," I say, a hint of desperation in my tone. "It's something I've wanted for... *forever.*"

"Then why the hesitation in enrolling for the upcoming fall semester? I'll warn you, a second gap year is generally not permitted. If you defer again, you may need to re-apply from scratch — which offers no guarantee of admission. No matter who your parents are." She pauses tactfully, steepling her fingers on the cluttered desk. The few visible stretches of varnish are marred with rings — the imprints of a thousand past cups of coffee. "I do realize there was a rather generous endowment to our institution made by the Valentine family, so an exception could be made... but we are not in the habit of holding spots in our freshman class for students who don't genuinely want to fill them."

God, I want to evaporate from my chair. If I could disappear into thin air, rather than continue this conversation, I'd do it in a heartbeat. This woman thinks I'm just another trust-fund brat buying entry into her university, with no actual interest in academics. I fight the impulse to squirm under her unflinching gaze. My voice comes out thready with humiliation.

"I didn't know about the endowment."

"Mmm." She sighs. "Be that as it may, we are still at a crossroads here, Miss Valentine."

Swallowing hard, I try to gather my thoughts. "Whether I defer another year is not entirely my decision to make. My parents believe it's important that I get some real world experience in the workforce before attending school."

"Again, all I'm hearing is what your parents think is important. What's important to *you*, Miss Valentine?"

"No disrespect intended, Ms. Vaughn — but it's somewhat difficult to disregard my parents, seeing as they're the ones paying my tuition fees."

"Fair enough." She sits back in her leather armchair with a small squeak of springs. "Despite what you may think, I am not entirely unsympathetic to your situation, Josephine. I've read your file. I've also seen the sketch portfolio you submitted when you applied for the arts program. You're a very smart girl with a heck of a lot of talent at your fingertips."

"Thank you."

"You're quite welcome. Your parents must be very proud — I can see why they want you working with them."

My mouth opens automatically, '*Of course they're proud*' poised on my lips. But the words never make it out. Because the truth is, Blair and Vincent aren't proud of me. Or, if they are, they've certainly never taken the time to tell me so.

In the stretching silence, a worried crease appears between Ms. Vaughn's brows. "Can I be frank with you, Miss Valentine?"

I nod.

"I know how difficult it can be to go against the grain, or let down those closest to you. That's why I think being here, at Brown, would do you so much good. The independence you'll gain from four years on this campus is an invaluable asset." Her head tilts in consideration. "But at the end of the day, you're the one who needs to make that decision. Not for your parents. Not for me. For yourself."

On my lap, my hands knit together tight enough to strain my knuckles. "And if they decide not to pay my tuition?"

She smiles wryly. "Then you will come to me and we will see what we can pull together in terms of student loans and financial aid — just like any other student who doesn't have billionaires for parents. With your grades and test scores, you should qualify for plenty of merit scholarships."

"Oh... I'd never thought of that."

"Hence, our meeting." She pushes back in her chair and rises to her feet. "Take a few weeks. Mull it over. Make sure, when you come back here for our next appointment at the end of July, you've contemplated what it is you really want from your future."

Just like that, our discussion is over. With a hand at the small of my back, she ushers me out of her office. Before she closes the door behind me, her eyes meet mine one last time.

"At the risk of sounding like a cheesy inspirational poster... You have the potential to be whoever you want to be, Josephine. No matter what your last name is, or what company your family runs." She pushes her glasses up her nose with a small smile. "Enjoy your Independence Day weekend."

"You too," I echo dully.

After I leave her office, my mind is awhirl with contradictory thoughts. I wander aimlessly for almost an hour, letting my feet choose paths at random. I have no particular destination in mind, nor am I in any great rush to return to Cormorant House.

It's strange to see the picturesque campus so empty. When I toured this university on a bright fall day nearly two years ago, long before I sent in my early decision application, it was packed with undergrads chatting animatedly as they made their way to classes, sitting on picnic blankets in grassy spots beneath the elm trees. Now, in the interim between semesters, there are only a handful of students walking the brick paths that crisscross the Main Green, eyes focused straight ahead as they shuffle between the imposing brick buildings that surround me on all sides.

I try to picture myself in their ranks — a backpack full of books, my head swimming with new knowledge. Learning from some of the best professors in the world. A year ago, nothing seemed like a more perfect fit for me. But these days, nothing seems to fit. The future I had envisioned for myself sits on my shoulders like a cashmere sweater accidentally put through the dryer cycle on high heat — scratchy on my skin and uncomfortably tight.

Feeling more lost than ever, I climb back into the Porsche and begin the long drive back to Manchester-by-the-Sea.

I drive the speed limit the whole way.

archer

I STAND at the end of the docks with a sputtering hose in my hand, spraying fish guts from the deck of the Ebenezer. It's my last task before I can head home — or, more likely, to Biddy's, where I'll wash down the memories of another monotonous day on the water with a glass or two of whiskey. Tommy is already long gone — off to unload our daily catch at the fish market across town, his old truck sagging beneath the weight of a half-dozen crates of live lobsters.

My stomach growls loudly, audible even over the steady spray of water. It's only mid-afternoon, but when your workday starts before sunrise, dinnertime comes early. The contents of the cupboards back at my ramshackle apartment are sparse at best. Stale, budget-brand granola bars and some instant coffee packets — not quite the same as the delicious home-cooked meals Ma spoiled me with for the first eighteen years of my life. At this point, I'd sell my good hand for a warm plate of her empanadillas.

I'm just about finished with the hose when the sound of footsteps rattles my focus. I glance down the docks. A lanky figure in a starched blue police uniform is making his way toward me, whistling lightly under his breath. The sight of a cop makes my spine go rigid. My hands tighten on the hose. My shoulders tense. It's involuntary. Since my arrest last summer, I can't walk past a fucking meter-maid on the street without remembering the cold press of handcuffs at my wrists; the flat intonement of an officer reading my rights beneath the fluorescent lights of my hospital room.

You have the right to remain silent. Anything you say can and will be used against you in a court of law. You have the right to an attorney...

My tension dissipates somewhat when the approaching policeman waves at me.

"Yo! Reyes!"

Fuck.

It's Chris Tomlinson. The relief I feel that I'm not about to be cuffed and hauled down to the station is quickly overridden by the annoyance of impending smalltalk. But he's already spotted me. There's no avoiding him.

Sighing, I walk over the to spigot and shut the valve. The flow of water slows to a trickle as I coil the hose and hang it back on its rack. By the time I'm done, Chris has reached my side.

"What do you want, Tomlinson?"

"What do I want?" He shoves me lightly on the shoulder. "Are you kidding me? I come to say hello for the first time in months and that's the greeting I get?"

Our eyes meet. His are brimming with good-natured humor, but if I look long enough, I swear I can see the pity lurking just beneath the surface. An ugly sensation snakes through my chest and lodges in my throat.

"Sorry, but I'm pretty busy here—"

"Is that so? 'Cause you don't look busy to me. In fact, it looks like you're just about finished for the day," he says cheerfully, hooking his thumbs into his belt and rocking back on his heels. "What do you say to a burger and a beer with an old friend?"

I'm silent for a moment, my jaw locked tight. I know I'm being a dick. Chris has been nothing but good to me, both before and after my accident. Most of the guys on my old baseball team hauled ass out of town about five minutes after flipping their graduation cap tassels; he was one of the only ones who stuck around. Which, unfortunately, gave him a first row seat to last summer's whole miserable saga — from my initial arrest to the dropped charges, from my first surgery to the painful physical therapy afterward. Chris even helped me move into my apartment last fall when my wrist was still too weak to lift the boxes up the stairs.

Despite all that, the thought of sitting down with him for a casual meal is anathema to me. With my face overtaken by a thick beard, my skin slicked with sea salt, and my clothes caked with dried fish scales, I feel unkempt. Uncivilized. Feral as one of the cats that roam the docks after dusk, scrapping for their dinners with razor-sharp claws.

"Maybe some other time," I tell Chris, already turning away.

He waits until I've made it a handful of strides before his voice halts me in my tracks. "I saw Valentine."

Spine rigid with fresh tension, I pivot slowly around to face him. "What?"

"Valentine." He shrugs lightly, as if we're discussing the weather. "Josephine. Jo. *Your* Jo. She's back."

I stare at him, trying to keep my rising temper in check. I can feel the anger beginning to swell, ticking in my jaw like a metronome. "And?"

"*And?*" He shakes his head. "That's all you've got to say? I tell you the love of your life just blew back into town and you don't have a single question? You don't want to know what she said? Or how she looked? Which was damn good, by the way. All that blonde hair blowing in the wind..." He looses a low whistle. "I never really appreciated how gorgeous she was, back in high school. Couldn't understand what you saw in her that was so different from any other girl at Exeter."

Of course not, I think scathingly. *You were too busy trying to screw everything in a skirt to notice a wallflower like Jo.*

"Anyway, I thought you'd want to know she's back. Didn't get the sense she'd be sticking around long, though."

I say nothing in response. I couldn't if I tried. My throat has closed up, full of all the words I can't say.

Chris stares at me with exasperation. When he realizes I'm not going to respond, he throws his hands up into the air. "I don't get you, Reyes."

"Great," I say stiffly. "Can I go now, officer?"

His stare turns hard. "You know, the funny thing is... Valentine doesn't seem to know about your accident last summer. In fact, from the sound of it, she thinks you're living out your baseball dreams on a pitching scholarship at Bryant University."

Again, I say nothing.

His steely stare never wavers. "If you don't want to talk to me, that's fine. Maybe I'll go talk to Josephine instead. I've got a feeling she would *love* to hear what you're really up to these days—"

I close the distance between us in two quick strides and grab him by the front of his fancy blue uniform. My right hand spasms in pain as my fingers curl into the fabric. "So help me God, Tomlinson, if you say a single word to her—"

He shrugs off my hold, glaring at me as he steps out of reach. "Chill, Reyes! Christ, I know you're angry at the whole damn world — and Lord knows you've got every right to be, after what you've been through — but I'm your fucking friend!"

My breaths are coming too fast, sharp bursts of air through flared nostrils. "I'm sorry."

He nods. Reaching up, he smooths his rumpled collar. "Good. You can make it up to me with a beer at The Salty Dog." His eyes drift to my rubber fishing boots. "You got a pair of sneakers stashed somewhere on that rust bucket you call a lobster boat?"

———

Thirty minutes later, I take a large sip of my beer on the front patio of The Salty Dog. Across from me, Chris does the same. The waitress didn't bat an eye when he ordered two drafts of Harpoon IPA — evidently, his uniform was the only identification she needed to serve us.

"Cheers, mate." Chris clinks his glass against mine. "Been too long."

I grunt out an agreement and take another long sip. Frankly, I can't recall the last time I've patronized an establishment other than Biddy's. It's strange to be seated at this picturesque seaside cafe, with overflowing flower boxes lining the street, tourists and local families jammed into the wrought-iron tables all around us. The smell of fried seafood fills the air like perfume — fish and chips, calamari, jumbo shrimp.

My stomach rumbles.

"I like the beard," Chris says lightly, scratching his own clean-shaven jawline. "Grow your hair a bit longer and you'll look just like Jason Momoa in *Aquaman*. The women of Manchester-by-the-Sea won't know what hit 'em."

I snort.

"I'm serious! Our waitress was totally checking you out. Didn't you notice?"

I hadn't.

Chris laughs. "Of course you didn't. You never did notice anyone except..." He trails off before he says her name. His smile fades a bit. "Man, I don't want to bring your head down by talking about this stuff. I just think you owe it to yourself — and to her — to have a conversation. Maybe if you got a little closure you could move on from this... phase... you're going through."

"Phase?"

"Some would probably call it a major depressive episode. Not *me*." He holds up his hands in surrender at my scathing look. "Just, like, maybe... a licensed therapist. Or anyone with eyeballs."

I force a smile. It feels foreign on my face. "Better?"

"Worse, actually." He frowns at me. "I'm not kidding. I'm worried about you, Reyes. You haven't been taking my calls. Lots of the guys from our old team are home on summer break — we hang out on the weekends. You should come. Everyone would love to see you."

"I'm busy."

"Lobstering," he says flatly. "Right. Of course. The only thing you seem to care about, these days."

"I have to make a living somehow."

He sighs. "Whatever, man. I'm not your career counselor. I'm just one buddy looking out for another when I see him starting to go down a dark path."

"I don't need you looking out for me. I'm fine."

"Are you? You don't look it. Frankly, you look like hell."

"Aw, shucks."

"Just calling it like I see it. Obviously you're not coping well with everything that's happened. But now that Valentine is back... maybe it's a chance for you to move forward. That girl was crazy about you for years. I'm sure that hasn't gone away, even if you haven't spoken in a while."

I shake my head. "You don't know what the hell you're talking about, Tomlinson."

"Then explain it to me."

My beer is almost empty. I signal the waitress for another. She smiles brightly as she bounces toward the bar, her dark ponytail swinging with each step. "There's no point talking about something I can't change."

"How do you know it wouldn't change things? If you told her what happened—"

"This is none of your fucking business!" I bark a shade too loudly. Several tourists' heads whip around toward our table, curiosity in their stares. I lower my tone. "I'm sorry. I don't mean to be such an ass about this. It's just..."

"Don't apologize. I should know better by now. Where Jo Valentine is concerned, you've never been able to keep your cool."

The waitress delivers my beer. I give her a nod of thanks before downing a large gulp. Chris watches me drink, not touching his own glass. He eventually clears his throat to break the silence. "You know, you don't seem surprised to hear she's back in town."

"Was that a question?"

"Just an observation."

I set down my half-empty glass. "I saw her last week."

"Seriously?! What did she say?"

"I never said I talked to her. I *saw* her. Out sailing around the islands one afternoon."

"Oh."

"Mmm."

"I'm glad you know she's in town. I didn't want you blindsided if you bumped into her on a street corner or something. Small town and all — you know how it is."

"I do."

We're silent for a moment, sipping our beers without speaking. Eventually, Chris shifts the conversation into safer waters — smalltalk about his new job on the police force, a brief rundown of a few teammates' summer plans. The latest gossip surrounding our former Exeter Academy classmates.

Lee Park founded a tech startup out in San Francisco.

Ryan Snyder flunked out of school first semester.

Andy Hilton came out of the closet.

Sienna Sullivan got fake tits.

I listen with a detached sort of interest, nodding along as if these people are still a vital part of my life. In truth, they feel as far removed from me as fictional characters in a novel. One I read so long ago, the plot is moth-eaten with holes, the details faded to an indistinct blur.

When we finally pay the check, Chris stands and reaches out for a handshake.

"It was good to catch up with you, Reyes. Don't be a stranger."

I clasp my scarred hand around his, struggling to hide my wince when he squeezes tight. "You know where to find me."

"You get a break from the docks, make sure you swing by my parents' place on Saturday. They're letting me utilize the backyard for a Fourth of July blowout. I've got four kegs on order. Making a metric ton of Jell-O shots. Even breaking out the Slip-N-Slide for the occasion."

"Very patriotic."

"Hey, I can think of nothing more American than drunk girls in bikinis on a hot summer day."

I laugh.

"Wow, was that a laugh?" Chris slaps me lightly on the

back as we exit the restaurant patio onto the sidewalk. "Watch out, Reyes. You keep that up, you'll blow your audition for Most Miserable Man in Manchester."

"Bite me, Tomlinson."

"See you Saturday!" he calls over his shoulder as he walks to his squad car.

"Not likely!" I yell back.

But he's already in the car, out of earshot.

SEVEN

josephine

FOURTH OF JULY weekend creeps in on the heels of a languorous week — one I pass the vast majority of lazing pool-side, inhaling fantasy novels in rapid succession. The most exertion I put into anything is periodically flipping over to even out my tan lines. I have all the motivation of a headless rotisserie chicken.

Judging by her ever-pinched expression whenever our paths cross — mainly when I pad into the kitchen to grab a snack or a bottle of coconut water — Mrs. Agatha Weatherby Granger is less than approving of my newfound indolence. That doesn't bother me. If she wants to be disappointed in my life choices, she'll have to get in line behind my parents. And Ollie. And my Brown academic advisor. And pretty much everyone else I've ever met.

Nothing a little Brandon Sanderson can't drown out, I think, burying my nose deeper in a paperback.

I'm finally forced to peel myself away from the pool on the muggy afternoon of July 3rd when the maintenance man arrives to clean the filters and check the chemical levels. Rather than face down the horror of my own thoughts, I decide to distract myself with some overdue errands in town. First the bookstore, then the pharmacy. My latest binge-read won't last the weekend, nor will my sunscreen supply. Plus, my contraband stockpile of sugary snacks is running dangerously low. Mrs. Granger may keep the Cormorant House pantry fully stocked at all times, but her reusable cloth bags from the organic grocery store never return home with the sour gummy worms I require for survival.

Tugging a sundress over my favorite blue bikini, I hop in the Porsche and drive downtown. The radio blasts a new JP Saxe song, his voice lamenting as he sings about the struggle to get over an ex lover. I jam my finger against the power button and continue driving in silence.

Love songs hold little appeal for me, these days.

It's slow-going — traffic crawls along so sluggishly, I think I might actually be moving in reverse. No one seems to be in much of a hurry to get anywhere. The roads are congested with cars and trucks, bikers and pedestrians. Red-white-and-blue clad tourists stroll the sidewalks, peering into boutique windows and taking pictures by the harborside. Banners hang from every street post, announcing firework display times and food festival locations in bold font. Everywhere I look, hydrangeas are bursting into bloom, just in time for the holiday.

There's something distinctly American about Independence Day in New England — a heady mix of summer heat and patriotism hangs in the air like perfume. Any town claiming even the loosest affiliation to the Revolutionary War drums up some sort of Colonial-era spectacle. Quaint parades of flag-bearers march down the main streets. History buffs reenact long-ago battles. Militia men fire muskets over the water in a cloud of gun powder as bagpipers play Taps for onlookers.

In abutting backyards, neighbors crack beers and flip

burgers while their kids run barefoot through sprinklers on lush green lawns. The strains of country music and classic rock drift from every rolled down set of car windows. After dusk, risk-loving residents blast off illegal firecrackers at all the local beaches, lighting up the sky in a show of defiant sentiment. Sometimes, the unofficial displays are better than the town-sponsored ones.

I catch myself caught up in the infectious energy of Americana as I stroll the aisles of the pharmacy, tossing items I don't need into my basket. I smile at babies, hold eye contact with strangers, make small talk with the cashier. It's possible — okay, *probable* — that I'm a bit starved for human interaction, these days. Aside from the occasional run-in with Mrs. Granger, I've been entirely alone since I returned from my meeting at Brown. And while I've always been quite content in my own company, as I drive back to Cormorant House with a lollipop in my mouth and a bag of contraband candy on my passenger seat, I find my eyes glazing over at the prospect of yet another solitary weekend poolside.

July 4th is not the kind of day you're meant to spend alone.

It's a day for barbecues and beach volleyball.

You could always take Chris Tomlinson up on his offer, a small voice whispers from the back of my head. *He's having that kegger tomorrow...*

I quickly dismiss the idea. The last thing I want is to attend a party where I'll be forced to make awkward chitchat with a bunch of people I haven't seen since high school. Or worse, where I might run into Archer.

I figure I'll be far safer going for a sail down the coast in Cupid.

I figure wrong.

———

Saturday dawns clear and bright. Every forecast calls for spectacular sunshine and steady wind. That's the only reason I feel confident heading so far from the familiar charted waters near Rockport and Gloucester — out past the channel markers, away from the speed-boaters on boozy harbor cruises, beyond the sight of shore-bound onlookers.

Later, they'll call it a freak storm. A white squall. A microburst. Unpredictable and unforeseen, even by the best professionals in the field. A meteorological event for the Fourth of July record books.

Frankly, it makes no difference to me what they call it, or how they account for the abrupt shift from lazy summer day to violent gale. All that really matters is, when those weather fronts do in fact collide... when I see the black-blue clouds spread across the sky like bruises... when I smell the sharp tang of ozone in the air around me... when I feel the sudden churn of tides beneath the boat... I know I am too far offshore to make it back to safe waters before the storm breaks.

I know it down to my bones.

I make a valiant effort anyway, refusing — even in those final moments of calm — to believe I am in any real danger. But as I point my bow north, toward home, the wind builds behind me like a wild thing at my back, growling with a menace that makes me nervous. Loosed strands from my ponytail whip into my face. I ignore the annoying flutter of tendrils, keeping my focus on the helm in my hand, the firm bench-seat beneath me.

No need to worry.

It's probably just a passing shower.

Steady gusts fill the sails to capacity and Cupid responds, picking up speed in accordance with the wind. The boat begins to heel, the opposite rail skimming the water as we fly over the rolling waves. She's never gone this fast before — we must be clocking speeds of nearly ten knots. It would be exhilarating if it weren't so terrifying.

Waves materialize out of nowhere, rolling swells that surge beneath the hull at a velocity that makes the rudder difficult to hold steady. The tiller shudders in my grip. My teeth clench together as I struggle to keep us on course.

Overhead, the sky grows taut with electricity, a rubber band stretched to capacity. A snap is imminent. I try very hard not to think about my mast sticking up into the sky, the only lightning rod around for miles.

Don't panic.

It'll pass.

Except... it's not passing.

It's intensifying.

The rain turns on as if by faucet — absent one minute, immeasurable the next. Fat raindrops plummet from the clouds in a thick curtain. They pelt the water's surface like machine-gun spray; patter so hard against the wood decking, they sound more like a tropical waterfall than normal precipitation. Within seconds I'm thoroughly soaked, my paper-thin sundress plastered to my body like a second skin. I wipe a hand over my face, clearing droplets from my eyelashes as I strain to keep my line of sight fixed toward land. Despite the rapidly darkening sky, I can still pick out the distinct bend of Beverly in the distance.

In the very *distant* distance.

I never should've sailed so far out. Not alone, and definitely not without a fully charged radio. I can't even recall the last time I plugged it in. When I reach into the storage cubby beneath my seat and retrieve it, a flutter of nervous butterflies erupt in my stomach. The power-indicator light is flashing. There's barely any juice — maybe enough for a single transmission. I'll have to save it for if things get really dicey.

Not yet.

I'm still okay.

I'm still in control.

I can still make it home.

My stubborn self-assurances fragment and fall away as the typhoon gains strength. Alarm bells begin to blare full-force inside me as I realize the boat is taking on water. It streams in from all sides, sloshing around my ankles with cold promise. Between the driving rain and the frothing spray off each swell, Cupid's built-in drainage scuppers can't keep up with the steady onslaught.

Still, the thought that I might capsize — or actually *sink* — seems absurd. How could I possibly sink five miles from home, in waters I've sailed a thousand times?

Impossible.

And yet...

The boat's incline worsens until I'm struggling to keep my seat. The opposite rail is practically submerged, the ocean a hairsbreadth from spilling inside the cockpit. I prop my sandaled feet against the opposite seat to steady myself. They're slippery against the rain-drenched fiberglass. My breaths are coming quickly now, sharp puffs of panic, even as I assure myself there's no way we'll flip. The Alerion 20 has a full-keel design, making it almost impossible to topple.

Somehow, in this moment, that knowledge does little to soothe me.

I let out the main sheet to allow some wind to spill from the sail, de-powering enough to flatten out the boat. The starboard rail recedes fractionally from the water. But no amount of trim adjustments can compensate for gale-force winds — they shove us forward at breakneck speed, relentless and ever-shifting.

My palms are clammy with fear and cold as I feel around in the storage cubby once more, groping one-handed in the dark for the fluorescent orange life-jacket stored there. A small, water-activated emergency strobe light is attached to the collar — one of those gratuitous features you roll your eyes at in the nautical equipment store, confident you'll never use such a thing.

That confidence is shaky now.

I can't take my other hand off the tiller long enough to fasten the lifejacket straps properly, so I simply pull it on over my drenched sundress. I know it's meant to make me feel more secure, but it does the opposite. The thick padding settles around my shoulders, surrounds my throat like a set of hands squeezing the air from my lungs. Suffocating me.

In the back of my mind, over the din of my hyperventilation, I'm able to recognize the fact that I'm beginning to panic. With effort, I struggle to regulate my breathing.

In through my nose, out through my mouth.

Inhale.

Exhale.

Again.

And again.

But no amount of deep breathing is enough to keep me calm when, mere seconds later, the first bolt of lightning flashes across the sky. The air catches in my throat as undiluted fear hijacks my nervous system. My eyes press closed involuntarily, waiting for the answering call of thunder. I flinch when it arrives.

Boom.

The radio is poised at my mouth even before the rumbles fall silent. I make sure it's set to Channel 16, the frequency for distress, and pray there's enough power left to send out a call. My thumb presses the side button as I relay a series of words I never thought I'd utter in a shaking voice that sounds nothing like my own.

"MAYDAY, MAYDAY, MAYDAY! This is the sailboat Cupid, out of Manchester-by-the-Sea." I suck in a sharp breath. "We are taking on water in a storm, just south of the Misery Islands. Require immediate assistance—"

There's a sharp beep as the radio dies in my hands. I swallow down a frustrated scream as I twist the power switch on and off several times, only to be met with a blank gray screen.

God damnit.

I have no way of knowing whether or not anyone heard my call. Whether they'll come to my aid, even if they did hear it. The muffled drone of distant fog horns reaches my ears every few moments — a sign I am not the only one blindly navigating through this unforeseen tempest — but it's impossible to pinpoint the origin. Those other boats could be ten meters or ten miles from me.

I'm on my own.

archer

JAMMING my finger against my cellphone screen, I send Tomlinson's call straight to voicemail. I'm not in the mood for another guilt trip about attending his damn barbecue this afternoon. I have a dozen traps left to haul and, from the looks of the clouds gathering on the horizon, not much time left to do it.

Funny — the marine forecast didn't call for a storm.

The rest of my traps will have to wait until tomorrow. With a sigh, I turn the Ebenezer back toward Gloucester. The faint murmur of the maritime radio provides an almost inaudible backdrop beneath the chugging engine. I put on a little speed as the clouds darken from slate gray to roiling ebony in a remarkably short amount of time, trying to outrun the imminent weather. Off my bow, I spot a handful of speedboats racing for the harbor, throwing frothy wakes into the air behind them.

Long before the storm rolled in, it was a quiet day on the water. Even the most dedicated lobstermen typically choose to spend the Fourth with family and friends. Tommy looked at me like I had two heads when I told him my plans to check the traps this morning, but he knows better than to argue with me by now. I may be the only bastard alive more stubborn than he is.

The waves build from a slow roll to a steady chop as I putter south, following the jagged Rockport coastline. In the distance, dark clouds reach skyward, rife with the promise of rain. I wouldn't want to be caught on the wrong side of that mess. In six months working on the water, I've never seen a squall move in so fast.

As I pass by Crow Island, I try — as always — not to look at the sprawling estate perched on the cliffside... but Cormorant House has a unique gravitational pull. My eyes move of their own accord to the place that was once my home. You cannot, of course, see the less-than-elegant outline of Gull Cottage from this vantage point — the staff quarters that I shared with Ma, Pa, and Jaxon are set back in the woods, out of sight, where they won't bring down the property values — but the imposing angles of the Valentine mansion make my chest tighten.

Is she inside? I wonder. *Is she pressed up against the glass of her gilded cage, staring out at the ocean, wondering why that old yellow lobster boat passes by her cove so often?*

It wasn't intentional. Not in the beginning, at least. But over the past few weeks, since that June afternoon I first saw her out sailing by Great Misery Island, I've found myself steering a bit closer to the shore than I used to on my route home. Looking across the sheltered cove to the private dock where a small red sailboat bobs. Loosing a breath I didn't realize I was holding when I see it's still there. Because that means maybe *she's* still there. Still within reach. Even if she's no longer mine to reach for. Even if the sight of her is the most acute form of torture.

Twisted, I know.

But if I've learned anything in the past year, it's that the only thing worse than seeing her is *not* seeing her. On the days her boat is gone from the cove, I seek her out at sea. It's almost involuntary — like a moth drawn to flame, I scan the surrounding waters for flashes of red as I go about my tasks, one eye fixed on the horizon as I restock bait bags and band crusher claws.

Tommy has surely noticed my recent distraction, even if he fails to understand its cause. He grumbles under his breath about my head being in the clouds — and, occasionally, up my own ass — but even that isn't enough to make me quit my painful new habit. I live for those fleeting glimpses of blonde hair; for those scant seconds when our paths intersect. I'm always careful to keep just far enough away that she can't recognize me. Not that she would. I doubt I bear much resemblance to the boy in her memories.

I justify my stalker-like behavior with flimsy excuses, telling myself it's fine to keep an eye on her, so long as she never knows I'm there. A guardian angel, watching from afar when she takes her sailboat out alone in the afternoons.

Just one mariner looking out for another.

I'd do the same for anyone.

My lies sound hollow even to myself.

The truth is, checking up on Jo is a habit so deeply ingrained, I can't seem to break it. I don't feel at ease unless I know she's safe. I don't feel alive unless I'm certain she's out there somewhere, existing. So now, as I round the small peninsula where Cormorant House looms and the cove comes into view... my hands tighten on the wheel until my knuckles turn white. Because the small red sailboat is missing from its spot at the dock. Which means Jo is out sailing.

Sailing in a storm.

My eyes cut to the ominous wall of black clouds billowing

on the southern horizon. It's heading straight for shore, cutting a swathe directly through an area there's a good chance she's out exploring.

Not that it's my problem, anymore.

She's not my problem, anymore.

But...

Fuck.

The first bolts of lightning split the sky over Salem Sound. I hope to God I'm wrong. But I know I'm not when I hear a distress call over the radio. I fumble for the knob, turning up the volume to hear it over the roar of the engine.

The voice coming across the line is faint. Muffled with static. And undeniably, heart-stoppingly familiar.

"MAYDAY, MAYDAY, MAYDAY! This is the vessel Cupid..."

Her transmission cuts off halfway through. It doesn't matter. The few snippets I managed to hear tell me everything I need to know.

Taking on water.

The Misery Islands.

Immediate assistance.

There's no choice.

No weighing of options.

No moment of hesitation.

The Ebenezer's engine growls in throaty protest as I push the throttle faster, foregoing the turn-off into the Gloucester Harbor channel.

Heading south toward the islands.

Toward the squall.

Toward Jo.

NINE

josephine

LIGHTNING STREAKS AGAIN, electrifying the world for the briefest of instants. I didn't realize how dim the sky had grown until it flashed momentarily back into focus; the craggy outline of Cape Ann is now almost indiscernible from the oppressive storm-front of rain and mist. Thankfully, the lumpy land masses that make up the Misery Islands are still visible off my port bow, my one remaining reference point in the darkness.

Hope sparks inside me — a fool's hope, perhaps, but I grasp at it with all my flagging courage. There's an anchorage at Great Misery. A small inlet, barely more than a shallow bay. Not a perfect spot to ride out such foul weather, but surely a better option than bobbing out here like a sitting duck, waiting to be struck by the next bolt of lightning.

Almost as if I've conjured it, another shockwave streaks across the atmosphere — a bolt of pure static power that severs the sky into neon shards. I count the seconds in my head: eight full heartbeats before the accompanying crash of thunder.

Eight miles away.

Too close.

And home is too far.

Just like that, my decision is made. Abandoning any aspirations of making it to the mainland, I adjust my course and head for the nearby islands instead. My sails groan over the howling wind, straining against their stays. The sheets grow taut beneath the pressure. I fear the rigging will not hold if the storm intensifies even slightly. The thought alone is enough to inspire true panic.

If the sails go, I'm screwed.

Ripping sails aren't my only worry. On this new course, Cupid is positioned perpendicularly to the building waves. Swells crash over the rails every few seconds, dousing my shins. The cockpit is beginning to look like a bathtub. The boat — not designed to carry this much weight — rides low, bulldozing forward like a field-plow through mud. Forcing her way through the water instead of gliding atop it.

With my free hand, I grab the plastic emergency bailer from the storage cubby and start to scoop out bucketfuls manually — one after another after another, a Sisyphean task. It's coming in faster than I can hope to expel it. Maybe if I had two hands to dedicate to bailing, maybe if someone else were here with me...

Maybes will not save me, now.

Minutes pass. Minutes of terror and breathlessness. Of shivers and shakes, born of cold and fear. I'm not sure if the wetness I'm wiping from my eyes is rain or tears. I'm not sure it matters, anymore. The islands are nearer, but so is the lightning. I count out heartbeats before each rumble of thunder. The crashes come closer and closer with every passing minute.

Six miles away.

Five.

Four.

Three.

By the time Cupid's bow rounds the southernmost point of Little Misery, the storm is practically on top of us. The water in the cockpit is up to my knees. I accidentally drop the bailer and watch it float out of reach with a disembodied sort of denial. It wasn't helping much, but letting it go tastes like accepting defeat. Like accepting the impossibility that I might actually...

Sink.

We are sinking.

The jib sail is the first to go; the material shreds into ribbons beneath the claws of a particularly strong gust as Cupid limps — waterlogged and graceless — toward the larger of the two islands. The main sail follows suit shortly thereafter, torn to useless flaps of canvas that whip around the mast in an ear-splitting racket. The tiller in my hands is now just a prop; I grip it more to keep myself aboard the flooded vessel than to attempt to steer. The waves are up to my waist, and rising.

With each swell, my pretty red sailboat — my most prized possession, the greatest source of material joy I have known in my lifetime — sinks a bit further beneath the surface. The thought of abandoning her, once an impossibility, is now an inevitability I cannot ignore. Not if I want to survive.

Surrendering the tiller, I tighten the straps of my life jacket around my abdomen. My flip flops, kicked loose in some undefined moment of chaos, drift away one after another. I watch them disappear over the stern, which is now fully swamped. Beneath the lifejacket, water splashes against my chest, seeps a cold path up my spine.

When the cockpit goes under completely, I half-swim, half-scramble my way up the deck, toward the mast. I wrap my arms around the metal beam as the ocean swallows Cupid beneath me in great gulps, praying a lightning bolt does not choose this moment to strike.

It doesn't take long to sink. In a laughably short amount of time, the water has me fully in its clutches. I gasp at the cold as my body begins to float. My numb fingers scramble for purchase on the rigging as the mast is dragged downward with the rest of the vessel. The emergency beacon at my shoulder activates automatically — a strobe blasting my retinas in rhythmic bursts of light, white then red then white, a looping pattern of distress designed to be spotted from a distance.

Against the thrashing waves, I struggle to hold onto the top of the mast — the only part of Cupid that has not yet been swallowed up — while trying not to get tangled up in the mess of shredded sails and stays. Between each white-capped crest, I glimpse the far off shore of Great Misery.

So close... yet so very far.

I'm a strong swimmer. Under normal circumstances, I could probably make it. On a clear day, without raging winds or ripping tides, I'd close the football-field's worth of distance between myself and solid ground with ease. I'd pass the hours sunning on the warm rocks, picking sea-glass fragments from the sand, watching glossy black cormorants dry their wings in the gentle breeze.

But it is not a normal day.

Directly overhead, lightning splits the sky. Less than an heartbeat later, booming thunder answers. I feel another few inches of the mast slip down into the depths, forever out of reach.

Now or never, Jo.

Even as I steel myself for the swim, even as I take a fortifying breath into my lungs and prepare to head for the island...

I know in my heart I'll never make it.

———

Looking back, I was a fool to think I actually stood a chance.

As soon as I start for shore, I know I'm done for. My arms flail for purchase against the raging currents, my legs kick futilely at the undertow dragging me off course. There is no order to this tide, no pattern to this surge. The ocean is a churning washing machine, ebbing and flowing at random, tossing me to and fro like a lone sock caught in the industrial cycle.

My attempts at swimming falter as I'm knocked sideways under the force of a white-capped wave. All I can do is hold onto my life jacket, fingers digging into the shoulder pads, praying it's enough to keep me afloat until help arrives.

If help arrives.

I try not to think about that as another set of waves slams into my chest like a one-two punch, strong enough to knock me backwards. My whole body goes under for a moment, head disappearing beneath the surface as I spiral upside down in the riptide. The world tapers down to nothing but dark water. Bleak, cold undercurrents cloud my vision, disorienting me until I have no idea which way is up. The emergency strobe is my only light source, a flickering reprieve from the blackness.

I kick for what I hope is the surface, knowing all the while that I might be swimming toward the bottom. Thankfully, the lifejacket does its job. My lungs are screaming for oxygen by the time it drags me back to the air. My head breaks clear and I gasp, swallowing a gulp of the Atlantic as soon as my mouth opens. I choke against the brine, coughing to clear my airway. I'm dizzy and nauseous, still reeling from my underwater somersaults. The last thing I need is seawater in my lungs.

In the tumult, I've lost all sense of direction. I cannot see even a sliver of land over the breaking crests anymore. Cupid is fully submerged, the glinting metallic tip of her mast lost to the ocean's fury. That should make me panic, but it seems I have grown numb — from the cold of the water, but also from something far more dangerous.

Hopelessness.

It spreads through me, a dull ache that moves outward from the center of my chest, where my heart pounds twice its normal speed, down my tired limbs.

And they are *tired,* I realize. *So very tired of swimming against currents they stand no chance of besting.*

So, there, bobbing like a cork at the center of a cyclone...

I stop.

Stop swimming.

Stop fighting.

Stop *living.*

The emergency strobe pulses weakly, a small speck of light in a dark expanse of sea. Overhead, the sky shakes with thunder. I crane my neck back, letting the rain pound onto my face. The blood in my veins is clotted with bitter resignation. I feel the storm surge swirl in deathly tendrils around my legs as I stop kicking.

I close my eyes as it drags me under.

archer

WHERE THE HELL IS SHE?

Rain pelts the windshield, too heavy for the pitiful wipers to keep up. I strain my eyes to see through the rivulets streaming down the glass. Even without the downpour making things difficult, my visibility is next to nothing out here. I'm guided forward by lightning flashes and gut instinct.

If only Tommy had invested in some radar for this rust-bucket...

God, he's going to be so pissed off if I sink. Not because he particularly cares whether *I* live or die. But if his precious Ebenezer ends up at the bottom of the Atlantic, he'll never get over it.

The swells are intensifying — the lobster boat rises and falls like a see-saw as it chugs southward, the bow lifting toward the sky, then crashing down again with a drenching spray of salt and foam. It's getting harder to steer; this vessel was designed to putter around the shallows pulling traps, not power through eight foot swells in the middle of a gale. If I don't turn back soon, the engine will be thoroughly swamped.

Just a little longer, I tell myself, gripping the wheel tighter as another wave rocks us sideways, toward the rocky shoals off the coast of Little Misery Island. *She's out here somewhere...*

But there's no sign of her anywhere. Not a single trace of Cupid or any other boat on the horizon. I tell myself Jo was smart enough to duck into a cove, to take shelter in one of the many inlets that pepper the shore around Salem and Beverly. She's a seasoned sailor. She can handle a little bad weather. Yet as I swing Ebenezer around the tip of Great Misery, I can't shake the nagging feeling in my gut.

It's the same neck-tingling sensation I had the summer we turned ten, when she fell off her bike riding back from the library and shattered the bones of her wrist. I found her on the side of the road, crying her eyes out, and carried her home.

It's the same chest-aching tightness I experienced the winter we learned to snowboard, when she got lost in the glades and couldn't find her way down the mountain. By the time I got to her, she was halfway to frostbite.

Call it instinct, call it insanity... call it whatever you like. Inside my heart, there's an internal alarm system programmed just for Josephine Valentine. When she's in trouble, I somehow always seem to know.

Or... I used to.

Maybe that internal alarm system doesn't work anymore. Maybe whatever part of my soul that used to be synced with Jo's has eroded over this past year of silence and miscommunication. Maybe she's perfectly safe in someone else's rescue boat at this very moment.

She's probably already back on shore, my mind whispers. *Go home, pour yourself a drink, and drown out all thoughts of that girl.*

But it's hard to listen to my mind when my heart is screaming something else entirely.

I've nearly given up when I spot something in the water. It's metallic — each time the sky flashes with lightning, it glints in the dark. As I pass closer, I realize it's the submerged top of a mast.

A sunken sailboat.

The sails, shredded to no more than rags, drift like ghostly fingers in the water. Half of the Valentine crest, hand-stitched with red thread, is still visible on the top section of the main sail — irrefutable confirmation of something I already knew in the marrow of my bones.

This is Jo's boat.

Panic and pain tangle into a knot and lodge inside my throat, blocking my airway. I'm barely breathing as I scan the surrounding waters for signs of life. There's nothing. Just black water and raging wind. I cup my hands around my mouth and scream at the top of my voice.

"JO!"

Against the storm, the sound barely carries, swallowed instantly by the darkness. The chance of her hearing me is slim to none, but I keep it up anyway, yelling until my voice goes ragged.

"JOSEPHINE!"

Despair claws its way up my throat as minutes pass with no response. I picture her caught in a line, dragged to the bottom of the ocean along with Cupid, and nearly break down at the thought.

"JO, CAN YOU HEAR ME?"

In these currents, she could've drifted halfway to Province-town by now. I motor in slow laps around the wreckage, back and forth, searching the swells in as much of a grid as I can manage, heedless of the intensifying squall unleashing hell all around me. The steering wheel fights me as I take on the building surf, shuddering beneath my grip. Water rushes by my rubber boots as it sloshes over the transom, then drains out the deck scuppers. Even standing beneath the relative protection of the semi-enclosed wheelhouse, I'm soaked to the skin beneath my rubber coveralls. My t-shirt is plastered to my chest; my hair drips onto my forehead.

I use a wet forearm to wipe water out of my eyes as I continue scanning the dark horizon. It feels futile. A fool's errand.

She's gone.

You were too late.

The thought is crippling. My knees are threatening to buckle beneath me when I finally see something bobbing off the bow. It's faint — barely more than a flicker amidst the rolling waves — but there's no denying it's there.

A light.

Blinking every few seconds.

Red then white then red again.

Recognition slams into me like a gut-punch.

The emergency strobe on a life-jacket.

"JO!" I scream, voice breaking on the word. Spinning the wheel around with impatient hands, I push the throttle into higher gear. The Ebenezer rattles in response, the overheated engine wheezing warningly, but I pay it no mind. My eyes are fixed on the blinking beacon, afraid to shift away even for a second. I won't risk losing sight of it.

Of her.

I shove the boat into neutral as I come up alongside her and lock down the wheel to keep the boat from drifting too much off course. I don't focus on the fact that the girl in the water is not responding to my voice. Or the fact that, even through the distorted glass windshield, she looks far too still. I put all my energy into the task at hand. Something inside me, beneath the roaring panic, functions on auto-pilot as I retrieve the boat hook pole we use to catch lobster buoys and bend over the transom to pull her in.

"Jo," I gasp as I catch sight of her face up close. Her eyes are closed. I can't tell if she's breathing. "Just hold on...."

Please, God, let her hold on.

The pole is slick with water; it's difficult to maneuver as I snag the collar-strap of Jo's lifejacket and tow her toward the side of the boat. When she's within arm's reach, I toss the pole blindly behind me and lean over the transom to grab hold of her lifejacket. It's no simple feat. The boat rocks riotously in the waves. Twice, I stumble off balance, nearly toppling overboard myself. Only by some small miracle do I manage to keep hold of both my balance and the limp girl in the water.

My right hand spasms in pain as I haul her waterlogged body up over the side. She's stiller than a corpse in my arms as we collapse backward onto the deck. Her skin is clammy with cold beneath my fingertips. I shake her lightly, saying her name over and over. Getting no response.

"Jo, come on." I slap her cheek. My voice breaks on her name, jagged with desperation. "*Josephine!*"

I lower her onto her back, pushing away my panic as I recall the steps to administer CPR. Jo made me take a course with her three years ago, when she was toying around with the idea of becoming a lifeguard at Good Harbor Beach. She changed her mind when she realized she'd have to socialize with chatty beachgoers all day long — not exactly an ideal summer job for an introvert. But by that point, we'd already taken the certification classes — pumping our hands against humanoid dummy chests in time to the song "Stayin' Alive" under the watchful gaze of several registered nurses on a YMCA gymnasium floor. My participation was more about keeping Jo company than actually acquiring life-saving skills. Never in a million years did I think I'd find myself in this position. If I had, I might've paid better attention.

Think, think, think.

What were the steps?

ABC.

Airway.

Breathing.

Compressions.

You can do this, Archer.

She needs you to do this.

My hands shake as I tilt back her chin. Her head lolls in my grip, a lifeless rag doll, as I position her face properly. Sucking in a large gulp of air, I pinch her nose closed, then bring my lips down on hers and breathe deeply into her mouth. One long exhale, then another. Her chest inflates as the oxygen rushes into her lungs.

I sit back, waiting.

Watching.

Praying like hell.

Still, she shows no signs of life.

Her heart isn't beating.

I remove her soaked life jacket. Interlocking my fingers together, I position them flat against her chest to begin compressions.

"You will not die," I tell her sternly as my palm pulses in steady beats. "I forbid it. You hear me?"

She's so still. And so small, I worry her ribcage will crack under the force of my hands. But I don't stop. My eyes never shift off her face. It's gone white with cold. Ghastly white. Ghastly white. Her lips are the only point of color — and it's not a good one. They're blue.

I keep up the compressions.

"You will live," I growl. My voice is gruff — with rage, with regret. My face is wet — with rain, with tears. I give her two more useless rescue-breaths, trying like hell to breathe her back to life. "Live, dammit. *Live.*"

My heart isn't the one that's stopped beating, but it might as well have. In this moment, staring into the face of the girl I love, the girl I have always loved, lifeless and limp... there are no words for the pain bolting through my bloodstream.

Jo.

My Jo.

Please, please, please.

Come back to me.

The thought that she's gone — not just from my life, but from the face of this earth... My mind refuses to process it. I cannot even think the word *dead*, let alone contemplate the possibility. I watch my own tears falling onto her pale face. My arms are beginning to ache, exhausted from my efforts. I'm not sure how long I've been doing this. Two minutes? Ten? I'm even less sure how much longer I can continue on before I admit...

She might not be coming back.

Something is breaking inside me, the longer I stare down at her. Painful memories claw at me, excruciating reminders of our past. A pigtailed girl with chalk-dust hands, playing hopscotch in the driveway. A gawky preteen at the pool, eye-rolling over the brim of her book as my cannonball splashes her pages. A stunning vision in a silk gown, ditching her senior prom date to spend the night with me.

So full of light.

Of *life*.

This cannot be the same woman I hold in my hands now. Blue and still and so very, very cold. So very, very empty. So very, very...

Dead.

A scream builds inside my throat, presses at the back of my teeth, demanding release. I let it out as I give one final compression. An animal sound, primal with anguish.

She's gone.

My Jo.

My world.

Gone.

My arms fall to my sides in defeat. My eyelids slam closed to trap the flow of useless tears. And as my agonized yell rends the heavens... another sound reaches my ringing ears. Not the slapping of waves against the hull, not the patter of rain, not the booming of thunder.

But a cough.

Small.

Weak.

Alive.

"Jo!" I gasp out, eyes flying open. I bend over her, cupping her face in my hands. "Can you hear me? Oh god, Jo! *Jo!*"

It isn't like the movies. She doesn't snap back into consciousness, sit straight up and throw her arms around me in a fit of joy. Water gurgles from her mouth like a kinked hose, a feeble trickle. She coughs again, more urgently this time, eyelids fluttering. She's drowning on the contents of her own lungs. I roll her onto her side so she can clear her airway. For a long moment, I simply hold her there, paralyzed by relief as I listen to her taking ragged breaths. Rubbing her back as she spits and coughs and wheezes her way back to life.

She's breathing.

Thank fucking god she's breathing.

Without warning, the boat rocks under a particularly large wave, wooden deck planks creaking ominously as the stern see-saws up and down. I grab hold of Jo before she's launched back into the water, pulling her into the circle of my arms. I'm afraid to embrace her too tightly, but I'm even more afraid to let go.

"You're okay," I whisper against the crown of her head,

holding her close. Her hair is slick with water, the strands plastered against her cheeks in a wet curtain. "You're going to be just fine, Jo."

Above us, the storm rages on, wild winds stirring the ocean into a fury that's liable to toss us directly onto the rocks. With no one at the helm to guide her, the Ebenezer spins in dizzying circles, completely untethered amidst the thrashing tides. But I can't bring myself to move to the wheelhouse. Can't bring myself to put even an inch of space between myself and the half-conscious girl in my arms.

Not yet, anyway.

For several long moments, I merely press my lips to her hair and listen to her breathe. Reassure myself that the thready pulse I feel at her wrist is not going to stop again. Allow my brain to catch up to my own thudding heart.

Lightning cracks.

Rains plummet.

Waves crash.

And I hold her.

She's alive.

She's alive.

She's alive.

josephine

I'M ALIVE.

In an unforeseen stroke of fate, I find myself breathing and back on solid ground. Or... not exactly *solid*. The first thing that registers in my sodden brain — besides the fact that I am, in fact, still able to use my brain — is that the ground seems to be shifting up and down like a bad carnival ride. I hear the distinctly fluid melody of waves crashing against the hull, and realize I'm still at sea.

Someone must've heard my distress call after all.

My eyes peel open, each lid heavy as an anvil. My surroundings are unfamiliar, but I've been on enough boats to recognize the inside of a wheelhouse, partially shielded from the pelting rain. Someone has propped me against the portside wall of the cramped space. That someone is standing with his back to me — one hand on the wheel, the other adjusting the frequency knob of a corded VHF radio. My mind feels sluggish as it works to catalogue his details.

Dark hair, slicked with rain.

Thick rubber boots.

Orange neoprene coveralls.

A lobsterman.

"This is the vessel Ebenezer," he's saying into the receiver, his voice barely audible over the steady drumbeat of rain against the deck. "We have responded to a MAYDAY call from the vessel Cupid. One sailor rescued from the water. She needs immediate medical attention. *Over.*"

There's a murmur of static across the line, followed by a muffled response from the Coast Guard operator monitoring the channel. I can't make out the individual words. The lobsterman lifts the radio to his bearded mouth again.

"We're tied-off to a day-mooring in Cocktail Cove on the north side of Great Misery Island at the moment, but we can't stay here for long — it's not going to hold in this weather. *Over.*"

I catch only fragments of the operator's response — words like *hurricane-force winds* and *take shelter* and *wait for rescue* — as a large swell rocks the boat sideways. Water crashes over the rail, sluicing across the flat bottom of the boat, draining out the scuppers. My heart, which has only recently resumed beating, quails within my chest.

I cannot go back into that dark ocean.

I will not make it out a second time.

My eyes fix on the man at the helm. My unknown rescuer. His knuckles are white with tension on the wheel. His tone is thick with impatience as he barks a response into the radio.

"*Wait it out?* That's your grand plan?" His head shakes, sending water droplets flying all directions. "That's not good enough. She needs medical attention now, not in two hours when you finally get your asses here. You're the fucking Coast Guard!" He sighs, then tacks on a terse, "*Over.*"

The hair at my nape prickles, standing suddenly on end. For a second there, beneath the frustration, the stranger almost sounds...

Familiar.

In fact... he sounds a bit like Ar—

No.

No, that's not possible.

I must be delirious from my brush with death.

I take a deep breath, trying to calm my jagged nerves.

"CPR was performed," the lobsterman tells the operator. "She's breathing but unconscious. *Over.*"

"I'm conscious," I say, my voice thready. Just getting the words out takes monumental effort. My throat aches like — well, like it's had half the Atlantic swallowed down and then forcibly regurgitated, I suppose. I try to sit fully upright, but every muscle in my battered body protests at the effort.

Who knew drowning would be so damn painful?

At the sound of my voice, the man at the helm goes stiff, the broad planes of his shoulders contracting beneath the fabric of his rain-soaked t-shirt. The receiver falls from his grip as he turns to me, swinging on its cord like a yo-yo, all answering transmissions abandoned. I suck in an involuntary breath as soon as I catch sight of his face.

That face.

Despite the thick beard, despite the sharp gauntness that has hollowed out his handsome features... the man staring back at me is instantly recognizable. Heartbreakingly recognizable. Seeing him hits me like an uppercut; knocks the wind from my tattered lungs. The world goes quiet, pounding rain and flashing lightning and churning sea no match for those burning hazel eyes, that aristocratic nose, the dark slashes of two furrowed brows. Suddenly, even simple things like breathing and blinking are utterly impossible.

Archer Reyes.

Is standing.

Five feet from me.

I never thought I'd see him again under any circumstance — let alone here, in the most unfathomable of places. Ship-wrecked in a storm. For a moment, I think I must be dreaming. Perhaps all of this is merely a nightmare conjured up by my bored subconscious. Perhaps I am safe at home in my bed, and any minute I will stir awake surrounded by throw pillows and a down feather duvet.

Yet, if I were asleep, I would not hear the desperate thud-ding of my own pulse, a mad tattoo in my veins. I would not feel the painful press of fiberglass digging into my spine. I would not shiver so violently in the cold breeze, or struggle to pull in each breath like a marathon runner passing the twenty-sixth mile mark.

I am here.

This is really happening.

I stare at the boy who smashed my heart into pulp, unable to say a single word. A million questions tumble inside my skull — infinite *hows* and *whys* and *what the hells* jumbled together into a confusing mental slurry. My tongue is lodged stupidly inside my mouth, refusing to function. I don't know what odd twist of fate has brought our paths crashing back on course... all I do know is, in this frozen moment, I cannot form even one coherent sentence.

He seems to be at an equal loss-for-words, because he doesn't make a sound. I watch his throat contract, Adam's apple bobbing roughly, and wonder if he's also having trouble breathing. I wonder if the sight of me haunts him, too — a ghost of the past, made present.

Once our eyes catch, they hold with magnetic force. Time seems to slip into slow motion as we stare at each other in silence. Tension builds, charging the air with an electric energy that rivals the lightning splitting the sky above our heads. The atmosphere practically crackles with it. Still, we do not move, or speak, or even breathe. We are a point of utter stillness at the center of the still-raging storm. The eye of an emotional hurricane.

Deadly quiet.

Endlessly still.

One move in any direction could be catastrophic.

The sharp beep of the radio makes us both flinch.

"Ebenezer, do you copy?"

Our eyes finally break contact as Archer bends to grab the receiver. He does not look at me as he raises it back to his mouth and replies to the Coast Guard. I watch his lips moving, forming words about our position and the state of the storm, but they barely register through an impenetrable fog of shock wrapped around my mind.

Taking a shaky breath, I climb slowly to my feet. My legs are unsteady beneath me, my bare heels pressed hard against the cold wheelhouse floor. I grip a nearby handrail to keep my balance and glance through the windshield, where two sets of wipers work double-time to clear the glass. The outline of Great Misery Island looms directly ahead, only a dozen or so yards off our bow. Even here, hooked to a mooring in the relative protection of the anchorage area, the sea churns like a pot set to boil. The lobster boat spins wildly on its tether in the ever-shifting tides.

One look at the bobbing white mooring ball tells me Archer was right — it's not going to hold us for long. The thin lines aren't designed for a boat of this size. Certainly not in conditions like this. They're going to snap under the pressure. It's only a matter of time until we break loose and are sent careening toward the rocky shoals that ring us on three sides.

Archer seems to realize the same thing. When I peer over at him, he's staring worriedly at the half-submerged mooring ball. There's a deep furrow between his brows. I can't seem to look away from it.

How many times have I smoothed that same wrinkle from his face? After he had a grueling baseball practice or lost an important game... when his brother Jax got arrested for drug possession or his father Miguel broke his arm falling off a ladder... Sitting at our spot up in the old boathouse rafters, I'd lean over and swipe at it with the pad of my thumb.

If you don't stop frowning, one day when they put your face on a baseball card, you'll be covered in wrinkles. Cheer up, Reyes.

I push the memories away with a painful mental shove. It'll do me no good to remember how things used to be.

How *we* used to be.

Feeling the weight of my gaze, Archer glances over at me. Our eyes lock instantly. The air goes stale, like someone's sucked out all the oxygen molecules.

"How are you feeling?" he asks lowly.

Confused.

Disoriented.

Scared.

Shocked.

"I'm fine," I say, my voice just as low.

He nods. Breaking eye contact, he clears his throat. "Fine enough to make for shore?"

My heart skips a beat at the thought of getting back in the water. "We should wait for help—"

"The Coast Guard isn't coming," Archer says bluntly. "Not until the sea calms down and the storm passes. That could take hours. We're on our own."

"Don't you have a cellphone?"

"There's no service this far from the main land. And even if there were, who do you suggest I call? StormChasers?"

Ignoring his sarcastic comment, I grit my teeth. "I don't think abandoning ship is the answer."

"We can't stay here. Even if the pendant lines hold — and that's a big if — we're dragging the mooring's anchor along the bottom every time a wave hits. We've drifted a dozen feet in as many minutes. At this rate, we'll be on the rocks long before help arrives."

"Then we should try to reach a harbor — Manchester isn't that far. The storm seems to be dying down—"

"There's another band of thunderstorms moving this way. We're just in a lull right now."

"But—"

"Enough!" he cuts me off tersely. "Jesus, Jo, you're smarter than this. You've spent more time on boats than anyone I know. You really think we're better off staying here?"

My chin cocks like a loaded gun. "I think getting in that water is insanity!"

"So is bobbing here like a cork, hoping for the sky to clear in a magical burst of rainbows and sunspots."

"Don't yell at me!"

"You're the one yelling," he points out with infuriating calmness.

"You... I..." I try to modulate my tone, but I'm practically shaking with anger. It flares to life in my chest, rising from long-simmering resentment to blind rage so fast I can barely process it. "I'm not leaving the boat, Archer."

"Still stubborn as a damn mule, I see."

"If anyone here is livestock," I say cuttingly. "It's *you*, jackass!"

We glare at each other for a long moment. In the silence, waves rock us up and down, down and up, an unpredictable undulation. I don't generally get seasick, but these conditions are enough to make even an iron stomach toss. Keeping one hand on the rail, I press the other to my midsection to quell the queasiness.

"Look — it's not just the storm," Archer informs me flatly. "We're almost out of fuel."

I whip my head around to examine the fuel gauge behind the wheel. The red indicator hovers below the quarter-tank mark. "We have enough to get to shore."

"Not in this weather, we don't. We'll burn twice as much powering through these rolling swells."

I look back at him, eyes narrowed. "Since when are you a maritime expert?"

"Since when are you so reckless?" he counters, tone thick with frustration. "You must've hit your head when you went into the water. Or did you block out the fact that your sailboat just sank? Because that's about the only explanation I can fathom for why you'd ever risk heading back out into open water, right now."

"You don't have to be such a jerk! I'm just trying to talk through our options—"

"The time for talking is over. This is my boat. That makes this my call. We're going to ride out the storm here, on the island."

As if on cue, the sky rattles with thunder, a sinister under-score to his words. I glance toward Great Misery. The shore isn't far, but the prospect of swimming does little to thrill me. I can still feel the scorch of leftover seawater in my lungs. Each breath burns with the heat of my all-too-recent brush with death. "We'll never survive the swim — not in these waves."

Archer sighs. "Then we won't swim."

"What?"

"You said you're not getting back in the water. Fine. I'll drive the damn boat right up onto the beach. There's a sandy stretch — we should be able to avoid most of the rocks."

"You can't do that," I gasp, jaw hinging open in horror. "The damage to the keel—"

"Fuck the damage! I don't care about the boat right now. I care about—" He breaks off, swallowing down whatever he was about to say. Swallowing down whatever he's feeling inside. When he speaks again, his voice is remarkably steady. "I already had to pull you out of the water once today. I thought you were dead. Hell, you *were* dead. So forgive me if I'm not willing to risk your life, or mine, again."

My jaw, still agape, shuts with a sharp click. I don't have a single valid counterargument left at my disposal, so I simply give a small nod to show I'm in agreement.

"There's a poncho in that compartment on your left. Put it on before you freeze to death," Archer instructs flatly. "I'm going to release the mooring lines. Assuming they haven't already snapped."

He doesn't meet my eyes as he walks out of the wheelhouse, into the relentless rain. Overhead, the sky snarls as another bolt of lightning cracks down on the horizon. I wait until he's out of earshot until I release the breath from my lungs — a great, rattling whoosh of air I've been holding for far too long.

Even if we make it out of this storm alive... we may wind up killing each other long before help arrives.

TWELVE

archer

TOMMY IS GOING to fire me — that is, if he doesn't strangle me first.

I wince, recalling the crunch of fiberglass against the seabed as I steered his beloved Ebenezer up onto the beach; the sound of splintering wood as I purposely ran us aground. I probably punched a dozen holes in the hull. I don't look back at the pathetic sight of her keeled over in the shallows, slowly taking on water, as Jo and I cut a path inland, leaving the rocky shore and pounding waves behind.

There's no point dwelling on it.

What's done is done.

Alone, I might've left the boat on the flimsy day-mooring and risked the swim, even with my damaged hand slowing me down. But once I saw Jo's face... once I realized how scared she was at the prospect of getting back into the water...

I couldn't put her through that again.

In the choice between Josephine Valentine and a floating rust-bucket, I'd choose Jo every single time. Frankly, in the choice between Josephine Valentine and just about anything... I'd still choose her.

Not that there was a plethora of good choices at my disposal, or anything. Our last communication with the Coast Guard — *"Just hang tight, we'll be there when we can!"* — didn't inspire much confidence in a timely extraction, and the storm has only intensified since we made it to land. I've no doubt the Ebenezer would've ended up on the rocks regardless. At least, that's what I tell myself.

Above us, a thick band of thunderheads rip apart the sky in savage strokes of light. Even here, beneath the shelter of sparse trees and scraggy bushes, the ground is slick with water from the deluge. I barely feel it anymore. My entire body is saturated — seawater and rain soaking into my clothes, sloshing around inside my boots. My skin is clammy with cold, my fingertips pruned and bloodless. A handful of steps away, Jo is shaking like a tambourine, borderline hypothermic. The chattering of her teeth is audible. We need to find dry ground before she freezes to death.

I glance around, trying to get my bearings. I've been to this island before — freshman year at Exeter Academy, our science class came by chartered ferry for a field trip. Officially, we were here to learn about local marine biology; unofficially, it was an excuse to spend a sunny spring afternoon away from the stuffy classroom. No one was particularly interested in actually learning anything — not even the teacher chaperones who'd tagged along to supervise.

The sole exception was, perhaps unsurprisingly, Josephine. Class Valedictorian, incorruptible nerd. While the rest of our classmates snapped selfies near the shipwrecked steamer decaying on the rocks, lounged on picnic blankets, and passed around smuggled joints in the ruins of the abandoned 1920s casino that sits atop the island, she dragged me down to the tidal pools on the opposite shore, determined to examine the unique ecosystems of each one.

Look at this, Archer! she commanded, crouched beside one of the larger pools, awe in her voice. *A whole world exists in this tiny little puddle, with its own food chain and social hierarchy. Predators, prey. Life, death, decay. Isn't that amazing?* Her grin was brighter than the sun.

That warmth is long gone, now.

I shake off the memories as I push aside a wet branch, eyes scanning the overgrown ground. The foliage has grown thick in the summer heat, green and lush with new leaves. Small black crabs scuttle out of my path as I walk, their pebbled homes disturbed by my footfalls. It takes me a few minutes to find what I'm looking for — a set of rocky steps, embedded in the low hillside. Moss creeps across the stones, a living carpet.

"Over here," I call over my shoulder to Jo. I have to shout to be heard over the rain. "I found the stairs."

She's a dozen feet away, searching a different stretch of bushes, but she turns at the sound of my voice. As she makes her way to me, she looks shaky and pale — her face slicked with rain, her feet swallowed by the spare set of boots I found for her in a cubby onboard, along with a translucent plastic poncho. It drapes her body like a shower curtain, offering meager water-resistance but little in the way of warmth. Her lips are blue; her eyes ringed by circles of deep exhaustion. Raindrops cling to her eyelashes like tears.

My throat goes tight as I look down into her upturned face. I'm bowled over by the urge to comfort her. I want to take her into my arms, to pull her close until the shivers stop. To hold her until the fear disappears from those sky-blue eyes.

Eyes that, at this moment, are fixed with sharp curiosity on my scarred right hand.

Shit.

In the numbing downpour, I didn't feel the tendons spasming beneath the weight of the branch I've been holding aloft, nor did I notice when Jo's attention shifted to the patchwork of scars left behind by my accident.

How much did she see?

I quickly release my grip, sending water droplets in all directions as the branch plummets. I tuck the damaged limb out of sight.

"Watch your step," I tell her, turning my back on her inquisitive gaze as I start up the steps. "It's slippery."

There's no railing, nothing at all to hold onto as we make our way up the embankment. The climb is steeper than I remember; the ascent slower in these conditions. But we can't stay on the beach — the rising tide has made that an impossibility. Soon, the small strip of exposed shore will be swallowed entirely by frothing swells; the shattered remains of the Ebenezer along with it.

At the top of the steps lie the ruins of an old clubhouse, a decaying skeleton leftover from the island's heyday, when rich vacationers used to flock here to drink and gamble away their summers. They should've known, on an island called Misery, the fun wasn't destined to last. A sweeping fire in 1926 razed the whole resort to the ground, effectively putting a stop to the stream of money-touting tourists. The owners never rebuilt all they lost in that fire; what didn't burn to ash was simply left to wither away in the elements.

After nearly a century, the once-glamorous casino has been reduced to a pile of rubble. Hope withers in my chest as I walk into the clearing, surveying our options for shelter. There's not much left. No walls, no roof. Not a single dry spot to ride out the storm. I'm beginning to think we climbed all the way up here for nothing, when I feel a hand curl around my forearm. The unexpected touch sends a jolt through my system; stops me in my tracks like an electrical shock. I glance cautiously down at Jo's fingers — small and slender and so very pale against my tan skin — afraid if I move too fast, they'll disappear.

"There!" She's pointing to our left, where a stone foundation slab juts out over the hillside, forming a narrow overhang. "Come on!"

Her grip on my arm slips away as she starts running toward the outcropping, those too-big boots sending mud-spatter in all directions as she tromps through puddles without a care. I suck in a sharp breath before I follow, swallowing down the hollow ache her touch set off inside my chest. One casual hand-graze, and I'm coming undone.

God, I'm pathetic.

I run after her, ducking beneath the low ceiling of hanging vines and heavy stone as I enter. The shelter is small — no more than ten feet across in any direction — but it's dry, and right now that's all that truly matters. Anything to get us out of the whipping wind and relentless rain long enough for some life to leech back into our bones.

We take up opposite sides of the cavelike space, each leaning on an earthen wall, staring at each other in the dim light as we catch our breath. Neither of us says a word. Tucked beneath the thick slab of rock, the storm is somewhat muffled. Muted. The world outside suddenly feels far-removed.

The silence stretches on, thick with things better left unsaid, questions better left unasked. Seconds curdle into minutes, stagnating the musty air between us. I focus on the faint rattle of Jo's breaths, relieved she's breathing at all. I don't think I'll ever recover from the moment I pulled her from the water, lips blue and lungs still. That's not the sort of memory that ever fades.

She simply stares at me, perhaps waiting for me to break this wordless stalemate. Waiting for me to fill in the blanks her dazed mind is no doubt struggling to piece together.

She'll be waiting a long time.

It's difficult not to stare at her. After a year of absence, of aching memory and throbbing loss, being this close — seeing every angle of her face at this proximity — is damn painful. I thought I knew her details by heart, but she's twice as beautiful as I remember.

Were her eyes always so blue?

Did they always cut into me so sharply, a knife slipped straight between the ribs?

Beneath the clear plastic poncho, her sundress is plastered to her skin, clinging to every curve, highlighting her perfect figure. Her nipples protrude against the thin fabric. I tell myself not to look, feeling like a bastard of the highest order when desire spikes through me, an unwanted current of electricity that shoots straight to my cock.

Not now. I grit my teeth and avert my eyes. *Not here.*

I chew the inside of my cheek so hard, I taste blood.

Jo breaks our stalemate first. Clearing her throat to shatter the quiet, she mutters a stiff, "I suppose I should thank you."

My brows lift in question.

"For saving my life," she tacks on. "Pulling me from the water. Thank you." Her well-mannered upbringing is beyond reproach — even when it comes to someone like me. Someone she can't stand. The girl would thank her mortal enemy if the right opportunity arose. She pauses for a long beat. "I guess I'm lucky you were nearby."

"Don't know if I'd call nearly dying *lucky*, but sure." I shrug lightly. "We'll go with that."

Her eyes narrow. "What I'd really like to know is *how* you happened to be nearby."

To this, I have no reasonable response. So I don't respond at all.

"I assume you heard my radio call..." She lets the statement hang in the air, unfinished, waiting for me to offer a proper explanation.

I don't.

I give her nothing. Nothing except a shallow, noncommittal nod.

Her brows pull inward, a furrow of frustration. When a full minute ticks by and still I remain silent, the furrow becomes a full frown.

Without the distraction of the storm, without the pressure of our lives hanging in the balance, she's able to examine me properly for the first time. Her eyes move rapidly over my face, studying me with an intensity that makes me want to shy away. Beneath the anger, there's an unmistakeable edge of incomprehension as she takes in the scruffy beard, the overgrown haircut, the hunched posture. I slide my hands deep into the pockets of my coveralls, hiding my scars from her pursuant gaze.

"So this is..." She gestures vaguely at my lobstering getup. "What, exactly? A summer job?"

I expel a sharp breath. "Something like that."

"I figured you'd be off at some glamorous training camp between collegiate seasons," she says bluntly. I do my best not to flinch at the not-so-subtle dig. "Isn't that what all you baseball hotshots do?"

I wouldn't really know.

I shrug.

My stubborn silence only seems to agitate her, stirring slow-swirling anger into a sweeping vortex of wrath. I watch her small hands curl into fists at her sides, a surefire sign she's struggling to remain in control of her emotions. "Are you seriously not going to say anything, right now?"

"What is it you want me to say, Jo?"

"An explanation would be nice, for starters!" She throws out her hands. "None of this makes any sense."

"I don't know what you mean."

"You know exactly what I mean. *You*! *Here*! On a freaking lobster boat like some freaking *townie*—"

My soul stills. For one frozen instant, I feel myself disappear into that word. That unwanted identity. It wraps itself around me in a chokehold, strangles the life from my lungs. Invasive as a deadly disease.

Townie.

The one thing I never wanted to become. The one life I was so determined not to live — stuck in this place, working like a dog to keep my head above water. Struggling just to make ends meet.

I see my whole miserable existence stretching out into a path of monotonous drudgery. Fifty years of hauling traps and gutting mackerel, until my back is bowed like a river reed and my legs give out — if I don't drink myself into a silk-lined box six feet under first, that is.

Exactly like Tommy.

"I'm just surprised, I guess," Jo continues, her tone softening slightly. "You're basically the last person on the planet I expected to see today. If Samuel Adams himself had pulled me from the water onto a schooner full of British tea bound for Boston Harbor, I think I'd be less shocked."

"Generally speaking, if long-dead Sons of Liberty start showing up, you should see a doctor."

"I'll keep that in mind," she says dryly. There's a short pause before she dives back in — a dog with a bone, she can't seem to let her curiosity go. "But I still don't understand... How are you here? *Why* are you here?"

"Do you scrutinize everyone who saves your life, or am I special?"

"I'm not trying to sound ungrateful," she insists. "I appreciate you saving me. I'm just having some trouble wrapping my mind around all of this."

"I don't know what you want me to tell you. I heard your distress call over the radio. I answered it. I would've done the same for anyone caught out here in the storm." My chin tilts away, avoiding her gaze. "It's Maritime Law 101 — you hear a MAYDAY, you respond."

She's quiet for a long time. I can practically hear the wheels turning in her head as she mulls over my response, weighing the density of my flimsy explanation. When she does speak again, its in such a whisper, I'm not certain I'm intended to hear it at all. "Fate sure has a funny sense of humor."

My shoulders tense. "Fate has nothing to do with it. It's just the price you pay for living in a small town. Stick around long enough, you'll bump into everyone you've ever met."

Her shoulders tense, too, a mirror of my own posture. "Except, last I heard, you don't even live here anymore. My mother told me your parents quit their positions and moved back to Puerto Rico..." She trails off. There's a shade of hurt in her words, but I barely register it over the rush of anger rising inside me. A hot flare of rage sparks inside my chest at the mere mention of Blair Valentine. When I think about her spinning some false narrative about my parents packing up and leaving Cormorant House voluntarily... leaving *Jo*, who they always saw as a surrogate daughter...

My hands curl into fists, aching to hit something.

"Then again," Jo mutters under her breath, "Leaving without a proper goodbye seems to run in your family."

My anger flares even hotter. I take a deep breath to calm my ragged nerves, but it's no use. My voice comes out sounding strange — eerily flat, devoid of any emotion whatsoever. "I said goodbye."

"Right." She scoffs. "The *letter*. How could I forget? It's amazing, really, that you managed to reduce eighteen years of friendship to a few scrawled lines on a piece of parchment. Incredible how you could walk away from your entire life without a single backward glance." Her hands clap together, a mocking round of applause that rings with startling sharpness in the small space. "Bravo, Archer. Really. I'm impressed. The level of sociopathy you display is rare. Scientists should study you in laboratories."

"What do you want from me? An apology? Fine. *I'm sorry*. I'm sorry your feelings were hurt when I left. I'm sorry they're still hurt after a year. I didn't realize I was required to keep you apprised of every change in my life." I narrow my eyes at her. "Funny enough, I haven't gotten any updates on *your* life since you moved to Europe. Switzerland, was it? Sounds glamorous."

"If you wanted to know about my life," she says frigidly, "Then you should've reached out to me. It's been nothing but stone-cold silence from you for a year, Archer. A *year*."

I glance up toward the ceiling. I can't stand to look at her while I'm lying through my teeth. "I guess I said everything I needed to say last summer."

It's a low blow. But it's the only thing I can think of to get her to back off. And it works — maybe a little too well, if I'm being honest. She reels back, spine pressing into the stone wall. Her breaths are shallow — with incredulity or indignation, I'm not certain. "What did you just say?"

"You heard me."

Her fury explodes, a torrent of words laced with bitter hurt that's been festering for twelve long months inside of her. "What the hell is the matter with you? I know we don't talk anymore, I know everything is strained and awkward and broken between us... but *I'm* not the one who made it that way. *I'm* not the one who walked out on this friendship. So if anyone has a right to be angry and annoyed right now, it's *me*. If anyone has the right to give the other person the silent treatment... once again... it is *me*."

"Silence is just fine, as far as I'm concerned."

"God, you've turned into such a prick!" She's practically shaking with rage. "Of all the people who could've pulled me from the water... This has to be some kind of sick cosmic joke."

"Don't worry. I'm sure the Coast Guard will be here any minute now, and you can go back to hating me from a distance."

"Not a nanosecond too soon," she snaps. She's glaring at me with such disdain, it's actually palpable in the musty air of the enclosed earthen space. "I can't believe I was ever stupid enough to consider you my best friend. To think you actually cared about me. That you might ever lo—" She bites off the words, forcing them back down her throat with a harsh swallow. "What a waste, you are. Waste of energy, waste of breath, waste of time."

I know.

I know I am.

And you deserve so much better than me.

"Well, then. Good talk," I drawl sarcastically. I force my features into a condescending smirk. It feels like a lie on my lips. "Glad we had a chance to catch up after all this time, old friend."

"Screw off, Archer."

She stalks to the mouth of the shelter, as far from me as she can possibly get without standing in the rain. Blowing out a long breath, I stare up at the ceiling.

It's going to be a long wait for rescue.

josephine

I'M VIBRATING — with rage, yes, but also with cold. It's freezing in this dank little cave. And Archer's icy disposition isn't helping matters.

An hour of frozen silence passes, the only sound that of the pouring rain against the crumbling casino ruins and the occasional rumble of thunder. I stand for as long as I can at the outermost edge of the overhang, staring into the distance, straining my ears in vain for the sound of helicopter blades or boat engines, a portent of rescue.

Eventually, exhaustion overtakes me. I peel the wet poncho over my head, spread it across the mossy ground, and sit down, legs pulled close to my chest to stop my shivers. I'm utterly worn out. Every part of my body aches like I've been thrown down a flight of stairs. It's not just physical, either — I am emotionally drained, a bone-deep sort of tired no amount of rest will cure.

A part of me knew if I ever saw Archer again, it would be difficult. But this is far more painful than I imagined it to be on the rare instances I'd actually allow my overactive mind to envision our paths crossing again. Maybe because, in my fictitious scenarios, we were always older. More time had passed. I'd be walking down the aisle of a grocery store in twenty years, reaching for an avocado, and there he'd be. Salt-and-pepper hair, a knowing smile. We'd nod politely and go our separate ways without a dramatic confrontation, no longer seeking closure or consideration. No mending of fences or water under bridges necessary, after so much time.

That, I could've lived with.

That, I could've swallowed without too much wounded pride.

That, I could've walked away from feeling, if not happy for him, at least at peace with the way it all played out.

But not *this*.

Anything but this.

This is...

Unimaginable.

One year was far too short. Too short for me to heal properly, and too short for him to have changed this much. He's radically different — grown so cold, so indifferent toward me, it's difficult to fathom we were ever inseparable. It's almost impossible to reconcile this brooding, bearded stranger with the boy in my memories, who I adored with an all-consuming sort of madness.

I curl my arms tighter around my body, wishing I would wake up from this nightmare. Somewhere out of view, I hear Archer pouring water from his boots, shrugging out of his wet coveralls. I fight the urge to cover my ears with my palms like a child, blocking out every sound he makes. Even if I did, there's no expunging thoughts of him from my head. My mind spins in dizzying circles, a torturous loop from which there is no reprieve. I'm so frustrated, I could pull my hair out at the roots.

Fall in love with your best friend. That's what everyone always says — in movies, books, television shows, you name it.

Fall in love with your best friend and you'll spend your whole life laughing. Fall in love with your best friend, and you'll never be alone. But no one tells you what to do if you fall in love with your best friend... and he doesn't love you back. No one warns you how damn painful it'll be to find the person you know, down to your bones, is meant for you... And he doesn't feel the same.

A realization like that can throw your whole world off its axis. It can make you question everything — about your concept of reality, about the choices you've made. About what makes you *you*.

Fundamentally.

Viscerally.

Inherently.

I've always thought that navigating the world of relationships is a bit like scanning the radio waves for a good station. Ninety-nine percent of the time, you're searching blindly — spinning the tuner with aimless fingers, seeking out a solid frequency amidst endless static. Occasionally, you might stumble upon one that comes in — not perfectly, not precisely, but clear enough to make out most of the words of whatever song they're playing at the time. To sing along for a few muffled tracks before moving on in search of a better fit.

These stations are our casual relationships.

Flings.

Acquaintances.

Ships passing in the night.

Good enough to pass the time, but ultimately not worth sticking around for.

And so, you spin on.

Rarely — so rarely, you begin to think it might be an illusion or an urban legend or a figment of your imagination — your tuner will land on a frequency that shocks you with its clarity. A broadcast that matches your tastes so perfectly, it blasts straight into your soul, vibrates you down to your core until every atom shakes with the sheer bliss of sound washing over you. A startling pulse of pure energy.

These stations are our soulmates.

Best friends.

True loves.

The ones with whom you feel that elusive *click* of camaraderie and natural connection — the kind that cannot be forced or fabricated with any amount of time or effort. A wavelength you could ride until your last breath, content in the knowledge that nothing else will ever echo quite as perfectly in the chambers of your heart.

For me... there was only ever one person who made me feel like that. Right now, he's standing six feet — and an emotional infinity — away from me.

Archer.

Freaking.

Reyes.

Last summer, when his frequency went dark without warning... when I found myself swimming solo through a world of meaningless static... a part of me shut down for good.

Closed off all connections.

Cut away all incoming signals.

I resigned myself to a life without love. Somehow, sitting in solitary silence felt safer than risking another erroneous bond. Being alone seemed infinitely smarter than letting someone in, only to get hurt again.

Better isolated by my own choices than cast aside by someone else's.

It wasn't until I met Oliver Beaufort last fall that I even considered opening up again. And, looking back, letting him in wasn't really a conscious decision I made, an intentional act I undertook. It happened so fast — *he* happened so fast — I didn't have time to put up any real resistance. He shot into my life like a brilliant beam of light in the darkness, chasing away my shadows with his sunny disposition and that southern twang and those charming manners before I realized it was happening.

And he stayed.

Despite the darkness, despite the damage. He waded straight into the static, grabbed me by the hand, and coaxed me back into the music. Every day since, for eight long months, he's done his best to prove everything I thought I knew about relationships entirely wrong.

I used to believe passion and pain were intrinsically intertwined, that you could not have one without the other. But it turns out, devotion does not have to split your soul in half in order to be real. Just because a heart can break, does not mean it should. And those all-consuming passions? They only do one thing in the end.

Consume you.

Far better to care for someone in careful moderation, without losing who you are in the process. Awful as it may be to admit, as much as I've ever allowed Ollie to adore me... I'm not sure I've ever let him all the way in. And I'm not sure I can ever truly love him — not in the way he deserves to be loved, anyway.

It's not his fault. I'm simply not capable of that kind of commitment.

Not anymore.

Not ever again.

It's selfish, surely, to let him stay with someone so emotionally stunted. But I can't help it. Can't change it. The doors to the innermost parts of my soul, the deepest chambers of my heart, are no longer thrown wide, allowing just anyone to walk inside and wreak havoc. They're double bolted and sealed shut with cement, soldered at the hinges and tempered with steel. Then blockaded with a few immovable boulders, just in case.

No one — not even someone as sweet as Oliver — is going to destroy me. It took far too long to put myself back together the last time.

Oh, god. Ollie. I glance up at the darkening sky, seeing my boyfriend's features in the edges of a storm cloud. *He must be getting worried. He hasn't heard from me all day.*

A wave of guilt washes through me as I calculate how long it's been since I last called him. Over twenty-four hours. I'd planned to check in after my sail, but obviously that's no longer an option.

I don't have a watch, but it's nearing dusk. Probably around six-thirty or seven. It doesn't matter. Time has little meaning out here, except to my stomach, which has begun to rumble with periodic demands for dinner. There's still no sign of rescue. No chopper blades echoing from incoming helicopters, no spotlight beams off the bow of rescue boats. And no way of knowing when they'll arrive, seeing as our one and only source of communication sank with the wreckage of Archer's old yellow lobster boat.

From our hideout atop the hill, we have sweeping views of the whole coastline, as far south as Hull. I sit at the mouth of our shelter, counting out the seconds between each flash of Boston Lighthouse — *one, two, three, four, five, six, seven, eight, nine, ten* — in the distance so many times, the numbers begin to sound like nonsense inside my head, a mantra of made-up syllables. The rain has finally tapered off, lessening from a thunderous torrent to a steady drizzle as the billowing clouds are swept up the coast, taking the lightning along with them.

In the squall's aftermath, the sky looks like it's been

through a fight — battered and bruised, streaked with black and purple. But as hints of light creep through at the western edges, diluting the darkness with softer tones, the horizon unfurls into the most spectacular sunset I've ever seen in my life. It's stunningly beautiful. Almost violet. I wish I had a camera to capture it.

Not that I need any more reminders of this day to look back on.

"Here."

A raspy voice cuts into my thoughts, startling me. I half-turn to find Archer standing just behind me, his hand extended outward. In it, there's a granola bar. He must've pilfered it from the boat before we abandoned her on the beach.

My brows go up.

"Go on," he says flatly. "Take it."

When I fail to comply, he sighs deeply before reaching down, grabbing my limp hand, and pressing the plastic package into my palm. I've barely curled my fingers around it when he turns on a heel and stalks away.

"Thank you," I whisper, my words halting. As awful as it is to be around Archer when he's acting like an asshole, somehow it's even worse when he's being kind.

"No need to thank me." His boots squeak as he takes a seat across from me at the opposite edge of the overhang, his back planted against the stone foundation. He's stripped down to a t-shirt and athletic shorts, his coveralls discarded in a damp pile in the corner. "Your stomach is rumbling so loud, it's going to drown out the sound of the rescue choppers."

There's the asshole.

I roll my eyes as I rip open the granola bar. The smell of peanuts and chocolate, sugar and processed oats hits my nose like a shot of heroin. Saliva rushes into my mouth. I'm so ravenous, I have to fight the urge to shove the entire thing down my throat. I hesitate only a beat before forcing myself to break the small bar in two. My fingers shake a bit as I extend it across the distance.

"Take half."

His brows pull together. "No, I—"

"If you pass out from hunger, I'm not lugging you down to the shore when the rescue boats arrive."

The ghost of a smile flits across his face as he leans froward and takes it from me. Our fingers brush — just a fraction of a second, barely the length of a heartbeat. But it's enough. Enough to send a volt of electricity through my nerve endings. Enough to make the breath catch in my throat.

My eyes drop quickly from his face, sliding away to study the ocean as I pop the first bite of granola bar into my mouth. I press my spine more firmly against the rock wall, almost to the point of pain, a desperate attempt to distract my mind from thoughts of the man sitting far too close for comfort. I chew slowly, trying to savor the snack, but it's gone all too soon. Afterward, I knit my empty hands together, wishing I had something to occupy them.

This momentary ceasefire is fraught with tension. I think, in some ways, I actually preferred our screaming match. That, at least, was clear cut. Black and white. This strange gray area we have entered — in which we are neither enemy nor ally, but both at once — is far harder to navigate.

The silence sits heavy in the air, every breath dragging its way in and out of my lungs with audible effort. Each molecule of oxygen riddled with unanswered questions, rife with unfinished business. I can feel Archer's eyes on my face, moving over my features in the gathering dusk. I keep my own gaze averted, afraid to look at him for fear of what I'll see in his expression. Angry scowl or softening acceptance... either option is equally dangerous to the heart thundering too fast inside my ribcage.

"Jo," he says, whisper-soft.

My teeth clench.

I cannot look at him.

I will not look at him.

"Jo, I'm—"

But whatever he is about to say to me is lost. We both hear it at the same time — the distinct sound of an engine, rapidly approaching. My eyes scan the water, seizing upon the sight of a ship. Gunmetal gray with a thick red stripe spanning the hull, the words U.S. COAST GUARD are visible even from this vantage point. Dual spotlights shine off its bow as it speeds toward the small cove where we made landing.

I glance over at Archer. The haunted look on his face is one I cannot quite decipher — one I'm not certain I want to decipher. When his eyes meet mine, I nearly flinch at the unexpected pain in their depths.

"We'd better go," he says flatly.

I swallow hard. "Right. We should."

Neither of us moves a muscle. We simply sit there, staring across the divide, paralyzed by all the damage we've inflicted upon each other; frozen by our utter inability to heal it.

"I'm sorry for yelling at you earlier," I tell him in a muted voice. And I mean it. "I really am grateful you saved me."

He nods stiffly. "Don't worry about it."

I open my mouth to say something — anything — but no words manifest. I have no idea how to speak to him anymore. Not the slightest clue how to bridge the strange gap between the thoughts in my head and my stupefied tongue. And Archer certainly doesn't seem inclined to make an effort in that regard. His silence is thick as the stone walls surrounding us. His expression closed off and cold, all traces of our cease-fire erased like they never existed.

He climbs to his feet without another beat of hesitation

and walks out of the shelter, headed for the rocky steps that lead back to the shore. After a moment, I heave a sigh and follow him.

Time to get back to reality.

Back to my life.

A life that no longer includes Archer Reyes.

archer

TOMMY STARES AT ME, his bearded jaw clenched tight. He's quiet for so long, I think I'll be forced to repeat myself.

"Did you hear what I said?" I swallow hard. "The boat, it's—"

"Do you want a drink?"

He doesn't wait for me to accept his abrupt offer; he merely turns on his heel and walks deeper into the dark house. The screen door slams shut between us with a bang loud enough to disturb the neighbors on a normal evening. Not tonight, though. Tonight, most people are down at the harborside, hoping to salvage their storm-dampened holiday with a fire-work show and some force-fed town spirit. Tommy's narrow, tree-lined cul-de-sac is ensconced in shadowy quiet.

I follow him inside, wiping my rubber boots on the welcome mat as I step over the threshold. It's a simple house — a single-story ranch with a low sloping roof, reminiscent of the 1950s. Unpretentious as the man who owns it. The spartan decor style is that of an aging bachelor. The only art on the walls are fading nautical charts hung in dark wooden frames.

What few knickknacks he possesses follow a similar theme — a vintage compass sitting on an end-table, a sawfish bill mounted over the fireplace, a collection of hand-painted fishing lures displayed behind glass.

A short walk down a dim hallway leads into a tiny, tidy kitchen with butcher-block countertops and striped navy wallpaper. I sit at a circular oak table while Tommy rummages through the cabinet above his refrigerator. It's odd to see him dressed in regular clothes. I'm so accustomed to the sight of him scowling at me over a stained yellow lobstering bib. Until this moment, I wasn't entirely confident the man had hair — I thought that low-brimmed Red Sox cap was permanently fused to his head. But there it is: a shock of thick white strands, neatly parted above his right temple.

He retrieves a bottle from deep in the cabinet, blowing a layer of dust off the cap before twisting it open. He's silent as he pours two fingers of brown liquor into a mismatched pair of tumblers. He sets one in front of me before settling into the seat across from mine.

"I was saving this bottle of scotch for the day I retired." He swirls his glass, watching the amber liquid form a tiny liquid tornado. "Guess this is as close as I'm going to get."

"Tommy, you have to know how sorry I am. If there's anything I can do—"

"You can start at the beginning," he cuts me off, taking a slow sip. "I'm listening."

I hardly know where to start.

I let a gulp of whiskey wash over my tongue and down my throat before I begin. Once I've started, the words come easily, pouring out in a torrent. I tell him everything, sparing none of the details — about the squall, the MAYDAY call, the sunken sailboat. I describe how I pulled Josephine from the water, cold and blue and needing CPR. The flimsy day mooring and the delayed Coast Guard response. The near-empty gas tank and the choice to abandon ship. The flashing spotlights of the rescue boat. The breakneck return to the docks. The paramedics waiting to whisk Jo away via ambulance without so much as a goodbye or a backward glance in my direction.

They wanted to take me to the hospital for an examination too, just to be safe, but I refused. These days, I barely have money for meals, let alone an exorbitant ambulance fee. The lobstering business may have some perks — days spent outside on the water, the occasional free fish dinner, no long commute to a stuffy office — but health insurance is not one of them. Whatever cuts and scrapes my body accumulated out on the water this afternoon will have to heal on their own time.

God knows I've healed from worse before.

I don't intend to confide in Tommy about my relationship with Jo, but as the telling of today's events unfurls, I find the past spilling out along with it. Before I know it, I've laid the whole story at his feet. Everything that happened last summer. The twisted path that lead me away from my family, from baseball, from the girl I loved, and to his doorstep last fall, full of scars — both surgical and soul-deep. It's the first time, the only time, I've told the story aloud since it all transpired. Chris has heard bits and pieces, fragments of the truth, but never the whole sad tale in its entirety. I had not realized how badly I needed to tell it — to expel it from my system — until I started speaking.

It's the most I've ever spoken to Tommy, by a long shot. It's also likely far more than my gruff boss bargained for when he sat me down to hear about his boat. But Tommy, quite unexpectedly, turns out to be a good listener. He lets my words wash over him without interruption, absorbing the story as he drains his scotch in measured, almost methodical sips. By the time I finish, his glass is empty and my throat is hoarse.

"Anyway," I say, pushing aside the rising tide of embarrassment inside me. "I'm not sure why I told you all that. The point is, I'm sorry about what happened with the Ebenezer, and I'm going to do whatever I can to make this right. I'll pay you back. It might take me some time — hell, it might take me the rest of my life — but I swear I will."

I fall silent, bracing myself for an interrogation — *How could you sink my sole source of income? How do you expect to pay me back for this loss?* — or, at the very least, some minor berating. Instead, Tommy merely turns his weathered stare my way and asks the one question I am wholly unprepared for. One that knocks the wind right out of my lungs.

"Do you want to stay here tonight?"

I blink, confused by the question. Confused by the kindness. Kindness I surely don't deserve. "Uh..."

"Couch ain't much more than a blanket over springs, but it's yours if you want it."

"My apartment isn't far."

"I know, kid." He pauses. "That's not why I offered. Seems to me, after the day you've had... I don't know. Just figured you might not want to be alone, that's all."

My eyes begin to sting. I blink rapidly, burying the rising emotion behind my lids. If I cry in front of Tommy, we'll both be even more uncomfortable. Which is hard to picture, seeing as we're already awkwardly near to having a Hallmark movie moment.

I clear my throat roughly. "Thanks for the offer, but I'm fine."

"Good." Rising to his feet, he reaches down and clasps me by the shoulder. "Go home, get a good night's sleep, and for God's sake, take a shower. You smell like day-old bait. We'll sort the rest out tomorrow."

I stand, feeling shaky with emotion. I'm exhausted. My

voice is choked, tight with unspoken gratitude. "Thank you, Tommy."

He's already walking out of the kitchen, toward his bedroom. His voice carries back to me from halfway down the hall. "These old bones of mine are beat. Heading to bed. You can stay as long as you like, just lock up when you leave, will you? And flip off the lights. You've cost me enough money today — no need to run the electric bill any higher."

A faint smile twitches my lips upward at the corners as I drain the dregs of my whiskey.

———

It's a balmy night, the skies clear and quiet in the aftermath of this afternoon's storm. I walk quickly, consumed by my own thoughts. It doesn't take me long to get back to my apartment. Tommy's neighborhood — a stretch of unpretentious houses tucked between a golf course fairway and a chunk of conservation land — is a ten minute walk from the inner harbor.

The weatherbeaten three-story walkup awaiting me at the edge of the docks isn't much to look at, with its sagging front porch and peeling paint, but the price was right and the landlord asked blessedly few questions when I found myself in need of an apartment last fall.

The bedroom is small; the bathroom even smaller. The tiles are mildewed, the grout yellowed with age. I peel off my damp clothes, step into the stall shower, and flip on the overhead faucet. I spend far too long beneath the spray, lingering long after the water has run cold. Pressing my forehead against the tiled wall, I wish I could wash every thought in my head straight down the drain, along with every emotion clanging inside the echo-chamber of my chest cavity.

If only.

My mind is as jumbled as my heart. Over and over, my thoughts return to Jo. I keep seeing her face. The look on it when she was loaded into that ambulance — such stark vulnerability, such sharp sadness. I was glad the door shut between us, if only so she wouldn't see my heart being physically ripped from my chest in that moment.

One of the paramedics, assuming I was her boyfriend, asked if I wanted to ride with her to the hospital. And I did. Of course I did. But instead, I just stood there like an idiot, throat clogged with emotions I couldn't begin to untangle, and watched her ride out of my life.

Somehow, it was even more painful this time around.

She's better off without you, I remind myself. *She deserves more than this life you're living, in a shitty apartment with no future ahead of you.*

The sudden buzz of my cellphone startles me out of my unpleasant thoughts. I grab it off my nightstand and examine the words blaring across the screen. A bolt of alarm shoots through me when I see my mother's name in insistent capital letters.

"Ma? What's going on? Are you okay? It's late."

"What's going on? *What's going on?* How can you so calmly ask me what is going on?" She gives me no time to answer these questions — merely bursts into a breathless tirade of Spanish that's difficult to follow. I catch a few key words — *Josephine, hospital, emergency contact* — before she switches back to our universal tongue. "*Mijo*, I'm the one who should be asking what is going on! I'm the one who answered the phone twenty minutes ago and learned what happened to you and Josephine in the storm today from a doctor at Beverly Hospital!"

Shit.

"Oh," I mutter.

"Oh?" She looses another stream of angry Spanish. "They say the Coast Guard was called in to rescue you both! They say she nearly died out there! And you didn't think to call me?"

I blow out a sharp breath and sit up on my bed. "I'm sorry. You must still be listed as Jo's most recent guardian. I had no idea the hospital would contact you."

"And if they hadn't? Would you have even told me what happened? Or do you think, just because you are no longer living under my roof, you do not owe your mother any explanation when terrible things go on in your life?"

"Of course I would've called you, Ma. Don't be so dramatic."

"You haven't even seen dramatic yet, *mijo*. This is me being calm. Why do you think it took me twenty minutes to call after speaking to the doctors? Your father has been leading me through deep breathing exercises so I don't scream your ear off through the phone!"

I wince. "I'm sorry, okay? I should've called. It's been a very long day. I'm tired. I didn't think."

"You scared me," she says. Her voice is marginally calmer, but remains thick with emotion. "For a moment, when I picked up the phone and heard it was the hospital, I was worried you'd been in another accident..." Her words press low beneath the weight of painful memories. "We almost lost you last summer, Archer. You have no idea how hard that was on your father and me."

Guilt sluices through me. Because I do know. I saw exactly how difficult my injuries were for them to come to terms with. In a way, the death of my baseball dreams hit them just as hard as it hit me. And on top of that loss, they also found themselves forced out of their occupations, along with the only home they'd known since arriving in New England twenty years ago.

They stayed for a few months, after everything fell apart.

They were right by my side as I moved through the phases of recovery — the surgeries, the hospital stays, the discharges, the physical therapy, the lingering pain. But even caught up in my own suffering, I was not immune to theirs. I could see the strain on their faces as they navigated their new reality — one son a broken mess, the other on the run from the authorities.

For months, they floundered to find new purpose in our too-small town. They moved around Manchester like ghosts, unmoored and unsure, living out of suitcases in a string of month-to-month sublet apartments with so little room, Gull Cottage looked palatial in comparison.

Eventually, when I felt enough time had passed, when I was ruled whole and healed by every medical professional in the Greater Boston area, I sat them down and told them it was time.

Time to go.

Time to begin again.

Somewhere else.

Somewhere far from here.

And where better than their home country? With the hefty severance payoff provided by Blair and Vincent, they were more than capable of purchasing a tract of land on the northern shore of Vieques, an island off the coast of Puerto Rico. In a small town abutting a sea of sparkling cerulean, Flora and Miguel Reyes did not have to be the raisers of a drug-addict, the banished staff of billionaires, the parents of a failed baseball star. They could simply be themselves.

Sure, they were resistant — at first to the idea of leaving in general, later to the idea of leaving me here without them.

Mijo, come with us.

There is nothing left for you here.

We can make a fresh start.

Together.

It took time, but I wore them down. Helped them pack up and drove them to the airport on a crisp October morning when the leaves were the color of fire. Stood on the other side of the TSA checkpoint and watched them disappear — Ma, crying her eyes out, Pa consoling her with soothing words I could not hear.

Some days, I wonder why I didn't get on that plane with them. Why I didn't cut my ties with this place as cleanly as I'd cut my ties to Josephine Valentine. But something deep inside — some stubborn-as-hell part of me — was unwilling to leave. Maybe because leaving felt like running away. Like letting Blair and Vincent and their piles of blood money win at some game I was never qualified to be playing in the first place.

Hell, I don't know.

"I'm sorry for yelling, *mijo*. It's just…"

"I know, Ma. How about this? I promise, the next time I'm caught in a freak squall and have to be rescued by the Coast Guard, I'll call you from the boat. Okay?"

"You'd better. Or I will fly back there and make you regret it."

I laugh lightly. "Don't worry. I don't plan on this ever happening again, if I can help it."

"I have to ask… How is it you came to be with Josephine? I thought, after last summer, the two of you weren't speaking. I thought, after her parents…" She clears her throat, nervous to even broach the subject of Blair and Vincent Valentine. "Have things changed?"

"No. It was just…" Jo's words from the island come back to me. "A freak twist of fate. That's all."

"Oh." Ma's voice is softened around the edges by a deep sadness. "That's too bad. I was hoping you'd found your way back to one another."

"You know that's not going to happen."

"But—"

"Look, I'm exhausted. I need to get some sleep now. I'm sorry for worrying you and Pa. I'll call you tomorrow and give you all the details, okay?"

"*Mijo*—"

"Night," I cut her off before she can say another word about my relationship with Jo, terminating the call with a sharp jab of my finger. Falling back against my pillows with a deep sigh, I stare up at the water-stained ceiling. My mind is awhirl with all that's happened in the past few hours. Exhausted as I am, I know I'll never be able to fall asleep. There's an electricity in my veins; a shockwave surging like an overextended generator through my every nerve ending.

For the first time in a long, long time... I realize I don't feel numb. Not at all. My heart, which has spent the past twelve months encased in solid ice, is pounding with emotions so strong, I think my ribcage might burst.

It doesn't take a genius to figure out the catalyst.

Not with her face burned into my retinas like a brand.

josephine

THE THIN BLUE curtain pulls back with a sharp yank. A middle-aged nurse steps up to the side of my hospital bed, her pale pink scrubs a cheerful counterpoint to the rest of my current surroundings. She shoots me a fleeting smile as she checks the sensors monitoring my vitals for the zillionth time, making small notes in the margins of my chart.

Since I arrived two hours ago, the ER doctors at Beverly Hospital have put me through a full gamut of tests. Electrocardiograms and X-rays, blood work and pulse oximetry. I've been poked, I've been prodded and, ultimately, I've been provided with information I already knew.

I'm totally fine.

"Can I go home now?"

"Just waiting on those final lab results. We want to be sure everything is ship-shape before we send you out that door." The nurse — Laura, according to her name tag, though she never formally introduced herself — pins me with a steely look. "You had quite a scare today. I still think you should take Dr. Pinkerton's advice and stay the night."

"I just want to be home, in my own bed. Preferably after

I've taken a hot shower to wash away all traces of this day."

She holds up her hands in surrender, then passes me a clipboard full of paperwork. "Fine, fine. In that case, we should have you out of here within the hour. Just fill out this discharge information and we'll get you on your way."

"What time is it, anyway?"

"Nearly midnight."

I settle back against the thin pillows with a sigh, fingers curled tight around the clipboard. The ER is buzzing with activity, even at this hour. The hospital staff blames Independence Day — *"Fireworks turn grown men into teenagers,"* Nurse Laura confided earlier — for the slew of traumas rolling through their doors tonight. So far, I've seen two blown-off fingers, four drunken teenagers in need of stomach-pumping, and one man with a BBQ fork stuck in his thigh.

Comparatively, my near-drowning is downright boring.

"Looks like you need the bed space, anyway," I point out, jerking my chin toward the automatic doors where two paramedics are wheeling someone new inside on a stretcher. I can't see much of the man, except a bloody bandage wrapped around his head, but I can certainly hear him — he's hollering loud enough to shake the walls, his words slurred into a drunken, indecipherable jumble.

"Jeeze," I mutter, eyes widening. "He's having quite a night."

"And we're the ones who'll pay for it." Laura shakes her head. "Drunk as a skunk, trying to shoot off a roman candle... Stupidity. Sheer stupidity. Lord, I hate this holiday." She hustles away to help, stopping after a few steps to call back to me, "Oh, I forgot to mention — you have a visitor coming. They should be on their way in here any minute now."

My heart lurches inside my chest. "Who? Who is it?"

But Laura is already long gone, off to help the paramedics

restrain the inebriated man struggling to escape the confines of his gurney.

Who could possibly be here?

My mind filters through every possibility of who is about to walk through those waiting-room doors, fixating on one distinct option with a disproportionate amount of hope — even though I know, deep down, there's no chance in Hell it'll be Archer. He wouldn't come here. Not in a million years. He couldn't wait to get away from me, earlier.

He spent the whole boat ride to shore talking to the Coast Guard officials, detailing everything that happened to us. When we reached the docks, where an ambulance was waiting to bring me here, he kept his eyes averted from mine as they loaded me onto a stretcher and into the back. I thought he might expire on the spot when the paramedic innocently asked, *"Will your boyfriend be riding to the hospital with you?"*

Given my own response — namely, shouting "NO!" with far too much volume from inside the vehicle — I'm surprised they didn't drive me straight to the nearest psychiatric ward.

I wince at the memory. Hours later, the embarrassment lingers in my system, palpable and paralyzing. I try not to think too much about Archer, but I'm haunted by the memory of my last glimpse of him, just before the doors slammed shut between us — standing in the darkness of the docks, his face flashing blue-red-blue-red-blue in the silent siren lights, his dark brows pulled together in an unreadable expression. We drove away, and just like that...

Archer Reyes is out of my life again.

The sound of kitten heels clicking against the linoleum floors jerks me out of my reverie. Glancing up, I see a familiar gray-clad form crossing to my bedside, her expression pinched as ever beneath the fluorescent hospital lighting.

"Mrs. Granger." I sit up more firmly in bed. "What are you

doing here?"

"What am I doing here? I think the better question, Miss Valentine, is what are *you* doing here?" Her voice is practically quivering with indignation. "And why did I have to hear about your being here from a very distressed Spanish woman in the middle of the night who claims to be your emergency contact?"

"Flora?!"

"Yes, *Flora*. Flora Reyes. At least, that was the name she gave when she called the estate earlier this evening, frantic to get in touch with your parents or any other responsible adult." She clutches her purse tighter. If she was wearing pearls, I'm sure she'd be clutching them too. "I won't even get into the impropriety of listing a former housekeeper as your primary point of outreach during a life-threatening scenario such as this, but I do urge you to, at the very least, select someone within the continental United States, who is actually able to be by your side."

"I forgot she was listed as my emergency contact," I tell her. And it's the truth. I really had forgotten. For most of my childhood, Flora and Miguel were a fixed constant in my life — far more so than my biological parents, often half a world away on one of their extended business trips. It made much more sense to call the Reyeses in the event of a medical crisis. It never occurred to me that I'd need to remove them from my medical files after they moved away. "I'm sorry, Mrs. Granger. She never should've bothered you. I know it's late, and—"

"*Bothered* me?" There's a fissure of strain showing in my housekeeper's unshakeable composure; her upper lip trembles with something that, in anyone else, I'd describe as downright disgruntlement. "It's my job to manage the Valentine house-hold. This certainly falls under that purview." She takes a few steps closer, her posture stiff as a board. "Now, if you are quite ready, allow us to take our leave — preferably before the drunkard across the room shatters my eardrums with his bellowing."

"There's still insurance paperwork to fill out—

She waves away the clipboard. "I'll handle all the particulars tomorrow morning. Come along, now. We'll get you back to Cormorant House and into a proper bed. One with actual sheets and pillowcases without stains from Lord only know's what. Honestly, the sheer nerve of calling *this*—" Her eyes cut a scathing path around the room. "—a hospital ward. I've seen prison systems with better aesthetics."

"I think the doctors are more concerned with saving lives than interior decor." I gasp with faux-outrage. "Where on *earth* are their priorities?"

She frowns at me. "There's no need to be glib, Miss Valentine."

"Sorry. I'm just tired. It's been a long day, what with nearly dying and everything."

"Mmm. In any case, I do hope you've saved some energy to speak to your parents. They're expecting your call."

My mouth gapes. "You told my parents about this?"

"Of course I did."

"Why would you do that?"

Mrs. Granger looks genuinely baffled by the question. "They're my employers. Why would I ever withhold information about their daughter from them?"

"They're very busy people, in case you hadn't noticed. There's no need to bother them with something this trivial."

"Nearly dying is *trivial*?"

I sigh. "Let's just say, when it comes to my general wellbeing, my parents are mainly concerned with things that could affect my academic performance and future earning potential."

"I'm certain that is simply untrue."

"Agree to disagree then." I swing my legs over the side of

the hospital bed and slide my feet into the scratchy microfiber slippers Nurse Laura was kind enough to leave for me. "Let's go."

Mrs. Granger looks pointedly at the wheelchair waiting by the end of my bed.

My eyes widen. "You cannot be serious."

"As you've no doubt learned by now, Miss Valentine, I am rarely one to play practical jokes. Now, take a seat."

"But—"

"Take. A. Seat."

I heave a martyred sigh.

And then I take a seat.

It's been the longest day of my life. I'm in no mood to argue. Frankly, I'm in no mood to do a damn thing except crawl beneath the covers of my bed and sleep for the next hundred or so years. Unfortunately, an unpleasant chat with my parents separates me from a solid night's rest.

Mrs. Granger drives me home in her beige-on-beige sedan as I begrudgingly dial the number of the executive office at VALENT headquarters from the passenger seat. Blair and Vincent take the call on speakerphone. They seem both annoyed I've interrupted the start of their workday and displeased that I've managed to sink my sailboat. They are altogether less worried by my brush with death and subsequent visit to the ER.

My father mumbles something about filing an insurance claim to recoup some of the financial loss, while my mother makes a pointed comment about how this never would've happened if I'd merely stayed in Switzerland, where I belong. By the time we hang up, my soul feels as battered as my body. I don't have any energy leftover to call Oliver. Which truly should make me feel a modicum of guilt. But I'm too tired even for self-condemnation.

Telling myself I'll contact him the moment my eyes spring open tomorrow morning, I take a scalding hot shower and collapse face-first onto my bed without bothering to change into pajamas. Given how tired I am, I assume I'll fall asleep instantly. But as ten minutes turn into twenty... as one hour ticks by, then two... sleep remains frustratingly out of reach. I toss and turn in my bed, unable to find a comfortable position. More though, unable to quiet my mind long enough to drift off into a blissful state of unconsciousness. Not with every waking thought wrapped up in Archer Reyes.

Here, safe in the silent darkness of my childhood bedroom, without the distractions of the storm, without the need to fight for survival... my battered brain begins to piece together some of the more puzzling elements of my day. Details I overlooked in the shock-laced aftermath of Cupid sinking are now lodged at the forefront of my mind. And they are not so easily dismissed.

I turn a single question over and over, examining it from every angle, like an archaeologist trying to make sense of an inexplicable artifact at a dig-site — an arrowhead from the wrong age embedded firmly in the topsoil, eons away from where it belongs.

Why the hell is Archer working on a lobster boat?

A star baseball pitcher at Bryant University wouldn't choose to spend his summer break hauling traps for minimum wage. Not even Archer, who has never shied away from a hard day's work. It doesn't make a shred of sense. Nor does the way he looked — which, to be honest, was like a shadowy mirror of his former self. Barely recognizable.

It wasn't merely the beard, obscuring his sharp jawline, or the fishing garb, or even the rather thin affirmation he gave when I questioned his chosen employment. It was something more. A look in his eyes that was never there before. A bitter darkness that reminded me a bit too much of his older brother, Jaxon.

Jax.

I haven't thought of him in ages. Last time our paths crossed, he was fresh out of prison — and seemed determined to land himself back there as soon as humanly possible, judging by the seedy company he was keeping. He's always run with a bad crowd, even back in high school; somehow, I doubt his fellow inmates provided any positive reinforcement.

For Flora and Miguel's sake, I hope I'm wrong. I hope he's managed to turn his life around and stay away from some of his more addictive habits.

Like heroin.

And fentanyl.

And oxycodone.

It always amazes me that two sons of the same blood could turn out so different. Where Archer is warmth and good humor, Jaxon is wrath and biting malcontent. Polar opposites, even before Jax developed a drug problem. At least, that's how it used to be. Something in Archer changed last summer. Something peeled away some of his happy outer shell and revealed a darker layer I never knew was there, hidden underneath. One I could not decipher, despite my best efforts. One that narrowed a bit of that demarcation line between him and his older brother.

Seemingly overnight, he became a different person. Guarded, defensive, brooding. And, perhaps most hurtful of all, completely uninterested in being my best friend. I was never able to figure out what triggered the change in him, or why he was so determined not to let me in on the secret. I suppose the answer was staring me in the face. I just didn't want to acknowledge it.

He might've been my best friend... but I was no longer his.

It shouldn't have come as such a surprise. After all, I'd spent a solid chunk of my teenage years worried he'd tire of me at some point. That my introverted inclinations would ultimately bore him — especially once he began to ascend the social pyramid at Exeter Academy during our senior year.

Why would he want to hang out with boring old me when half the varsity cheerleaders were lining up to date him?

Even if Archer hadn't intentionally pulled away, our friendship would've changed eventually. At separate colleges, leading separate lives, we would've drifted apart naturally, as so many high school friends do, finding ourselves with scarcely anything in common by the first Thanksgiving recess of freshman year.

But bracing for a schism and living through one are different beasts entirely. I'd be lying if I said I was not left reeling by the sharp sting of his rejection last summer. I'd be lying again if I said twelve months of space somehow supplied me with closure.

The sad truth is, I've spent a year pushing down the pain instead of healing it, burying my grief beneath the weight of a new relationship instead of working through it properly. And now, like a fool, I find myself disintegrating all over again; the loss bubbling up from the deep like a volcano gone temporarily dormant.

How pathetic is that?

One afternoon in Archer's presence, and I'm slammed right back to where I started, heart ripped to shreds like the letter he left when he ended our friendship. Unable to think straight with my head so clouded by him.

Questions I still lack answers to tug at me with vicious fingers.

What could've happened last summer to change him so completely?

Were those scars I saw on the hand he was so quick to hide away?

Which pieces of this infuriating puzzle am I still missing?

After the events of today, it has become abundantly clear to me that I do not know the whole story of Archer Reyes. My thoughts scatter into a million fragments, then reform into implausible shapes. In the darkness, I begin to wonder ridiculous things. To postulate improbable scenarios, if only to fill in the gaps in our story. Anything to explain why he's here, working a summer job so outside his skill set I can hardly wrap my head around it.

Unless...

It's not a summer job at all.

It's just...

A job.

My eyes widen in the darkness as the possibility bounces inside my skull, a ping-pong ball of chaos, upending the ground beneath my feet. Questions come at me so fast, I can barely keep track of them all.

What if, for some reason, Archer never went away to school?

What if he's not playing baseball at all?

What if, however crazy it seems, he's become a full-time lobsterman?

I try to dismiss these strange inklings as no more than the delirious effects of an overtired mind. But, once considered, they are not so easily brushed aside. With each passing hour, I become more determined to follow the threads of suspicion braiding together inside my chest into a tight knot that threatens to block my airway. I become equally aware that, after hours of tossing and turning in vain, nodding off to a peaceful sleep is an unattainable impossibility.

Throwing on a pair of yoga pants and a sports bra, I slide my feet into rubber sandals and head downstairs. The house is empty, the silence absolute. I cross the kitchen and slip out the back door, onto the terrace. The night air is thick with humidity. It's nearly dawn. On the eastern horizon, the sky is tinged with the faintest shades of pink and yellow, the first fingertips of sunrise creeping into focus.

I don't dwell on my own intentions as I walk down the sloping lawn toward the cove. My heart gives a great pang when I look out over the dock, barren and useless in Cupid's absence. The heart-pangs only intensify as I turn my back on the sea and head toward the stone building hanging halfway out over the water. Sucking in a sharp breath, I grasp the door handle and push my way into the boathouse before I can talk myself out of it. The door shuts behind me with a creak that vibrates my bones.

My pulse pounds in time to each footfall on the paneled flooring as I walk deeper into the dim space. There, at the interior slip, sits my father's navy blue Hinckley picnic boat. She gleams with a fresh coat of paint, even in the low light. The mere sight of her triggers a series of memories, flashing rapid-fire across my mind: Archer and me, tangled together in the berth, exploring with greedy fingers and love-starved lips that fateful night last summer.

Prom night.

The night that changed everything.

But I am not here to reminisce on things that make my soul ache. I am not here for the boy who took my virginity, with his vacillating intentions and abrupt changes of attitude. I am here for the version of him I'd rather remember. The boy I grew up with. My fiercest protector, my closest ally. My best friend.

My Archer.

The climb up the ladder is longer than I recalled. The rungs are coated with dust beneath my grip. No one has been up here in over a year, that much is evident. At the top, I hunch-walk my way to the rafters' edge, ducking my head to avoid the sloped roof, dodging around obstacles whose locations I memorized by heart long ago. I'm barely breathing as I step into the small cleared area of the loft so often frequented by Archer and me during our childhood.

Our spot.

I lower myself to the floor and swing my legs over the edge of the rafters. The sun has now made its presence known in full, brightening the sky to a dozen shades of pastel, like watercolors on an artist's palette. A single shaft of light shoots through the window pane, illuminating a plank on the wall beside me. There, carved into the wood by two twelve year olds with a stolen pocket knife, are two sets of initials.

AR + JV

I trace the roughly gouged edges with the tip of one finger. Tears gather behind my eyes as I think about those two kids, pressed shoulder to shoulder, giggling as they left their lopsided mark with the tip of the blade. Innocent fools with their whole lives still ahead of them. Not yet damaged by the world and all those who inhabit it.

Back then, we were certain of absolutely nothing — nothing, except the most important thing of all: that no matter where our paths led, we would be there together at the finish line. Through thick and thin. Inseparable until the end of time.

AR + JV

4EVR

I sit there for a long while, tears dripping down my cheeks in silence as the sun slowly cants higher into the sky. The beam of light eventually moves away from the carved letters, shifting sideways across the floor.

Letting us fade once more into the shadows.

SIXTEEN

archer

I WAKE UNGODLY EARLY the morning after the storm. My body is conditioned to rising before dawn even when I'm dead tired. I walk my usual route to the harbor, more out of habit than anything. There's no real reason for it — with the Ebenezer shattered to bits by the Atlantic and Tommy embracing his early retirement, I'm staring down the long road of unemployment.

For the briefest of moments, I contemplate looking for a different line of work. Something with a salary and healthcare benefits. Something less back-breaking. Something that will get me out of my shitty apartment, out of this pit of despair I've fallen into. Out of my whole fucking life, frankly.

Wishful thinking.

I'm qualified for exactly nothing. Without a college degree and five years of entry-level experience under my belt, I'll be laughed out of any salaried white-collar interview in town.

Face the facts, an ugly voice whispers from the back of my mind. *You're only good for changing bait bags and banding crusher claws. You'll only ever be a grunt worker. A lackey.*

Loser.

Failure.

Townie.

My thoughts are dark as the pre-dawn horizon. I hasten my pace, as if to outrun them, getting to the harbor just as the first trucks are rolling in, their headlights dim beams in the shadowy parking lot. I recognize several of the local lobstermen stepping out onto the pavement, already wearing their rubber boots and coveralls, breath steaming the air as they sip coffee from thermoses and bark low orders at their stern-men. I brace my shoulders as I make my approach.

In my gut, I know it's highly unlikely I'll be able to find another lobstering gig this late in the season — most captains locked in their crew months ago. But I ask around anyway, growing more frustrated with each fruitless conversation.

Sorry, son.

Already have a stern-man.

Check back next spring.

The sun rises higher in the sky as my hopes plummet. By late morning, I've made the rounds down every dock without a lick of success to show for it. Fists clenched, teeth gritted, I take the long way back to my apartment. My nose twitches at the fishy smell as I pass by a row of trawlers bobbing on thick, braided lines at the commercial pier. Long-haul vessels, rust stained and salt coated, with large dragger nets suspended on wooden booms from either side.

The men who work on these rigs return to land only once every few weeks. I've seen them on the stools at Biddy's, with their empty-eyed stares and stern-pressed mouths. They look devoid of life — like all that time on the water, away from humanity, has stripped something vital from their bones.

That sort of work has never appealed to me, but I'll be forced to consider it if things grow desperate enough. I need money and for that, I need a new job. The small nest egg I've been stockpiling from my lobstering wages won't keep me afloat for much longer.

The last slip on the pier hosts a particularly ugly trawler. It's a depressing sight to behold, with its corroded side panels and splintered booms. Next to it, the Ebenezer would've looked like a luxury cruiser. As I meander past, eyes moving absently over the name REINA in faded paint across the stern, a deck-hand emerges from the cabin, his hands braced around a black plastic crate of fresh fish from the ice-hold. Our eyes meet for the briefest of moments across the space, and I feel my feet falter.

Because I'm staring at my brother.

His hair is a few inches longer, his tattooed sleeves bear a considerable amount of fresh ink, his rangy build is packed with more muscle than before... but it is indisputably, unquestionably Jaxon.

"Well, well, well," he drawls, walking down the gang-plank with measured steps. "If it isn't my baby brother."

My jaw is clenched so tight, I can't form a single word. Rage, red-hot, pumps through my bloodstream, burning me up from the inside out. It takes all my self-control to keep from charging at him, fists flying. To hold back from pummeling him into the planks beneath my feet.

"From the look on your face, I'm guessing you weren't expecting to see me." Jax grins, a flash of straight white teeth. "I must say, after a year, I thought maybe you'd be a little less pissed about everything that went down last summer."

My feet are rooted to the dock. My jaw is locked so tight, I'm no longer breathing. The act of pulling air in and out of my lungs feels too risky. If I open my mouth to let in oxygen, I'm not sure I'll be able to contain all the fury from pouring out in a deadly torrent.

Jax continues walking down the gangplank, closing the

distance between us with a casual stride that makes me want to wrap my hands around his throat and squeeze until that gloating look disappears from his face. His eyes never shift from mine; his grin never wavers. "What, nothing to say to me? No, *'Hey, bro, how are you?'* No, *'Wow, Jax! I've missed you, let's hug it out?'*"

With each mocking syllable that slips from his venomous lip, my self-control slips a little more.

"Where are those fine manners of yours? The ones Ma and Pa were always bragging about? *'Why can't you be more like Archer? He's so polite. So good. So perfect.'*" He makes a tsk sound with his tongue. "Guess you aren't so perfect anymore, though, are you?"

Somehow, I manage not to react. But my patience has grown precariously thin.

Reaching the end of the gang-plank, Jax steps onto the dock. Only a dozen feet separate us, now. I tell myself to turn and walk away, to be the bigger man, but my feet are no longer cooperating. All I can do is stand there, stock-still, as he brings us face-to-face.

"You know..." There's that grin again — laced with equal parts mocking and malice. "I'm disappointed, brother."

It's that word that finally breaks me.

Brother.

Of all the things Jaxon Reyes has been in his life, he has never once acted like a sibling to me. Not a role model, not my hero, not anyone I could possibly look up to or idolize. And he never even cared to try.

"*You are not my brother,*" I hiss, the words bursting from my chest like cannon-fire. "You're dead to me."

He laughs. Laughs, like it's the funniest thing he's ever heard in his life. "Oh, Archer. You always did hold a grudge."

"A grudge?" I laugh, too, but the sound is so bitter, so

joyless, it's really more of a bark. "You think that's all this is? You broke our parents' hearts. You ruined my life. You ripped our family apart."

"Speak for yourself. I'm doing just fine here."

"That's rich! You're a criminal. You're wanted by the police for drug possession and parole violation," I remind him, none too gently. "Some *brotherly* advice? Turn yourself in, Jaxon."

"That won't be happening." His eyes turn cold as he takes a measured step toward me. "And while we're giving one another advice... Before you get any grand ideas of dropping a dime to my PO about where I've been spending my time, allow me to suggest you keep your fucking mouth shut. You should know better than anyone, the crew I run with these days does not screw around when it comes to people who complicate our business."

"So you're still caught up with the Latin Kings, then?" I shake my head, scoffing. "Why am I not surprised to learn you're just a lackey for some two-bit drug lord?"

"You don't know what the fuck you're talking about!" Jax snaps, fury rising swiftly. "I'm no one's lackey. Most of the shit we've got going on right now is thanks to *me*. The boss knows that, and he respects me for it. Which is more than I could ever say for you. Or our parents. You all treated me like a screw-up from the moment I was born."

"Well, if the shoe fits..."

His mouth twists into a snide smirk. "I guess it was a hard pill for you — the precious Reyes golden boy — to swallow. After all that work, all that dedication... you're going to end up no better off than our parents. Just another blue-collar stiff, slaving for the man. About as far from the lights of Fenway Park as you could find yourself." He laughs, like this entire scenario is hilarious to him. "Me? I'm making something of myself. I'm going places. Take a look at yourself in the mirror, Archer. Can you say the same?"

That's it.

The final straw. The camel's back breaks. And my my control, already stretched perilously tight, breaks right along with it.

"*Bastard!*" I roar, hurling my body down the docks headlong in his direction. "You ruined my fucking life!"

Jax sees me coming a mile away. And, judging by the eager expression on his face, he's been craving this altercation for a long while. "I didn't ruin your life, brother. You did that all by yourself."

"Fuck you!"

His smile is laced with vengeance as his arm cranks backward in preparation to throw a punch. He's always been bigger than me, but even after my injuries I'm still faster. I duck his powerhouse right hook and slam into him full-force, catching him in the midsection with my left shoulder. The impact tosses us both off balance. We tumble down onto the docks in a pile of limbs.

Rolling across the splintered wood, we curse at one another as we trade jabs. We're clawing like wild animals, all sense of sportsmanship abandoned. He hauls me into a headlock, one thick arm roping around my neck. I jerk my skull back into his nose with a sharp snap that makes him scream. There's a grim satisfaction burning in my veins when I realize I've likely broken his nose.

Good.

He deserves it.

He deserves all the pain I can possibly inflict.

And then more.

My damaged hand screams in pain, pulsing violently as I clench it into a fist and send it flying into Jaxon's left eye socket. I'm probably undoing six month's worth of physical therapy, but in this moment I am unable to summon the common sense to care. All that matters right now is retribution. Making my older brother suffer the same way he's made me suffer. A fair trade of devastation, delved out in frantic punches and uneven uppercuts.

By the time bystanders from nearby vessels manage to pull us apart, we're both banged up. My lip is swelling to twice its normal size; Jaxon's left eye is turning a deep shade of eggplant. Blood trickles from both his nostrils — his nose is definitely broken. Panting for air, our eyes stay locked in twin glares as we're hauled in opposite directions by the intervening fishermen.

"This isn't over, little brother!" Jaxon's voice carries to me on the wind, each word imbued with gloating malice. "I'll see you again. Soon. Count on it."

I don't say a word. Turning on my heel, I shrug off the restraining grip on my shoulders, spit a gob of bloody saliva into the water, and walk straight toward the only place I know will offer a modicum of comfort.

———

I've been at Biddy's for nearly an hour when the stool beside mine screeches against the hardwood floor as someone drags it backward. I glance over just as a burly, bearded man in his late thirties settles his large frame onto it. I recognize him instantly. One of the regulars. He's here even more often than I am. Harvey, the bartender, sets a frothy beer in front of him before his ass is fully on the seat.

"You're Mahoney's deck hand, aren't you?" he asks, taking a long sip.

I shrug noncommittally. The last thing I want to do is make

smalltalk with a stranger — not after the week I've had. Not ever, really. I guess my *fuck-off* expression needs practice.

"I'm Deacon Hayward. Everyone calls me Dee."

Everyone knows Dee Hayward. He captains the nicest lobster boat in the harbor, a forty-footer tricked out with all the bells and whistles.

"Reyes," I offer flatly, my voice half-muffled as I swallow down a gulp of my whiskey.

"What happened to your face, Reyes?"

"I tripped."

"Into someone's fist, from the looks of it."

I grunt noncommittally.

"Message received — none of my business. I'm not looking to make your day worse, kid. Just wanted to stop over and tell you I heard what happened yesterday. About the Ebenezer, sinking in the storm."

I grunt again.

"Not many secrets on these docks. Word travels fast." Dee takes another sip of his beer. The foam clings to his thick beard as his throat works. "Don't beat yourself up too much, kid. Insurance will cover the loss, payout should be plenty for a new boat — or an early retirement. Tommy should be thanking you, far as I can see it. That old rig of his was cursed right from the start. We all told him it was bad luck to give a boat a man's name, but did he listen? Of course not. That's Tommy Mahoney for you, though. Stubborn as a damn mule and twice as ornery."

My lips twist.

He's not wrong.

"Talkative chap, I see." Dee chuckles. "Perfect fit for Old Tommy. He never was a chatterbox, either."

"We get along just fine."

"That so? Well, I'm glad to hear he hasn't scared you off the

141

trade entirely. Miserable bastard, he is. Not that you can blame him. Never met a man who's lost so much in one short lifetime."

I glance sharply at him, curious despite myself. "What do you mean?

"You don't know? Ehh, I guess that's no surprise. He wouldn't tell you himself. But Tommy Mahoney used to be a family man, if you can believe it. Beautiful wife, three kids, the whole shebang."

This surprises me. I'd figured someone like Tommy had been alone since the day he was born.

"What happened?" I ask.

"House fire. Tommy was out early one morning, hauling some traps. Came home to find the place burned to ash. His family in their beds along with it. Not even the dog made it out."

I stare into the dregs of my whiskey, swirling it around the bottom of the glass. My chest feels uncomfortably tight. Suddenly, my bad day — my bad *year* — doesn't seem so bleak. "Jesus."

"Nightmare-fuel, truly. Not sure how a man recovers from something like that."

"Suppose he doesn't."

Dee nods. "No one talks about it... and I ain't even sure how true it is, so don't quote me or nothing. But back then, rumor was that Tommy left a stove-burner lit when he went out fishing that day. Fire started in the kitchen, traveled up the stairs while they were all still sleeping... Smoke got to them before they had a chance to run for it." Shuddering, he takes another long sip of his beer. "Losing your family in a freak fire is one thing. Finding out you're the one responsible for setting it... Well, you can see why Old Tommy is the way he is."

I feel like I've been clobbered over the head. My chest is

tight; my throat blocked with emotions I can't seem to swallow down, no matter how many sips of whiskey I take. I don't know if Dee is expecting a response, but he's not going to get one. I'm incapable of formulating any sort of speech.

There are no words.

Not after hearing that.

In silence, my eyes trace the spiderweb of scars that thread across my wrist, onto the back of my hand. The tangible damage, a visible reminder of the life I've lost. Much as I hate to look at them, I think I'd prefer this sort of damage to that Tommy bears. That undetectable, untraceable kind that snakes its way around your soul and sucks the life from your bones.

"Shit, I'm sorry. Didn't mean to bring your head down, kid." Dee clinks his glass against mine and laughs stiffly to fill the silence that's descended over us. "Mostly just came over 'cause I wanted to tell you that I've seen you around the docks. You're a hard worker." He pauses carefully. "One of my stern-men just up and quit on me. Right before peak season, the son-of-a-bitch. I assume you're out of a job, what with the Ebenezer sitting on the bottom of Salem Sound. You give me a shout if you're looking for a new gig."

Before I can reply, Dee grabs his beer and vanishes into a shadowy corner, where several other regulars are shooting pool on an ancient table with peeling green felt. Leaving me there to nurse my drink and wonder how on earth I'm ever going to meet Tommy's eyes again.

That's the thing about seeing someone else's damage.

You can't ever unsee it.

Harvey doesn't even ask if I want another round. He simply leans over the bar and pours, until my glass is once more full of amber liquid. I drink until the world goes out of focus, stumbling home on unsteady legs under the cover of darkness. But even after I've fallen into bed, water-stained ceiling swimming in and out of focus overhead, I cannot shake the desolation clenched like a fist around my heart, or the grim sadness pounding through my veins like poison.

Jo.

Jaxon.

Tommy.

I pull a pillow over my face and scream until I run out of air.

SEVENTEEN

josephine

"I'M GETTING on the next plane."

"*Ollie.*" I sigh for the third time in as many minutes, my exasperation increasing exponentially with each breath. I try to keep my voice level. "Please. You're overreacting about all of this."

"You nearly died yesterday. Forgive me if I'm a bit frantic at the moment."

"I told you, I'm totally fine."

He's silent for a long stretch. "I just don't understand why you wouldn't want me there to support you after an ordeal like this."

"It's not necessary, that's why. I know how busy you are at VALENT. I'm not going to drag you halfway across the world when there's no justifiable basis for it."

"So... that's the only reason?"

"I don't follow."

He hesitates a beat. "There's no other reason you don't want me coming there, right?"

"Of course not!" My pulse is pounding as the words rush out. "Why would you even ask something like that?"

"You've been so distant since you got there. You barely call me. You don't answer my texts or emails. I feel like... like I'm losing you."

My eyes press closed. God, I'm the worst girlfriend ever. "I'm so sorry, Oliver. Really, I am. Being back here has been a bit more difficult than I thought it would be. I promise from now on I'll reach out more. I'll communicate so much, you'll be sick of me."

"That, I assure you, would be impossible." I can hear the smile twisting the edges of his voice. "I miss you, Josephine. Geneva has gone gray in your absence."

My heart pangs. He's so sweet, it makes me ache. Not with longing, but with something closer to contrition. "I miss you too, Ollie."

"Do you?"

"Of course I do."

"Okay. Okay, that's good to hear."

His sharp exhale of relief is audible across the line. My guilty conscience rears its ugly head. The poor man is starved for reassurance and affection.

"It won't be this way forever," I remind him.

"Does that mean you've made a decision about your attendance at Brown?"

"I have another meeting with my academic advisor in a few weeks. I'll have to tell her whether or not I'm enrolling for next semester when I get there."

"Ah. I see."

There's an awkward silence. I get the sense he's waiting for me to tell him my decision right now, while we're discussing it. But I can't do that. Because that would require me knowing what I'm going to decide. And the truth is, I have no clearer picture of my future in mind than I did the last time we spoke. I still have no idea what to do about Brown, about VALENT, about Archer. About anything.

"Well," Ollie says somewhat stiffly. "I have a meeting in a few minutes with your parents about the marketing budget for next quarter…"

"All right."

"So… I'll guess I'll let you go, then."

"Have a good meeting. I hope Blair and Vincent aren't too unbearable."

He doesn't laugh. His voice is quite serious as he says, "I love you, Josephine."

My eyes press closed. My grip tightens around my coffee cup.

Why is it so difficult to say it back?

"I love you, too."

The call clicks off. The screen goes dark. And those three little words sit heavy on my tongue, tasting more and more like a lie with each passing moment.

———

It's half-past two when the outer gate buzzer rings. I hit pause on my episode of *The Great British Bake-Off* when I hear it. Typically, Mrs. Granger is the one to handle the comings and goings at Cormorant House, but since she's out at the grocery store — no doubt stocking up on a pantry's worth of sickeningly healthy snacks — I'm the one who answers the intercom. The stranger — a wizened, white-haired man of middle years who looks like he's spent more than a few decades in the sun — introduces himself politely as the "boat maintenance man."

I buzz him through the gates and peer out the front window as his sagging Ford rolls slowly around the circular driveway. The truck bed is full of empty lobster traps and bait-storage crates.

"You're not Mrs. Granger," the man says by way of greeting, climbing down out of the cab.

"No," I confirm. I stick out my hand, and he envelops it firmly inside his. His grip is callused, rough in a way that only comes from years of hard labor. "I'm Josephine Valentine. This is my parents' house."

Something like recognition flashes across the man's expression, but it's gone far too quickly to decipher. "Josephine, is it? I'm Tommy Mahoney."

"Nice to meet you, Mr. Mahoney."

"No need for formalities. Just call me Tommy. Everyone else does."

"Okay. Tommy it is, then." I shoot a smile at him. One he does not return. I'm not offended; I get the immediate sense that smiling is not something he does often. "Unfortunately, there's not much work for you to do today. My father's Hinckley is still here but Cupid, my Alerion, sank in that freak storm yesterday, just off the coast of Great Misery."

"You don't say."

My head tilts sideways at the wry note in his voice. "Yeah, it was a real bummer. I've had her for years. Losing her feels a bit like losing a limb."

"Tricky weather, that was. You're lucky you got out alive." Two salt-white brows arch. "Anyone come to your aid out there?"

"Thankfully, there was a lobsterman nearby and willing to lend a hand. I'm not sure I would've been so lucky if he hadn't heard my distress call and shown up to pull me from the water." I pause a beat, laughing humorlessly under my breath. "Though I seriously doubt he sees it that way."

"Now, why would you think a thing like that?"

"Oh. Uh..." I swallow hard, instantly regretting my words. "He ended up sinking his own boat, trying to save me." Aiming for nonchalance, I shrug. "Not sure it was a fair trade, in his eyes."

Tommy says nothing. But his eyes — the palest shade of blue I've ever seen, made more so in contrast to his sun-weathered skin — scan my face so intently, it's like he's trying to see into my soul. Normally, this might make me uncomfortable, but there's something oddly comforting about his closed-off demeanor. I find myself wanting to tell him all my secrets. Knowing he would keep them.

Maybe I do have a concussion, after all.

Finally, Tommy drops his eyes. With an awkward cough, he shifts his weight from one foot to the other. The silence has stretched on for far too long.

"Sorry," I say sheepishly. Embarrassment heats through me, burning the tips of my ears. I'm sure my cheeks are flaming red. "I don't know why I told you any of that."

"No need for apologies. And no need for such thoughts. I'm sure that man — whoever he is — doesn't feel that way. Any mariner worth his salt would happily sacrifice his boat for his girl."

"Oh," I blurt. "I'm not his girl. I'm just—" I break off abruptly, unsure why I'm bothering to explain my twisted saga with Archer to a total stranger. "It doesn't matter."

"Whatever you say." Tommy pauses. "Though if you're feeling guilty over things, you could always do something to make it up to him."

I blink slowly, stupefied by the suggestion. "Such as?"

"Home-cooked meal goes a long way with most men."

"Oh. That's a good idea. It's only... we aren't on the best of terms, these days. I'm not sure he'd appreciate me showing up with a thank-you casserole, butting into his personal life like that..."

"That boy's life could use some butting into, trust me."

"What?" I ask, certain I've misheard him.

"Nothing, nothing." Tommy's mouth twists sardonically. "Just blowing hot air."

"Okay..." Shaking off my confusion, I downshift the conversation back to business. "Anyway. Do you need me to show you to the boathouse?"

"No, I've been here plenty of times before. I know the way."

"All right. Mrs. Granger should be back soon, but if you need anything in the meantime, I'll be at the pool."

He gives a short nod and, after wordlessly retrieving his tool kit from the back of his truck, walks down the pebbled path that leads through the gardens, toward the water. Just before he's out of earshot, he stops to glance back at me. His gruff voice carries on the wind.

"Hey, Josephine!"

"Yes?"

"Don't bring him a casserole. Make him a pie. No man says no to a pie. Especially apple. With a big scoop of vanilla ice cream on the side."

He turns and walks off before I have a chance to respond, whistling lightly as he goes.

It's a nice enough suggestion. Though, if he knew the slightest bit about my relationship with Archer, he'd know it's going to take a lot more than baked goods to repair things between us.

———

After yet another sleepless night tossing and turning, going over everything that happened on the Fourth of July again and again and again, until I want to pull my hair out by the roots, Tommy's suggestion doesn't seem quite so ludicrous.

When the sun's first rays of light begin to leak through my curtains, I kick off my duvet and swallow a scream of sleep-deprived frustration. Over the past few days, my confusion about Archer has solidified into a mass of quiet rage I cannot push down, no matter how many times I try to swallow it. All the words I want to say — to scream — at him are lodged at the back of my throat, making it harder and harder to breathe with each passing hour.

None of my usual mind-occupation tricks are working. Nothing provides a true distraction. Not burying myself in books, not lounging at the pool, not scrolling aimlessly on the internet for hours. Even the possibility of a long sail has been taken away from me, given Cupid's current location.

In my overtired, increasingly ornery state, perhaps my better judgment is compromised because I decide to take matters into my own hands. To get the bottom of things, once and for all. At this point, I figure I've got nothing left to lose.

It's time I got some answers.

Past time.

I pay special attention to my hair and makeup, fussing with my reflection in the mirror until I'm satisfied with the girl staring back at me. She is not the same innocent introvert who left this place last summer, heart shattered and head hanging low. That girl is long gone. In her place stands a young woman in a chic linen dress, with a direct gaze and unflinching confidence. At least, that's what I'm hoping I look like. I have a feeling, as soon as I find myself face to face with Archer, my carefully cultivated self-possession will crumble to dust and fly away on the wind.

I'll have to track him down first, though.

I hop behind the wheel of the Porsche and head toward the

only lead I possess. It doesn't take long to reach the police station — situated smack in the middle of Manchester-by-the-Sea's idyllic downtown, a stone's throw from the harbor. With a force of a dozen total officers, it takes even less time to locate Chris Tomlinson inside the white-columned building. In fact, he's the first person I come across, sitting at the front desk manning the reception area.

"They've got you on phone duty, huh?" I ask, smiling sunnily at him as I step through the front doors. "Not out fighting crime?"

"Oh, you know. The glamorous life of a rookie."

"They let you use a gun yet?"

He scoffs. "They barely let me use the stapler."

"Give it time. I have a feeling that by the end of the year, you'll have graduated to a three-hole-punch at the very least."

"Hardy-har-har." He narrows his eyes at me across the desk. "So what brings you here today? I assumed, since you blew off my Fourth of July cookout, you were already on your way back to France."

"Switzerland."

"Not my point, Valentine."

"Sorry." I blow out a breath. "I sort of... need a favor."

"Let me guess. You want my help getting out of a speeding ticket."

"Not exactly."

"Parking violation?"

"Nope."

"Jaywalking fine?"

"No."

"Then what the hell do you need help with? If you couldn't tell by this whole secretary-duty thing, I don't have an excessive amount of pull on the force yet. There's only so much I can do. My powers are limited."

"This favor is not crime related, Chris. Relax."

"Oh." His brows pull together. "Then what is it about?"

I murmur a single word.

"What was that?" Chris asks. "You mumbled."

"Archer," I repeat, marginally louder.

"Still couldn't quite make out—"

"Oh for the love of God," I hiss. "*Archer!* Archer Reyes. My old friend, your former teammate. Don't make me say it a third time."

"All right, all right. No need to yell at me." He holds his hands up in surrender. "I'm not messing with you. I'm just surprised to hear you asking about Archer when, the last time I saw you, you were pretty adamant about forgetting his general existence."

"That was before I bumped into him."

Chris's face pales. "*Shit.* When?"

I give him a brief summary of my Fourth of July, skimming over all but the most vital details — the sudden storm, the boat sinking, the eventual rescue. His brows pinch tighter and tighter together as I talk.

"I guess I'll give you a pass on missing my barbecue," he says when I finally trail off into silence. "Nearly drowning is a pretty good excuse."

I choke out a hoarse laugh. "Thanks."

"So I'm guessing, when you saw Archer, it wasn't a reunion of hugs and happy memories...?"

"Definitely not." I heave a sigh. "It was pretty much the opposite in every way imaginable."

"Sorry to hear that."

"It's not your fault."

"Well, I hate to be obtuse, Valentine, I'm just still not exactly sure how this all concerns me. I don't have insight when it comes to you and Reyes and your strange relationship."

"There is no *relationship*!"

"You know, it's a crime to lie to a police officer."

"Spare me. You're a glorified secretary with a taser."

"She comes to me for help, then she insults me..." He shakes his head in faux-serious hurt. "I'm gravely wounded by your lack of respect."

"Do me a favor and set that aside for a second. I came here because after seeing Archer..." I trail off, struggling to put my thoughts into words. "The way he looked... Those scars on his hand..."

"Ah." Chris grimaces. "You have questions."

"Yes. I have so many questions, I can't see straight. I can't sleep at night. And you're the only person I can think of who might have the answers."

Suddenly, he's avoiding my eyes like the plague. "It really isn't my place to say anything about what went down with Archer last summer."

"Last week, you couldn't wait to fill me in!"

"Yeah, well, that was before Archer practically tossed me across the docks for mentioning your name."

My heart skips a beat. "He did *what*?"

Chris shakes his head. "It doesn't matter. You're a sweet girl, Josephine. I like you. I really do. But I have to stand with my boy Reyes on this front. Bros before—"

"So help me, if you call me a hoe right now..."

"Fine. Pricks before chicks. Men before hens. Guys before girls with pretty blue eyes. Males before—"

"Please stop now."

He leans back in his office chair, pinning me with a look. "I'm sorry. I really can't say more."

I chew my lip, trying to hold back the words fighting for freedom. "Can you at least tell me..."

"What?"

"Is he okay? Because... he didn't seem okay."

Something in Chris' expression goes dark. "*Okay* is a relative term."

"Is he in some sort of trouble?"

"Trouble is also a relative term."

"Tomlinson, I swear I will hurt you. I may be petite, but I woke up with violence today."

"Shaking in my boots, over here. But I'm still not spilling the tea. Sorry, Valentine."

I make a sound of vexation somewhere between a growl and a groan.

"Hey, don't shoot the messenger! This is not my story to tell. If you want to know the truth about last summer, it's going to have to come from Reyes."

"If you won't give me any details, then you at least have to tell me where to track him down. Because other than roaming the fish docks of Gloucester Harbor for a bearded lobsterman who only vaguely resembles the boy I grew up with, I'm not sure where to start."

"The docks are actually exactly where you want to start," Chris informs me, heaving a sigh of deep martyrdom. He pulls the cap off a pen and scribbles something down on a notepad. Tearing off the top sheet, he passes it to me. "Here."

I glance down at the piece of paper. Beneath the MBTS police department letterhead is an address in navy ink. I don't recognize the street name, but it has a Gloucester zip code.

"What's this?"

"Answers."

"What sort of answers?"

"Relax, it's not a serial killer's den of iniquity. It's Archer's apartment."

My brows lift. "He has an apartment? But, what about Bryant—"

"Sorry." He mimes zipping his lips closed. "That's all I can give you."

"Fine. Thanks. I guess."

"My pleasure."

I pocket the paper and turn for the door. I might've come here for clarity, but I'm leaving even more confused than I was when I arrived.

"Don't be a stranger!" Chris calls after me as the doors swing shut at my back. "Come visit any time! I'll let you use the stapler!"

I shake my head, laughing softly under my breath all the way across the parking lot.

EIGHTEEN

archer

THE KNOCK that sounds on my door at nearly ten that evening is soft. Hesitant. As if the person doing the knocking is half-ready to run off before I have a chance to open it.

Wondering who the hell could possibly be at my apartment this late, I jam my thumb against a button on the television remote, muting the sounds of the cheering crowd at Fenway Park on my screen, shove to my feet, and stomp to the entryway. It's probably Tomlinson — the guy just can't seem to take no for an answer, despite the three texts I've already sent declining his offer to watch tonight's Red Sox game at the Salty Dog over a beer and a plate of nachos.

Need to tell you something, he insisted in his last message.

Life-threatening? I replied.

Not exactly.

Then it can wait, I sent back, before flipping my phone into DO NOT DISTURB mode. I'm not good company at the moment. My bottom lip is still swollen to twice its normal size, courtesy of Jaxon's beefy knuckles on the docks yesterday, and I have a pretty nice shiner blooming over my left temple.

As I walk to the door, I press the bag of frozen peas more firmly against my brutalized face. I don't bother pulling on a shirt or even brushing the crumbs from my sweatpants as I grab the knob and yank it inward.

"Tomlinson," I say over the screeching hinges. "I told you earlier, I'm not in the mood fo—"

The words fall off my tongue as the bag of peas falls out of my hands. I hear it hit the ground at my feet with a dull thud, but I don't look down to see where it landed. My eyes are locked on the girl standing at my door. One of her small hands is still aloft, frozen in place mid-knock; the other is holding a pie dish covered in foil. The scent of baked apples and cinnamon sugar fills the narrow hallway where she's standing, her upturned face illuminated by the flickering fluorescent light.

For a moment there's only silence, interspersed by the occasional buzz of a moth flying repeatedly into the bare bulb overhead. I swallow sharply, trying to make sense of this implausible scenario: Josephine Valentine, standing on my doorstep in the middle of the night, holding a fucking pie.

Whatever careful speech she undoubtedly rehearsed in the mirror before coming here quickly disintegrates when she catches sight of me.

"Your face!" she blurts, horrified eyes sweeping across my features. "God, you look awful!"

I say nothing in response.

Seeming to realize this might not be the most appropriate of greetings, she coughs lightly and adds, "Are... Are you okay?"

I don't know how to respond to that. So I don't. Her eyes flicker toward her feet, avoiding mine. She's nervous, that much is plain to see. Probably not half as nervous as I am, but I'm hopefully doing a better job at hiding that fact.

"Sorry. I guess it's not really my business."

I clear my throat. My hand is gripping the door knob so tight, it's losing circulation. "What are you doing here, Josephine?"

She flinches, almost imperceptibly, when I say her name. As though just hearing it from my lips is enough to cause her physical pain.

I just can't seem to stop hurting her.

"I..." she hedges uncomfortably. Her voice is small enough to tell me this interaction is not going at all how she'd planned. I bet she regrets her decision to ever darken my doorstep. "I brought you a pie."

My eyes flash briefly to the dish in her hands before returning to study her face. The way she's chewing her bottom lip is driving me to distraction. There's a lock of hair falling out of her braid, into her eyes; I cross my arms over my chest to give them a task, so I won't reach out and tuck it back for her. My tone is glacial.

"You brought me a pie."

"It's apple," she hurries on, words rushing together in a breathy stream. "And it's probably not very good. Honestly, I've never made a pie before. I just wanted to give you something. As a thank you. You know... for... well, for saving my life the other day in the storm." She extends the pie out toward me, clearly wanting me to take it from her hands.

I don't.

The pie hovers in the air between us, caught in suspended animation. The natural thing — the normal thing — would be to take it from her. But my arms remain immobile, crossed over my chest. If I release them, I worry I'll do something stupid, like push the pie dish aside and haul her straight into my arms.

"So..." She sucks in a shaky inhale, clearly trying to maintain her composure. "Yeah. That's it. That's all she wrote, folks!" A nervous chuckle pops from her lips. She quickly

159

clamps them together, stifling the sound. "Anyway. Thanks. I guess I already said that, huh? So... thanks *again*."

The pie creeps another inch toward me. Her arms are now fully extended; the dish is almost brushing my bare abdominal muscles. There's a part of me that aches to take it from her hands. To accept her awkward little peace offering and invite her inside — not just into my apartment, but into my life again. Into my soul again.

But I can't.

I have nothing to offer her anymore.

Frankly, the fact that she's here — on the doorstep of my shitty apartment, getting a first-hand glimpse into just how far from grace I've fallen — is setting off bombs of mortification inside my chest, a series of rapid-fire explosions that rock me to my core. Smoky self-loathing billows up into my airway; my voice comes out choked with it.

"I never asked for a thank you. Or an unannounced visit, for that matter."

"That's kind of the whole point — if the person has to *ask* for a thank you, it's not a real show of appreciation, now is it? And since I don't have your phone number anymore, I couldn't really announce my arrival." Her shoulders have gone stiff. Around the pie dish, I sense more than see her fingers tighten as her ire rises. "Would you prefer a carrier pigeon? Some sort of smoke signal? Telegram? Flash mob? Whatever the case, next time I'll be sure to give you ten business days' worth of notice." There's a marked pause in her stream of sarcasm. "Not that there's going to be a next time."

"A standard greeting card would've sufficed." My eyes narrow, a thought suddenly occurring to me. "How did you find out my address, anyway? Last I checked, I'm not listed in the yellow pages."

Her lips press closed. "Does it matter?"

"Yes."

"I don't see why."

"Then you're being intentionally imperceptive."

She's silent, avoiding my eyes. It doesn't much matter, though. There's really only one person who could've told her where I am; only one mutual point of contact with that information at his disposal.

I'm going to kill Tomlinson.

I shake my head slowly, lips pursed in a show of annoyance. "Did you bring a bribery pie down to the police station to get your information, or did he give it to you for free?"

"Don't be mad at Chris. He didn't tell me anything."

"Except my fucking address."

"What is this, your secret lair?" She rolls her eyes. "Spare me. It's an apartment, not Superman's Solitary Fortress."

"Fortress of Solitude."

"Ah yes, by all means, *now* is the time to correct me on my improper geek references!" Her scoff is mocking. "I didn't care about your comic book phase when we were twelve and you made me borrow the entire collection from the Public Library because you were too embarrassed to check them out yourself. I definitely don't care, now."

The casual reference to our past hits both of us at the same time. We are so far removed from those two gawky kids we used to be — the ones who huddled in the boathouse rafters on summer nights, holding flashlights under a flannel blanket, tracing our fingertips across the inked pages. Reading snippets of dialogue in cartoon thought bubbles, laughing at the pop-art caricature drawings until our eyes grew too heavy to continue and we nodded off, a tangle of limbs, only to be awoken hours later by the sound of the lawn sprinklers going off before dawn. Scurrying back to our separate beds before anyone realized we were missing.

I'm not the only one who remembers. I can see the memories lurking in Jo's eyes, playing out on the surface of her sky-blue irises like a projector screen of pain. For a moment, neither of us says anything. I'm afraid if I let a single word escape, all the rest will flood out after it. Words like *I'm sorry* and *I screwed up* and *I don't know how to fix this.* Useless words that will get me nowhere.

Nowhere except deeper into misery.

Jo finally shatters the increasingly stale silence, hissing out a plea through gritted teeth. "Take it already."

"What?"

"Take. The damn. Pie."

My eyes flicker to it, then return to her face. "Why?"

"My arms are getting tired, that's why!"

"Then take it home. Give it to someone else." I swallow harshly. "I don't want it."

"What kind of psychopath doesn't accept a fresh-baked pie?" She jerks the dish another inch forward, so the rim bumps my stomach. "Just *take* it!"

"You're acting like a crazy person."

"And you're acting like a total dickhead!" She glares at me fiercely. "Which shouldn't be much of a surprise, given that seems to be your new standard. Tell me, when the aliens abducted you last summer and switched out your brain, did you get a say in the new personality type they installed or was it a surprise to you too?"

"Cute," I mutter flatly. "Are we done, now?"

"No, we are not *done now*," she snaps. The pie dish is quivering — whether from sheer anger or from her overexerted arm muscles, I'm not certain. "I came here to find out what the hell is going on with you, and I'm not leaving until I get some answers!"

"I thought you came here to thank me."

Her mouth drops open. "Um. Right. I..."

"So, the pie is a ruse, then."

"No." She shakes her head vigorously. "Of course not. I truly did want to thank you! But I..."

I press my eyes closed as she stammers into silence.

I want her gone.

No.

I need her gone.

Having her here is too hard. Looking at her this close, hearing the little catch in her voice, watching the light flicker over her features... and not being able to touch her, to laugh with her, to offer her comfort in the midst of her confusion...

It's absolute torture.

It's like getting a tiny taste of something delicious that you know, down to the marrow of your bones, you'll never again have access to. You'd be better off never tasting it. Because every other flavor, for the rest of your life, will be dull by comparison. That one sample of perfection will haunt you until you leave this earth.

Not a gift; a curse.

An echo.

A ghost.

Having half of you would be worse than none at all, Jo told me once, last summer. I understand that now, more acutely than ever before. I'd rather not see her at all than do this constant dance of self-deprivation; rather our paths never cross if it means constantly pretending not to care.

I rip my own heart from my chest over and over again, trying to protect hers. And every time, it gets a little harder. Every time, a little less of me comes back to life after she walks away from me.

So... end it.

Make this the last time.

Make sure, when she leaves...

She does not come back.

Not ever.

My anger, long-simmering, boils up to the surface before I can stop it. I'm suddenly furious — furious at Jo for coming here; furious at myself for fucking everything up so thoroughly; furious at the whole damn world for being rigged against us from the start.

My eyes snap open. Whatever she sees in their depths makes her own eyes widen in surprise. Her mouth opens to ask something, but I don't give her the chance. Letting my arms fall to my sides, I take an abrupt step forward, onto the landing, forcing her backwards. Using my body to crowd her away from my threshold, toward the stairwell. She retreats instinctually, unprepared for my sudden advance.

"You *what*, Jo? Thought you'd come here and pepper me with questions? You thought you'd hand me a pie and bat your eyes at me and... what? We'd be best friends again? Just like—" I snap my fingers; she flinches at the sound. "*That?*"

"You don't have to be cruel."

Oh, but I do.

It's the only way to make you go.

I tilt my head, considering her. "Whatever you came here looking for... Whoever you came here looking for... I can't give it to you." Bitterness unfurls on my tongue, coils into a strangled sound. "So you might as well turn around and go back to your perfect life, with your perfect parents, and your perfect future. That's where you belong. Where you've always belonged."

"What does that mean?" Her gaze sweeps over my face, trying to make sense of my words. "Whatever world I belong in, you belong to it too. You always have."

A bark of cold laughter bursts from my chest. I can't hold it back. "I never belonged to your world, Jo. Not really. And we both know it. I was just your little pet — a stray you collected from the pound, shoved into a fancy collar and allowed to mingle for a while with the purebreds. A charity case."

Her head is shaking. So is her voice. "That's not true and you know it! You're twisting things! Rewriting history. Making it sound like—"

"Like, what? Like I wasn't the boy from the poor immigrant family? Like you weren't the princess of privilege?"

"That never mattered to me. It never mattered to you, either."

"Of course it mattered!" I'm yelling, now, my fury rising like a tide. "The fact that you think it didn't matter only further proves my point."

"Which is what, exactly?"

"The world isn't the safe little bubble we pretended it was, growing up at Cormorant House. We aren't kids anymore."

"I know that!"

"Do you?" I ask ruthlessly. "Because you aren't acting like it. You're acting like a five-year-old, whose world still operates on pinky promises and giggles and the golden rule."

"So in your eyes, I'm a monster because I look for the best in people? Because I search for sliver linings? I didn't realize that was such a terrible crime!" Her volume shoots up in proportion with her anger, rising to meet mine. "God, Archer! I came here today— against my better judgment, I might add — because I wanted to make sure you were all right! Because, the other day, after the storm... I felt like something with you was just... *off*."

I suck in a sharp breath, trying to keep my composure. I should've known she'd put two-and-two together. She's too damn perceptive. She always was. Thankfully, right now, she's too upset to do anything except yell in my face.

"I came here to find out why you're here. Why you're not at Bryant, or some intense summer training camp, where you're supposed to be. Why you're working as a lobsterman instead of off conquering the world of collegiate baseball."

She's a hairsbreadth away from the truth.

So close.

Too close.

I feel exposed.

Caught in a headlight beam.

Frozen in place.

Her face is flushed with exasperation as she glares up at me. Her hands are wrapped tight around the pie dish, a white-knuckled grip. "Honestly, I figured something must be seriously wrong. That something must've happened — something so bad, maybe you felt like you couldn't tell me about it. But if this is what I get in return — insults and anger and snide remarks — I'm not sure why I bothered." She bares her teeth at me, a smile lacking all warmth. "I guess I'm an idiot for caring at all. I mean, why the hell would I want to find out what's going on with you, when you've made it so abundantly clear you don't want me involved in any facet of your life?"

I suck in a deep breath. Hold it in my lungs until it starts to ache. And then, on a bitter exhale, I mutter, "Good fucking question."

"Wow. I just..." She's trembling with anger, vibrating with it from head to toe. "I cannot believe you're being like this."

"Like what, Jo?"

"*This!*"

I take another step toward her, forcing her to retreat further into the hall. She pulls the pie toward her body, arms jerking backward to accommodate my sudden nearness. With only the dish to separate us, our faces are no more than a few inches apart. We're so close, I can see every freckle dotted across the bridge of her nose; every dark eyelash surrounding her furious blue eyes; every pillowy curve of her bow-like mouth.

Stop looking at her mouth.

"Why, Jo?" I loom over her, eyes never shifting from hers as venom leaks from my lips in an uncontrollable stream. "Why can't you believe it? Because you can't even fathom a world where something doesn't go your way?"

"*Excuse me?* What has ever gone my way?"

"Oh, I don't know — you mean besides the millionaire parents, oceanfront mansion, valedictorian status, world at your fingertips..."

"That's rich, coming from you — All-Star pitcher, most popular guy in our graduating class, adored by one and all... not to mention the golden son of two parents who actually gave a shit whether he lived or died!"

"Is that seriously how you saw our time at Exeter? Is that how you've got it sorted in your head — you, the neglected wallflower, and me the metaphorical prom king?" I laugh, though I'm not finding any of this amusing. Not in the slightest. "That's fucking hilarious."

She's stiff as a board, her spine ramrod straight with tension, her words icy with wrath. "No, Archer. That's not hilarious. That's *accurate.*"

"Right." I laugh again, even more bitterly. "Okay. Sure. Whatever you say."

"Stop that."

"Stop what?"

"Laughing at me like I'm delusional, when you're the one not making any sense."

"What doesn't make sense?"

"I don't understand where all of this is coming from! I

don't understand why you're bringing all of this up, out of nowhere!"

"Of course you don't."

"Don't patronize me."

"Then don't be so naive. Don't you get it? In the real world, we never would've met if your parents hadn't hired mine to scrub their fucking toilets and mow their fucking lawn." My eyes narrow on hers. "We were never meant to be friends! We were never meant to be *anything*."

"What does it matter how we met?" She blinks rapidly, like she's trying not to cry. *God, please don't cry. Yell, scream, holler. Hit me. Do anything except cry.* "All that matters is that we did. We did meet. We did become friends. We did matter to each other." She pauses. "Even if you want to pretend otherwise."

Fuck.

"Right." I swallow hard. "Well. If we did... you said it yourself. *Did*. Past tense."

"You—" Her eyes, to my horror, fill with glossy tears of frustration. "You don't get to just brush me aside like garbage! You don't get to just act like this— this— this unrecognizable monster for no reason at all!"

But I do have my reasons.

My jaw locks tighter. "I'm sorry I'm not following the perfect script you apparently wrote for me in your head before coming here, Jo, but that's not how life works. You don't get to be angry with me for having the audacity not to recite the lines you were expecting to hear."

"I'm not angry with you for that. I'm angry because you used to be my best friend in the entire world and now you can't even look me in the eyes for more than three seconds straight. I'm angry because you were the only person I could confide in, about anything and everything under the sun, and now we don't even speak. And most of all, I'm angry because I don't understand *why*."

Her voice cracks, the words breaking apart beneath the strain of her agony. Hearing it breaks something inside of me, too. I can't breathe. The pain in my chest is an anvil, compressing my lungs. Her eyes hold a plea — for clarity, for compassion. For all the things I cannot give her, no matter how much I might like to.

"If you'd just..." She sucks in a breath. "If you'd just tell me what I did, maybe it would make sense to me. If you'd let me in on whatever it was that made you throw away almost two decades of friendship, maybe I'd finally have some closure. Maybe then, I'd be able to stop going over it and over it and over it in my head like a goddamned crazy person."

She attempts a laugh, but there's nothing funny about the noise that comes out of her mouth. It's laced with so much grief, my stomach flips with nausea.

"Maybe I *am* crazy," she whispers. "That's the only real explanation for why I can't let this go, after all this time. That's why I can't stop thinking there must be some better rationale for what happened between us last summer. That's why I keep trying and trying and trying with you, when it's so very clear you want nothing to do with me anymore. Right?"

She's looking at me with pure desperation in her eyes. Heart in her throat, cards on the table. Setting aside all her pride to beg me — *beg me* — for the slightest confirmation.

Hearing her like this...

Seeing her like this...

It is a knife, straight to the heart.

And I know, this is it. This is the moment. The chance to rectify everything that went wrong. The long-awaited peace offering. The olive branch, extended outward with a shaky hand.

It takes every ounce of strength I possess not to take it. To stand there, an immovable statue, unyielding in my apathy. Meeting her desperation with incalculable coldness.

For a suspended moment, she simply stands there, waiting for me to say something. Waiting for me to explain things to her. Waiting for even a crumb of validation.

When I don't...

When a full minute slips by without the smallest crack in my detached demeanor...

Her gaze changes. Shifts, along with the world beneath my feet, as Josephine Valentine — a girl who has loved me longer and better than anyone on this earth — finally sees what everyone else does: that I am not even worthy of breathing her air. As she releases her hold on the last shred of hope she was clinging to that things between us might get better... and finally....

Finally...

Finally...

Lets me go.

"Fine," she says simply. I sink a little deeper into my own self-abhorrence as the hurt on her face hardens into grim resolve. "That's fine."

Just go.

Just leave.

I can't take any more.

But she's not finished. Her voice cracks. "You know... you were always cocky, Archer. Sometimes you were a little too blunt, the way you'd phrase things or respond to certain situations. Occasionally, you'd snap and show your temper. But you were never outright cruel. You were never mean just for the sport of it." The shuddering breath she pulls into her lungs seems to steady her a bit, but it's not enough to camouflage the depth of her devastation when she says the last words I'm certain she will ever waste on me. "If this is who you are now... If this is the man you've decided to become... then you're right. Coming here was a waste of time."

I shrug, shouldering the disgust I feel at my own actions with a familiar facade of indifference. The smirk on my face only adds to the charade as I jerk my chin toward the stairwell behind her. "You know where the exit is."

She physically recoils a step. I watch the shock of my callousness make impact. A flurry of emotions plays across her features, giving me a front-row seat to the exact moment she decides I'm not worth it; that her parents were right all along: she really is better off without me in her life.

Great, I tell myself, swallowing hard. *I'm glad she's finally up to speed.*

"Fuck you, Archer Reyes," she says in a stark whisper. "You can go straight to Hell, as far as I'm concerned. And you can stay there."

With that, she drops the pie. Two seconds of free-fall, then — *crash.* The ceramic dish slams against the tile floor, shattering on impact with a clatter that sounds like gunfire. I don't even look down as chunks of flaky crust and cinnamon-coated apples fly in all directions, covering the walls around us like blood spatter at a crime scene, flecking my bare feet and sweatpants with crumbs.

I just watch her go.

Watch her pivot on her heels in an angry whirl, hair flying around her slim shoulders in a curtain of gold. And when she's gone, when the sound of her stomping down the stairs has faded, when the slam of the front door echoes up to me on the landing... I sink down beside the ruined remnants of the pie she baked especially for me, put my head in my hands, and try to breathe around the black hole of misery yawning inside me. Try to remain conscious as it widens from my chest to my limbs to the top of my skull. As it stretches to fill the air of the dingy stairwell. The apartment beyond. The building itself. As it reaches up into the sky, blackening the horizon in every direction. Encompassing everything, until the whole damn world goes dark.

And in that unending darkness...

I feel the last bit of light inside of me sputter out and die.

NINETEEN

josephine

I HATE HIM.

I thought I hated him before, last summer, when he left me behind with a broken heart. But then, my rage was tempered by heartbreak, dampened by despair. In retrospect — and in comparison — that anger is the palest of flames. A flickering ember, next to the raging inferno that blazes through me as I drive away from Archer's apartment.

My hands are a death grip on the wheel. I can barely see the dark road in front of me through the tears. Scrubbing at my face with my sleeve, I fly through a stop sign without fully braking. I pay minimal attention to the route I'm taking back to Manchester — winding my way south along the coast, a narrow road that takes me over the drawbridge at Blynman Canal, past the historic spires of Hammond Castle, through the sleepy streets of Magnolia.

It's dark outside. Quiet. The kind of lazy summer night you're meant to spend lying in the grass counting fireflies or sipping cold tea on a creaky porch swing. In another life, I would've taken Cupid out for a sail under the stars, drifting from constellation to constellation in the slow currents, the waves a rocking lullaby against the hull. But Cupid is rotting somewhere at the bottom of the Atlantic — along with all my other hopes and dreams.

I drive faster, pressing the gas pedal almost to the floor, eager to put as much space between me and Archer as I possibly can, as quickly as I possibly can. Thick humidity hangs in the air, only a light breeze to stir it. With the convertible's top down, my hair whips into a messy tangle, erasing the extra care I took to curl it this afternoon. Strands stick in the thin layer of gloss I applied to my lips.

Trying to look pretty for the boy who hates your guts.

Feeling like an idiot of the highest order, I swipe my thumb roughly across my mouth, wiping all traces of my foolishness away.

It doesn't take long to get home. Before I know it, I've reached the turn to Crow Island. But as I think of Cormorant House awaiting me on the other side of those high stone walls — dark and empty, a perfect echo-chamber of all the thoughts I am desperate to escape — I find myself rolling right past it. Heading into town. Heading anywhere, really, that might offer a small distraction.

I choose my route at random. Left, then right, then left again. I don't expend any thoughts on my destination. I also try not to examine my own feelings too closely. I know if I do, I'll be facing an unpleasant reality; namely, that I'm almost as angry at myself as I am at Archer. My own stupidity is hard to swallow.

How could I be so idiotic?

How pathetic can I possibly be?

Showing up unannounced.

Baking him a pie.

A freaking pie.

What did I expect? That a few slices of hand-baked dessert

would somehow mend all that is broken between us? That he'd see me standing there on his doorstep, fall to his knees, and beg forgiveness for destroying our friendship?

God.

Archer was right.

I really am naive.

———

There's one big problem with a town this small: pretty much everything closes as soon as the sun sets. Europe, this is not. There are no late-night eateries, no all-hours dining options for night owls to indulge their cravings. The only shop in Manchester-by-the-Sea that stays open past seven is a small convenience store in the middle of town, owned and operated by the same family for as long as I've been alive.

Its narrow aisles don't offer much in the way of variety, but I'm not looking for a Michelin-Star experience at the moment. I grab a jumbo bag of gummy bears from the candy section, swipe a ginger-berry juice from the cooler, and head for the cash registers with my puffy, post-crying eyes downcast. A middle-aged man rings up my purchases in silence as I search for a ten dollar bill in the depths of my purse, blessedly abstaining from smalltalk.

The sound of the bell over the front door makes us both look up from our tasks.

Two identical blonde girls walk — *strut* might be more accurate, actually — into the tiny shop, their matching, chin-length platinum bobs almost translucent in the harsh convenience store lighting.

"—so I told him, if he expects me to go all the way to Ibiza, I'm flying private or I'm not flying at all," one of the girls is saying.

"Naturally," the other adds.

"Like, if he *really* wants to see me, he'll send the jet. I'm not flying first class like some sort of peasant."

"First class is the new economy."

"Put that on the family crest."

They dissolve into giggles. Their laughter dissipates when they spot me standing by the cash register.

"Oh my god!" Odette squeals.

"Oh my *god*!" Ophelia screams.

"Josephine Freaking Valentine!"

"Back from the dead!"

"Back from Switzerland," I correct lowly, but neither of them seems to be listening as they race toward me at top speed. Before I can brace for impact, they've thrown their arms around me — ensconcing my frame in a huddle of long limbs and a cloud of expensive perfume. They don't pause long enough for me too answer a single question before firing off another.

"Where have you been hiding?"

"Why didn't you tell us you were back in town?"

"Chris Tomlinson said he saw you but we didn't believe him!"

"He thinks he's a big shot, since they made him an officer."

"As if we haven't seen him passed out on a pool table after downing, like, sixteen Jell-O shots in a row." I can practically hear Ophelia's eyes rolling in her head.

Odette snorts. "Give a man a badge, suddenly he's an upstanding citizen."

"Ridiculous."

"Totally."

I manage to squirm free of the twins' embrace, backpedaling until my butt bumps the counter. "Funny enough, Officer Tomlinson pulled me over for speeding the other day."

They gasp in unison.

"In his defense, I *was* speeding," I point out. This factoid falls on deaf ears.

"What a dick!"

"Total dick!"

"I'll tell you what, we do *not* miss the Exeter boys."

"We've moved on."

"Upgraded!"

Odette winks in agreement. "To *men*."

"Ones with emotional maturity."

"And high-limit credit cards."

The twins high-five.

"Good for you," I say weakly, for lack of a better response.

A low cough sounds from behind me. I turn to find the solemn cashier staring pointedly, his hand outstretched for payment. I cast an apologetic look his direction as I fork over my cash, as if to say, *Please do not lump me in with these two lunatics.* He makes no comment as he opens the drawer to retrieve my change, but I can practically feel the waves of judgment rolling off him.

"So, Jo, what have you been up to?" Ophelia asks.

"Nothing much," I say, turning back to face them, gummy bears cradled against my chest like a shield.

"Puffy eyes and a bag of candy," Odette notes, eyeing my purchases with a shrewd gaze. "Guessing you had a rough night."

I shrug. "I'm fine. Just hungry."

"Your smeared mascara says otherwise." Ophelia's head tilts in contemplation. "Do we need to hurt someone?"

"Because we will," her twin adds, a bit too eagerly.

A nervous laugh pops from my lips. "No, no. Definitely not."

They trade a glance.

"Come on." Ophelia loops one arm with mine. "You're coming with us."

"No, I—"

"Don't protest," Odette orders, attaching herself to my other side, so I'm effectively sandwiched between them. "We haven't seen you in, like, ages. We're going back to our place."

Ophelia squeals again. "Girl's night!"

"But—"

"No more *buts*, Valentine."

"It'll be fun, we promise!"

"Our parents are away in France for the summer. Plus, we have a metric ton of wine in the cellar just begging to be consumed."

"You can tell us all about whatever stupid boy made you cry."

"And then we can decide how best to punish him!"

I sigh as they drag me out of the store, into the night. I don't bother putting up any more resistance as we walk across the parking lot, where their bubblegum pink Land Rover is parked beside my classic green convertible; a fittingly odd reflection of our mismatched friendship. I know from experience, it's futile to deny the Wadell twins when they've fixed their sights on something. And, tonight, that something seems to be me.

———

Less than an hour after following the twins back to their house — a massive Tudor-style brick mansion with a series of soaring gabled roofs and a facade of dark timber framing —

I've got a glass of priceless Dom Pérignon from the Wadell wine cellar in one hand and a store-brand yellow gummy bear in the other.

A perfect pairing.

Ophelia and Odette are sprawled on opposite sides of the enormous white leather sectional that dominates their parents' living room, staring at me with identical expressions of incredulity as I catch them up on all that's happened since I last saw them.

Geneva.

Oliver.

Brown.

Cupid.

Chris.

Archer.

When I finally trail off into silence, I take a large gulp of champagne for strength. The bubbles dance over my tongue and down my throat, exploding in my empty stomach like liquid fireworks. For a long while, the twins are quiet, sipping their own champagne as they process the load I've just dropped on them.

"Wow," Odette says finally, draining her last bit of Dom. "That's—"

"*Intense.*" Ophelia blows out a puff of air. "Especially the shit with Archer. No wonder you left. If I were you, I never, ever would've come back here."

"I told you, I have to make a decision about Brown." I shrug with a calmness I do not feel inside. "Otherwise, I probably would've stayed away forever."

"You know what? Screw that. And screw Archer Reyes," Odette says, sitting suddenly upright. "No idiot guy should have the power to scare you away from your home."

"Or to keep you away from your friends!" her twin adds.

"He's not worth it. Especially when you have a new hottie to occupy your days!"

"And nights." Odette winks.

I laugh awkwardly. "The thing about Ollie is..."

"What?"

"He wants to wait until he's married to have sex."

The twins gape at me.

"You must be kidding."

"Josephine, please tell us you are kidding."

I lift my hands in surrender. "Serious as a heart attack."

"Wow. No sex until marriage," Odette murmurs, like the thought is incomprehensible.

"Not even *oral?*" Ophelia asks, genuinely mystified.

I drop my head into my hands and groan. "*Guys.*"

"Fee, you're embarrassing her!"

"I'm legitimately curious, though!" She looks at me pointedly. "Does he know *you're* not waiting? Or is he under the impression you'll be trading v-cards on your wedding night?"

"Whoa, whoa, whoa!" I hold up my hands. "Who said anything about getting married?"

The twins glance at each other. "He's what, like, twenty-three?"

"Twenty-four."

"Mmm. And you've been dating how long?"

"Eight months."

"Mmmm. And he's close with your parents?"

"I mean... He works at their company, so, yeah."

"*Mmmmm.*"

"Stop *mmmmm*-ing!" I protest.

Ophelia waves away my words with a flick of her wrist. "I'm just saying... It smells like marriage to me."

"It smells like nothing of the sort!"

Odette's eyes narrow in thought. "You didn't answer my

question though. Does he know Archer already rounded your bases? Slid into your home-plate, so to speak?"

I squirm a bit on the loveseat. "He doesn't know a thing about Archer. I didn't see any good reason to share that particular story with him."

"So, he doesn't know." Ophelia whistles. "That's probably for the best. Men tend to place a lot of significance on our maidenly deflowering."

"Seriously." Odette rolls her eyes. "You'd think breaking a freaking hymen is some kind of natural testosterone booster, the way they go on and on about it."

"Sis, haven't you heard?" Ophelia waves her arms through the air like a witch casting a spell. "The virginal hoo-ha has magical powers to enhance virility — like powdered rhinoceros horn and shark fin soup!"

The twins both throw their heads back in a fit of laughter.

"Ollie isn't like that," I insist, trying not to sound defensive. "Even if I did tell him, he wouldn't care." I swallow hard, wishing it would clear the lump of uncertainty lodged in my throat. "This is really not that big of a deal."

"Uh huh."

"Whatever helps you sleep at night."

I glare at them in turn. "I thought you two invited me over to cheer me up, not to judge my boyfriend's sexual preferences."

"Sorry! Honestly. We aren't trying to be judgmental. We just don't understand... *why?*"

"Does he have... you know... some sort of *problem?*" Odette asks. "Anatomically?"

"No. Not that I'm aware of." I shrug. "He's from the south. He was raised in the Bible Belt. He's religious."

"*Religious.* Oh. So his problems are psychological."

"Ophelia!" Odette glances at me. "She didn't mean that."

"I did, actually," her twin mutters.

I can't help laughing. "Really, I'm fine with it. The one and only time I had sex didn't exactly go well, remember? I'm not in a rush to replicate those results."

Odette purses her lips. "Archer really did a number on you, huh?"

"He did totally ghost her, after she'd spent, like, her entire life in love with him."

"*Ophelia*," Odette hisses again. "That wasn't very sensitive."

"So? It's the truth." Ophelia glances at me. "No offense, Jo."

"It's fine." I shake my head at the ridiculousness of this situation. "You guys did warn me, after all."

"We did?"

"Yep. Back at Exeter, on graduation day. You told me Archer's disappearing act was because he might not feel the same, after we slept together."

Ophelia blinks slowly, pushing her frame upright. "Wait. That was on graduation day? The day he ghosted?"

I nod.

"Are you sure?"

"Tough to forget the day you had your heart ripped out of your chest. Especially when that same day, you're forced to get up on stage and give a speech about conquering the future and fulfilling your life's potential." I pause a beat. "Why do you ask?"

They trade a loaded glance. "The timing of it all..."

"It's just..."

"Just *what?*" I ask, feeling my blood pressure skyrocket. "What aren't you saying?"

"Graduation day," Odette murmurs, looking at her twin strangely. "Isn't that the same day..."

Ophelia nods. "Yeah, I'm pretty sure."

"Guys." My teeth are suddenly grinding together as tension ripples through me. "Explain. Please."

They look at me with the same expression — sympathy mixed with a strange hesitation I can't interpret. "We didn't realize..."

"You must not know about the accident."

"What accident?" I ask.

"Archer's accident."

For a second, time goes still. The breath halts in my lungs. "I don't know what you're talking about."

"Look, we don't know the full story, but..." Odette heaves a sigh. "Right around the time you left for Switzerland, we found out Archer was in a pretty bad car accident."

"Totaled his truck," Ophelia jumps in.

"Flipped it right over."

"Rumor was, that's why he missed our commencement ceremony."

"He was in the hospital for a few days, recovering from surgery."

"No," I whisper. The rejection comes out thin, a breath-starved sound. "No, that's... it's... Where did you hear this?"

Ophelia shrugs. "Chris Tomlinson got drunk at a party last year and told us about it. He said he wasn't supposed to say anything, that Archer didn't want people knowing he was hurt, but..."

"Can you blame him?" Odette grimaces. "If I was a star pitcher and I completely shattered my throwing arm right before my first college season, I wouldn't much feel like talking about it either."

His arm.

His pitching arm.

Shattered?

No.

There's no possible way.

My mind spins, trying to process this information. Cycling through a million emotions at once. Even as I recognize the ring of truth in their story... Even as my mind presents a memory of Archer on the island, tucking his hand from my sight — fast but not fast enough to hide the surgical scars... Even as the mystery of him living in Gloucester, working as a lobsterman, finally starts to make sense... there is a part of me that cannot accept their words. Cannot process the magnitude of what they are telling me.

"No," I say again. The only word I seem to be able to voice. "No, that can't be right."

Odette's nose wrinkles. "I mean, yeah, there's probably more to the story. We only got the SparkNotes version from Tomlinson before he passed out that night."

"And the next time we tried to talk to him about it, he told us to butt out of other people's business."

"So rude!" Odette mutters.

"Totally." Ophelia shakes her head. "We just, like, wanted to know if Archer was still in the hospital or not. We would've sent flowers or something."

"I think he was there for a long time. A week or two, maybe? We definitely should've sent flowers."

"Oh well. Too late, now."

Nausea is stirring inside me, the champagne and gummy bear concoction in my stomach churning in a noxious cyclone. It takes all my strength to keep from retching all over their oriental carpet as I shake my head back and forth. "No. No, you're... That's not possible. None of this is possible."

"It's just what we heard."

"Then you heard wrong!" I snap. "Archer can't have been in the hospital with a broken hand on graduation day, because on that day... He came to my house. He left a note. It was his handwriting. It said—" I swallow hard, trying to get myself under control. "It said we'd made a mistake, sleeping together. That he just wanted to be friends. That he was going away for the summer, to an elite training camp, and that we should take some time apart."

"He came to your house?"

"Yes!" I'm practically yelling.

"You actually saw him there?"

My mouth opens. Closes. Opens again. "I... No. Not me. Not personally."

"So, who said they saw him?"

"My..." The anger leeches out of my voice, leaving behind nothing except a quivering sort of confusion. "My mother did. My mother said she saw him... She said... She said..."

"Okay, Jo," Ophelia says gently. "Maybe we're wrong. There's no need to cry, honey."

"I'm not crying," I tell her. But when I reach up and touch my face, I find that I am. Tears are dripping down my cheeks, leaking in a stream I cannot seem to stop. "I'm fine. I'm just confused. None of this makes sense." My voice cracks, breaks open. Anguish pours out of me in a flood. "Nothing has made sense in so long. I don't even remember what my life felt like when things were normal. No matter where I turn for answers, I hit another roadblock. It's like I'm trying to put together a puzzle, but someone's thrown away the box and I'm missing half the pieces and—"

The rest of my words are overtaken by jagged sobs, the force of them rocking my body back and forth. As I fall to emotional pieces, the twins get up off the sectional and move to sit with me on the loveseat. It's only built for two, but they cram their bodies in beside mine anyway, pressed close with their heads on my shoulders and their arms wound tight around my back.

"Don't worry. We'll figure it out," Ophelia whispers from my left side. "We'll help you find out what really happened last summer. We'll make Chris cooperate, even if he's reluctant."

"Yeah," Odette agrees from my right. "I mean, if there's one thing we're good at, it's getting what we want out of unwilling men."

"And in the meantime, we have plenty more champagne."

Laughing through my tears, I extend my empty glass for a fresh pour. "Bottom's up."

archer

I SIT on a weatherbeaten bench by the harborside, nursing a strong cup of coffee from the cafe on the corner and watching the boats pass by. The local sailing school is in full swing — grade-schoolers in fluorescent life jackets pepper the waters, their Optis and Lasers racing back and forth in jagged tacks as they head out for the day. The fleet is chased by a hard-bottomed inflatable with two high-school aged instructors at the wheel, yelling out directions that carry on the wind.

Hold your tiller like a microphone, Max!

Anya, your sail is luffing! Pull it in!

Patrick, we aren't in international waters — peeing off the stern is public indecency!

A ghostlike smile pushes at my lips as I remember the first time I went sailing. I was ten. Seasick as a dog, but entirely under Jo's spell as she barked orders at me like a tiny drill sergeant. She was so thrilled to share her biggest passion with me; she radiated so much joy, it made me happy just to be around her.

"Whatever you're smiling about right now doesn't take away from that ugly black eye," a wry voice announces.

In the days since the fight, my bruises have worked their way through half the color wheel, fading from mottled purple to puce green and finally to the sallow shade of yellow-brown I now bear. Draining the final sip of my coffee, I toss the empty cup into a nearby trash bin before glancing over at the man who's just taken a seat beside me on the splintered wood bench.

"Whose fist did you run into?" Tommy asks.

"My brother's."

"I hope you returned the favor."

"More than once."

He nods in approval. "Good. From what you've told me, he had it coming."

"This and more."

"Wanted man, isn't he?"

"Last I checked."

"No wonder he's working on a long-hauler. It's much easier to stay in the wind when you're offshore three weeks out of the month. No parole officers on the high seas."

I cut a sharp glance at Tommy. I never mentioned where Jax was working. "Where'd you hear that?"

"Word gets around." He shrugs. "Not many secrets on these docks. At least, not when you've worked them as long as I have." He pauses, laughing lightly. "Make that *had*, seeing as I'm officially retired."

"How's it feel?"

"Going to take some getting used to. Mind you, I still have some small side jobs to keep me busy — boat maintenance for some rich folks up in Manchester, that sort of thing. Maybe I'll finally learn to sleep in after forty years of waking up before the rooster crows. Hell, I might have myself a leisurely breakfast. Kick up my heels. Even read the newspaper."

"Do they still print newspapers, old man?"

"No one likes a smartass."

"Wasn't aware I was competing in a congeniality contest."

"If you were, you certainly wouldn't win." He glances back at me. "Your brother — he's working on that old outrigger, right? Over by the commercial warehouses?"

I nod. "Reina."

"La Reina. *The queen*." He falls curiously silent. A seagull gives a croaky call as it soars overhead. It's nearly across the harbor by the time Tommy speaks again. "Fitting boat name for the Latin Kings, I suppose."

Startled, I look over at him. "What?"

"Did you think your brother and his crewmen were filling those holds with fish? Don't be a fool. Everyone around here knows they use that old rust bucket for one product and one product only — and it don't require refrigeration, if you catch my drift."

"They're using the boat to move drugs up the coast," I mutter. Jaxon's cocky words the other day come back to me in a rush. *Most of the shit we've got going on right now is thanks to me.* Yep. This has my brother written all over it. I grind my teeth together. "I should've known. As soon as I saw my brother on that boat, I should've realized he was up to something. It's not like he'd bother working an actual job."

"Have to hand it to him — it's a smart plan." Tommy leans back against the bench. "Far less regulation here in Gloucester than in a big city like Boston. They pull in once a month with a full hold of heroin, load it into bait crates, pack it into waiting fish trucks... Product is on its merry way across the state by sunup."

"They're probably supplying all of Massachusetts."

"All of New England, more likely."

"Jesus Christ."

"Jesus has no hand in this." Tommy lets out a low whistle. "Satan, on the other hand..."

"I should've known," I repeat, frustration bleeding into every word.

"Well, you know now. Question is... What are you going to do about it?"

"What do you mean? What can *I* do?"

"You can turn your brother in, for starters. He's a wanted man. Violated his parole. The authorities would be more than happy to toss his keister back in the can."

I run a hand through my hair. It's grown so long, the tips brush the top of my shoulders. "I should. I should've called the other day, the moment I saw him on the docks. God knows it's what he deserves."

"So why didn't you?"

"I don't know."

"That's a bullshit answer."

I sigh. "I don't want to cause my parents any more pain, okay? They've been through enough."

"Pain is inevitable." Tommy's voice turns gruff. "Every parent knows when they have kids, they're setting themselves up for a lifetime of it. Reproducing is like cutting off chunks of your own heart and sending them out into the world, hoping like hell they don't get too banged up, but knowing in your gut there's no avoiding it. You can't prevent the pain from happening. All you can do is be there when it does."

There's no missing the undercurrent of agony laced through his words. The story Deacon Hayward told me about Tommy's family flashes through my head. I feel strangely guilty knowing the grim details of his personal tragedies. If he wanted me privy to that story, he would've told me himself. It's like I've spied through a window into my intensely private boss's soul without permission.

There's no way in Hell I'm about to broach the topic of the fire, and all he lost in it. So I merely clear my throat and say, "I'm not planning on having kids anytime soon, Tommy."

"That's not what I meant as a takeaway." He shakes his head. "My point was, your parents don't need you to shield them from pain — no matter how you'd like to, no matter if you believe it's somehow your responsibility to do so. They're your parents. They're the ones who are supposed to protect you, not the other way around. Don't believe me? Call and ask them what they think. See how they react when they hear what your brother is up to, these days."

I squint out at the harbor, trying to keep the small sailing class in my line of sight. They're nearly out of the channel now — ten white dots on the horizon, skimming across the sun-dappled waves without a care in the world. I wish sometimes I could turn back the clocks to when I was ten years old, and my biggest worries were whether I'd be able to save up enough for a real pitching glove before tryouts. I'd do it all over, minus the mistakes.

"I hope he's caught. I hope he pays for what he's done. But turning in my own brother — no matter what he's done to me — seems... I don't know. Low. Base. I accused Jaxon of betraying his own blood... destroying our family... If I turn him in, how am I any different?"

"You're not defined by his actions any more than he's defined by yours. Every man is responsible for holding his own. From the sound of it, Jaxon made his bed a long time ago. Letting him lie in it doesn't make you a bad person. It just means he's getting his comeuppance."

We lapse into silence for a moment, both lost in our own thoughts as we stare out at the water. After a long stretch, I glance over at him.

"There really should've been a sunset and a swelling musical score to accompany that motivational speech."

"Wiseass." His lips twitch. "Anyway. I didn't drag you down here to give you advice."

"Oh? Then why am I here, exactly?"

"Just wanted to see how you were."

"Really?"

"Don't sound so surprised. You'll wound my delicate sensibilities."

I snort. "Apologies."

"Heard Dee Hayward offered you a position on his crew."

"Guess word really does get around these docks."

"You planning to take him up on his offer?"

"I don't exactly have many other job opportunities knocking on my door. I was planning on heading over to talk to him this afternoon."

"Before you do that..." His tone is casual. "I might have something better for you."

My brows skyrocket. "What do you mean?"

"Easier to show you than explain." He pushes to his feet, his arthritic limbs stiff. "Come on, kid."

————

Tommy leads me down the docks, heading for the Ebenezer's old slip. My curiosity mounts as we approach and I see, in place of the battered vessel, there's an unfamiliar lobster boat bobbing gently against the tide. She looks fresh off the assembly line, with a coat of bright yellow paint — closer in shade to a cheery sunflower than the dull mustard of her predecessor — gleaming in the mid afternoon light and newly purchased lines holding all forty-plus feet of her in place. My eye catches on the metallic glint of a brand new electric pulley system hanging over her starboard side, designed to haul in traps at the push of a button. New aerator tanks line the stern, awaiting her first haul.

I whistle lowly as I take in the sight. "Wow."

"Gorgeous, ain't she?"

"Nicest boat in the harbor by a mile, Tommy. Not even Deacon Hayward's rig can hold a candle to her."

"Glad you think so."

I glance over at him, bemused. "So all that talk about retirement was a bunch of crap, then?"

"Nah. She's not for me."

My brows arch. "Oh?"

"She's yours."

I start in shock. "Come again?"

"You heard me." He jerks his chin toward the shiny yellow boat. "She's all yours, kid. Courtesy of the fine folks at my insurance agency. Turns out, the Ebenezer made me more money by sinking than she ever did in high season."

"But Tommy, that's your money."

"I have more money than I need already and no one left to spend it on. What am I going to do with a stack of bills? Wipe my ass with them?"

"Buy a house!"

"I have a house."

"Pay off your mortgage!"

"Been paid off since 1992."

"Then go on vacation!"

"I don't want to pay money to relax in some strange place. You know what I want? I want to sit on my couch and watch my television. I'm tired."

"Still. You can't just give me a boat. That's insane!"

"I can and I did and I won't hear any argument on the matter. It's done. I had the title papers drawn up with your name and everything. Already transferred my lobstering permit to you with the folks down at the Fish and Wildlife Department. Just need a notary to sign and you're officially a commercial captain." He looks at me, his expression the closest to *giddy* I've ever seen on that typically dour face. "Go on. Take a good look at her!"

Shaking my head, half-certain I've nodded off on that sun-drenched bench and am drifting in some vividly detailed daydream, I walk the length of the boat, bow to stern, taking in her details up close. I run a hand along the beam, marveling at the glossy fiberglass decking and flush-mounted cleats. She really is a thing of beauty. By the time I reach the rear section, there are practically tears in my eyes.

"Tommy, this is too much." I shake my head. "I'll never be able to—"

My words break off suddenly as I spot the name plastered across the stern in curvy, capital-lettered serif font. He's christened the boat something so unexpected, I blink three times to make sure I'm reading it right. I reach up and rub them — hard — but the word does not waver from my vision.

JOSEPHINE

My eyes fly to Tommy's. He's standing a handful of feet away, hands in his pockets, looking rather proud of himself.

"Fine name for a boat, don't you think?"

"Why?" I choke out, throat tight. "Of all the names—"

"You know why, kid."

I shake my head, rejecting his words. "You don't understand. She's not— we're not— "

"You're not what? Not together?" He shrugs. "And whose fault is that?"

My eyes narrow. "You don't know a thing about it."

"Actually know quite a bit. Or did you forget you spilled your guts out at my kitchen table a few nights back?"

"It's not that simple."

"Never is. Love is messy and inconvenient and always arrives at the wrong time. My late wife—" He sucks in a sharp breath, seems to steel himself, as if just mentioning her is enough to cause him pain, even after all this time. "She was the best thing in my life. But before we got together, before we stopped dancing in circles and admitted we wanted to walk the same direction instead... Trust me, it was one long headache. She was feisty as a panther; I'm stubborn as a mule. Led to a lot of miscommunication. Lot of useless arguments. Looking back, that's the thing I regret most... knowing I wasted even a minute with her. All that time fighting was time we could've spent loving each other. Do you know what I'd give to get those minutes back, now that she's gone?"

My stomach is a ball of lead. "Tommy..."

"Life is short. So goddamn short. And it'll knock you off balance long before you've found your sea legs. That don't mean you give up. That don't mean you stop fighting the tides." His eyes flash with emotion as he takes a step closer to me. Such a show of passion is completely out of character for this reserved man. It rattles me. Shames me. Hits me square in the chest. "You got knocked down, kid. Last summer, everything that happened... everything you lost... it sent you sprawling. But it's time to find your feet again. Because wallowing in misery, hating yourself, numbing your pain with whiskey every night isn't going to fix a damn thing."

"It's not fixable."

Tommy smacks me upside the head.

"Ow!" I rub at the spot he walloped. "What was that for?"

"For being obtuse. Your dreams died. *You* didn't." His eyes soften. "You're better than this. Deep down, you know it."

"And if I'm not?" I'm horrified when my voice cracks.

"What's the fucking point of standing up if I'm just going to get knocked on my ass again?"

"Then it's a good thing you've got people around you to help. Plenty of hands stretched out, trying to haul you back to your feet. You just won't let yourself take them."

"It's no one else's responsibility to save me."

Tommy snorts. "That self-sacrificing hero-complex of yours is out of control, kid."

"I don't have a hero-complex!"

"Always taking on other people's problems. Always trying to save everyone else. Never recognizing when he himself needs saving. All you need is a blue spandex suit and some superpowers."

"Hilarious."

"Not joking." He looks at me, hard. "Even Superman needs something to live for. And even Superman needs help sometimes. He wouldn't get far without Lois Lane, I'll tell you that much."

"I can't believe you read comic books."

"Only the classics, kid. Not a fan of the new age stuff."

"Fair enough." I raise my brows. "Still not sure how Clark Kent is relevant to anything in my life."

"Past time you patched things up with your own Lois, don't you think?" He looks pointedly at the name plastered across the stern of the boat.

My eyes follow, fixing on the gold and black lettering. "Josephine Valentine doesn't want to listen to a thing I have to say, believe me."

He wallops me upside the head a second time.

"Ow! Stop that!"

"There you go again. Lying to yourself. Just like you lied to that girl."

"Even if I told her the truth, it wouldn't change anything," I grit out, rubbing my head. It's beginning to throb. "We're from different worlds. I have nothing to give her."

"Then make something of yourself! Tear up the script you thought your life was going to follow and write a new one."

"You make it sound simple."

"It won't be simple. It will be the hardest thing you ever do. But whatever lies on the other side of that struggle has got to be better than *this*." He gestures at me. "We don't get infinite chances in this life, kid. We don't get unlimited opportunities to fix the things we've broken."

I know he's thinking of his family again. Of the fire, and the destruction it left behind.

"Some mistakes truly can't be fixed," Tommy says starkly. "But yours can. So stop pissing away your days. It's starting to piss me off."

We stare at one another. He looks mad as a hornet. I'm feeling prickly as a porcupine. But beneath that surface-level anger, there's no true fury. There's a feeling I can't look at too closely, because if I do I might do something stupid. Like hug him. My glaring eyes might do something crazy. Like tear up.

"Tommy—"

"Oh, don't go getting all mushy on me now, kid. Just promise me you'll treat Josephine right."

"The boat or the girl?"

"Both."

TWENTY-ONE

josephine

I CLOSE the front door as softly as I can manage, but the click of the latch still makes me wince. My head is splitting. Even through the dark lenses of my polarized Prada sunglasses, the world is far too bright; every sound that reaches my ears is ten times its normal decibel. I haven't been this hungover since...

Ever.

By the time we fell asleep last night — or, technically, in the wee hours of the morning — we'd put a sizable dent in the Wadell wine cellar supply. When I woke this morning, blinking blearily against a shaft of blinding midday sun, I was sprawled on the white sectional, barefoot in an unfamiliar, oversized t-shirt, my thoughts as fuzzy as my tongue. There was no sign of Odette or Ophelia. They must've stumbled off to their beds at some point, leaving me passed out on the cushions. I'd scribbled a short note on a Post-It — THANKS FOR LISTENING. XX - JO — and stuck it to their coffee machine before slipping out the side door.

I had to pull over twice on the ride home to throw up.

Serves me right for drinking half my body weight in champagne. It felt good in the moment — each sip washing away the memories of my confrontation with Archer, until my head felt as empty as one of the bubbles in my glass. Until I couldn't even recall why I'd felt so pathetic and broken and lost in the first place. But now, in the cold light of day, all those feelings have not only returned, but are compounded by the ceaseless pounding at my temples and queasy swirling of my gut.

My ill feelings further amplify at the sound of approaching kitten heels in the hallway, heading my way. I make a break for the stairs, but it's too late. My foot isn't even on the first step when she steps into the atrium and brings my walk of shame to an abrupt halt.

"Miss Valentine." Her voice hits me like a slap. "You've returned."

Wiping my expression clear, I turn to face her. I know what she must see — borrowed t-shirt, bedhead, bare feet, black circles beneath my eyes. I'm a disaster. And she's the picture of poise in her gray blouse, buttoned straight to the collar. Not a single wrinkle on her skirt. Not a single lock of hair escaping her low chignon.

"Good morning, Mrs. Granger."

"Morning? It's nearly afternoon."

"Right." My smile is weak. "Good afternoon, then. If you don't mind, I'll just be on my way upst—"

Her voice stops me again. "I was quite distressed when I arrived this morning and found you missing. Your bed not slept in, no sign of you. In another hour, I'd planned to phone the police and file a report."

"I'm just in time, then."

The silence is frosty.

"I apologize if I worried you," I say. "I spent the night with some friends. We lost track of time. When I realized how late it was, I was too tired to drive home."

Not to mention too toasted to remember my own name, let alone get behind a wheel, I add silently. In this case, a bit of omission is necessary. The judgment rolling off my housekeeper is potent. She says nothing — merely starts at me in frosty silence, her thin eyebrows arched in an inscrutable fashion.

I'm far too hungover for this.

Sighing, I run a hand through my messy waves. "I'll call next time, okay? I'm sorry for worrying you."

"It's not my place to worry—"

"*Agreed,*" I mutter.

"—but I hardly think your parents would approve of this untoward behavior."

"Then it's a good thing they aren't here."

Her eye twitches — the only ripple of displeasure visible in an otherwise placid mask. Awareness slams into me as the moment drags on. I scoff in disbelief. "You already called them, didn't you?"

"They have a right to know that their daughter is acting like such a... a..."

"A *what?*"

Her chin jerks slightly. Whatever name she was about to call me — probably something along the lines of *two-bit floozy* or *woman of loose morals* — remains stubbornly lodged on her tongue. I lean over the bannister, breathless with sudden anger. "You had no right!"

"I had every right!" she retorts haughtily.

"Is this why you're here, Mrs. Granger? To spy on me? To report any and all indiscretions to my parents? Because in case you've forgotten, I'm a legal adult."

"And I am the keeper of this household!"

"Of this household, perhaps. But you are not *my* keeper."

We face off across the drafty foyer, our mutual displeasure seeming to magnify and echo back at us from all sides. When I speak again, my voice is stone-cold. "Let's get something straight: If I choose to stay out all night, if I choose to join a biker gang, if I choose to tattoo my body from navel to nose... none of that is your concern. You are not judge, jury, or executioner, Mrs. Granger. If I offend your thick moral fiber, well, I'm sorry about that." I pause, spine stiffening. "Actually, I take it back. I'm not sorry."

I stomp my way up the stairs without a backward glance. I'm rather giddy from the rush of actually standing up for myself for once, instead of letting my parents — or their minions — steamroll me into bumbling apologies and cowed subservience. A bit of that levity evaporates when Mrs. Granger's voice follows me across the upper landing.

"Your mother is expecting your call, Miss Valentine. If I were you, I wouldn't keep her waiting."

I slam my bedroom door so hard, the frame rattles.

God, could this day get any worse?

———

It could indeed.

"What were you thinking? Staying out all night?" my mother hisses into the phone. "Are you trying to jeopardize your future with Oliver? Have you lost your senses? You know the Beaufort family is from good southern stock, where propriety and manners still reign supreme. They will not be so keen to welcome you into their ranks if you continue to spiral out of control!"

Of course she wasn't concerned for my safety — merely the possibility that I might upset my potential in-laws and thus derail any future business dealings between the two family companies. The Beaufort bloodlines are old as their money, an empire built on oil and tobacco dating back well over a century. From what I've heard from Oliver, his parents — and grandparents and great grandparents and great, great grandparents — are steeped in tradition stronger than the sweet tea they serve at their bi-monthly luncheons.

Appearances are everything.

"Mother." I glance at my bedroom ceiling, trying to get a handle on my ever-increasing exasperation. My hair, still wet from my shower, drapes over my shoulders in a damp curtain. "I hardly think having a sleepover with my friends is cause for all this overreaction. And even if I'd been out all night smoking crack and getting knocked up—"

"Do not even make jokes about such things!"

"—it wouldn't matter to the Beauforts," I finish tersely. "Oliver and I aren't engaged."

"*Yet.*"

I swallow a scream. Unless she knows something I don't, she's wildly off-base. "Have you taken up tarot card reading since I left? Purchased a magic crystal ball that predicts the future?"

"I don't need to be a psychic to see where this relationship is heading. Men like Oliver are not frivolous. They do not flit around indecisively. They move through life with intention. And I assure you, men like that look for the same qualities in their spouse."

Her pointed pause informs me I am not currently up to par.

"I'm not even twenty," I grumble. "Don't you think I'm a little young to be discussing lifelong commitments?"

"I married your father at eighteen. Look at all we've built since then. Look at all we've accomplished. Do you think I'd be able to say the same if I'd waited a few years longer to settle down? Dated a slew of useless suitors with nothing to offer? No. I taught you better than that. Men of calibre are not an abundant resource, Josephine. When you find one, you keep him. You'd be a fool to let Oliver slip away."

"Who says I'm letting him slip away?"

"He did."

"He *did?*"

"He may as well have." Her voice is practically smug. "He confided in me that you've been distant since your departure. I assured him you would be coming back soon, and all would be well again."

My frustration bubbles into furious betrayal. I can't believe Oliver is having pow-wows with Blair and Vincent, discussing me like a science experiment gone wrong.

"Your father and I both agree," Blair continues, "It's past time you ended this little charade of independence and returned to Switzerland, where you belong."

"Charade? I'm here to figure out my college plans, not audition for Cirque du Soleil."

"You cannot possibly still be considering attendance at that institution."

"Brown is an Ivy League school!"

"Barely. How you could pass over Harvard and Oxford in favor of that haven for pot-smoking artists, I'll never understand."

"Stop. Just stop." I press my eyes closed. "You know I want to study design. It shouldn't come as such a surprise to you that I'm not willing to change my plans in the blink of an eye."

She laughs. It holds no joy. The sound is cold, biting. It makes me flinch, even thousands of miles away. "Isn't it time to let go of that infantile pipe dream? I thought you'd surely seen the light, working here at VALENT these past few months. I was certain, once you got firsthand experience at an organization like ours — one that actually makes a difference in this world, one that actually matters — you'd let go of this silly notion of *art* and *fashion*." She says the words like curses. "How can you chase such an insubstantial pursuit when we are offering you the reins to our empire? How can you turn your back on your birthright?"

"I never asked for that future. I never wanted to be heir to the VALENT throne."

"This isn't about what you want, you foolish, selfish girl. This is about obligation. We are your parents. You will come to heel or we will bring you to heel."

"What are you going to do, Blair? Kick me out of the house? Cut me off?"

"Where is this attitude coming from? This newfound streak of obstinance is unlike you."

"Maybe I'm just finally growing a little backbone," I mutter. "Maybe I'm tired of bending over backwards, trying to please you and Vincent."

"Please us?" Her tone freezes over, each word blasting across the line in arctic gusts. "You don't please us, Josephine. You have always been a disappointment. I thought we might correct that, allowing you to stand by our side, permitting you to be a part of our life's joy—"

Ah yes, their life's joy.

Their company.

Not their child.

Never their child.

"—but it seems I was gravely mistaken. It seems, despite my best efforts, you are determined to throw away all our hard work. Everything we've invested in your future. For what? A failed foray into fashion, followed by a miserably ordinary existence?"

Her words sluice through me like a blade.

You have always been a disappointment.

I wish I was strong enough to ignore the pain that sentiment causes. Wish I didn't still crave what all children crave from their parents — love, affection, a semblance of pride. I should know better, after two decades' evidence to the contrary. I am no more than a puppet on their strings, my actions meticulously choreographed from the day I was born.

What other facets of my life have they attempted to orchestrate?

I'm breathing hard, trying and failing to control my emotions. The blood between my ears rushes like a river, flooding the banks, unearthing things left buried for far too long.

"What happened last summer, Blair?" I ask quietly. "That day Archer came here and left me that note. What really happened?"

She sucks in a sharp stream of air. I'm not sure which one of us is more thrown by the question — me in pitching it or her in fielding it. Blair certainly never offered up any details, and I'd never asked. Last June, I was so buried in heartache, so consumed by the haze of pain and confusion, I never wanted to hear the specifics.

I want to hear them now.

"Blair," I prompt.

"What does the Reyes boy have to do with anything? It's ancient history."

"Not for me."

"Don't tell me you've been in contact with him. Really Josephine... after what he did to you last summer...." She makes a *tsk* sound. "Are you so foolish to open doors better left closed?"

Apparently.

"Just tell me!" I insist. "If you've nothing to hide, if you've told me the truth, then tell me what happened. Spell it out."

"He came. He dropped off the note. I assure you, we did not exchange any words — or, if we did, they were not worthy of remembering. That shouldn't be a shock. He was never exactly... verbose."

I let her veiled insults slide by, too focused on more important clarifications. "So he came here. In person. You spoke to him. Face to face."

"Didn't I just say so?" she snaps, her unshakable calm momentarily slipping. "If you're just going to pepper me with nonsensical questions, I'm hanging up the phone."

I swallow hard, working up my courage. "The funny thing is, I've got it on good authority Archer couldn't have come here that day. Because he was in the hospital, recovering from a nasty car accident."

Silence blasts over the line.

"So I'm wondering," I continue, with a violent sort of softness. "Why you said you saw him if you didn't?"

"What does it matter if I saw him or not?"

"Then you didn't see him."

Her silence is answer enough.

"How exactly did a note in his handwriting end up here?"

A note that broke my goddamn heart.

A note that shattered my whole world.

A note that, now, makes absolutely no sense to me.

"What does it matter if he put it in my hand or left it in the mailbox?" she asks. "And why do you care either way, Josephine? I thought you'd finally moved on from this. Have a little self-respect and stop clutching at straws. *He didn't want you.* It's rather pathetic to keep pretending otherwise. Not to mention a waste of your time. And mine."

Tears gloss my eyes in the time between two heartbeats. Her words, true or not, cut me to the quick. Some of my anger has been tempered by shame when I murmur, "I just don't understand why you'd lie and say you saw him if you didn't. It doesn't make any sense—"

"What doesn't make sense is you asking me continually about a boy who was never fit to wipe the mud from your boots, let alone stand by your side," Blair hisses. "What doesn't make sense is that any daughter *of mine* would get wrapped up with the son of *the help* in the first place!"

I flinch. Archer's words the other day slam into my stomach like a lead fist.

I never belonged to your world, Jo. Not really. And we both know it. I was just your little pet — a stray you collected from the pound, shoved into a fancy collar and allowed to mingle for a while with the purebreds.

I've never seen him that way... but it's clear my mother does. I wonder what's more offensive to her — the fact that I deigned to give my heart to someone she considers beneath our social standing, or the fact that, despite the illustrious legacy she and my father have worked so hard to build, Archer has never shown any desire to align himself with the Valentine family. I'm certain she cannot fathom why a poor boy raised with nothing would not covet all the trappings of her privilege.

But then, she never did see him clearly. Never took the time to get to know him in more than the most insubstantial of ways. If she had, she'd have realized long ago that Archer isn't infatuated by wealth or stirred by celebrity status. His dreams are clearer cut, his longings more purely distilled.

Family.

Stability.

Baseball.

"If your interrogation is over," Blair says sharply, pulling me back to the present, "I have meetings to attend."

"I still have questions—"

"Honestly, Josephine! I've grown tired of your pointless questions."

"They aren't pointless to me. And I wouldn't have so many of them if you'd been honest with me in the first place!"

"Enough! I will not entertain your baseless accusations—"

"They aren't baseless if they're true!"

"—about last summer. I am not discussing this anymore. I do not have to explain myself to my child. Certainly not when it comes to that... that... waste of space, Archer Reyes." The receiver practically crackles with her wrath. "He is in the past. Leave him there, Josephine. I mean it."

"Or what? What will you do, mother?"

But my angry inquiries never reach her.

The line has gone dead.

———

I spend the following hour seething and pacing. I cut a path back and forth across my bedroom so many times, I'm certain there'll be a permanent groove left behind in the rug. The phone call with Blair rattled me more than I'd like to admit. I'm a mess of frustration and paranoia. Everything I thought I knew about last summer has been thrown off kilter. Like a conspiracy theorist, I tug at the loose threads of my life, searching for hidden schemes.

Great. Next, I'll be questioning the moon landing and convinced the earth is flat.

I redial the VALENT offices, hoping to pry more answers from my mother through sheer force of will, but I'm told she is in a meeting. Unreachable, until further notice. Try back tomorrow. I'm fed a similar line when I ask to speak to my father.

"Then connect me to Oliver Beaufort."

"Mr. Beaufort is out of the office today," the receptionist

says apologetically. I'm certain she can hear my patience dwindling. "If you'd like to leave him a message—"

"Forget it."

I disconnect and fall back onto my bed with a huff. Blair told me nothing, but her silence was evidence enough. Whatever happened to Archer last summer, she knows more about it than she's willing to share. More, even, than Chris Tomlinson or the Wadell twins, if I had to guess. Short of getting answers from Archer himself — which went over about as well as a hand grenade, at my last attempt — I've reached a dead end.

Why do you even care? a snide voice whispers from the back of my mind. *Knowing the truth won't change anything. Archer may've had an accident, he may've lied about All-Star camp... but that doesn't mean he lied about how he feels. Didn't he make things crystal clear the other day, when he practically threw you out of his apartment?*

I feel like a dog chasing its own tail, going round and round in dizzying circles. I rack my brain, replaying blurry memories of last June, trying to sort the tangle of possibilities into something that makes even a little bit of sense, but there are no answers to be found inside my head.

Only more questions.

With the earth giving way beneath my feet, I'm dangerously off balance. I dial Oliver's cell number, desperate for a shred of stability. I crumble further when the call goes straight to voicemail without a single ring. I try his landline instead. A sharp beep precedes his pre-recorded answering service.

"You've reached Oliver Beaufort," his deep voice says, twanging with familiar warmth. "Please leave a message and I'll get back to you as soon as I can. Thanks."

I terminate the call.

Where is he?

It's late in Geneva. He should be home from the office by

now, or at least on his way there. It's unlike him not to answer his phone. I'm shaken by the distinctly unpleasant possibility that my mother was right. That I've truly driven him away for good by being so distant lately.

Perhaps that's for the best, that same snide voice whispers inside my head. *Perhaps that's what you wanted all along.*

"No," I say aloud. "That's not true. I love—" I swallow hard. Try again, with fresh conviction. "I love Oliver. I do."

I tip my head back and look at the ceiling, attempting to hold in my tears. It takes a few shaky breaths, but I manage to keep them from welling over and flowing down my cheeks. When my chin lowers, I feel marginally more in control. At least, I do until my eyes drift out the large bay window that overlooks the water, and I spot something strange.

There's a sunshine-yellow lobster boat puttering into the cove. It looks like it's headed straight for our private dock. I move closer to the window, trying to peer at it from a better angle, but it's hard to make out any details from this distance. In another minute, my view will be obscured completely by the boathouse.

Probably some guy having engine trouble, I think, a pang of sympathy stirring in my gut. *He must've put into the first port he spotted.*

Shoving my feet into a pair of old Sperry topsiders, I head down to the docks to offer the stranger some assistance.

archer

CORMORANT HOUSE LOOMS before me as I putter into the cove. I drop my throttle down low and turn the wheel lightly with the tips of my fingers, marveling at the responsiveness of the brand new boat.

My boat.

The thought alone makes a laugh catch in my throat. I'm still not quite used to the idea. After Tommy's completely atypical show of generosity, the crazy bastard acted in a far more typical fashion — disappearing down the docks with his hands in his pockets and a faraway look in his eyes. His final orders lingered long after his departure.

Take her out for a spin, kid. See how she handles.

I offered for him to come along, but he told me the maiden voyage is something a captain should experience solo. So, off I went — cruising out of Gloucester Harbor, passing a fleet of inbound vessels returning with a fresh catch. It was one of those spectacular July days without a single cloud to mar the infinite blue sky, only a light breeze to stir the surface of the waves. As I puttered around, testing the features of my new rig, morning yielded into afternoon, but intense heat continued to blanket the coastline. The air was syrupy with humidity, even as the sun began to crest in the midday sky, and I knew it would be hot as hell even come nightfall.

A scorcher.

(Or, if you're blessed with a thick East Boston accent like so many of the guys who work on the docks — a *scor-chah*.)

I'm not entirely certain how I ended up here. Maybe the temperature is to blame. Heatstroke makes people do all sorts of crazy things, doesn't it? Too much hot air got to my head, upending all sense of intelligent thought and reason...

Right.

I snort.

I don't have a sufficient explanation for my actions. All I know is, one minute, I was motoring down the Cape Ann coast, telling myself I should check our long-neglected traps off Magnolia Point... and the next, I was here. In the little cove where I'd spent so much of my youth, with the Valentine mansion rising up behind it like a mountain range of turrets and pitched roofs.

The estate is far more intimidating at this proximity than it ever appeared during my distant drive-bys. As I close the final distance, my heart begins to pound a frantic drumbeat inside my chest. I grip the steering wheel harder as I navigate toward the dock, ignoring my jangling nerves as I drift to a stop in the space formerly occupied by a bright red Alerion sailboat. My fenders bump gently against the wood planks as I shift into neutral, shut the engine, and scramble overboard. I'm securing the stern line around a sturdy cleat when approaching footsteps rattle the boards beneath my feet.

I glance up.

Straight into a set of sky blue eyes.

They widen as they meet mine, clearly shocked by my presence. She freezes a dozen feet away, her expression flickering between so many emotions, I can't decipher a single one of them. She's in cut-off jean shorts that make her legs look a million miles long and a sleeveless linen blouse. Her long blonde locks are damp around her shoulders, a shade darker than usual. She wears no makeup, fresh from the shower.

It's hard to look at her, she's so damn beautiful.

I rise slowly to full height, holding the breath in my lungs until it starts to burn. Never shifting my gaze from hers. Not daring to move an inch into her space, for fear she'll run away. Or, worse, come closer. Within arm's reach. Within lip's reach. Close enough for me to pull her up against my chest and beg forgiveness. Beg absolution. Beg anything, so long as she'll give me a chance to repair all I've broken.

I push aside the thoughts.

"Hi," I say dumbly, clearing my throat. I don't know much about how this interaction is about to go, but I do know this: I'm the one who has to speak first this time. I'm the one who has to take the leap of faith. After our last interaction — the things I said to her — I'm just lucky she hasn't punched me in the face.

Not yet, anyway.

"What are you doing here?" The question trembles from her lips. Her eyes look glossy — as though she's already on the brink of tears.

Isn't that the question of the century?

What the fuck am I doing here?

I fist my hands at my sides, trying to hold myself in check. "I don't know," I tell her honestly. "I was just motoring down the coast and then I... suddenly found myself here."

She stares at me. "You found yourself here."

I nod.

She mulls that over for a moment. I can't read her eyes, nor her expression, but after a while they drift away from my face to study my lobster boat, moving over the bow with frank curiosity. "New?"

"Yes."

"Yours?" She steps closer, skimming her hand along the rail. Her fingers dance lightly against the fiberglass. I watch them, swallowing hard around the lump in my windpipe. Trying not to think about those hands — how they feel on my skin, how one small brush is enough to unravel me completely. I'd give just about anything to feel their weight again. To lace one with mine and walk down a street together, just a normal couple on a normal day.

No fractured past, no perilous future.

She turns to me, brows raised. I realize I haven't answered her question.

"Yes. She's all mine."

"Looks expensive," she notes.

"I wouldn't know. She was a gift."

She whistles lowly. "Some gift."

"My boss — the owner of the boat that sank — bought her with the insurance payout. He's ready to retire. He had no use for her, so she's mine now."

Another whistle. "Some boss."

"He is." I'm rattled by her composure. She's eerily calm. Not the good sort of calm. Calm like the sky before a storm. Still as the clouds before lightning touches down. I get the sense, if I push the wrong button, she'll strike out with similar lethal force.

"Jo."

Her eyes slide to mine. "Archer."

God, if she only knew what that did to me. Hearing my name on her lips. Watching it move through her mouth as her stare burns into mine.

It would send a weaker man to his knees.

"I'm sorry," I force myself to say. My voice is so raspy, it barely makes it past my lips. "Last time, with the pie... at my apartment... what I said to you..."

Her brows lift. Waiting.

"I was out of line."

"For which part?"

"All of it." I suck in a breath. She's not making this easy on me. Not that she should. "I was cruel. I was an asshole. I was honestly just trying to make you leave, any way I could. Because I thought..."

Her head cocks. A rogue curl falls across her face. She doesn't bother tucking it back behind her ear. "Thought what?"

"I guess I thought pushing you away would be easier than explaining everything."

"Easier." She hums. "Right."

My brows furrow. Is this the same girl who, only days ago, showed up at my doorstep demanding answers? "I guess I'm saying, if you still have questions..."

"Oh, I don't," she murmurs, surprising me greatly. The last time I saw her, she was brimming with them. "I don't have a thing to ask you. Frankly, I'm tired of asking questions. It never seems to get me anywhere."

My jaw tightens. "Jo—"

"Why don't I tell you what I know, instead?" she interjects. I see a flash of fierce temper lurking in the depths of her eyes, but she buries it away quickly beneath her frigid composure. "I know about the accident. I know you flipped your truck, totaled it completely. I know you've still got scars on your wrist. I know the bones shattered so bad, you were hospitalized for a long time." She pauses. Looks away from me. Her voice goes absent, as though she's only half there. As though we're discussing something trivial, like the weather, not the event that stole every hope and dream I'd ever had. "I know you're a liar."

I don't dare move.

Don't dare speak.

"You said you came here to explain things. But I don't trust your explanations, Archer. And I don't want your evasions or elaborations." Her eyes find mine once more, and this time they're completely unguarded. Two blue pools of abhorrence, blasting straight at me across the small distance between us. "I just want you to answer plainly. Whatever I ask. True or false. Confirm or deny. One word, nothing more." She pauses, breathing hard. "Can you do that?"

I nod.

"Good." She seems to steel herself. "First... that note you wrote last summer..."

I go still as I wait for the other shoe to drop. Right now, in this fractured moment, she could ask me anything and I'd answer her honestly. If she wants me to admit I lied about my feelings for her, I'll do it. I'm ready. I cannot keep pretending otherwise. I cannot keep lying to her. Even if it means the Valentines send their lawyers after me with more threats, even if it means staking my word — whatever little its worth — against theirs. Even if it means telling the girl I love it was her parents who crushed our chance at happiness.

Screw Blair and Vincent.

Screw the repercussions.

Screw everything but us.

"You lied when you said you were going to that All-Star camp," Jo continues, watching me closely. "You never went away. You were right here all along, recovering from your injuries. True or false?"

"True."

"You lost your scholarship last fall. True or false?"

"True."

"You never went away to college. True or false?"

"True."

"You work as a lobsterman full-time, not as a summer job. True or false?"

"True," I croak. My throat is so tight, I can barely release the word from my vocal cords.

She takes a step nearer. "Your accident happened on graduation day — that's why you missed the commencement ceremony. True or false?"

"True."

She nods. She already knew these answers. Deep down, beneath the lies, some part of her has probably always known.

"You can't play baseball anymore," she whispers finally, a long unspoken secret. "True or false?"

"True." I run a hand through my hair. "It's all true."

Her eyes follow the movement of my hand, tracing the scars spiderwebbed across the surface. Memorizing the damage. They never shift away as she mutters a single word.

"Why?"

"Why what, Jo?"

"Why *lie*?" She practically spits the word at me. Taking two steps forward, she plants both hands on my shoulders and shoves me backward. I nearly trip over a dock line and sail straight into the water, only managing to right myself at the last moment. "Why keep all of this from me?" She keeps coming, shoving me again. I backpedal down the dock, aware I'm rapidly running out of footing. "Why hide the truth?"

"What was I supposed to do, Jo? Call you up and say, 'Hey, I know you're heading off to start your life in Switzerland but, by the way, I'm in the hospital with a broken hand, and my whole future is fucked?"

"*Yes!*" She screams the word so loud, three black

cormorants burst into flight from a nearby rock. "That's exactly what you were supposed to do!"

"How could I do that?"

"How could you *not*?"

"I'm sorry, okay?" I roar at her. "I fucked up. But you don't know what it was like, that day—"

"How could I, when you hid it from me?!"

I grit my teeth. "I'm not defending myself. I'm just saying, it's not as clear cut as you're making it sound. If you'd been there—"

"I *would've* been there if you'd let me!"

"I know that!" I yell back. "Don't you think I know that?"

"I have no idea what you know or don't know! I'm pretty certain your brain stopped working sometime last spring when you started screwing cheerleaders—" That earns me another shove; I rock backward on my heels, absorbing the blow. "—and pushing away your best friend!"

"Would you stop screaming for a second and hear me out?"

"No!" She pushes me again. I'm nearly out of dock. One more shove, and I'll be sent sprawling into the ocean. Her anger has reached a boiling point. Nothing I say will calm her, in this moment. My words are falling on deaf ears.

Threading her hands up into her hair, she casts her eyes heavenward. "God! What the *fuck*, Archer? What the actual fuck? This is un-*fucking*-believable!" She's swearing. She never swears. She's looking at me like I've ruined her life, which sends guilt spiraling through me.

I was wrong to come here.

Wrong to listen to Tommy.

Wrong to hope this could ever be mended.

I should've just let her hate me for the rest of my life.

Her head shakes back and forth. "I don't understand you!

One day, you're saving my life, the next you're telling me to scram. Now, you show up here unannounced—"

"I didn't come here to upset you."

"Then why did you come?"

"To apologize."

"To a girl you claim you can't stand? Shouldn't you be *happy* I'm feeling like this?" Her hands fly out in a sarcasm-laced display of jazz fingers. "Surprise! I'm miserable! Mission accomplished!"

"I don't want you miserable." My voice is so low, she has to lean in to catch my words. "I never wanted that, Jo. I only ever wanted to protect you. And somehow, it all got screwed up. Somehow, all I've managed to do is hurt you." I glance down at my sneakers. "I'll go, okay? I'll leave. And you can just... pretend I was never here."

When she shoves me, I don't see it coming. I go head over feet off the edge of the dock, straight into the cove, with a splash that rattles the wind from my lungs.

I surface, spluttering for air.

My eyes sting with salt, searching for her.

She's already gone.

———

I'm winded by the time I manage to haul my waterlogged body back up onto the dock. Not to mention drenched to the bone. Thankfully the fading afternoon sun is still warm. I set my soaked sneakers on the rail of the lobster boat and squeeze the worst of the water from my jeans, then peel my t-shirt up over my head. I'm wringing it out as best I can manage when I hear the sound of approaching footsteps.

My head swings around. To my surprise, Jo is standing

there holding a towel from the boathouse. She extends it toward me, a peace offering.

"I shouldn't have pushed you in," she says, by way of apology. "That was petty of me."

"I'll dry."

For a moment, we're both quiet. I sponge droplets from my stomach and arms, then put the towel over my hair and shake like a wet dog. When I'm decently dry, I look for Jo and find her sitting on the edge of the dock, staring out at the cove. All traces of her anger have vanished on the wind, but I move with extra caution anyway as I drop down beside her.

It's a position we've sat in a million times before — side by side, four feet in the water, two backs to the world. But there's nothing familiar about this new tension between us. We are in uncharted waters, a million miles offshore, with no lighthouses or stars to guide us back home. I have no idea what to say. Where to start. Perhaps she doesn't either, because the silence drags on for a long time.

Finally, she clears her throat and speaks, still not looking at me. "These past few days... since I came back home, since I saw you again... I've felt like I'm losing my mind. Truly, like I'm going mad. Ever since you came back into my life, everything I thought I knew, every shred of closure I've spent a year chasing... it's all just fallen to pieces. I can't sleep at night, because the memories..." She sucks in a pained breath. "I forget to eat, I'm so caught up in my thoughts. And now you're sitting here, right next to me, so close and so far, and I can't even *breathe* properly—"

"Jo. Look at me."

She does. Her eyes are full of tears. I'm pretty certain mine are too, since they're stinging like hell. I could blame the salt water, but I'd be lying to myself.

"I begged you," she whispers so gently, it's a knife to my

gut. "At your apartment. With the pie. I actually *begged* you. I was so desperate for a single grain of truth in all the lies... so tangled up, trying to get answers... and you made me think I was insane. You sent me away like... like... some piece of garbage you didn't want anymore."

"What do you want me to say? That I'm a bastard?" My voice shakes. "*I'm a bastard.* That I screwed up? *I screwed up.* That I'm sorry? *I'm sorry.*" Without thinking, I take her by the shoulders. Callused hands on silk skin. The moment we touch, we both flinch. Like an electric shock has jumped through us both. Her mouth parts, a small gasp sliding from her lips. My words are shooting sparks. "I'm so fucking sorry, Jo. I'll never be able to put it into words. I'll never be able to explain—"

"Try."

Like it's so simple.

My hands tighten on her shoulders. Almost unconsciously, my thumbs begin to rub small, soothing circles against her skin. Whether I'm soothing her or myself, I'm no longer sure. It takes me a while to find the words.

Just start at the beginning.

This part is easy to tell.

The rest will be harder.

"You know last spring, my brother was released from prison."

Her eyes widen. Whatever she'd expected me to say, it was not this, but she nods for me to carry on.

"When he first came home, things were fine. Even good, for a little while. But pretty quickly, they started to unravel. *He* started to unravel." I expel a breath. "Turns out, while he was behind bars, Jaxon made some powerful enemies."

"Not shocking, given his personality," Jo mutters.

"Agreed. Long story short, he found himself in need of protection. And he got it... but it came at a price."

"A price?"

"He joined a gang." I hold her gaze. "The Latin Kings."

She gasps softly. Even someone like Josephine Valentine, daughter of privilege, has heard that name. A name synonymous with drugs, guns, and dangerous criminals.

"Those men last summer..." Jo whispers, her eyes spinning with thoughts.

The hair on the back of my neck goes up. "Men?"

"The scary ones with the tattoos... I think their names were Rico and... Barbuda? Barbazon? Bar-something. They came looking for Jaxon." Her eyes widen. "And... for you."

"*What?*" My hands fly from her in an exasperated jerk. "How could you not have said something about this?"

"Oh, as if you share anything with me. Please." Her eyes roll. "*Hello, pot! Meet kettle!*"

"God, Jo! Those guys are seriously bad news. You can't keep things like that to yourself — not when they threaten your safety. You should've told the police. You should've told *me*."

"How was I supposed to tell you anything last summer?" she retorts, her rage flaring back to life like an ember hit with a shot of pure oxygen. "You were barely talking to me! Do you really think I was going to chase you down and say, 'Hey, Arch, just a quick FYI, there are some seriously bad thugs looking for you and your dickhead brother. They cornered me in a parking lot and majorly freaked me out.'"

"They cornered you," my voice is scary soft, "In a parking lot."

"Don't look at me like that! All vengeful and brooding. You don't get to be mad at me. First of all, it was a year ago. Second of all, I'm mad at *you* right now. Stay in your lane."

"You could've would up hurt or worse—"

"Like you did?" She stares suddenly at my damaged wrist, her mind making the connection in a single leap. "Did those men have something to do with your accident? *Was* it an accident? The Wadell twins said you flipped your truck..."

"Yes and no. It's complicated." I pause for a moment. "Those men in the parking lot — they were enforcers for the Kings. They followed me around all last summer, looking for my brother. Threatening to hurt anyone I cared about if I failed to deliver."

Her eyes are working with thoughts. Turning over my words. Weighing each of them for significance. "That's why..."

"Why what, Jo?"

"Why you started acting so weird... Pushing me away. Holding me at a distance," she murmurs, looking rather rattled by the realization. "You were trying to protect me."

"Yeah, well. Some good it did. They found you anyway."

There's a long beat of silence. Jo looks away from me, out over the water. In profile, her tension is apparent; jaw locked tight, pulse a quicksilver tattoo in her jugular vein. Her next question is asked through clenched teeth. "Why were they so determined to get Jaxon?"

"He owed them money. They wanted him to pay it off by dealing for the gang. Not pot or coke, either. Hardcore stuff. Heroin. Fentanyl. Oxy. Meth. They saw him as a linchpin for the North Shore — an access point to get their product in the hands of rich prep school kids with big piggy banks." I sigh deeply. "But when Jaxon proved less than cooperative with their grand plans... they didn't react well. So they took my parents captive. As leverage."

"They *took* Flora and Miguel?!" Jo explodes in shock. "Oh my god!"

"Mmm. The morning of graduation... I woke up with you, in the boathouse..." My eyes drift over her shoulder, to the stone building at the end of the dock. I swallow sharply, pushing the memories aside. "When I checked my phone, there was a message from Rico, demanding I bring Jaxon to him. And along with that message, there was a picture of my parents, held hostage. They..." My voice cracks. "They were duct taped to chairs. They looked so fucking scared. They looked like... like they thought they were about to die. I swear, my heart stopped in that moment. I don't think it started beating again until I knew they were safe."

I hear her pull in a gulp of air. Cautiously — so very, very cautiously — her hand creeps into mine. We both tense at the contact, freezing for a split second as the world jolts on its axis.

Jo recovers first. Her fingers wind with mine. Our palms meet. She squeezes gently. Offering me strength. It's more than I deserve, after everything I've done to her.

But I squeeze back.

Hard.

"I didn't stop to think," I continue, ignoring the way my pulse is thundering between my ears. "I didn't pause. I didn't wake you. I just... reacted. Threw on my clothes, hopped in my truck, and headed straight there. I called the cops on the way."

"And then?" she prompts. She's practically vibrating beneath the strain of holding in her questions. It's taking every bit of her self-control to let me get the rest of the story out uninterrupted.

"My own fault, really. I was so focused on getting there, I blew right through a red light. Never saw the truck coming. Sure as hell felt it, though."

She lifts our interconnected hands close to her face — hers, so small and fine-boned, mine a mess of scars. She examines the damage through a haze of gathering tears.

"The truck flipped three times. When it finally stopped, I was hanging upside down by my seatbelt. Shattered glass everywhere. Metal frame crushed like a soda can. I've never been in so much pain. Thankfully, I wasn't conscious for long.

The blood loss..." I shrug as lightly as I can manage. "I passed out. When I woke up, I was in an ICU bed."

In handcuffs.

Charged with my brother's crimes.

At your parent's absolute mercy.

I omit those details, for the moment. Jo looks like she's struggling to process everything I've just told her; I hesitate to pile on too much at once.

"God, Archer." Her voice is shaking. "I can't even imagine... That must've been terrifying. Your parents. The accident. All of it."

I give a shallow nod. I can barely breathe, let alone speak with her so close to me. Touching me. Her hand in mine. The scent of her hair stirring in the breeze around us. The press of her bare thigh against my damp jeans.

Need surges through me, a molten tidal wave. Need to hold her tight in my arms. To press her back against the wood dock, claim her mouth with mine, and watch her come apart beneath my fingers. To bring us back together — not with words, but with our bodies.

I want to make love to her until I've undone all the damage.

Until we both forget the past.

I don't care how long it takes.

Carefully, like it's made of glass, she sets my hand down on the dock. Looking up into my face with brimming eyes, her lashes fan across her cheeks as she blinks back tears. "I had no idea any of this happened to you."

"I know."

"I wish you'd told me. I wish..." Her head shakes. "A lot of things."

"Me too, Jo." I swallow hard. "A lot of things."

"But what about your parents—"

"They're okay," I assure her, hearing the worry in her voice.

225

"The police stormed the place they were being held and arrested the men responsible. Flora and Miguel are just fine, trust me. They're probably tanning on a beach in Puerto Rico as we speak."

"And Jaxon?"

"Still on the run. Still with the gang. Wanted for parole violations and a slew of new charges." I swallow roughly. "If he's caught... he's probably going away for life, this time."

"And... you?"

"I woke up in the hospital with a broken wrist. Three cracked ribs. Some pretty bad bruising. Bit of internal bleeding. Oh, and this souvenir." I push back the long hair that flops over my forehead to expose the scar that stretches across my temple. I try to smile, but I can tell it's less than convincing when Jo's sadness spills over, streaming down her cheeks in a torrent.

"Don't cry," I plead, horrified. "Please, Jo, don't..."

My words evaporate as she leans in to me. I watch tears drip down her face, plummeting from her chin like rainfall. Her face is so close to mine, I can count her freckles, one by one. Her hand shakes as she reaches up to trace the jagged line that extends across my hairline. The scar tissue is extra sensitive, every nerve ending heightened. I hiss out an involuntary breath when her fingers make contact.

Fuck.

In my jeans, my cock is beginning to become a problem — pressing against the zipper with increasing insistence every time she touches me. I shift, trying to lessen the throbbing ache, but it does no good.

"Jo..."

"I can't believe you almost died!" She snaps furiously, through the flood of tears. "I can't believe you almost died and I wasn't there! I don't care how bad things were between us —

you should've called me! You should've let me be there for you! Why wouldn't you let me be there for you, you idiot?"

And this is where our story takes a turn.

Where the telling gets tough.

How can I look into her eyes and tell her about her parents? How can I make her understand that, when I found myself backed into a corner with my spine against the wall and no way out... it was Blair and Vincent who put me there? That it was a Valentine bank account that paid for my silence?

As I struggle to find the words, she smacks me on the arm. "I'm so angry at you, Archer Reyes!"

"I know, Jo."

"I could kill you myself for almost dying!"

"I know, Jo."

"This is just... it's too much! I can't... I don't..."

"I know, Jo. I know."

"I... you..." Her face crumples completely as emotion overtakes her. And then, before I can even brace for it, she's falling forward onto my chest. Plastering her body against mine like a wrecking ball of anger and sorrow and hurt and frustration, all wrapped up in one petite blonde package.

Tears drip against my torso, tracking wet paths from my pecs all the way down my stomach. Her fists land soft punches against my bare skin as she sobs, an ugly cascade of pent up pain.

I can't take it from her.

I can't make it better.

All I can do is hold her — stroking her hair in long, rhythmic moves. Absorbing her grief as best I can.

"Just breathe, baby," I whisper against the crown of her head as I hold her, so softly I'm not sure she can hear it. "Let it out. I'm here."

I'll always be here.

TWENTY-THREE

josephine

IT TAKES a long time for my tears to slow from sobs to hiccups. By the time they fade into silence, the sun has begun to slant toward the western horizon. The sky above us is streaked with color; the waters of the cove look like stained glass on a church steeple. Beneath my ear, Archer's heart beats steadily on. His arms are still wound tight around me, cradling my body against his chest.

It's difficult to reckon with the fact that I dissolved into an emotional puddle after he described nearly dying. And he comforted me — even after I pushed him off the dock. Even after I lashed out at him. The sting of embarrassment pierces me straight between my cry-swollen eyes.

My emotions are a tangled mess — as is typical, where Archer is concerned. But I must admit, I do feel better after expelling some of them through my eyeballs. My internal well was at capacity, overflowing. Now, in the aftermath of my small breakdown, I feel blessedly empty. Hollowed out. Once again able to breathe without hyperventilating.

Archer is quiet, just holding me without saying a word.

"I'm sorry," I whisper.

"For what?"

"Hitting you. And pushing you into the cove." I pause. "And saying I wanted to kill you. I don't want anything to happen to you. In case that wasn't obvious from the small waterfall of tears I just leaked all over your chest."

A chuckle rumbles through him, vibrating his whole body. It feels nice against my cheek. Treacherously nice. I force myself to pull back, to peel away from him, straightening my spine so I'm sitting upright. His arms fall away instantly, but I see a flash of regret move in the depths of his eyes. Like he doesn't quite want to let me go.

Our faces are close. Bathed in sunset hues, beneath the beard, beneath the *man*... I see the face of the boy I built my life around. Some of the demons have vanished from his eyes. Some of that tight-held pain has slipped from his expression.

My Archer.

"You're still in there, aren't you?" I whisper. "I thought you were gone for good."

He's watching me guardedly. I can't read his expression at all, but I can see the tension in his body even before I hear it in his voice. "I'm not the same guy I used to be, Jo. I wasn't lying the other day when I told you the Archer you came looking for is gone."

"Maybe we can get him back."

"There is no getting him back." His eyes press closed. His breaths grow shallower, as if he's drowning beneath the weight of pain. "Don't you understand? That guy you miss is gone. Dead. He died that day, in the accident." He pauses harshly. "Sometimes, I wish I'd died with him."

"Don't say that!" I cry. "Don't you ever say that, Archer Reyes!"

"Why? It's the truth. Every path I ever walked... every dream I ever had... they all disappeared that day."

I can hear it in his words — raw anguish. Unadulterated loss, untempered by time's passing. He has not yet begun to heal from the damage inflicted last summer. His body may be functioning, but there are deep scars etched across his soul. The kind I'm not sure ever truly disappear.

I wish I could reach into his ribcage and take some of that pain off his heart. But I know I can't. This is something he has to work through on his own. And even if he'd allow me to be there for him — to support him, like I used to, back when he still needed his best friend — I'm not sure it's my place. Not anymore. I'm not sure where we stand. He's dropped so many truths at my feet in the past few minutes, I haven't yet begun to process how I feel about any of it, let alone what it means for our relationship.

Are we still enemies?

Are we back to being friends?

Or... are we something else entirely?

Thinking too hard about any of it makes my head ache. I push aside the past, the future... everything but the present. Moving forward in small degrees. One minute at a time. One truth at a time.

"You say your plans disappeared, Archer? Then I guess you need to find some new ones," I tell him with as much gentleness as I can manage. "Because living like this, in the absence of hope... it's not living."

His head is shaking, rejecting my words before they're fully out of my mouth. "You couldn't possibly understand, Jo. You've never lost a thing in your whole damn life. I lost everything. I lost my *dream*."

"And I lost *mine*!" I snap back, the words rushing out before I can stop them. "You lost baseball? I lost *you*. I lost *us*." A tear streaks down my cheek and I brush it away angrily with the sleeve of my sweater.

His face pales, going ashen white against a radiant backdrop of red-pink sky.

I shove to my feet, unable to look at him as I continue. "You say I couldn't possibly understand? That I've never lost anything? Of all the cruel things you've ever said to me, Archer Reyes — and there have been many — that's the cruelest by a mile."

He gets to his feet, following me down the dock. Matching me stride for stride. I feel a hand curl around my bicep, wrenching me to a stop. Whipping me around to face him.

The look he's giving me — passion, pure and palpable — makes my knees quake, but I infuse my limbs with iron and anger, refusing to crumble before him like a paper doll for a second time. I do not cave to the urge to fall into his chest. Instead, I dig in my heels, glaring up with every ounce of fury I can muster.

"I was in love with you," I tell him, point blank. A bullet at close range, straight to the heart. He rocks back on impact. I keep going. "For years. I was so in love with you I couldn't see anything else. Anyone else. And maybe it wasn't the same for you, maybe you couldn't love me back in the way I wanted you to, but you were the most important thing in my life. And when you pushed me away, you broke my goddamn heart. Because I didn't just lose the boy I loved. I lost my best friend. I lost the person who meant more to me than anything in this world."

We're both breathing hard. I'm stunned I've just said all that, but once I started there was no stopping it. Everything spilled out in a torrent. Part of me aches to take it all back, to somehow snatch my words from the air and shove them inside, deep down, where he can't hear them anymore. But another part of me is relieved I can finally take a clear breath for the first time in a year without my heart lodged in my throat.

Archer lurches forward and I swear, in that instant, he's about to pull me into his arms and crush me against his chest. I backpedal away as his hands graze my shoulders, knowing if he touches me, all my resolve will evaporate like steam.

"Jo, just wait—"

"No! I'm done waiting for you. I've waited my whole life for you, and it's gotten me nowhere."

"That's not fair. There are things you still don't understand—"

"Oh, I understand. I understand completely. Trust me." I laugh, but the sound is agonized. "But that's the problem, isn't it? You *don't* trust me. You never have. Not like I trusted you. Not enough to tell me the truth about what was going on last summer."

"God dammit, Jo, come back here!" he calls after me as I turn and start walking away from him again. "You don't get to just say you love me and then— *Dammit!* Would you just stop for a second, you infuriating girl—"

I don't stop.

I've reached my emotional limit for the day.

I hear a deep masculine growl of frustration. The sound of his footsteps stop. I think he's given up pursuit until his voice slams into my back like a sledgehammer.

"You were my dream, too."

I stop short. The breath freezes in my lungs. Goosebumps break out across my skin, skittering from the crown of my head to the soles of my feet.

I don't turn to face him.

I stand stock-still, listening as he closes the steps between us. He comes up behind me, pressing his chest against my back. Absorbing my trembles with the broad frame of his body.

His chin comes down to rest on my shoulder. I feel the heat of his breath against my ear. I gasp as the hard evidence of his desire grazes my ass through the thin denim of my cut-off shorts.

I want nothing more than to lean back into his touch, to melt beneath the sensation of his body pressing deliciously against mine.

But I need one more truth from him first.

One last truth.

The only truth that really matters.

"You lied about the rest of that letter, too," I breathe, eyes pressed tight closed to shut out the world around us. Dulling my senses to everything outside the circle of his arms. "When you said you didn't feel the same. When you said sleeping together didn't mean anything. When you said we should just go back to being friends." I pause. Inhale. Exhale. "True or false?"

His mouth moves against the shell of my ear.

But it's not his voice I hear.

Not his answer I receive.

"Josephine? Darlin,' is that you?"

———

My eyes fly open.

To my utter disbelief, Oliver is walking down the stone steps beside the boathouse. His eyes are wary, full of questions, as he steps onto the dock. His blond hair catches the day's last rays of sun as he approaches. The lenses of his wire-framed glasses refract like dusky pink headlights.

I jerk like I've been sucker-punched. Archer's arms fall away from me so fast, you'd think my skin had scalded him. We spring apart, two magnets with opposing charges.

"Ollie! What on earth are you doing here?" I practically run to him, desperate to create a bit of space between me and the man standing behind me.

Ollie leans down to press a quick kiss against my lips. I try not to flinch away, hyper-aware of Archer's intent gaze.

"I came to check on you, of course," Oliver says, like it should've been obvious. "I was worried. You sounded out of sorts on the phone after your boat went down."

"I told you I was fine!"

"I'll be the judge of that."

Archer's stare burns into my back like a hot brand. I do my best to ignore it, but it's not easy. There is a storm brewing inside me. One I cannot tame or temper. My stomach rolls with nausea. My veins churn with an uncomfortable emotion that, after a few seconds, I identify as guilt. I try to quell it with flimsy assurances that I haven't done anything wrong. That I haven't cheated on my boyfriend. That I haven't somehow — and quite illogically, might I add — betrayed Archer by *having* a boyfriend in the first place.

As hastily as I can manage, I extract myself from Oliver's arms. Nerves jangle as I glance back and forth between the two men. Two radically different men. One bare-chested and bearded, his skin tan from long days working in the sun, his hands callused with evidence of long labor; the other every inch the business man, a gleaming Rolex at his wrist and platinum cufflinks on the sleeves of his custom-tailored suit.

Oliver, a sunny southern breeze; Archer, a storm cloud with sentience.

They are night and day.

Worlds apart.

And me, standing between them.

They stare at one another with equal parts curiosity and

wariness. Both smiling strangely stiff smiles that do not reach either of their eyes.

"Aren't you going to introduce me to..." Oliver trails off. Beneath his friendly facade, there's a ramrod tension in his posture he can't quite hide.

"Right. Of course. This is—" I look at Archer and clear my throat uncomfortably. "This is Archer Reyes. He's... an old friend."

A ghost of a smile touches my *old friend*'s mouth.

"I'm Oliver Beaufort. And any friend of Josephine's is a friend of mine," Ollie says amiably. He sticks out his hand to shake. "We're a package deal, you see."

"I do see." Archer's eyes flicker to me for a heartbeat before he steps forward and grips Oliver's hand. The air seems to crackle with tension as they shake... and shake... and *hold*. The moment drags on forever, neither of them willing to release first. My eyes widen a bit when I see their knuckles are turning white. I'd bet my bottom dollar, if you put an acorn between their palms right now, it would crack wide open.

Archer's surgical scars have gone pale beneath Oliver's grip. He must be in excruciating pain. If he is, he keeps it well concealed, his indifferent mask never flickering. I let out a relieved breath when they finally break apart.

"Funny," Oliver says after a long moment, winding his arm around my back as soon as it's free; pulling me close like I'm a prize he's won in their contest of wills. "Josephine never mentioned an old friend."

Archer smiles coldly. "She never mentioned a boyfriend either."

"She's not one to brag." Oliver forces a laugh at his own joke. Archer does not join in. When silence descends again, it's even more stagnant than before.

"So," I squeak. "Uh—"

They both look at me.

I fight the urge to squirm like a bug beneath a magnifying glass.

Kill me now.

I glance up at my boyfriend. "Sorry, Oliver — I'm just so stunned to see you standing here, I'm at a bit of a loss for words. I had no idea you were flying in."

"Wouldn't have been much of a surprise if I'd warned you first, darlin,' now would it?"

"Right," I agree weakly. "When did you get here?"

"Touched down just over an hour ago. I came straight here from the jetway." Oliver glances at Archer. "Josephine's parents were kind enough to lend me the company Gulfstream for the journey. Can you believe that?"

"Oh, I'd believe just about anything when it comes to Blair and Vincent."

I glance at him sharply, eyes narrowing at the cutting edge in his tone.

What's that all about?

Oliver doesn't seem to notice anything amiss. "They're great, aren't they? I'm lucky to have two bosses who don't mind me dating their daughter. Or taking a personal leave to surprise her halfway across the world." He grins wide, a flash of bright white teeth. "Hey! Here's a thought. You're an old friend — maybe you can convince Josephine to fly back to Switzerland with me in a few days. Everyone knows it's where she belongs."

Something inside me quails.

Archer's jaw is locked down tight. He doesn't look at me when he speaks, but his words are low; nearly guttural.

"She's all yours, Beaufort."

With that, he turns and stalks away, disappearing down the dock in a handful of strides. I watch him go — muscles in his broad back rippling, long legs carrying him swiftly away from me — and have to swallow down the urge to lean over the edge and vomit straight into the water.

"Not the friendliest chap, is he?" Oliver murmurs, watching Archer untie his dock lines and step aboard. "I guess all those stereotypes about grumpy New Englanders aren't too far off, after all."

"He's just..." I shake my head, trying to clear it, then force my eyes away from the yellow lobster boat. "A little rough around the edges, right now. He's been through a lot since I left."

"Hmm." Oliver looks down at me. "You've been friends a long time."

Despite the curiosity lurking beneath the words, they are not phrased as a question. He sensed the strange, electric intimacy between Archer and me a mile off.

I nod. "Since we were kids."

"You never told me about him."

"No," I say softly. "I didn't."

There's a long silence. Oliver stares at me, weighing my words. Parsing hidden meaning from the gaps I've left unfilled. "I'm guessing you dated," he says with forced nonchalance. "First boyfriend?"

"No. We never dated."

Not exactly.

His brows furrow for a few seconds, then smooth almost instantly back into his familiar open expression. "So, I don't have anything to worry about."

I swallow hard. Trying not to think about the almost-moment I just shared with Archer. Trying not to wonder where that moment might've led, had Oliver not interrupted us.

Nothing happened.

So why do I feel so guilty?

"No, Oliver. You don't have anything to worry about."

"For a minute, when I first walked up... I thought maybe he was the reason you came back here or something."

I jolt in surprise. "I told you, I came back here to sort out my academic leave with Brown. That's all. I promise."

"Good." He's not looking at me. His eyes are sweeping around the cove, examining the view in the setting sun. "Gosh, it's beautiful, here. I can see why you love it." His arm tightens at my waist. "I'm glad I'm finally getting to see it in person."

I lean a bit closer to him, wrapping my arm around his lower back. "Me too."

"That old boathouse is amazing, by the way. I love how it hangs over the water like that. I'd love to see inside. Maybe you can give me a tour?"

I hope he can't feel how I stiffen. The thought of him in the boathouse — a space I cannot step foot inside without being swamped by memories of Archer — is hard to reconcile.

"Oh. Uh. Maybe later." I gulp for air. "It's really dusty in there."

"I don't mind a bit of dust."

"*No*." I can hear the tightness of my own tone. "I mean... Not right now, all right?"

Oliver's brows lift toward his hairline. "Darlin', are you okay?"

"I'm fine. Honestly, I think I'm just a little bit shocked you're standing here."

He nods, turning away from the boathouse to examine the rest of the cove. "Good shocked, right?"

"Great shocked."

"That's my girl." A smile lights up his whole face at my words. It wavers a bit when his eyes snag on something in the distance. I turn to see what's bothering him and feel my own half-smile vanish — along with all the air in my lungs.

Archer's lobster boat is heading out of the cove, into open water. With the waves lapping gently at his bow and the sky above streaked a million shades of red, the idyllic nautical scene looks like an oil painting you'd see hanging in a Winslow Homer exhibit. But the beauty is not what steals my breath; rather, the name written across the boat's stern in unmissable bold letters.

JOSEPHINE

My mouth falls open. My legs nearly give out beneath me. My arm around Ollie's waist is just about the only thing keeping me upright.

In thick silence, my boyfriend looks down at my face — just once, just for a heartbeat — before turning his attention back to the cove. He stares after the departing boat until it's passed the channel markers and rounded the point, motoring back toward Gloucester Harbor. Only when all signs of Archer are out of our view does he loose a long breath.

"*Never dated* — that is what you told me, right?"

———

We stare at each other across the kitchen island, both holding cups of tea. Mine has gone cold, still untouched. More a prop than anything. I don't trust my queasy stomach to hold it down, at the moment. I notice an unfamiliar tension in Oliver's fingers as he grips the porcelain cup, lifting it to his mouth for a long swallow.

I can't blame him for being tense. I've spent the past half hour telling him about my history with Archer. Our childhood here at Cormorant House. The complicated dynamics of last spring. The tangled web of half-truths we wove in the summer that followed. My words catch as I talk about prom night. The morning after. The note. The year of silence. The storm.

I don't share the details of Archer's accident, or the situation with his brother Jaxon. That's not my story to tell. But everything else pours out. Even things I'd planned to keep to myself — like the fact that I'm no longer a virgin. Or the fact that I have Archer to thank for that state of affairs.

It's difficult to share everything with him, but I figure it's the least I can do. Oliver has only ever offered me honesty; he's owed the same in return. By the time I finish speaking, my heart beats woodenly inside my chest and my eyes are heavy with the weight of unshed tears. I wait for him to respond with bated breath, fully prepared to defend myself for any judgment.

I don't regret my choices. I only regret that not telling you about those choices is causing you pain now.

As usual, Ollie surprises me. He doesn't fixate on my virginity. He doesn't judge me at all.

"Thank you," he murmurs instead, knocking the wind out of me with those two little words. "For trusting me enough to share."

"Thank you for listening."

"I had a feeling something like this might've happened." There's no accusation in his voice — only a grim sort of resignation. "I could sense you pulling away, day by day. That something — or someone — was *pulling* you away from me. It's why, the first chance I got, I hopped on a plane here."

"Are you angry with me?" I ask. My voice is shaking. "I swear to you, Ollie, nothing happened between me and Archer. I would never be unfaithful."

"I know. I trust you, Josephine. But I don't trust him." Storm clouds of anger move across his typically sunny expression. "He hurt you."

He had his reasons, I think instantly. My first instinct — as always — is to spring to Archer's defense. A long-ingrained habit I can't seem to break.

"Do you still love him?"

The question makes me flinch. "I've barely spoken to him in a year, Oliver!"

"That's not what I asked."

My lower lip is trembling. "When it comes to Archer and me... things are just... complicated."

"Not complicated. *Unfinished.*"

"No, Ollie," I say immediately, rejecting his gentle correction. "It's over. It never even started, actually."

"Just because you didn't put a label on it doesn't mean it wasn't real. He may not have ever been your official boyfriend, but you gave him your heart all the same. He holds a piece of you in his hands. A piece I've spent a year wondering about." He shakes his head sadly. "When I first met you, I could see how sad you were. How broken. I knew whatever guy came before me had done some serious damage. And I made it my mission to fix that damage. To repair what he'd broken. To bring back that light in your eyes."

A tear slides down my cheek. "I know you did."

"But it's tough to be an antidote if you don't know anything about the poison. I've done my best."

Reaching across the table, I take his hand in mine. "You've done more than I ever deserved, Oliver. More than any other man would have, in your shoes."

"As usual, you sell yourself short."

"You've been so good to me." My voice cracks. "If you want to leave... I'll understand. I won't hold it against you."

He blinks. "*Leave?* Why would I leave?"

"I just thought... after hearing all that, you wouldn't want..."

Me.

You wouldn't want me anymore.

"I didn't fly halfway around the world to break up with you, Josephine."

"So it doesn't disappoint you that I'm not a..." I falter on the word *virgin*.

"Disappoint me? No, it doesn't disappoint me. If anything, it makes me a bit sad that we won't get to experience our first times together. But I would never judge you for something you can't change. That's not who I am. I'd never leave you because of something you did long before we met. That's not how I operate. Darlin'... I'm not going anywhere." His brows lift swiftly, as though a thought has just occurred to him. "Unless that's what *you* want?"

"No! No, I..." I swallow hard. "Of course I want you to stay."

"It's going to take a lot more than an ex-boyfriend to scare me off, Josephine. He can have your past. I want your future." He squeezes my hand gently. "I want *our* future."

My eyes fill with tears. I don't know how to respond. "Oliver..."

Something in his expression changes. I see thoughts working behind his eyes; see a new sort of resolve settle into his features as he stares across the kitchen island at me. He gives a small nod, as though he's made a decision, and clears his throat. "I was going to wait to do this. To find the perfect time. To plan some silly romantic moment with flowers and candlelight... But I just realized something. I don't want to wait another second to start building a future with you. And I'm tired of carrying this around in my pocket like a pipe bomb, set to go off."

"What are you talking abou—"

My words fall short when he suddenly pushes back his stool, rises to his feet, and comes around the kitchen island. Before I can do so much as stand, he's dropped to his knees on the tile floor. He fishes around for something in his pocket, then lifts it toward me. In his hand, there's a small velvet box.

Time stops.

"Josephine Valentine..." Oliver is smiling at me with tears in his eyes and I try to smile back but my lips won't cooperate. Something inside me is screaming out objections I can't discern over the roar of blood rushing between my ears. My heart rails against my ribcage like a feral animal, desperate to break free of its confines. "I knew the moment I met you that one day, I'd make you my wife. We're cut from the same cloth. We understand one another without even trying. And together, I think we can change the world."

He opens the box. Sitting atop a bed of pale silk, there's a dizzyingly large diamond. It catches the light, twinkling. It must be at least four carats. I can't even fathom the cost of such a purchase.

"Please," Oliver says. "Do me this honor. Make me the happiest of men."

I look up from the ring, into his eyes. My mouth opens, but I can't speak. All that comes out is a soft sort of wheeze.

He smiles.

The ring lifts higher.

"Josephine... will you marry me?"

TWENTY-FOUR

archer

DARK HAS FALLEN by the time I reach Gloucester Harbor.

The docks are empty, the waters inky. Beneath the dim pool of light cast by a nearby electric pole, I tuck my boat in for the night — locking the cabin doors, double-checking her lines twice. I keep my mind laser-focused on the tasks at hand. It's easier to think about ropes and cleats and fenders than to let my attention wander inward.

To Josephine.

Thinking too hard about the events at Cormorant House sets my teeth on edge. My stomach clenches every time I revisit the image of her standing there beside perfect, blond Oliver. He looked like just the kind of mate her parents would choose for her. Well-dressed, well-spoken. No doubt in possession of a rich pedigree.

He's the ideal guy.

He's everything I'm not.

I should've known she's moved on. That her heart — the one I was so foolish to think might still be mine to reclaim — is already spoken for.

Did you think she'd wait for you forever?After the way you treated her? my inner voice sneers, mocking me as I coil the spare spring line. *Did you think she was somehow still yours?After all this time?*

The voice barks out a laugh.

You utter fool.

Tommy was right when he said we don't get unlimited chances in this life. I have no one to blame but my own damn self for missing mine. I know that with certainty. Just as I know I'll spend the rest of my however-many-years on this planet regretting the fact that I lost Josephine Valentine.

Cursing under my breath, I turn away from her namesake vessel, bobbing quietly in the slip, and begin the slow walk home. Part of me — the same pathetic part I've been listening to for far too long — craves the comfort only a barstool can offer. Liquid oblivion, served up in a lowball glass at Biddy's.

Six weeks ago, six days ago — hell, maybe even six hours ago — I might've listened. But a different part of me, newly awakened after a long slumber, overrides the urge to numb my pain and insists, quite annoyingly, that I feel it instead.

The truth is, I've spent months looking for solutions in the bottom of a whiskey bottle. It's gotten me nowhere. Given me nothing. I look at the man I've become — this shell of the person I wanted to be — and see that many of my wounds are self-inflicted. Some of my damage has nothing at all to do with the pins in my wrist or the scars on my flesh.

Somewhere along the way, I gave up on myself. I stopped fighting. I let my spirit die, just as surely as if I'd died that day in the accident. I believed I was worthless. A waste of space. Not worthy of love or redemption or understanding from anyone.

Not even from myself.

Especially not from myself.

And yet...

Cut adrift in a maelstrom of misery, hands reached out. They found me in the storm and dragged me back to shore, thrashing the whole way. Fighting them tooth and nail. Certainly never thanking them for their attempts at salvation.

I hear Chris, talking around a swallow of beer.

I'm worried about you, Reyes.

I owe it to him.

To be less absent.

To be less angry.

I hear Ma, voice cracking with worry.

We almost lost you last summer, Archer. You have no idea how hard that was on your father and me.

I owe it to them.

To take care of myself.

To take charge of my life.

I hear Tommy, telling me plainly.

Wallowing in misery, hating yourself, numbing your pain with whiskey every night isn't going to fix a damn thing.

I owe it to him.

To be better.

To do better.

I hear Jo, words brimming with emotion.

Living like this, in absence of hope... it's not living.

I owe it to her.

To try harder.

To live harder.

And finally, so faintly I have to strain to catch the words, I hear my own voice inside — thready, weak... but there all the same. Growing louder with each passing second.

They all believe in you.

Isn't it time you believed in yourself, again?

———

I'm so caught up in my thoughts, I'm not paying much attention to my surroundings. I don't see the man standing in the shadows near my slip until I pass within inches of him. I nearly jump out of my skin when he steps into my path.

"About time. I thought you'd never show up, little brother."

I stop short. Overhead, the lamppost buzzes as moths dive-bomb into the bulb. It's the only sound for nearly a minute. Tension mounts in the air as we stare at one another. My fists curl at my sides. My voice is clipped with impatience.

"What do you want, Jaxon?"

He tilts his head, angular features half in shadow. "To talk."

"Like I told you last time — we have nothing to talk about. We have no relationship. As far as I'm concerned, you no longer exist."

"See, that's where you're wrong. We're family. We'll always be family. There's no changing your blood."

"Stay away from me. I'm warning you—"

"Warn away. You forget that I know you, Archer. Your bark has always been worse than your bite." His lips tug up at one side. "And your actions speak louder anyway. You didn't call the cops. You didn't dime me out."

"So?"

"If I didn't mean anything to you, I'd be in a cell right now. Or on the run again. But my boys kept watch for days and... nothing happened. No one came. You kept your mouth shut."

"A mistake I'll rectify very soon, trust me."

Jaxon shakes his head. "Nah. I don't think so, bro. You're loyal. Even if you don't want to admit it. Even if you hate it." He pauses for a long beat, staring at me. "In my circles, we reward loyalty."

"I'm not in your circles."

"What if you could be?" There's a strange excitement in his eyes. "When I saw you the other day, I realized how much I missed you. How much I miss our family. And then, when you didn't turn me in... I realized you must miss me, too."

He's fucking delusional.

Or high.

Or both.

"I had an idea," he continues, stepping closer to me. "Of how I can help you."

"Help *me*?" I hiss. "What makes you think I need your help?"

"You seen yourself lately? I barely recognized you the other day." He smirks. "You're my little brother. You'll always be my little brother. It's my job to look out for you."

"Jaxon—"

"I want you to come work for me," he cuts me off. "*With* me."

"You must be joking."

A flare of temper shoots through his eyes. "You don't understand. This new gig I'm running is foolproof, Archer. The money just pours in, hand over fist. More than you could ever need."

"I don't need money."

"Everyone needs money." He scoffs, as though I'm an idiot. "You want to buy a mansion for Ma and Pa? *Done*." He snaps his fingers. "Just like that. You want some state-of-the-art experimental surgery to fix your hand? *Boom*." He snaps again. "You could play baseball again, Archer. You could pitch again."

I shake my head, trying to shut out his words. They're too good to be true. I know that deep down. But just the thought — however improbable, however unlikely — that I could potentially get back my dream...

No.

Jaxon takes another step toward me. "You want to impress that rich girl you were always chasing around? Give her the life you know she's expecting? *Easy*." Another snap. "You could finally turn Josephine Valentine into Josephine Reyes."

My eyes spring open. Fury fills me, infusing my every nerve ending until I'm practically shaking with the force of it. "Stop talking, Jaxon. I mean it."

"You'll be set up for life!" he continues, not sensing the danger. "You'll never have to work again. Never have to struggle again. And we... We can be brothers again."

"You must be high."

"I'm not!" he insists, but his pinprick-pupils say otherwise. "I've changed. Unlike you. Same old Archer — too proud to ever accept help. No wonder you're alone. No wonder Ma and Pa couldn't wait to leave you. No wonder your girl left you, too."

"*Shut up!*" I roar, stepping forward and grabbing him by the shirt front. I mange to shake him a few times before he shoves out of my grip. "For once in your life just shut up!"

"What the fuck!" He pushes me back, eyes flashing with temper. "I came here to offer you the chance to make something of yourself... To turn this dead-end life of yours around..."

"I'd rather work as a poor lobsterman for the rest of my life, barely scraping by, than take part in your new business ventures, brother."

"And why's that?" Jaxon asks with terrifying softness.

"You think I don't know what you're up to? You think it's some big secret that you're running drugs up and down the coast with that old trawler?" I glare at him so hard, I'm surprised he doesn't burst into flames. "How long do you think you can keep that up before the cops catch wind? Or before one of your crew turns on you in exchange for a lesser sentence?"

"That will never happen," he snarls. "You don't know what

you're talking about. You don't know my crew. You don't know anything."

"I know, if you're smart, you'll turn yourself in. Serve your time. Stop running."

"Do I look like I'm running?" He shakes his head, stepping closer to me. "I'm not going anywhere."

"Then you're an even bigger dumbass than I thought."

"Is that a threat?"

"That's a fact. Plain and simple."

"Let's get one thing straight, Archer. You're either with me or you're against me. I made you a fair offer. I held out my hand to you. And instead of taking it, you spit in my face. So whatever comes next... remember you only have yourself to blame. Remember you're the one who chose war when he had a chance for peace."

"What are you going to do, Jaxon? How are you going to hurt me? I have nothing left for you to break."

"That's where you're wrong, little brother." His eyes drift over my shoulder, to the yellow boat bobbing in its slip. I follow his gaze and see his eyes are lingering on the name plastered across the stern. The bold letters are clearly legible, even in the darkness. "You think you have nothing to lose. You think you're untouchable. But if you breathe a word about my business to anyone, you won't be the one who suffers. I promise your precious Josephine will pay the price."

My heart squeezes tightly. "She's not *my* Josephine. She's not even a part of my life, anymore."

"Is that so?" A smirk twists his lips. "Strange, then, to name your boat after her."

"That's not— I didn't—" I shake my head. "You've got it all wrong. That girl means nothing to me."

"You told me that lie once before. I didn't believe you then. I don't believe you now." Jaxon smiles. "Take care, Archer."

"If you so much as *breathe* near her, Jaxon," I call after him. "It'll be the last thing you do as a free man."

His laughter carries back to me. He's nearly out of sight, passing through a distant pool of light where the dock meets the gangway up to the parking lot. "More threats?"

"No. That's a vow."

I wait until I'm sure he's gone before I pull out my cellphone and tap the screen to dial one of my most recent contacts. It rings twice before a familiar voice blasts over the line.

"Hello?"

"I need you to meet me tomorrow morning," I say, without preamble. "It's important."

TWENTY-FIVE

josephine

THE VELVET IS whisper-soft beneath my fingertips. I turn the jewelry box over and over in my hands. I do not open it. Every time I do, the princess-cut diamond nestled within dazzles my eyes, ensnares me like a crow so enamored with a shiny object, it does not see the plate-glass window directly in its flight path.

Such a small, little thing.

Such enormous implications.

It's the middle of the night. Or, it was. The faint lightening on the eastern horizon tells me it will soon be dawn. From my perch in the boathouse rafters, I watch as slate gray lightens to ash, then to dove. A blush colors the cheeks of morning, staining the sky with the hues of hidden feelings. The pale pinks of infatuation, those faint reds of self-doubt.

I should go inside. Oliver will soon be stirring awake in the guest room down the hall from mine. I wasn't offended when he chose to sleep there instead of by my side. Honestly, I think we both needed a bit of space after last night's proposal. A bit of breathing room, to allow the sting of rejection to fade.

I shut my eyes, wishing I could shut out the memories.

Wishing I could rewind the moment I screwed everything up by not taking the ring immediately from his outstretched hand, sliding it onto my fourth finger, and flinging my arms around the neck of my new fiancée.

I tried to accept.

I swear I did.

But for some incalculable reason, instead of saying *yes, of course I'll marry you!* what came out of my mouth was a mumbled, *I need some time to think about this.* Instead of making Oliver happy, I watched in horror as all the light faded out of his eyes, as his jubilant expression clouded over with bitterness.

So that's it, he'd whispered haltingly. *You're saying no.*

I'm not saying no!

Well, you're not saying yes.

Ollie, it's just so fast!

We've been together almost a year.

That's fast!

Who cares? If we want to be together...

This isn't just about us. Our families—

Your parents love me. I already feel like I'm part of the Valentine clan.

And what about your parents?

They'll adore you!

How do you know?

Because I adore you.

Oliver...

Just say yes, Josephine.

I can't! Okay? Not right now. Not yet.

There was a long beat of silence, the air thickening with unspoken accusation.

This is because of him, Ollie hissed. *Isn't it?*

Who? Archer?!

He's got your head all confused.

This has nothing to do with him!

Whatever you say.

Please... Can we just talk about this?

Not right now. I'm exhausted. I'm going to bed. With that, he'd closed the box with a snap that made me flinch, set it on the counter, and walked out of the kitchen without a backward glance. His parting words hit me like a bullet as he paused briefly at the threshold. *If you want to talk about this tomorrow, we can. But... maybe I'm not the one you need to be talking to, Josephine. Maybe the clarity you seem to be looking for has to come from... someone else.*

I didn't even have time to respond before he vanished down the hallway. Heart in my throat, I stood in the empty kitchen, listening to his leather loafers traversing the atrium, ascending the stairs. Carrying him as far from me as he could get within the confines of Cormorant House.

Even now, hours later, I'm haunted by his words. Much as I want to dismiss them as nothing but jealous speculation, I cannot deny their ring of truth. Oliver is right — I cannot give him an answer. Not until I've heard an answer of my own from Archer. Not until he's explained what he meant yesterday.

You were my dream, too.

God, it's a mess. All of it. My entire life. Every time I think I've found my footing, the very ground beneath my feet shakes and shifts, tectonic plates jolting without warning. I do not know what my path forward looks like. All I know is, I will not walk into the future with my heart still tethered to the past. I will not ride into the fairy tale sunset burdened by the baggage of a broken relationship. I will not accept a ring from Oliver with my fingertips still tingling from the warmth of Archer's skin.

My grip tightens on the velvet box, squeezing so hard the

lid skews out of alignment. I'm consumed by the strangest urge to crush it into dust, if only to remove the heavy weight its existence has placed upon my shoulders. To hurl it into the ocean lapping below, where the waves could banish it to the depths as if it never existed. Maybe then, Oliver and I could go back to the way things were before — before the proposal, before the rejection, before everything got so very complicated.

A wide yawn cracks my face in two. I've been up all night thinking and have nothing to show for it except deep circles under my eyes and restless energy buzzing through my limbs. I long for the universe to send me a sign. Some cleverly disguised message to prompt me down the correct path. But that's not really how life works, is it? There is no mystical interference reaching down from the heavens to show me the way, no omnipotent hand stirring the pot.

In absence of a higher power, I'd take some sage advice. But there are no wise Exeter Academy teachers to dispense wisdom, no guidance councilors to gently pivot me, no Flora or Miguel to prod me along with calming words. I'm on my own. I guess that's the difference between adolescence and adulthood. When you're a kid, you're surrounded by people telling you what to do, how to live. Your every action is dictated, every breath orchestrated. Then, you graduate. And, at the ripe old age of eighteen, you're thrust into the cold reality of the real world without so much as a map or a compass.

There's no one to clean up your messes. No one to ground you or teach you to tie your shoes the proper way or press cold compresses against your brow when you're burning up with fever. All you can do is muddle along in the darkness, picking directions at random and hoping they're the right ones. Hoping they don't lead anywhere too terrible. And eventually, when you take a wrong turn, when you wind up somewhere you never thought your feet would carry you... you stand alone at the precipice of disaster. Watching the metaphorical shit hit the metaphorical fan, powerless to stop it. Bracing for the fallout with the only person you can really count on to be there for you, no matter what.

Your ride or die.

Your constant.

Your own damn self.

I hear the sound of a car rumbling down the circular driveway, tires crunching on pea stone. It must be Mrs. Granger, arriving for the day. She's early; the sun is barely up. I jolt to my feet, prepared to race back to the house if it means beating her there and avoiding any judgmental looks at my raggedy state — barefoot with grass stains on my toes, a baggy sweater layered over thin pajamas. In my haste, the velvet ring box slips from my fingers and hits the ground, skating across the dusty floorboards and disappearing beneath an old, chipped nightstand.

The rafters house a hodgepodge of similar castoffs from the mansion, dragged up here over the years to turn the space into a proper clubhouse. Boxes of spare boat parts and retired household appliances are stacked haphazardly beside paint cans and myriad tools.

Cursing my clumsiness, I drop to my knees and peer beneath the old nightstand. I can't see much of anything in the dimness, so I grope around blindly until my fingers brush something velvet. It's only after I've pulled the jewelry box into view that I see it's not the one I was looking for — not small and square, but wider and flatter. The kind crafted for a necklace or a bracelet instead of an engagement ring. The crushed velvet exterior is not black but champagne colored, and coated in a thick layer of dust.

It's been up here a while, that much is clear. Less evident is who left it behind. It certainly isn't mine. I seldom wear jewelry — especially not the kind that comes in a fancy velvet box. Yet, no one else comes up here. So the owner remains a mystery.

Some forgotten family heirloom, perhaps?

Doubtful. The Valentine jewels are locked away in a safe somewhere, meticulously catalogued according to size and value. I tell myself it's not my business. To put it back down and continue my search for the ring, but my fingers aren't cooperating. Curiosity wins out. Rather than placing the box back on the dusty floor, I flip open the lid.

And very nearly drop it.

My fingers shake as I reach out to trace the pendant. Thin cords of gold twine together, forming an elegant coil. It's a shape I recognize instantly, both from my nautical experience and also from the old legends. A fisherman's knot. A knot that, once fastened, will not fray — no matter how the elements strain it, no matter if meddling hands tug at it. Pressure only makes it stronger, only tightens the bond, until the ropes grows so tight they might as well be fused together.

I've always loved the symbolism. I've long believed that true love, like that knot, is unbreakable. Not merely capable of weathering the worst of life's storms, but stronger because of them.

Or... so I used to believe.

So I used to hope.

After my heart shattered last summer, I lost some of that naivety. Some of that romantic sentimentality slipped out of my disposition. But here, in my hands, I find it returned to me. Cast in gold. Covered in dust. Forgotten for a time, but not gone. Merely tucked away, out of sight, until I was ready to rediscover it.

There's a message printed on the inside of the lid — gold lettering against white silk.

Josephine —
I saw this in a shop window and knew it was yours.
Like my heart.
Happy 18th Birthday.
— Archer

My heart is in my throat. I don't think it's beating, anymore. I don't think I'm breathing, either. And I don't care. My mind is one big blank, the buzz of static between my ears impossible to think through. I don't need to think, anyway; my hands are moving on autopilot, no executive functions necessary.

Pulling the necklace from the box.

Reaching beneath the thick curtain of hair around my shoulders.

Clasping the tiny chain.

Allowing the pendant to settle against my skin.

It's the perfect length, hanging just long enough to nestle in the hollow where my breasts curve inward. The gold is warm against my skin, radiating heat beneath the fabric of my thin pajama top. For a long moment, I press my palm flat against it, wondering why this gift — one that arrived a year too late, one I was likely never meant to receive in the first place — was so very easy to claim as my own... when I could not accept a far more significant piece of jewelry offered to me mere hours ago.

The sound of a car door slamming jolts me back to reality. I need to get back to the house before Oliver comes looking for me. The last thing I want to do is give him a tour of the boathouse right now. Bending swiftly, I rummage beneath the nightstand once more, eventually locating the ring box in the darkness. I tuck it into the pocket of my sweater without opening it — alongside the now-empty necklace box — and hurry toward the ladder. My hands are clammy on the rungs as I descend. My heart beats a strange song I do not recognize.

Half hope, half terror.

A haunting, inescapable percussion that follows me all the way up the lawn. My bare feet make no noise on the cold flagstones. I cross the terrace to the side door into the kitchen; it swings inward on silent hinges. But the stealth goes to waste. When I step inside, Mrs. Granger is already in position at the stove, brewing a pot of coffee. She glances at me, brows arched to her hairline. Somehow, she manages to pack a thousand snide comments into that one fleeting look.

"Oh. Hi." I gulp like a fish out of water. "Good morning."

"Miss Valentine."

"I was just out getting some fresh air."

"Mmm." Her eyes narrow a shade. "Will you be in need of breakfast?"

"Just coffee for me, thanks. But my boyfr—fianc—" I break off, coughing nervously. "My *guest* Oliver may want something."

"Mr. Beaufort already left for the day."

"Excuse me?"

"We crossed paths in the driveway as I was arriving several minutes ago. He asked me to inform you of his plans to work from the VALENT offices in downtown Boston today." She pauses for a beat. "He attempted to say goodbye, but you weren't in your bedroom."

I press my eyes closed, sighing. "Like I said, I was out getting some fresh air."

"He was worried." She pauses. "Perhaps because it's so unusual for you to rise before noon."

It's a struggle not to flip her off as I stalk to the coffee pot and pour myself a massive cup. Lord knows I'm going to need it. I manage to keep my snarky replies trapped behind a frigid smile as I leave the kitchen and stomp my way upstairs. The guest bedroom door is shut tight; no sign of Oliver. My pace hastens as I pass by, eyes fixed toward the end of the hall. My own door is slightly ajar. I know for a fact I left it closed. I can almost picture Ollie standing there at the threshold, one hand on the knob, confused gaze searching for me in the empty room and coming up short.

God, what must he think of me?

I don't let myself look too hard for an answer to that question. Once inside, I close the door with a firm click and lock it for good measure — just in case Mrs. Granger gets any ideas about walking in unannounced. I need a shower, but first... I need to find a place for the two jewelry boxes burning holes in my sweater pockets. I can't keep carrying them around. They're heavy as anvils, an emotional weight I'm ill-equipped to bear.

I slide open the middle drawer of my desk, shove aside a stack of pens, and drop the velvet boxes in the very back. Out of sight, out of mind — that's how the saying goes, isn't it? Somehow, I doubt it will be that simple to stop thinking about the two pieces of jewelry — or the two men who purchased them for me — but I'm willing to give it a shot.

The drawer is already half-shut when my eyes catch on something buried beneath a pile of crumpled receipts. A thick notebook with a sage green cover. My old sketchbook. Not the design portfolio I submitted to Brown when I applied for their arts program; this one I used as an outlet for random bursts of creative energy during my junior and senior years at Exeter Academy. Its margins contain everything from cartoon doodles to charcoal self-portraits to paper collages cut from magazines.

Familiarity courses through me as I pull it free and flip it open to a random page. The drawing that greets me sends a jolt through my whole body. Archer stares out at me, inked with a blue ballpoint pen. His brow is furrowed in concentration. The line of his jaw is so sharp, just running my fingers across it might give me a paper-cut.

I turn the page.

Archer again — younger this time, sketched with pencil. He's on the pitching mound with a glove in his hand.

I turn another page.

Two kids in shades of pastel sit in the rafters, legs swinging in the air, shoulders pressed tight together. Even in profile, the girl's expression is brimming with adoration.

Page after page after page, I find different variations of the same thing. Archer. Archer happy, laughing, head thrown back with joy. Archer sad, hazel eyes burning with feelings. Archer frustrated. Archer frowning. Archer grinning.

Archer, Archer, Archer.

I slam the sketchbook closed with a pained laugh.

No wonder I left it behind. It's basically a tribute to my unrequited love for Archer Reyes. If he ever saw this — if anyone ever saw this — they'd think I was some sort of obsessed stalker, in need of psychiatric deprogramming. I shove the book back into the drawer and slam it shut with so much force, a picture frame rattles off my desktop. When I bend to retrieve it, I see it's a black and white photograph of two kids, no more than six or seven, sitting beside a sand castle down by the cove.

The little girl's blonde hair is in messy, braided pigtails. She's laughing. So carefree, it hurts to look at her. The little boy is more serious, a solemn counterpart to her airy delight. His hands are steady as he shapes a turret with a plastic shovel. His eyes aren't on his work, but on the girl sitting across from him.

I remember that day.

Remember Flora snapping the photo. Remember Jaxon running down the beach like a wild thing, flattening our masterpiece into a lumpy mound in two seconds. Remember Miguel telling us not to cry, because sand castles aren't meant to last forever. The incoming tide would've swept it away soon enough. And, after all, wasn't the real fun in building it?

I set the frame back on my desk, swallowing hard to clear the lump from my throat.

Okay, Universe — you win.

Message received.

I asked for a sign.

No need to keep hitting me over the head with them.

Sinking down to the floor, my fingers curl tightly around the pendant hanging from my neck. The gold knot digs into my palm with a sharpness I feel all the way down to my bone marrow. With a screech, I drop my head into my arms and curse myself for ever seeking divine interference.

When am I going to learn to stop tempting fate?

I sigh. "Maybe when I start listening to it."

archer

A LOW WHISTLE greets me as I step past the chain-link fencing, onto the field.

"Well, well, well! Look at this handsome devil!" I can hear the grin in his voice. "Who are you and what have you done with my friend Reyes?"

I rub my clean-shaven chin, still not used to the sensation. "Flattery will get you nowhere, Tomlinson."

"I'm serious! I almost didn't recognize you." He steps out from the dugout holding a bucket of baseballs, a bat tucked beneath one arm. He's in a faded Exeter t-shirt and a black cap with the outline of a wolf — our old mascot — embroidered above the brim. "Not that the man-bun look wasn't working for you. It's just nice to see you looking more like your old self. Less scruffy. Out of rubber fishing gear."

"Stop, you'll make me swoon."

"Is that a new Henley you're wearing? Just for me? I'm flattered."

In truth, the haircut was a spontaneous decision, made without any forward planning on my walk through downtown Gloucester this morning. I passed by the barbershop on a corner in the square just as the window sign flipped from CLOSED to OPEN. Before I knew it, I was sitting in a red leather chair with a warm towel wrapped around my after-shaven face as a cheerful, chatty man named Jerry trimmed a year's worth of overgrown mop from my head.

When he'd spun me around to look in the mirror thirty minutes later, a stranger was peering back at me through the glass. With cropped brown hair and clear hazel eyes, he bore a striking resemblance to the guy once known around these parts as Archer Reyes... if you could overlook the faint scar at his temple and the new wariness in his stare.

"What prompted this radical change?" Chris asks.

"Radical? It's a haircut, not a face tattoo. Relax."

He rolls his eyes and walks toward home plate. "Grab those mitts in the dugout, will you? I need to get the field set up before the team arrives."

I do as he says, ferrying the equipment toward the patch of ground reserved for home plate. There's an uncomfortable tightness in my chest as I move across the infield, my sneakers smudging the fading white lines chalked on the dirt. It's been a long time since I stepped foot on a baseball diamond — even a small one like this.

Owned and maintained by the city, the field at Stage Fort Park lacks the luster of the Exeter Academy sports arena, with its state-of-the-art overhead lights, solar-powered scoreboard, and imported astroturf. Here, the grass is overgrown, the bleachers are rusting, and the dugout benches are splintering. Obviously, not much was left over in the town's beautification budget for little league parks.

Despite its somewhat neglected state, the location can't be beat — perched beside the harbor, every player from shortstop to the distant outfield is afforded sweeping water views from just about every angle. I let my eyes scan the coastline, squinting against the morning sun. Early-risers stroll along the paved boardwalk, passing beneath a row of American flags waving proudly in the wind. An outdoor yoga class is gathering by the gazebo. Families meander toward Cressy Beach, folding chairs tucked beneath their arms and colorful coolers in tow.

"What are we doing here, Tomlinson?"

"I told you on the phone — my little cousins signed up for a summer tee-ball league. It starts in an hour."

"And you volunteered to help with the gear?"

"Not exactly." He grins wryly. "Their coach bailed on them. Something about unforeseen family commitments... Sounds like a bunch of crap, if you ask me. My guess is, the dude realized he was about to take on twenty-five hyperactive six-year-olds who've never held a bat before and got cold feet."

"Can't exactly blame him..."

"Guess not." Chris shrugs. "Still, it sucks for the kids. They were excited to learn."

"Can't they find a backup coach? It's tee-ball, not Red Sox spring training. I'm sure almost anyone could teach them the basics."

"Glad you feel that way." His grin widens. "Since I told them we'd do it."

"*We?* As in you and me?"

"Yep."

"Tomlinson," I growl. "You can't be serious."

"I swear on Ted Williams." He laughs. "After you called me last night and asked to meet, the idea hit me like a bolt of lightning! I hung up with you and called the league. They were thrilled to have two former varsity players at their disposal. Of course, at this point, they probably would've been thrilled to have just about *anyone* willing to wear a whistle and wrangle wild youths..."

My mouth opens.

Shuts.

Opens again.

No words come out.

"Before you say no, promise me you'll at least consider it," Chris continues in a rush. "It's only a couple days a week. Think of the kids! They'll be devastated if the camp is cancelled."

My eyes swing around the empty field. In some ways, even now, even after everything... this dirt triangle feels more like home to me than any other place on earth. I've spent more cumulative hours of my existence standing on a pitching mound, hurling fastballs, than I have doing any other activity besides the autonomous ones, like breathing or sleeping. Being here again, inhaling that unique perfume of leather and wood and grass and chewing tobacco that permeates the air at every stadium in America, rattles my senses awake. Calls back a million memories. All the joy and sweat and blood and tears, all the tough-to-swallow losses and hard-fought victories. Every moment with my teammates — fighting and laughing and bickering and bonding.

Amazing how something like a scent can trigger flashbacks to things you thought you'd buried forever, six feet under in a cedar casket. I remember the first time I ever stepped foot on a diamond. I couldn't wait to get back out there the minute practice ended. I saved every penny of my measly allowance for months until I was finally able to purchase a glove of my own. And once I brought it home from the sporting goods store, once it was *mine*, I'd refused to take it off — except to eat and occasionally bathe — until Jaxon started to notice my attachment and I realized it was far safer off my hand than on it.

He's always had a nasty habit of destroying the things he covets.

"Look, if you really don't want to do this, I won't force you.

I can do it on my own. But... You're the best player I've ever known, Reyes," Chris says, calling my attention back to him. He's standing by home plate with a bat slung across his shoulders, hands dangling over either end. "I know you can't pitch anymore. Not like you used to. But it'd be a shame to let all that talent go to waste, in my humble opinion. Especially when you could share it with some kids who probably need a bit of inspiration."

"I'm not exactly a motivational speaker. Kinda doubt I'm cut out for coaching."

"That's bullshit and you know it. Half the time, Coach Hamm used to let you lead our warm-ups and drills during practice back at Exeter." He stares at me, a pleading look on his face. "Come on, Reyes."

I sigh. "Fine."

"Fine? As in, you'll do it?!"

"I'll do it."

"Fuck yeah!" Chris grins, drops the bat, and hauls me into a back-slapping hug. "Thanks, man. Knew I could count on you."

Some of my assurance wavers at the thought of anyone counting on me. It's been a long, long time since someone did. But I shake off the self-doubt and, with a grin that feels out of place on my face, push my way out of Tomlinson's arms. "All right, all right. I agreed to be your co-coach, not to give you one of my kidneys. Don't go overboard."

"Oh, admit it. You're excited too, Reyes."

I roll my eyes. "Now that you've effectively conned me into a coaching position, can we please get back to important things? I asked you to meet me for a reason."

"Right. The mysterious favor." He shoots me a curious look. "What is it?"

I reach up to run my hand through my hair, a nervous

habit, and am startled to find there's no hair to run through. My arm drops uselessly back to my side. "It's my brother."

"Jaxon?"

"Mmm."

"Let me guess — he's causing trouble again."

"*Trouble* might be an understatement."

"So when you asked to meet me... you didn't mean as your pal. You meant..."

"As a policeman." I nod stiffly. "Yeah. I'd like your advice, if you're up for it."

For the next few minutes, I tell Chris about my last two run-ins with Jaxon at the docks, along with Tommy's theory that they're running drugs up the coast with the old trawler. As I talk, my old friend's typically playful demeanor drops away, replaced by intent concentration. In that moment, I can see the officer he's on his way to becoming; the man whose shoes he's on the precipice of stepping into. And I know it wasn't a mistake to bring this to him.

"Long story short," I say, sighing as my story winds down. "Jaxon is paranoid. He's also violent, especially when he's on drugs. He's unpredictable. Worst of all, the bastard isn't entirely stupid. He's got some kind of sixth sense for knowing when shit is about to hit the fan and somehow manages to Houdini his way out of the crosshairs every time."

"I sympathize, I really do. But I'm not sure how I can help."

"Your father is the police chief. You're an officer."

"This isn't really our jurisdiction. The MBTS force is more accustomed to parking tickets and traffic details than taking down local crime syndicates." His brows lift. "Why not take this to Jaxon's parole officer?"

"You mean the same parole officer who did such a great job watching him last summer?" I snort. "Let's just say, I don't have the most faith in his abilities to track down my brother, let alone take him into custody. If I call him and he goes strolling up the docks to confirm my story for himself..." I shake my head. "Jaxon's crew will clock him a mile away. They'll just cast off their lines and disappear. And then..."

"He'll come after you. Jaxon. He'll know you dimed him out."

"I don't care about me," I mutter. "I care about..."

"Valentine." Chris swears lowly. "I get it. I do. But, setting my pride aside for a moment, I'm not sure I'm qualified to help you here. You could take it to the state police or the local FBI bureau, I'm sure they've got a crime division for cases like this—"

"Last summer, I was nearly arrested for something I didn't do. Since then, I don't have much faith in law enforcement. But I trust you, Chris. I trust you more than I trust some random desk agent who looks at me and sees a kid with a recent arrest for drug possession—"

"Those charges were dropped," he interjects. "Your record is clean."

"And the fact that I share the same last name as they guy I'm accusing? You don't think they'll pick apart my story? For all I know, they'll toss me in jail right along with my brother as a co-conspirator."

"Now who's being paranoid?"

"Look, I—" I swallow down my stubbornness, my pride. Bury away my natural instincts to do everything on my own, to handle every problem in my life without admitting I might possibly need a little bit of assistance sometimes. "I can't do this by myself. I tried that last summer, and... it didn't exactly turn out in my favor."

Thoughts are working in the depths of Chris' eyes. "If we could get a warrant for the trawler, we could raid the docks. Take them by surprise. Call in Coast Guard support to block the channel. A coordinated strike to make sure Jaxon can't slip through the net again and ensure that no more drugs move through our harbors." He's silent for a long moment. "The main issue is, it's a bit of a Catch-22 — we can't raid the docks without a warrant. Can't get a warrant without some evidence of wrongdoing to bring to a judge."

"What kind of evidence?"

"Could be anything. Pictures of illegal paraphernalia or weapons, video of them loading drugs on or off the trawler, an audio confession—"

"I can get a confession."

His eyes widen. "What?"

"You get me a wire to wear, I'll get you my brother's confession." I pull in a breath. "I'll get enough evidence for them to send Jaxon away — for good, this time."

"Hell no, Reyes. You're not putting yourself in danger on the off-chance Jaxon is dumb enough to talk to you."

"Oh, he'll talk to me. He loves to brag. And he's convinced himself that our brotherly bond is strong enough to make me forget that he ruined my life."

"If he realizes you're there to record him, there's no telling how he'll react."

"I'll be fine, Tomlinson."

"I don't like it."

"You don't have to like it. You just have to make it happen."

"I'll talk to my father. He's got some connections at the District Attorney's office we can reach out to, who'll send this info up the right channels. When I have a more concrete plan, you'll be the first one in the loop."

"But—"

"I know you don't trust the system. I know it hasn't done you any favors in the past. But you said you trust me. So trust me enough to do this the right way. Trust me when I tell you I'm not going to screw you over."

I suck in a deep breath, trying not to succumb to the panic clawing at me. It's the same sense of urgency I felt the morning of graduation, when I realized my parents' lives were at stake. I'd hopped in my truck without a second thought to my own safety. Without considering anything but getting to them as soon as humanly possible. I thought I could do it all myself. And I paid a high price for that arrogance.

It's a mistake I have no intention of repeating. Still, my anxiety that something will go wrong — that I'll unintentionally put Jo's life in danger again — makes my heart thunder twice its normal speed.

"Thank you, Chris."

"Don't thank me yet." His lips tug up in a wry smile as he looks beyond me, to the parking lot. I follow his gaze, watching in horror as a horde of children descend upon the field from a fleet of SUVs and minivans. "Thank me after we survive our first practice."

"Christ," I mutter, following him toward the dugouts. Three nervous mothers are already gathered there, waiting to talk to us about allergies and emergency contact numbers and all manner of things I'm not remotely prepared to respond to with any sort of eloquence. I paste a smile on my face and pray it doesn't look as stiff as it feels.

———

Three hours later, the first session of tee-ball camp is finally over. The last child in our care has been passed off to their nanny. I'm covered in dust. My pitching hand is practically convulsing. My voice is hoarse from yelling out instructions.

My ears are ringing from the nonstop chatter of first-graders. And I can't wipe the stupid smile off my face.

There's a lightness in my soul I haven't felt in ages. Maybe it was the kids — that boundless energy, that infectious enthusiasm, those high-pitched giggles. The way their faces lit up when they managed to hit the ball off the tee. (Except for little Lennie, who definitely needs a pair of prescription glasses.) Maybe it was simply being back on the mound with a mitt on my hand, doing something I used to love with every fiber of my being. Whatever the case, I haven't had such a good morning in a year.

Chris offered to drop me off at home, but I told him I was happy to walk. That was twenty minutes ago, when the sun was shining brightly overhead and the sky had all the makings of a perfect July afternoon. Now, as fat raindrops begin to plummet the pavement around me from a fast-moving cloud front, I'm regretting my desire for fresh air.

I pick up my pace from a walk to a jog. I'm not far from my apartment — three blocks, at most. But by the time I round the corner onto my street, I'm soaked to the skin. My white t-shirt is plastered against my chest, my jeans and sneakers are squelching with each stride. I'm so intent on reaching the triple-decker at the end of the row, I don't even notice the green sports car parked in front, rain pattering violently at the ragtop roof. Not until I'm practically on top of it.

The vintage 1965 Porsche Cabriolet would stand out on any street in America. It's a gorgeous bit of craftsmanship. It looks especially out of place in my low-rent neighborhood, wedged between a beat-up sedan and a rust-flecked pickup truck.

My stomach plummets to the cracked asphalt beneath me. My feet slam to a halt in a puddle. Cold water splashes against my legs. I barely feel it. There's no time to recover my composure or catch my breath. All I can do is stand there like a statue, watching as the driver's side door flies open and a girl steps out, into the rain. Her blonde hair is already damp in the time it takes her to round the hood and step into my path. Her light blue sundress is turning navy as it absorbs the downpour, drop by drop.

I swallow hard. She's so close, it's painful. Only inches away. I stare down into her upturned face, mesmerized by the droplets clinging to her eyelashes each time she blinks. Her lips are pursed tightly, signs of strain apparent in every plane of her expression as she attempts to keep her emotions in check. Her voice betrays her, though — it's shaking, every syllable over-saturated by the depth of her feelings.

"Hi."

"What are you doing here?" I ask softly. I'm scared if I speak too loudly, she'll bolt like a spooked horse.

"I had to come. I had to see you."

"Why?"

"You know why." Her throat contracts, the muscles working visibly beneath her skin. "Our conversation wasn't finished."

"Maybe it should be."

"What do you mean by that?"

"There are parts of this story you might not want to hear, Jo. Things that..." I shake my head. *Can I tell her about her parents' true nature? Can I shatter whatever illusions she still harbors about her loving family?* "It could do more damage than good."

"How can you say that? The truth is always better than a lie. Even if it hurts."

"Spoken like someone who hasn't yet been hurt."

Her eyes flash. "I've been hurt plenty. Trust me."

"I know." I try to keep my voice even; it's a struggle. "Maybe that's why I'm so hesitant to do it again."

"You never change, do you? God, Archer! How many times do I have to tell you? I'm not some little girl who needs to be shielded from the horrors of life. You can't protect me from everything!"

"Not from everything," I agree.

But I can protect you from this.

"Did you mean what you said the other day?" she asks suddenly. "Or was that just another lie?"

"Which part?"

"That I..." She presses her eyes closed, unable to hold my gaze as she says it. "That I was your dream, too"

I inhale sharply. It takes a moment to find my voice. "Even if I did... Does it matter anymore?"

Her eyes snap open. "Of course it matters!"

"Does your boyfriend know you're here, Jo?"

She pales slightly, rocking back on her heels like the question packs a physical punch. "I don't want to talk about him right now. I want to talk about us. You and me."

"There is no you and me. There's just two people who used to be friends, spinning in useless circles because neither of them is smart enough to let go."

"Is that really what you believe?" Her eyes fill with tears, red-rimmed and glossy. "Or are you just saying that to push me away?"

"I don't need to push you, Jo. You're already gone. You just haven't admitted that to yourself yet."

"I'm not gone! I'm standing right here!"

"For how long?" I ask lowly. "How long until you get on your private jet with that perfect Ken Doll and fly back to your new life?"

Her mouth snaps closed with an audible click. "I... I don't know."

"How long until your parents tug on your leash and yank you back to Switzerland?"

"You have no right to say that to me!"

"You're right — it's not a leash. It's more like a pair of shackles." I scoff, bitterness rising into the back of my throat like bile. "Blair and Vincent must be *so* pleased to have their precious daughter by their sides, right where they've always wanted her. No more silly dreams of art or design, no more charcoal-smeared fingertips or hours wasted sketching. Certainly no more playing with the poor boy in the servants' cottage. You're their perfect little doll! And, as an added bonus, now you've got the perfect, parent-approved boyfriend accessory!"

"What do Blair and Vincent have to do with any of this?"

"Everything!" I snap before I can stop myself. "Your parents... if you only knew..."

"Knew *what*? What really happened last summer?" She jumps on the fragment of truth, clinging to it before it slips away. "I know there's more to the story. More than just your accident. Something doesn't add up. My mother told me you came to the house to drop off that letter..." Her voice breaks when she mentions it, as though just thinking about the things I wrote still causes her deep pain. "I caught her in the lie, and now she won't tell me anything more. Won't even discuss the matter."

"Blair Valentine isn't being cooperative? *Shocker*."

"You're one to talk."

"Do yourself a favor — leave it alone. It's ancient history."

"Ancient history?" Her voice rises another octave. "Maybe for you, but not for me. I think I deserve to know why you lied to me about going to All-Star camp. Why you didn't tell me about your accident. Why you *broke my goddamn heart* in that letter. And don't tell me it was to protect me from Jaxon's shady friends or keep me from getting dragged into danger."

"Your heart must not have been too badly broken," I mutter darkly. "Seeing as you moved to Switzerland and immediately fell into bed with someone else."

She slaps me — a hard, clear hit across the cheek. I flinch, more in surprise than any actual pain. Judging by the stunned look on Jo's face, she's just as caught off guard by her actions as I am. "Oh, god, I—"

I rub at my smarting cheekbone. "I probably deserved that."

"No, you didn't. I shouldn't have... I'm sorry." Her bottom lip is trembling; she sinks her teeth into it to stop the quivers. Reaching up to brush at her face, she clears the mix of rain and tears from her cheek. "Not that it's any of your business," she says stiffly. "But I didn't fall into bed with anyone. And even if I had... you don't get to be pissed about it. You don't get to judge me for how I pieced myself back together this past year. Not when you're the one who broke me."

"I'm sorry. I was out of line. I don't have any right to talk about your love life."

There's a tense moment of silence. We're both drenched. There's water pooling in my sneakers, dripping down my neck. My white shirt has gone completely see-through, plastered against every plane of my chest. I hold Jo's gaze, watching as a shiver moves through her body. The water has sculpted her sundress against her every curve. Loose tendrils of hair frame her face. The summer sunshine has exposed a riot of freckles across the bridge of her nose.

She looks so beautiful, standing there.

A single bright spot against the dull, gray landscape all around us.

A supernova in the bleak, bottomless universe.

And I'm a fucking black hole.

"Go home, Jo."

Her teeth set in a stubborn clench. "I'm not going anywhere until you tell me the truth. I don't care if I have to stand out here in the rain all night."

"Suit yourself." I turn to walk away from her, up the front stairs to my apartment. She races around me, beating me there, blocking my path with her petite frame. Standing on the bottom step, she looks directly into my face with defiance etched across her features. We're eye-to-eye.

"You don't get to walk away from me," she tells me plainly. "Not this time. You don't get to push me away. I'm not going."

"Don't you get it? You don't belong here." I gesture around me at the block, with its overgrown grass and cracked asphalt. Josephine Valentine fits in here about as well as her convertible. "You belong back at Cormorant House. You belong with a guy who'll make your life easier — not complicate it even more."

"You only met him for five seconds—"

"Five seconds were enough."

Her tears spill over. "So you're just bowing out? Walking away? Taking the easy road—"

"*Easy?*" I practically shout, my voice cracking out like a whip. My blood is suddenly boiling with rage. "What exactly about this do you think is *easy*, Josephine? Being forced to walk away from you was the hardest thing I've ever done in my life! Harder than losing my baseball career. Harder than having my scholarships pulled. Harder than getting the bogus charges dropped—"

"*Charges?* What charges?"

I plow on. "Harder than all the surgeries. Harder than physical therapy. Harder than saying goodbye to my parents. Harder, even, than knowing you've found someone else.

277

Someone who actually fits into your world. Someone who'll make a perfect addition to the Valentine family." I grab her by the shoulders and pull her closer, my fingertips digging into the damp material of her dress. "Do you really think, if I'd had any choice in the matter, I would've let you go? Do you honestly believe, if I hadn't been backed into a corner with no other options, I would've willingly sat back and watched you stroll off into the sunset with another guy?"

"What do you mean, *forced*?" she asks desperately. "Who forced you?"

"It doesn't matter," I mutter tightly.

"Stop saying that or I will strangle the life out of you, Archer Reyes, I swear to God!" She's yelling now, too, her eyes full of rage that mirrors mine. Her face is so close, I can feel the heat of her breath on my lips with each word that flies out of them. "It matters. *We* matter. More than anything."

I laugh, but the sound is broken — broken, right along with the dam inside me. The one that's been holding back everything I haven't been able to tell her. Every painful truth, every disastrous lie. I try like hell to patch the holes, to brace it back shut, but it's too late to halt the flood roaring from the deepest banks of my soul in an unstoppable river.

If she asks me one more time, I'll tell her.

Everything.

Her mouth opens, the question poised there.

A question I have to stop her from asking, any way I can.

I don't think.

I just act.

My hands tighten on her shoulders. I yank her closer, our bodies colliding with a jolt of pure static electricity. And then, before a single whisper can escape her lips, my mouth slams down on hers.

TWENTY-SEVEN

josephine

IN MY AP BIOLOGY class last year, we read a chapter about the psychology of human desire. A scientist named Maslow introduced a theory that our needs are arranged in a pyramid, with the most vital, life-sustaining elements — food, shelter, water — at the bottom, and our more superfluous aspirations — self-esteem, spirituality, emotional stability — stacked atop. The theory goes, you can't move up the pyramid if your bottommost layer is incomplete; essentially, you can't build on a shaky foundation. For most people, this means having a roof over your head, a steady supply of nutritious meals, and a sense of safety.

But I think my pyramid is built different.

I think *I'm* built different.

Because there's another vital element at the base of my pyramid, shoved in right alongside the basic necessities. Something that keeps my lungs pumping and my heart beating just as surely as the water in my glass or the food on my plate. An element I cannot function without — not with any sort of vitality, not in a way that prevents merely scraping along, day by day, enduring the monotony of my own existence with grim perseverance.

Him.

The moment his mouth crashes down on mine, I feel my whole world shift, a seismic click deep inside that snaps my very soul into place. He kisses me, and for the first time in a year, my internal pyramid finds its proper footing. As our arms wind around each other, desperation in every touch, fingers shaky with desire... I realize why I've spent the past few months so off balance, so out of sorts.

Archer Reyes is as vital to me as oxygen.

Without him, I cannot transcend to a higher state of happiness or fulfillment. Without him, I'm stuck perpetually at the base of my pyramid, grasping uselessly at everything around me in the hopes that I might fill the void he left behind.

But nothing else can fill it.

No one else can fill it.

A growl rattles in his throat as he kisses me harder, deeper. His tongue in my mouth, his hands in my hair. My bones turn to water, dissolving uselessly beneath his touch, but it doesn't matter. He's holding me so tight, I no longer need my knees to support me.

A cry moves in my throat as the kiss intensifies, desire sparking from an ember to a flash fire in a matter of seconds, but the sound gets swallowed up instantly. I press closer, wishing I could disappear into his touch, wishing I could climb under his skin and never come out.

Close isn't close enough.

I crave more.

I crave everything.

All of him, stripped bare.

His weight.

His hands.

Above me.

Inside me.

Making me whole.

Shattering me to pieces.

"Jo," he gasps, his mouth finally breaking from mine to drag in oxygen. "God, I need—"

"Me too," I whisper, barely able to get the words out. My lips are already fusing with his again, my willpower no match for the magnetic force of attraction between us.

I need.

I need.

I need.

My nerves sing with desire as my fingers grip the back of his neck, stroking the wet fabric of his shirt. I'm trembling head to toe against him. The emotions are so strong, there's no holding them back. They pour out in a torrent, leaking from my eyes in a flood. I can feel tears streaming down my face, mingling with the rain falling down all around us.

We move like two longtime dance partners, our moves so in sync you'd think we choreographed them decades ago. No need for words, our bodies do the talking. Archer's hands hitch under my thighs at the exact moment my legs wind around his waist. We both moan at the moment of impact. Flush against me, separated only by the damp fabric of his jeans and the whisper-thin material of my underwear, his erection is hard as steel.

Normally I'd be scandalized by just the thought of standing on a street corner with my sundress up around my ass, in plain view for anyone walking by to see. But I can't think straight. Not with Archer touching me. Holding me. Devouring me with his teeth, his tongue, his lips.

Tightening his hold, he rubs his body against mine, a torturously slow grind, and I nearly come just from the intoxicating buzz of friction. He never pulls his mouth from mine as he walks us slowly up the front steps, onto the porch. I hold his shoulders tighter as he grapples blindly for the door knob and shoves it inward. We stumble across the threshold, still intertwined. And then, before I can blink, we're up the inner stairs, on his landing, standing before the door to his apartment.

The last time I was here, I smashed a pie on the floor and stormed off.

I'm enjoying this visit more.

Archer presses me against the wall, his weight pinning me in place, as he shoves the key into the lock. The door gives way and so do we — falling inside in a tangle of limbs, landing on the hardwood floor with a thud that knocks the wind from both our lungs.

"So..." I laugh breathlessly, straddling him. "This is your place."

I see the ghost of a smile, hear the fragment of a chuckle before he flips me over onto my back and rolls on top of me. The door slams with a bang as he kicks it closed with one foot. Bracing one arm on either side of my head, his weight settles between my legs — bone-crushing in the best kind of way, setting off a hollow ache that demands to be sated.

When he tears his mouth from mine, he's panting hard. I stare up at him, feeling drugged. Dazed by lust and desire. I can barely process the fact that this is happening. All I know is, I don't want it to stop.

Not now.

Not ever.

"I can't believe you're here," Archer murmurs. There's a vulnerability in his eyes that shakes me to the core; the hazel of his irises are molten with longing and disbelief, as though he doesn't quite trust that this is real. That I'm here, in his apartment, in his arms. "I thought I'd never get the chance to touch you again. I thought..."

A tear snakes from my eye, down my cheek. He watches it fall, tracking its path from my jawline down the length of my neck, creating a tiny puddle in the hollow of my throat. His eyes widen fractionally as he spots something. I watch disbelief bloom over his expression before I recognize its trigger-point.

The necklace.

At some point in our frantic tumble, the gold knot worked itself free from where I'd tucked it into the neckline of my dress. Archer's eyes flicker up to mine for the briefest of seconds as he pushes off me and sits up, creating a bit of breathing room between us. I mourn the press of his body against mine, but I don't dare say a thing as he reaches out a shaky hand to touch the pendant, moving so slowly you'd think it were made of the most fragile glass. As he takes it in his palm, his knuckles brush the bare skin of my clavicle — perilously close to the top curves of my cleavage — and I fight back a shiver.

"Where—" The word breaks in his throat. His voice is rough, almost hoarse with shock. "Where did you get this? I thought it was lost."

"I found it in our spot."

His eyes flash to mine. "The boathouse?"

"You didn't leave it there?"

He shakes his head. "No, I... I left it on the dock last summer, on your birthday. I wonder how it got into the rafters."

"Maybe Flora or Miguel found it. Or one of my parents."

"I'm pretty sure Vincent or Blair would've left it to be swallowed up by the tide. They aren't exactly my biggest fans."

A faint ember of annoyance flares to life inside me. I sit up, bringing our faces even again. The pendant falls from Archer's palm, swinging down to rest against my chest. His eyes never shift from it. I stare at his face, trying to work out my sudden brewing anger. Something is bothering me, but I can't quite put my finger on what.

"Why did you leave it on the docks?"

"Seemed as good a place as any."

"So you never planned on giving it to me?" I ask, temper flaring. As the fog of lust clears from my head, my annoyance gains clarity. "You never planned on telling me how you felt?"

He's watching me carefully, now. Perhaps sensing my gathering ire. "No, Jo. I never planned on telling you how I felt."

"Felt?" I stress. "Or *feel*?"

"What do you want me to say? That I love you? You need those three words to make this real?"

I recoil. "If all I needed were words, I wouldn't be here! If all I needed were words, I would've accepted Oliver's perfect proposal! He said all the right things. He was romantic and kind and straightforward. He didn't play deceitful little games or make my head spin!"

Archer goes completely still, like a snake before a lethal strike. His tone is dark, shaky with tightly leashed anger. "He proposed to you?"

"Yes, he proposed to me!" I snap. "Why? Does that shock you? That someone else wants me?"

"Did you say yes?"

"I..." I break off. "I told him I needed time to think."

"Time to think?" he says harshly. "Or time to come over here and screw me out of your system once and for all?"

"Fuck you, Archer!"

"You nearly did," he mutters. "What would your fiancé say about that?"

This moment — once blissful — has taken a turn, somewhere along the way. How very quickly our passion slipped back into painful reminders of the past.

"This was a mistake," I say, my voice shaking. "I shouldn't have come. I'm sorry I bothered."

I start to push to my feet but he catches me around the waist, pulling me back against his body. I feel him breathing hard, his chest pumping in and out like a mechanical piston.

"If you want a label for my feelings, I'll give you one. I'll say the words. But I don't need to tell you something you already know. Something you've always known." Turning me around to face him, he takes my hand and presses it flat against his chest on the left side, where his heart thunders like a violent summer storm. With his face clean-shaven and his hair trimmed to normal lengths, he looks so much like his old self it makes my stomach somersault violently. "Josephine. This heart of mine isn't mine at all. It's yours. You've owned it from the start. It may beat inside my chest, but it belongs to you. It always has. It always will."

I hold my breath.

His lips brush mine. "I love you. I will love you until I stop breathing. Until I leave this earth. And if there is an afterlife, I'll love you there, as well."

Our mouths crash together again, a crushing kiss that leaves me panting for air and clinging to his shoulders for support. I shake my head as we break apart, confusion swamping me despite the waves of desire crashing through my system.

"But you didn't tell me. I don't understand... if you love me, why aren't we together? Why have we spent the past year apart? Why did you let me think you didn't w-want m-me?" I hiccup, trying to keep from sobbing. I'm borderline hysterical. "I s-still d-don't un-understand."

"I know you don't. But if you give me a minute, I'll

explain." His voice is gentle as he grips my face between his palms, staring deep into my eyes. "When I woke up in the hospital last summer, my injuries were the least of my problems. The truck I crashed... It turns out, Jaxon had stashed his drugs inside. When the police found them at the scene..."

"They assumed the drugs were yours?"

He gives a shallow nod of confirmation. "They arrested me. Drug possession, intent to distribute, trafficking... I woke up handcuffed to my hospital bed."

"Oh my god, Archer."

"There's more." His fingers tighten on my cheeks. "I was still in so much pain from the surgeries, from my accident... I knew my baseball career was over. Instead of heading to college, I'd be heading to a federal correctional facility to serve time for my brother's crimes."

"But surely the cops had to know you didn't do anything wrong! Surely they had to listen to you—"

"As far as they were concerned, they'd caught the criminal red-handed, at the scene of the crime. Another Reyes kid caught up with drugs. Another bad seed, like his big brother. No great surprise."

Anger flares inside my heart. "You're nothing like your brother."

"Yeah, well, the cops weren't much interested in listening to any alternative theories. And I didn't have the money to pay for my hospital stay, let alone some fancy lawyer who could make them listen."

"So what did you do?"

He hesitates for a long beat. I see the pain in his eyes and know, whatever comes next, is going to level me. "Someone offered me a way out. A deal with the devil, in a manner of speaking." He presses his eyes closed, unable to look at me. "God help me, I took it."

"What kind of deal?"

"They made the charges go away using their political connections. They made sure my family — my parents — could have a fresh start." I swallow. "But there was a catch."

Foreboding is unfurling inside me. My mouth is growing parched. "A catch."

He can't seem to say the words. And, much as I need to hear them, a part of me isn't ready to. A part of me knows, whatever he's about to tell me...

It will change everything.

"Who offered you the deal, Archer?" I force myself to ask.

I wait. Wait for him to answer, wait for the other shoe to drop. It nearly kills me not to physically shake the answer out of him, but I force myself to stay still and quiet. Force myself not to flinch when his eyes open again, regret and self-loathing spilling over each time he blinks.

"Your parents."

———

Part of me goes numb as he tells me the rest. I detach emotionally, unable to be fully present in my body as he describes how Blair and Vincent orchestrated our separation. Much as I want to deny his words, much as I wish he's making it all up... I know better. Beyond the ring of truth in his story, there is the undeniable fact that I know, from nearly two decades of firsthand experience, exactly what my parents are capable of. I can envision it so clearly in my mind, it's almost like I was there that day. I can almost see their expressions — that mix of haughty entitlement and blue-blooded superiority — as they pushed us around their chessboard like pawns. Each move a perfect calculation, designed for maximum impact.

Something breaks inside me as the story unfolds in painful fragments.

Something I thought had broken a long time ago. Something I thought I no longer possessed.

Hope.

My last shred of hope that I might someday forge a normal connection with the people who brought me into this world. My last sliver of optimism that maybe, in the distant future, our relationship might develop from begrudging tolerance to parental affection.

I've spent my life telling myself I didn't mind that Blair and Vincent didn't love me. Pretending that them treating me more like a feather of achievement in their cap than their beloved offspring wasn't a deep wound in my soul. But as I listen to Archer speak, as I hear how they manipulated an untenable situation to their own advantage... I know I've been lying to myself.

The pain of it cripples me.

I do not cry or scream. I do not rage in Archer's arms. But deep inside me, a cavern of despair tears wide open, swallowing me in slow degrees. It spreads through my whole body, leaving me hollowed out. Empty of every feeling but one.

Broken.

"Jo," Archer is saying from somewhere very far away. His hands shake me lightly. "Jo, look at me."

My eyes drag to his. I can barely focus on him.

"I'm sorry," he whispers. There are tears glossing over his gorgeous hazel eyes. "You have to know how sorry I am. How much I've hated myself since that day — for agreeing to their plan, for hurting you. Every minute since I wrote that letter, I've wanted to take it back. Every second since I lost you, I've wished I'd been able to find some other way out."

I blink at him, incapable of words. If I open my mouth, I have a feeling all that will escape is a scream.

"Jo..." He swallows roughly. "Are you okay?"

"Am I okay?" I laugh. The laugh catches in my throat, turns to a sob. I try to swallow it down, but it won't budge. "No. No, Archer, I'm not okay."

I jerk back, out of his grip, and scramble to my feet. I can't sit still another second. If I do, I'll fly apart into a thousand pieces, an explosion of emotional shrapnel. I pace in small loops across the tiny apartment, hands in my hair, mind racing ten times its normal speed, pulse thudding like a percussion band. Archer remains on the floor, watching me with wary eyes.

"I should've known," I mutter. I'm not sure if I'm speaking to him or to myself. I'm not sure it matters. "I should've realized they had a hand in breaking us apart. Anything I've ever wanted that fell outside the parameters they deemed socially acceptable..."

"You couldn't have known." His voice is bitter. "They outplayed me. Outplayed us."

"They're masters at it," I say hollowly. Is that *my* voice — so exhausted? So strained? "They've been doing it my whole life." I laugh-sob again. "They'll keep doing it forever. It's who they are. It's how they operate."

"I'm sorry."

"Why are you sorry?" I shake my head. "I've been treating you like the villain this whole time when you're the victim in all this. I should be the one apologizing. If my parents weren't such monsters..." My hands tighten in my hair, tugging the roots to the point of pain. "God, I hate them. I hate them so much. I never want to see them again."

He sighs. Something in the sound makes me look at him.

When I see the expression on his face, my brows shoot up my forehead.

"What? Why are you looking at me like that?"

"They're your parents, Jo." He climbs to his feet. Walks toward me with cautious, measured steps. "Your family. No matter how you might wish otherwise at this particular moment... they'll always be a part of your life."

I shake my head, rejecting his words. But even as I do, I wonder if I'll truly be able to excise Vincent and Blair out of my life like a fatal tumor. They won't react well to their formerly obedient offspring attempting to cut ties. Even if I manage to slash my biological tethers... I know them well enough to know they won't ever let me live in peace without them. They'll make it their mission to dismantle any future I attempt to build, to derail any business I launch down the tracks. And with limitless funds and infinite connections at their disposal... they'll more than likely succeed.

They didn't reach the pinnacle of success by accident. When it comes to their enemies, they're utterly ruthless.

I begin to pace again.

"You see now... why I didn't want to tell you..." Archer murmurs knowingly. "I thought I could at least spare you this pain."

"And what about you? You'd just continue taking all the blame? Letting me hate you?" My rage is nearly blinding. I'm furious — at him for hiding this secret, at my parents for ruining everything, at myself for not seeing the truth sooner.

"I'd rather you hate me forever than see you in this much agony. I'd rather watch you marry someone else than make you this miserable."

"That's not your call to make!" I whirl around to face him. "If you really loved me—"

"I do love you, Jo."

I flinch at his words. Words I was so desperate to hear, only moments ago. Words that now, only cause me more pain.

"I can't—I just—" I'm standing on the precipice of a full emotional breakdown, mere seconds from falling to the ground and curling into the fetal position. I need space to breathe. I need time to think. Most of all, I need to be alone. "I'm sorry. I have to go."

Before I fall apart completely, I race for the door. Archer's voice chases me out onto the landing.

"Jo, wait!"

But I don't wait. I fly down the stairs, nearly losing my footing on the bottom step. My field of vision is blurry with tears as I race out of the building, into the rain. I'm sobbing in full as I climb into my car and slam the door closed. My hands are shaking so badly, I can barely get the key into the ignition.

I don't allow myself to hesitate as I pull away from the curb. But as I race down the street, away from Archer's apartment, my gaze slides up to the rearview mirror. For just a second, I catch sight of him standing in the middle of the road, rain pattering all around him, staring after me with a look of such indescribable loneliness, a fresh flow of tears gathers behind my eyes.

I turn the corner with a sharp jerk of the wheel. But the image of him standing there haunts me long after I've driven out of sight.

TWENTY-EIGHT

archer

I KNEW TELLING her wouldn't be easy.

I had no idea it would be so damn hard.

After Jo drives off, I stand beneath the shower faucet until the water runs cold. There's no washing away the dirty, broken feeling inside me. My soul itself feels stained with regret.

Wishing I'd told her sooner.

Wishing I'd never told her at all.

Wishing I had something to distract my thoughts.

My hands splay against the wall, my forehead coming down to rest between them on the cold, hard tile. I'm consumed by memories of the look in her eyes as I shared the truth about her parents.

Betrayal.

Pure, undiluted.

The broken, bitter sting of it sucked the light right out of her, a poisonous leech. I've been there. I know what she's going through; spent time in the exact circle of Hell in which she now finds herself. I worked my way out, step by anguished step. It didn't happen overnight.

Much as I want to go after Jo, to support her as she spirals through denial, anger, bargaining, depression, acceptance... there's nothing I can say to comfort her. Not right now. Not yet. She needs time to work through her thoughts on her own; time to digest the monumentally heavy load I've just dropped on her shoulders.

How much time, I don't know.

How long does it take to process a betrayal of this magnitude?

For someone like Josephine — a girl who is so naturally good, so naturally giving — to experience such deeply personal duplicity... I can only pray the experience doesn't change her on a fundamental level.

Don't worry, a self-loathing voice snarls. *She has a fiancé to comfort her, remember?*

I sigh and shut off the water.

My cellphone is ringing when I emerge from the bathroom. I race to it, thinking it might be her, but of course it's not. Even if she had my number, she wouldn't call me. Not after today. My brows lift as I see Tomlinson's name on the caller ID screen. It's been less that four hours since we left the ball field. Somehow, it feels like an eternity.

"Miss me already?" I ask upon answering.

"Terribly," he responds. "So much, in fact, I've spent the last hour talking to my Dad about your proposition."

"And? What did Chief Tomlinson have to say?"

"He called a friend in the DA's office to ask about best procedure. Apparently, there's already an open investigation into increasing gang activity in the North Shore area."

I nod. "I'm not surprised this is already on their radar. Everyone at the docks is talking about it; they treat it like an open secret. The Kings aren't exactly being discreet. And a crew of tattooed ex-cons doesn't really fit into the Yankee Doodle demographic."

Chris chuckles. "Be that as it may, sleepy little harbors like

Gloucester, Manchester, and Rockport have become prime locations for smuggling drugs from offshore rigs onto dry land. And since many of those drugs come all the way up the coast from our southern neighbors...."

"It's federal jurisdiction."

"Correct." He blows out a breath. "My Dad's contact at the DA said they've escalated the investigation. Kicked it over to the Drug Enforcement Administration — the DEA — to take point. There's a special task force in place to coordinate with the Coast Guard for water coverage, plus local police departments for additional ground support the day of the raid."

"So it's really going to happen, then. They're planning to raid the docks."

"Depending on some things."

"Such as?"

"You, mostly."

"*Me*?"

"Look, Reyes, I'm going to be honest with you — you could be the break the DEA needs to crack this operation wide open. Apparently, they've been trying to get enough evidence to justify a warrant for weeks. But your brother's crew is being especially careful. Speculation isn't enough. Rumors aren't proof. Surveillance teams have gotten jack-shit, watching the warehouse from afar. They need someone inside. On that trawler."

"To confirm there are drugs present."

"Not just drugs. They also need intel on how many men are in Jaxon's crew. Plus, what kind of heat they're packing. The last thing anyone wants is a shootout at a commercial port with all kinds of innocent bystanders caught in the crossfire. The US government can't afford a WACO-style fuckup."

"I don't know anything about guns. Even if I get onboard..."

"They don't need specifics. Just a general count, along with a basic description." He pauses. "Three gangbangers with some basic pieces they bought out of some dude's trunk makes for an entirely different scenario than a full crew locked and loaded with serious, semi-automatic firepower at their disposal. You feel me?"

"I feel you, Tomlinson."

"The DEA guys will tell you more in person. What to look for, what to take note of when you're onboard. Entry points, potential exits, hidden compartments. They'll walk you through everything — the wire you'll be wearing, the camera."

"Camera?"

"It's tiny. Size of a dime. You won't even know it's there."

"I'm more worried about Jaxon knowing it's there..."

"Don't worry. You'll get a full debrief before they send you in. That's your chance to sort through any performance anxiety."

"I don't get performance anxiety. You must be thinking of yourself, Tomlinson."

"That's the cocky bastard I know and love." I hear the grin in his voice. "Reyes, I mean it — you may be going in alone, but you're not going in unprepared. These agents at the DEA are professionals. They know what they're doing. They know how to keep you safe."

"Mhm." I breathe deeply, pinching the bridge of my nose with two fingers. I'm struggling to wrap my mind around all of this. Trusting the system to work for me instead of against me... Putting my faith in the police to handle things efficiently, when they've fumbled so spectacularly in the past... It's a foreign sensation. It doesn't sit naturally inside my skin. My body is in full fight-or-flight mode, the hair on the back of my neck standing on end, my pulse hammering inside my veins.

"You still with me, Reyes?"

I clear my throat. "I'm here."

"You still up for this? I'm asking, because... Well, they want to bring you in for a debrief as soon as possible."

"When?"

"Tonight."

"*Tonight?*"

"That a problem?"

"No," I mutter. "I just didn't think this would happen so fast."

"In the DEA's mind, your brother's crew is highly prone to pulling up anchor at the first whiff of law enforcement sniffing around their business. They want to make a move before that happens."

"Right." I suck in a gulp of air. "Okay. That makes sense."

"Are you sure you're ready for this?"

"Ready as I'll ever be, Tomlinson."

"I'll come pick you up in a few hours, then."

When we disconnect the call, I take a series of deep breaths, forcing my frantic heartbeats to slow. When I'd wished for a distraction from thoughts of Jo back in the shower, I'd certainly never expected *this*.

A reckless part of me is glad for any diversion. Even a dangerous one that could backfire disastrously. But an eerily calm part of me is too laser-focused on the endgame to think about the potential danger.

Jaxon, out of my life.

For good this time.

Behind bars, where he belongs.

Where he can't hurt the people I love anymore.

Where he can't threaten the girl I love, anymore.

This is happening.

There's no backing out, now.

And, as I stare into my closet, wondering what the fuck one wears to discuss becoming a confidential informant in a sting operation, I realize I don't want to back out. I want the mess my brother created wiped clean.

I'm done with the past.

My gaze is locked on my future.

Our future.

Jo's and mine.

TWENTY-NINE

josephine

MY TIRES CRUNCH against the driveway as I pull to a stop in front of Cormorant House. The mansion looks foreboding as ever in the darkness as I shut the engine and climb out into the night. The rain has finally stopped, but a drizzly mist hangs in the air. It clings to my hair and coats my skin as I walk up the front steps to the imposing front door.

This is the last place I want to be, tonight.

My parents' domain.

Each step against the flagstones positions me a bit more firmly back under their thumb. I do my best to shake off the sensation and force myself to keep moving. I feel like a lamb walking blithely into a slaughterhouse — even as I assure myself it won't be for much longer.

This little lamb will have to grow a spine.

And some sharp teeth, to bite back.

Mrs. Granger's tan sedan is — blessedly — gone from its usual spot on the side of the house. Part of the reason I'm home so late is rooted in my undeniable desire to avoid a confrontation with my parents' spy. The other reason is that I spent the afternoon driving all the way to Providence, stopping only to fill up my gas tank. With my red-rimmed eyes fixed on the road, it was harder to succumb to the urge to sob my eyes out.

I've cried enough for a lifetime, today.

My heart has not even begun to sort out the tornado of emotions that ripped through its chambers, leaving a path of destruction in its wake. I need some time alone to pick through the rubble; to see what is left standing, once the dust settles. But I feel markedly better after my impromptu visit to Ms. Vaughn's office.

To say my advisor was surprised to see me sitting in her waiting room is an understatement of massive proportions. Yet, she was gracious enough, not only finding space in her schedule to accommodate me, but talking me through the options in a concise, compassionate manner.

I left with dry eyes, a clear mind, a packet of scholarship applications, and an informative pamphlet on student loans.

My feet feel made of lead as I force myself to punch in the front door code and step inside the house. It's dark in the atrium but there's a shaft of low light coming from my father's office. The door is slightly ajar. Sucking in a deep breath, I move down the hall and push it open all the way, half-expecting to see Vincent sitting there behind the imposing wood desk, signing VALENT contracts with a four-hundred-dollar fountain pen. But the man hunched over the stack of papers is several decades younger than my father. His blond hair is golden in the glow of the lamp, his facial hair sharply groomed, his blue eyes obscured by a smart pair of glasses. He glances up when I stop at the threshold.

"Hey, darlin,'" Oliver drawls, sitting back in the sumptuous leather chair. His expression is unreadable. "Where've you been all day?"

A series of images — Archer's hands in my hair, Archer's

lips on my neck, Archer's hips pressing me hard against the floorboards — flashes through my mind. Guilt stirs awake, coiling around my heart and settling there like a pair of iron shackles.

Cheater, a low voice snarls. *Unfaithful, ungrateful girlfriend.*

In retrospect, it's hard to imagine I could get so caught up in lust, I forgot about my commitments to Oliver, my sense of loyalty, my moral compass. And yet, even now as I stand here crippled by a disquieting amount of shame, I cannot pretend to wish it never happened. Nor can I pretend to regret it. I find, selfish as it may sound, I cannot regret any sequence of events that led to hearing the truth from Archer's lips.

I love you. I will love you until I stop breathing. Until I leave this earth. And if there is an afterlife, I'll love you there, as well.

"I took a drive," I say in a hollow voice, not moving from my spot by the door. "Down to see my advisor at Brown."

"Oh? I thought your appointment wasn't until next week."

"It's not."

His head cants to the side as he considers this. "You made a decision, then. About next semester."

My teeth spear into my bottom lip to keep it from wobbling as I finally force myself to unglue from the doorjamb. As I sink into the seat across from him with shaking knees, I'm again struck by how much he reminds me of my father. No wonder my parents are such big fans of our relationship. They've spent twenty years trying to mold me into a more suitable version of myself, but Oliver Beaufort couldn't be more perfect in their eyes if they'd mail-ordered him from a specialty son-in-law catalogue.

He sets his pen down with great care, then lifts his eyes to mine.

"Josephine," he says softly. His hands are folded on the desk. "You can tell me. I promise not to be angry, whatever your decision about Brown." His hands flex into a white-knuckled ball. "And about the ring."

He's staring at me patiently, not a shred of condemnation in his entire being. And I know, looking at him... This is a good man. He would accept me without question, flaws and all. He would spend a whole lifetime making me so safe, so secure, I'd never again be hurt. Never cry my eyes out in the middle of the night until my pillowcase is damp with misery. Never curl into a ball and hug myself close, trying to physically contain the pain inside my chest. This man would not shatter my heart; he would safeguard it.

This should be the man I choose.

This should be the man I build a life with.

This should be an easy decision.

A no-brainer.

A given.

But in my traitorous, treacherous heart... in my stubborn, stupid soul... in the very marrow of my damaged, deranged bones... something screams out that the easy decision is not always the correct one. That the way things *should be* does not always reflect how they are. That you cannot choose who you fall in love with any more than you can choose your genetic makeup.

Archer Reyes is coiled in my DNA.

Flaws and all.

Pain and all.

We are both broken. But somehow, our breaks fit together like two halves from the same fracture. And I'd rather be a mess by his side than perfect with anyone else.

The silence has stretched on for far too long. My empty ring finger suddenly feels uncomfortably conspicuous. I set the pamphlets on the desk and tuck my own hands out of sight.

Oliver's eyes move across the glossy words printed on the front.

"Financial aid?" His brows are arched. "Why would you need financial aid? You parents..."

"My parents won't be paying for my education." I suck in a breath. "My parents won't be paying for anything in my life from this point on."

"Josephine, what are you talking about?"

"I'm done taking their money. It's not worth the strings attached."

"What strings? What are you talking about?"

"I'm talking about Blair and Vincent wielding their fortune like a weapon."

"They're philanthropists—"

"They're also controlling, condescending monsters with an infinitesimally small margin for making mistakes. At least where their daughter is concerned." I shake my head back and forth. "I don't expect you to understand, Oliver."

"I'm trying to understand, Josephine. I am. But to do that properly, I'll need a better explanation about what's going on."

"What's *going on* is I found out just how far my darling parents are willing to go to control my life. What's *going on* is I realized they're never going to let me be free — not while I'm still beholden to them financially."

"You talk like they're keeping you in a cage."

"They are, though! By keeping me at VALENT... by getting me to give up on my own dreams, in order to carry on their legacy... Don't you see? I'm in a cage of their expectations. A prisoner to the conditional love of two people who are supposed to love me unconditionally."

His posture stiffens. "Forgive me. I didn't realize Geneva has been such a terrible prison for you."

"Ollie... you know that's not what I meant. Geneva is lovely.

You are lovely. But that doesn't take away from the fact that being there... deferring my own dreams just to win the approval of two people who I now see are never going to give it..." I shake my head. "I can't do it anymore. I won't do it anymore."

"So you're staying. You're going to Brown in the fall."

I nod. "I spoke to my advisor. She thinks she can help find me a few academic scholarships. I'll apply for financial aid. Take out loans. Whatever I have to do to make this work." A thrill moves through me, electric and wild. I've made my decision. And it's remarkably liberating. I'm empowered in a way I haven't in so long, I barely recognize the feeling. My voice practically rings with conviction. "I'm going to study design in one of the best arts programs in the country. I'm going to work my ass off. And one day, I'm going to build an empire of sustainable fashion that flips the whole industry on its head."

There's a prolonged silence. Oliver is looking at me with a strange mix of trepidation and confusion. As though I've just pulled a rug out from beneath his feet without warning.

"Why are you looking at me like that?" I ask. "You knew I was planning to pursue design. I showed you my portfolio months ago, when we first met. We talked about this."

"I guess... I didn't think you were serious."

My eyes narrow. "Why wouldn't I be serious?"

"Josephine..." He hedges, avoiding my question. He's getting a bit red around the collar. "This is all happening so fast. And it's such a big decision. Don't you think you need to give it a bit more time?"

"I've given it a year."

"Let's sleep on it. Okay? We can talk it over in the morning. Or, better yet, we can fly back home to Geneva and discuss it with your parents."

I go still.

He doesn't seem to notice. He tries to smile through his growing agitation. "Maybe there's a way you can incorporate some of your passions into future plans at VALENT."

"No." I shake my head, rejecting the words. I can hardly believe he'd suggest something like that. "No, that's not what I want."

His smile is losing the battle against a growing scowl of frustration. "Fine. If that's how you feel... *fine*. But I wish you'd hesitate before flying off the handle. I wish you'd at least talk to Blair and Vincent."

"I don't want to talk to them. All they do is lie, and deceive, and manipulate."

"That's not fair."

"It is, actually."

"Your emotions are running high, right now. This is a big decision. You can't make it recklessly."

"I'm aware it's a big decision. But it's *my* big decision to make."

"*Your* decision?" He yells the words, his anger exploding. It's startling. I've never heard him yell before. I've never even seen him lose his temper. "We're practically engaged! Don't you think I should have some say in you moving halfway around the world on a whim?"

I flinch. "A whim?"

"You know what I mean!"

"No, Oliver. I don't know what you mean. Why don't you explain it to me?"

He doesn't heed the warning in my tone — the one that says *back off, don't push me, you're on dangerous ground already.* He's too caught up in his own anger to notice mine. "For Christ's sake, Josephine. You're talking about abandoning your family legacy! Everything your parents have built! For what — to chase some silly dreams of fashion?"

"My dreams are not *silly*." The words come out like ice, my voice cold as an arctic breeze. "Nor are they any less important or less valid than yours."

"I'm sorry. I didn't mean to imply..." He grits his teeth, trying to get his tone under control. "I just think you're overreacting. You want to attend Brown? You want to study design? Then do it. But you don't have to cut your parents out of your life to do those things."

"Yes, I do! You aren't listening to me! I don't want to fold my dreams into theirs. They aren't egg whites in a cake batter, Oliver. I won't be absorbed into someone else's recipe. Not anymore. I need to break away from them. If you knew what they'd done—"

"What have they possibly done? Besides support and love you all your life?"

"I can't believe you're blindly taking their side, without even hearing me out."

"By all means..." He gestures flippantly, breathing hard. "Explain."

"They lied to me, for starters! Last summer, they fabricated a whole story to get me on that plane to Switzerland. They orchestrated a separation between me and my best friend in the world. They basically blackmailed him into—" I press my eyes closed along with my lips. "Listen... What matters is, I no longer trust them. They don't have my best interests at heart. They never have. They never will. They're only interested in what I can do to advance the Valentine name."

The silence stretches on, lengthening from uncomfortable to unbearable. When I gather the courage to open my eyes and look at Oliver, he's wearing an expression of such acute disappointment, it hits me like a bullet to the heart.

"I see what's happening here." He laughs, but there's no mirth in the sound. "This isn't about which university you want to attend or what you want to study. It's not even about your parents. This is about *him*."

"Oliver—"

"Do me the courtesy of not lying about it, Josephine. I think you owe me that much."

My lips press tight together.

Oliver rises slowly to his feet, hands bracing against the desk. "Did you fuck him yesterday?"

"No," I breathe, feeling color rush to my cheeks. "But..."

"But?"

"We kissed." I blink hard, holding back tears. "I'm sorry. It happened. I'm not going to lie to you about it or pretend otherwise."

He takes off his glasses and sets them down. He's panting with anger, his shoulders rigid with tension. "Well, I'm not going to compete with some... some... lowlife *fisherman* for your heart."

I stare at him, not recognizing the man before me. It's like staring at a stranger. I tell myself Oliver Beaufort is kind, generous, welcoming. Warm, open, affectionate. He is not this person — this man with thinly veiled superiority and the cold blue blood of elite society.

Or... A small voice pipes up insistently. *Maybe he's not bothering to wear a mask anymore.*

"I can't believe you just said that," I whisper. "You sound just like my parents."

"Yeah, well. Unlike you, I don't see that as such a terrible comparison. I quite like your parents."

I shake my head. Sadness is blooming inside me, along with another emotion. It takes me a moment to recognize it as relief. I'm relieved, looking at this man before me. This seemingly perfect man who, it turns out, may not be so perfect after all.

"Can I ask you something?"

He sighs deeply. "You can ask me anything you'd like, Josephine."

"If you had to choose between me and my parents... between a future as my husband or a future as a senior vice president at VALENT... which would you pick?"

He looks up at me sharply. His eyes widen, then narrow. I can almost see the wheels turning inside his head, thoughts spinning round and round as he tries to compose a suitable response.

"See..." I murmur. "If you were the right man for me, you wouldn't have to think nearly that hard about the answer, Ollie. If you truly wanted me — *me*, Josephine, not my family connections, or a permanent place in my parents' good graces, or my last name — you wouldn't have to weigh the pros and cons for more than a nanosecond. Because when you love someone, you choose them. No matter what. Above everything and everyone else."

He blinks at me, like he doesn't have a clue what I'm talking about.

"I can't marry you," I tell him softly. "I'm sorry, Oliver."

"You— you've gone completely mad! That's the only explanation for this change in your behavior!" His face is pale. He's practically spluttering. He yanks at his tie, loosening it as he begins to pace behind the desk. "First you demonize your parents. Now, you're lumping me in with them? Rejecting my proposal, like it's nothing?!"

"It's not nothing. I never said it was nothing. But it's not right — not for me, not for you. This conversation has shown me, beyond any shadow of a doubt, that we would be miserable for all our days as husband and wife."

"You cannot be serious!"

"How could I marry someone who can't choose me over my

parents?" I rise to my feet, locking my knees to keep them from collapsing beneath me. "How could I ever trust you to be my partner?"

"You talk about marriage like a child," he snarls. "When it comes down to it, lifelong commitments aren't about passion or desire; they're about basic compatibility. Perhaps in a few years, when you're capable of rational thought, you'll see what I mean."

"I may talk about marriage like a child, but you talk about it like a business acquisition!"

"Because it is! It is nothing but a merger between two families. The Beauforts and the Valentines are a good match. Cut from the same cloth. A seamless stitch." His tone grows disdainful. "And you're walking away from that... turning me down... for what? Some fleeting feelings of lust for an ex-boyfriend that will vanish after a few bouts between the sheets."

I can't quite swallow down my fury. "I think it's time for you to leave, Oliver."

"You're going to regret this. You don't belong with someone like him," he says bluntly. His pacing stops as abruptly as it began. "He hurt you before. He'll hurt you again. And when he does... I won't be here to pick up the pieces."

"You may be right. Archer may hurt me again. He may not be perfect. I'm certainly not. If we do have any sort of future together, it won't be easy." I suck in a breath. "But I'd rather fight every day to make it work with someone who loves me without question than live out my life as no more than a line-item on a business contract between our bloodlines. I deserve more than that. And so do you, Oliver. I hope you realize that, someday. I hope you meet someone who makes you realize that."

He retrieves his briefcase from beside the desk and walks

stiffly to the door. At the threshold, he pauses for only a brief moment.

"Have a good life, Josephine," he says.

He leaves, then.

He does not look back.

THIRTY

archer

"CAREFUL WHERE YOU SWING THAT, ROSS," I call across the field, halting the unruly first-grader where he stands. His small hands — still holding the wooden bat — freeze midair, poised to bring down a dizzying blow on the head of a ginger-haired kid with freckles and glasses, waiting for his turn at home plate.

The last thing we need is a concussion injury. It's only our second practice.

Crossing my arms over my chest, I shake my head at Ross until he sighs, steps back, and drops the bat to the dirt. He huffs his way to the back of the batting line to wait for his turn — and, no doubt, find another unsuspecting victim to antagonize.

"Cocky little shits, aren't they?" Chris mutters from beside me on the pitching mound.

I bark out a laugh. "The arrogance of youth."

"That one isn't just arrogant. He's a troublemaker. All the makings of a class clown." He pauses. "He's also my little cousin, so I may be biased."

"He reminds me a bit of you as a kid."

"Oh, come on! I wasn't that bad."

"I seem to recall an incident involving spit-balls and the coach's daughter—"

He smirks. "Fine. Maybe I *was* that bad. But we couldn't all be you, Reyes. So calm, so focused. Early to every practice. Always offering to carry the equipment and help clean litter off the bleachers after our games. A coach's dream."

There's a strong sense of irony, looking back — the devilish son of the police chief a constant source of trouble; the angelic boy from the wrong side of the tracks forever overcorrecting for his criminal connections. I don't bother pointing out to Chris that not all of us have the privilege of acting out. Even in elementary school, I knew I had to work twice as hard to be seen as anything except *just another Reyes kid*. From my very first tee-ball team all the way through varsity, I bent over backwards to distinguish myself from Jaxon's actions. In a way, I'm still doing it. Only this time, it's not on a baseball field and the stakes are much higher.

"Any word from the DEA?" Chris asks, reading my mind.

"Not since the other day. They're watching the harbor, waiting for the trawler to come back into port. Could be any minute, now. They said they'll call as soon as that happens."

"They want to raid the boat with a full hold."

"Mhm." My eyes follow the swing of the redheaded kid. He's butchered three separate attempts at hitting the ball off the tee and his self-confidence is deflating faster than a week-old birthday balloon. At the back of the line, Ross sniggers something cruel that makes the whole line of kids laugh. I keep my eyes on the batter. "Jimmy, look at me."

Beneath the brim of his plastic helmet, his eyes find mine. I see a double-dose of humiliation, lurking beneath the shimmer of impending tears. Poor kid can't take much more taunting. "Hey — don't give up. Adjust your grip — remember how we showed you earlier? Where are your hands supposed to go? Up a bit farther. Yep, that's it." I nod at him. "Now, try again. You've got this, buddy."

He grins crazy-big when his next swing makes definitive contact, sending the ball across the infield with a sharp crack. Chris and I both cheer encouragingly, clapping our hands and stomping our feet. He won't be the next David Ortiz, but at least he can hold his head up high as he walks to the back of the line to join Ross.

"Next up!" Chris calls. "That's you, Matthew. Hey! What's our rule? Put on your helmet before you step out of the dugout, remember?" My co-coach slides a glance at me as the next batter steps up to home plate. "Four hours with these kids, and I'm questioning if I'll ever reproduce."

"Don't worry, Tomlinson — reproduction requires you find a woman willing to tolerate you. You've got nothing to worry about."

"*Ass.*" He shoves me playfully. "Speaking of women... how's Valentine?"

"Don't go there."

"What? I'm curious. Sue me."

Curiosity aside, I have no intention of telling Chris a damn thing about me and Jo. Not our heated kiss three days ago, not the radio silence she's been broadcasting since. I don't need his opinions on how badly I butchered that conversation — I've been beating myself up enough all on my own. Nor do I need any reminders that, even as we speak, she may be accepting that stodgy asshole Beaufort's marriage proposal.

"I..." I adjust my baseball cap, pulling the brim lower to shield my eyes. "I'm giving her a little space."

"You've given her a year of space! Try a new tactic."

"Hilarious."

"I wasn't joking. When has giving Josephine Valentine space ever gotten you anywhere?"

"Who's Josephine?" A kid named Uriah asks, jogging up to us. His shoelace has come untied — I bend to help him. His small hands hold my shoulders for balance. "Is that your giiiir-llfriend?"

"See, everyone wants to know," Chris taunts from above. "Come on, Coach Reyes. Is she your *giiiiirlfriend*?" He stretches out the word into two elongated syllables, just like the six-year-old. I tighten the final loop and point back toward the dugout.

"Off you go, Uriah."

He runs off without so much as a *thank you*. I rise back to full height, glowering over at Chris. "Was that necessary? The whole team will be giggling about my so-called girlfriend in about thirty seconds flat."

He holds up his hands defensively. "I stand with the first-graders on this one."

"That's not a shock. You do share the same maturity level."

"You still haven't answered the question."

"Because it's none of your business."

"I'm your best friend!"

"And?"

"And, that means we tell each other shit."

"What is this, a slumber party?" I roll my eyes. "Do you want me to french-braid your hair, too?"

"No. It's not long enough for a braid."

I snort. "Pity."

A few seconds later, every boy waiting in line for his turn to bat cups his hands over his mouth and, like a dismally off-key choir, chants in unison, "*Coach Reyes and Josephine, sitting in a tree, K-I-S-S-I-N-G.*"

My head swings around toward Chris, who looks like he's desperately trying to swallow down a laugh. My glower is lethal. "Are you happy now?"

"First comes love, then comes marriage, then comes a baby in a baby carriage!" They dissolve into a flurry of giggles.

Chris loses the battle against his amusement, bending at the waist with his hands braced on his knees and laughing himself breathless. The sight ignites a fresh round of hilarity from the batter-line.

"Perfect," I mutter. "Now you're encouraging them..."

It takes five full minutes to get the boys back under control, calm enough to stand in a line and start practicing their swings once more. When Chris and I finally return to our spot by the pitcher's mound and slide our gloves back on, ready to resume practice, he has the good grace to look somewhat chagrined.

"I'm sorry, Reyes." Chris chuckles. "But you have to admit, that was pretty funny."

"Uh huh."

"I'll buy you a beer at the Salty Dog after practice wraps up. A peace offering, to wash away some of your child-induced trauma." He pauses. "Demons, the lot of them."

"You're the one who signed us up to coach," I point out.

"That was before I knew how wild these kids were going to be!"

"You thought six-year-old boys would be easy to handle?"

"Yeah, yeah, yeah. I'm not the brightest bulb in the box. Whatever." He pauses. "Hence the need for post-practice beers."

"You're up first, Joey!" I call, pointing toward home plate, where a fresh baseball is sitting atop the tee, awaiting the next batter. "Take your time. Find your stance. Then give it your best swing."

The kid misses completely.

"Try again, Joey!"

"I'm buying," Chris offers from beside me. " I'll even throw in a plate of fries, to sweeten the pot."

"Can't," I say absently. Most of my attention is fixed on the kid at bat. His next swing makes contact with the ball; I bend to snatch it from the grass as it rolls toward me. "That was great, Joey!"

"Why not?" Chris asks. "Look, I promise not to ask about Josephine. I just want to hear more about the meeting with the DEA. That's all."

"There's not much to tell. I spent two afternoons sitting in a conference room with some federal drug enforcement agents, telling them everything I know about Jaxon's operation — which isn't much — and listening to them go over every possible contingency plan once I'm onboard the Reina."

"So the mission is a go? This is actually happening?"

"Why are you so surprised? You're the one who set this in motion. You're the one who got me in contact with the DEA."

"I know, I know. But I didn't think it would happen so quickly."

"Generally speaking, the United States government isn't a big fan of letting drug-lords continue their operations unchecked."

"Evidently."

"They want this handled before another shipment of heroin hits the streets." I pat my pocket, where my cellphone sits at the ready. "Just waiting on their call. The second Jaxon returns to port, they're wiring me up and sending me in."

"Archer..." He sounds surprisingly serious. "Are you absolutely certain you want to do this?"

I shrug. "Not much choice in the matter. I'm the only one who can get onboard that ship and get the evidence the DEA needs to make any credible arrests. They can't search the holds without just cause. I'm going to get it for them."

He absorbs this information in silence. Shoulder to shoulder, we watch as another young boy steps up at bat. His stance is all wrong, but he hits the ball on his first swing. It sails past us on the right, rolling toward third base.

"Good job, Keith! You'll be hitting homers in no time," I call, nodding my approval. "Next up! Come on, Jared. Reset the ball on the tee. Yep, just like that. You've got it, buddy."

"You're good at this," Chris remarks.

"Wrangling first graders into compliance?"

"*Coaching.*"

I shrug without comment.

"I mean it! You're a natural."

"It's tee-ball. Anyone can coach tee-ball."

He looks at me appraisingly. "Ever thought about applying your skills on a higher level?"

"No."

"Maybe you should. You know, Coach Hamm was always talking about bringing on an assistant coach at Exeter... someone to handle the JV team..." He grins. "You could call him. He'd be thrilled to hear from his favorite former player."

"Give it a rest, Tomlinson."

"Give what a rest?"

"Your mission to be my personal savior. I appreciate the concern for my future, but it's not necessary. It's frankly a bit condescending, coming from a guy who once agreed to swallow a goldfish on a dare."

He groans at the mention of the koi incident. "Fine. Message received. No more life advice from me. We can just drink beers and talk about sports, like the hyper-masculine Neanderthals society expects us to be."

"Afraid you're on your own for that." I chuckle. "I'm taking a hiatus from drinking."

He looks at me in surprise. His mouth opens to comment, but he merely nods and shuts it when he sees the expression on my face. "Fine. I can deal with no beers. You still eat burgers though, right? Because going vegan is where I draw the line..."

josephine

THE BUZZ of the front gate makes me look up from my laptop screen. My heart leaps inside my chest.

Archer?

I'm desperate to see him.

I'm also terrified to see him.

The last time we were in the same room, we nearly combusted in a supernova of lust. I couldn't think straight through the haze of desire that clouds my mind whenever I'm in his presence. I thought time might help me sort through some of my messy emotions, thought space might let me better articulate my thoughts... but in the handful of days since our heated kiss, my blood has cooled only marginally — a low simmer of need that hums in my veins at all times. It will take no more than the brush of his fingers, the skim of his lips, to ramp back up to a rolling boil we cannot contain.

In this moment, I don't care.

Abandoning the student housing application on my laptop, I jump to my feet and race for the front door. My heart deflates as I peer at the image projected from the front gate camera — a Pepto-Bismol-pink Land Rover idles in the driveway, with

Odette and Ophelia Wadell grinning from behind the dashboard.

"Yo, Jo! Let us in!"

I buzz them in with a martyred sigh and head out onto the front steps to await their arrival. Music blasts from the rolled-down windows as they race up the driveway in a blur of bubblegum pink. The car is barely in park before they're bounding toward me, platinum blonde bobs bouncing with every step. They strut up the front walk like they own the place. They're dressed in matching neon bikinis and designer flip-flops, with sheer sarongs wrapped artfully around their willowy frames. Odette is carrying a beach bag with towels and sunscreen; Ophelia is toting a cooler that I know from experience contains all manner of alcoholic beverages.

"This is a surprise," I say, holding open the door and allowing them inside. "Did I invite you over for a pool party and completely forget about it?"

"Nope. This is an ambush!" Odette informs me happily. "We had no choice. You're not answering your phone."

"It goes straight to voicemail," her twin adds. "What is this, the Dark Ages? Are we supposed to send you a fax or something if we want to hang out?"

"Sorry." I shrug. "It's on silent-mode."

"Why?"

"Dodging my parents calls."

"We repeat — why?"

Oh, no reason... besides Oliver returning to Switzerland and promptly informing them about the broken engagement, not to mention my intent to attend Brown in the fall... thus eradicating everything they've ever wanted for me in a single crushing blow...

I woke this morning to the insistent vibrations of my cell-phone on my nightstand. Even after I sent the call through to voicemail, it proceeded to buzz so many times, I thought it might dig its way down through the earth's crust, all the way to the molten core. When I turned it off completely, like clockwork, the landline began to ring on five-minute intervals. I unplugged the damn thing, for lack of any better options.

Only a few more days, I console myself. *Then I'm out of here.*

"Hello?" Odette and Ophelia are blinking at me. "Anyone home in that head of yours?"

"Sorry." I laugh. "Lately things in my life are... complicated."

"Great! We love complicated. You can tell us all about it over frozen margaritas. Where's your blender?" Ophelia doesn't wait for an answer; she's already headed for the kitchen.

"Go get your bikini on." Odette bumps her shoulder against mine and pushes me lightly toward the staircase. "You look like you could use some sun. You're pale as an old man's inner thigh."

"Thanks," I say wryly.

"Oh, relax. I said, *'You're pale'* — not, *'You look like you've been locked in your room watching reruns of* The Great British Bake-Off *for the past week like a sad little loser who's allergic to sunlight.'*"

"Ouch! That was harsh."

"Go."

I turn and head upstairs to find a swimsuit, too tired to argue with her. Mostly because she's sadly correct in her assumptions — I have, in fact, been locked in my room watching reruns of *The Great British Bake-Off* like a sad little loser all morning. Something about watching strangers create delicious confections through a high-def screen has a calming effect.

My life may be spinning out of control, but damn, would you look at that beautiful five-layer buttercream cake?

In the kitchen, the sound of the blender flips on. I let the hum of crushing ice carry me down the hallway to my bedroom, and tug on the first bikini my hands land discover.

———

Over two rounds of frozen margaritas, the twins listen to my tale of woe. I tell them everything about Oliver's proposal and my parents deception. I even tell them about Archer. By the time I'm done talking, the ice in my margarita has turned to water beneath the scorching midday sun and both of them are looking at me with fascination.

"Sorry," I murmur, sipping the watery drink. The sugared rim of the glass hits my tastebuds with lip-smacking sweetness. "You guys came here to hang out and instead I've just spent an hour talking your ears off."

"Oh my god, do *not* apologize." Ophelia grins. "Your life is always so much more interesting than anyone else we know."

"Seriously," Odette adds. "You could have, like, your own reality show."

I shudder at the thought of a camera crew following me around, documenting my every move. "Introvert, remember? That's my version of Hell."

"Lame." Ophelia sighs. "We'd make great guest stars. That's all I'm saying."

"Oooh, yes!" Odette giggles. "The fabulous BFFs who sweep in to dispense advice about boys."

"And occasionally, give fashion tips."

"I'll keep that in mind." I laugh and set down my drink. "But I'm more interested in boy-advice than fashion at the moment."

"Have you heard from Oliver since he left?"

I shake my head. "No. And I don't think I will. Ollie isn't the type to change his mind or circle back. He's the quintessential businessman — by now, he's already assessed the pros and cons, accepted the cause as lost, and moved into damage-control mode."

"This is why we don't date businessmen!" Odette gulps her margarita. "So boring. So predictable. So entirely *repressed*."

"That's also why we don't date virgins," Ophelia mutters lowly. "Good riddance, as far as I'm concerned. He can take his four-carat diamond and shove it up his own ass. It'll be the most action he sees for a while."

I roll my eyes. "His problem isn't his commitment to celibacy. His problem is his commitment to my parents, above everything — even me."

"You were *so* right to kick him to the curb."

"You deserve a guy who'll put you first, Jo!"

"Thanks, guys. I appreciate that."

Ophelia makes a drum-roll with her hands on the beach towel. "And behind door number two, we have another bachelor contending for our heroine's heart...."

Odette cups her hands around her mouth and mimics the sing-song tones of a television game-show host. "Arrrrrrcher Reyessssss!"

"Hilarious," I mutter, reaching for the pitcher and topping off my glass with another serving of watery margarita. "Really, you guys should do a stand-up routine."

"Oh, come on! We're just teasing."

"You always get so serious when the conversation shifts to him."

"Because..." I gulp my drink and settle back on my chaise lounger. The sun is so hot, sweat is beading against my brow. "I don't know how to speak casually when it comes to Archer. Nothing about our relationship is casual. It's one big, complicated mess."

"What's so complicated?" Ophelia asks. "He told you he loves you!"

"He explained why he pushed you away last summer!" Odette chimes in. "And, honestly, it's a pretty good reason. Your parents... *Wow*. I thought ours were controlling, but I have a whole new appreciation for them after hearing what yours pulled on you."

"Why do you think I'm so torn up about this? My family destroyed his life. He's spent the past year suffering... all alone... because of me."

"Because of your parents! Not because of you."

"Logically, I know that's true. But emotionally..." My eyes are stinging. I blame the bright sunshine overhead. "How can we have any sort of shot at a future together, with such a heavy past tied around our ankles? We don't stand a chance."

"First of all, you don't know that." Ophelia glares at me. "Second of all, you owe it to him — to yourself — to try. After all this time, all this suffering... All this pining for one another..."

"Serious pining," Odette confirms.

"You can't just let him walk out of your life again. You'll regret it forever."

"What if he doesn't want to see me?"

"Why would you think that?" They both look confused.

"He knows where I live. He hasn't come. If he wanted to talk to me, he would."

They trade a glance. "Jo, honey... we hate to break this to you, but you're going to have to be the one to reach out this time."

"*Me?*"

"You." Odette is nodding vigorously. "The guy poured his heart out to you and you just..."

"Ran," Ophelia confirms.

"I needed time to process!" My voice is defensive. "My whole life had just exploded."

"Right. You needed to take a beat. And you took it." Odette begins to apply a fresh coat of sunscreen to her arms. "Now, it's time to stop hiding and tell him how you feel."

"He knows how I feel," I say immediately.

"Does he?" Ophelia takes the sunscreen bottle from her twin. "Maybe he knew how you felt last summer. Before the accident. Before he lost his future. Before he lost baseball. But has he ever heard you say you love him *now*? As he is? Have you told him you still want a future with him — even if that future looks totally different than the one you always imagined?"

I blink slowly, processing her words. In truth, I've always seen it as a given. An indisputable fact.

I love Archer Reyes.

I've always loved Archer Reyes.

And I always will love Archer Reyes.

It didn't occur to me that he might question that unshakable state of reality. I suck in a sharp breath. "You think... he might actually believe I don't love him anymore because of his injuries? That I might think less of him because he's not going to be some big-shot MLB star?"

"I don't know," she says gently. "Maybe you should ask him."

My brows arch. "Call him up and say, 'Hey, Archer, just so you know I'm still in love with you and I want to make a go of it as a couple, despite our track record of monumentally screwing everything up every time we've tried in the past?'"

"A little wordy for my taste," Odette murmurs. "But sure, it gets the point across."

I snort.

Could it really be that simple?

Could we really just choose to step over the wreckage, hand in hand, and walk forward together?

The twins are right. I owe it to myself to try. If I don't, I'm as big a hypocrite as Oliver. Hadn't I, only yesterday, told him that if you really love someone, you fight for them? No matter what?

"Don't worry, Jo." Ophelia pats me gently on the back. "It's all going to work out. You'll see."

"And if not... we have more margarita mix."

I sit up straight on my lounger, suddenly alarmed. "Wait. You want me to call him now? Like, right this minute?"

"No time like the present."

"But..." I swallow weakly, trying to think of an excuse to get me out of this. As much as I want to talk to Archer, I don't want to do it with a rapt audience. "I can't. I'm not ready."

"You're ready," they chorus in unison.

"I don't even have his phone number saved in my new phone."

"Use mine." Odette plucks it from her purse and hands it over. "Go on. The passcode is 666."

"Um," I squeak, staring at the phone like it's a venomous creature. "I..."

I'm saved by a most unlikely source — the tight voice of Mrs. Granger, cutting across the sunny afternoon like a grim reaper's scythe. "Miss Valentine."

My head whips around. She's standing a half-dozen feet from us, glaring from me to the near-empty pitcher to the twins with undisguised distaste.

"Mrs. Granger. It's Saturday. I didn't think you were working today."

"Mmm. So it would seem." She pauses, nostrils flaring. "I need to speak with you — now, if you please. I will wait in the kitchen."

She stalks away, leaving us in silence. I glance at the twins apologetically. "Sorry about that. I'm guessing her sudden appearance has something to do with my parents. If I don't deal with her, she'll just come back."

"Guess that's our cue, then."

"Just because I have to go doesn't mean you do! Stay. Tan. I'll be back eventually. Unless Mrs. Granger plans to knock me unconscious, wrap me in styrofoam, and ship me back to Switzerland against my will."

"She seems the type." Ophelia stretches her arms over her head. "Text us if you need extraction."

"The clouds are moving in anyway." Odette drains the final sip from her glass. "Besides, you know we'll be back for more gossip once you've made up with your man."

Ophelia points at me. "Spare no details!"

"Okay, okay. I promise," I say, laughing.

The twins gather their belongings, layer on their sarongs, and slide on their sandals. They each give me a long hug before they depart.

"Don't wait too long to tell him how you feel," Ophelia whispers in my ear. "I know it's scary to open yourself up to hurt again. It's tough to play the game. But I think it's way more terrifying to sit on the sidelines. Love isn't a spectator sport. So put on your helmet and step up to the plate."

"Did you just make a baseball metaphor?"

She shrugs, grinning at me. "Seemed appropriate, given the man in question."

"Thanks, O."

She chucks me lightly beneath the chin, then follows her twin down the garden path that leads to the driveway. I take a fortifying breath before I turn for the house — and the miffed housekeeper awaiting me inside.

———

Mrs. Granger is standing in the kitchen, as promised. Her expression is no more welcoming now than it was back at the pool.

"Miss Valentine."

"Mrs. Granger." I fold my arms over my chest. This might be more intimidating if I weren't clad in a polka dot-bikini. "What seems to be the problem?"

"I received a phone call from your mother this morning. It seems Cormorant House is to be shuttered for the season, starting next week. The access codes will reset at midnight on Monday."

The day after tomorrow.

I exhale softly.

It's a blow — one I was foolish not to anticipate, but a blow nonetheless. I should've known they'd kick me out as soon as I dared rebel. Not that I particularly wanted to stay. I've already inquired with the Student Housing office at Brown about alternative accommodations in the undergraduate dorms — I could have a placement on campus by mid-August. Despite my desire to leave this place behind... it's still somewhat surreal to hear that my parents are just as keen to cut ties.

Surreal, but not exactly surprising.

Kicking me off their property — via the housekeeper, no less — is just the kind of cold, calculated move my parents make in their business endeavors. I no longer serve their endgame; as such, I will be excised from their life without hesitation. Without so much as a conversation.

No more support — financial or otherwise.

It's somewhat exhilarating.

Terrifying, but exhilarating.

I'm free.

I have no idea where I'll be sleeping starting tomorrow. I have no money to my name except that left to me by my grandparents in a small trust, and the meager salary I earned as an intern at VALENT. But in this moment, I don't mind.

I'm finally free.

"This will be my last full day here on the property," Mrs. Granger tells me flatly. "I've already begun emptying out the refrigerator and covering the furnishings with sheets. I should be done in a few hours. If you need help packing your belongings—"

"That won't be necessary." My voice is just as flat. "I don't plan to take much with me."

I want nothing that reminds me of this place.

"Tomorrow, the boat maintenance man will come to deal with your father's Hinckley and secure the boathouse. You will be here to let him in, I presume?"

"Sure, I'll be here."

"Excellent." She nods. There's a long pause. "There's just one more matter then..."

My brows lift. "What is it?"

"I gather the closing of Cormorant House has something to do with Mr. Beaufort's rather abrupt departure." She pauses. "It seems, in his haste, he left behind a rather personal item..."

"Ah. The ring." I pinch the bridge of my nose. "Of course. I'd forgotten."

"No matter. If you'll bring it to me, I will see it delivered back to the proper hands."

"It's in my bedroom. I'll go get it."

I quickly retrieve the ring from its hidden spot in my desk, and return to the kitchen. Mrs. Granger is waiting there with her purse clutched in her hands so tightly, I doubt she has any blood circulation in her fingers.

"Here," I say, passing her the small velvet box. I feel not

even the slightest twinge of regret as it slips from my fingers. "Thank you for handling this."

"Very well, Miss Valentine." After tucking the box into her purse, Mrs. Granger pauses. "For what it's worth, I think you're making a grave mistake — letting a gentleman like Mr. Beaufort slip through your fingers."

"For what it's worth? I don't particularly care about your opinion, Mrs. Granger."

"Your mother was right — you are a willful girl."

"I'm sure she meant that as an insult. But I think I'll take it as a compliment." My mouth tugs up at one side. "Thanks for all your help with the house. You can go, now. I'll take it from here."

archer

DESPITE THE CALM assurances I made to Tomlinson at the ballpark this morning, when the DEA agents call me in ten hours later, I find I'm far more nervous than anticipated. We've walked through the plan multiple times, going over every possible contingency. It's simple enough, on paper.

Head down to the commercial docks after dark.

Approach the old trawler slowly, so they know I'm not a threat.

Ask to talk to my brother.

Get onboard, if possible.

Get confession, if possible.

Get pictures, if possible.

Get out cleanly, if possible.

Frankly, there are a few too many *if possibles* for my liking. But agents Pomroy and Stanhope don't seem ruffled. They both emit an unflappable energy, staring at me through flat eyes that have seen too much. Even now, crouched in an unmarked black van six blocks from the harbor, surrounded by surveillance equipment and government-issue weaponry, they don't seem at all nervous about the myriad ways this could go wrong.

"Okay, Reyes. Our teams are in place. Coast Guard is standing by to move in and block the harbor, if we need them. We've triple-checked the tech. Signal is clear as a whistle."

I try not to fidget at the mention of the recording device I'm wearing. I'd pictured something like I'd seen on old reruns of Law and Order — a wire taped to my chest, a bulky recorder box strapped to the small of my back. The reality is far more technologically advanced. I hadn't even realized, when they handed me a plain gray button-down to layer over my plain white t-shirt twenty minutes ago, that the top button is not a button at all. It's a camera. The device is so cleverly hidden in the fabric, you'd never know it was there — recording your every word, automatically snapping photographs every twenty seconds. The wires are stitched in the seams, invisible to the casual observer.

I'm counting on that.

Just as I'm counting on Jaxon's deluded sense of familial loyalty to buy me entrance onto the trawler.

"What do you do if they don't let you onboard?" Pomroy asks, narrowing his eyes at me.

"Abort the mission. Walk away."

"And what do you do if they start to suspect you?"

I sigh. This is about the hundredth time he's asked me this question. "Make an excuse. Get out."

"And if you can't get out?" Stanhope chimes in.

"I use the extraction code."

"And then?"

"Find cover until you arrive, guns blazing, to haul my ass out."

Pomroy's slate-gray eyes narrow. "Don't be a wiseass. This isn't a joking matter."

"I know that."

"Maybe he's not right for this op," he says, glancing at his partner. "Maybe we should wait for a different chance to get the intel—"

Stanhope shakes her head. "You know as well as I do that if the Reina crew heads back out on another run down the coast tomorrow, it could be weeks before they come back to port. Assuming they come back to this port at all. If they don't... all our groundwork here will be for nothing."

Pomroy glowers. "I still don't like it."

"Well, I don't like your cologne. We all make sacrifices for this job."

"It's a risk."

"A calculated one," she rebuts stubbornly. "And you know what they say. No risk, no reward."

"You're not the one taking the risk, Stanhope." Pomroy turns his gaze toward me. His eyes hold a severity that makes my stomach turn. "You sure you're ready for this, kid? You sure you realize what's at stake, here?"

Only my life.

I meet his steely stare head on. "My brother already took one future away from me. I won't let him take this new one I'm trying to build. You say it's a risk, and I hear you. But I don't think you understand... I'm risking far more by not doing anything. By letting Jaxon control my destiny. By letting the threat he poses to the people I care about keep me isolated."

Pomroy nods slowly. "Okay, then."

"We're ready," Stanhope tells the man sitting at the back of the van, manning the comm-station. I hear him relaying commands to the net of units spread around the harbor, prepared to move in at a moment's notice. The thought is comforting. I keep it close to my chest, like a shield, as I step out of the van, into the night, and begin the long, lonesome walk to the docks.

———

The rusty old trawler bobs innocuously at her slip, giving no indication of the danger lurking inside. Nerves churn in my stomach, clawing their way up my throat, as I approach with measured footfalls that sound like gunfire on the wooden planks.

The harbor is quiet, the frenzied daytime rush sedated by the blanket of night that's fallen in the past few hours. Even the clanking of rigging and lapping of tidal waves seems muted. Perhaps everything is muffled by the roar of blood rushing between my ears.

Someone is up on deck. I feel a set of eyes tracking my movements even before I spot the small red flare of a cigarette against the dim backdrop of sleeping vessels. I don't recognize the voice that whips my way, but I do recognize the threat in it.

"Wouldn't come much closer, if I were you."

I stop walking. In the dark, I can't make out the stranger's features, so I fix my eyes in the general direction of his silhouette. I clear my throat. "I'm here to see my brother."

There's a tense silence as he absorbs my words. "You're the kid?"

So, he's heard of me. "Archer."

He grunts, walking along the railing from the bow to the mid-section of the ship, where a narrow gangplank extends onto the dock. His boots clang against the metal as he descends halfway down. I wonder if they're steel-toed. I wonder if he's planning to curb-stomp me before I've even made it on the fucking boat.

"Jaxon didn't mention you were coming by," the stranger says, eyeing me suspiciously. His hair is close-shaved, his eyes are cold.

"He doesn't know." I shrug casually. "Is he here or not?"

He crosses his arms over his chest and stares me down. I notice his left hand bears a crown tattoo I recognize — the Latin King's signature ink. I make a point not to glance at it, keeping my eyes locked on his. I can't help flinching as he whistles without warning, a piercing sound that shatters the still night.

"Yo! Boss!" he yells over his shoulder. "Someone's here to see you." He looks back at me for a long moment. "Wait there."

I stand stock-still as the man turns and walks back to his spot at the bow, disappearing back into the darkness like he's part of the night itself. Only the occasional flare as he takes a drag from the cigarette butt reveals he's still there, watching me from the shadows.

Jaxon emerges a few seconds later. He says nothing as he makes his way down the gangplank, coming to a stop a few feet from me. His pinprick eyes flicker back and forth over my face, restlessly reading my expression. There's a tightness in his shoulders, a coiled sort of tension in his clenched fists.

"What are you doing here, Archer?"

"Can't a little brother come say hello without a reason?" I strive for a light tone.

"Not after the way we left things last time." His voice is hard with anger. "You've got a lot of nerve, showing your face in front of me."

"That's why I came. All right? I wanted to apologize for being such an ass the other night. You were trying to look out for me and I didn't even give you a chance. I was in a shitty mood and I bit your head off for no reason." I grit my teeth. "I'm sorry, Jax."

"Why the sudden change of heart?"

"I thought about what you said — about us being family. Being connected by blood. With Ma and Pa gone, it's just you and me left around here. If we're fighting... I've got no one. I'm alone. And I'm sick of being alone. I'm even more sick of scraping by like some pathetic loser, hauling lobster traps. I can't do it for another fifty years, Jax. I won't make it."

He nods, but his eyes are still wary. "Thought you said you'd rather be by yourself than be my brother. That you'd prefer being a poor lobsterman for the rest of your life than taking my help."

"Maybe... I need your help after all. Maybe... I was wrong."

"Wouldn't be the first time."

"Nope." I try out a laugh, though inside I'm burning with resentment. "Probably not the last, either. I am a Reyes, after all."

"That you are." Some of the ice melts out of his expression. "Glad you've pulled your head out of your ass in time to see the light."

Pushing down the urge to punch him right in his smug, self-satisfied face, I force myself to step closer and stick out my hand for him to shake. "What do you say? Can we be brothers again?"

Closing the distance between us, he slides his hand into mine. Instead of shaking it, he hauls me forward, into a tight embrace.

"Brothers," he echoes, thumping me on the back hard enough to rattle my lungs. "Family. Forever. We're gonna build a dynasty around here, Arch. We're gonna show everyone who tries to fuck with us that the Reyes name deserves respect." He pushes me back, punching me in the shoulder. "Now, come on. I'll introduce you to the crew."

My pulse is pounding as I step onto the narrow gangplank. I follow Jaxon up the incline, trying to keep my breaths shallow as I step onto the ship. She rocks lightly with the incoming tide, swaying against her dock lines.

"Welcome aboard the lovely Reina. Our queen of the seas."

Jaxon's grin is a flash of white in the darkness. There's a manic edge to it. I wonder if he's been sampling whatever products fill the holds beneath our feet. "That's Cisco up on the bow. You've already met. And down here..."

I follow him into the main cabin, squinting against the sudden burst of light against my retinas. It takes a moment for the spots to clear from my visual field. When they do, I find myself standing in a fairly large room with wood-paneled walls and round, portal windows dotted every few feet. There are three men seated at a built-in table to my right, playing a round of poker. Two handguns sit beside the stack of cards. A clear plastic bag of something white and granular rests beside an ashtray.

The room goes completely still as we enter. Even the smoke trailing from their cigarettes seems to halt midair. I try to breathe, try to remember that there's a team of highly trained agents only moments away if these men decide to squash me a like a bug against a windshield — which is pretty much what their expressions are broadcasting.

Fuck.

"That's Lopez," Jax points to a middle-aged man with massive fists and a teardrop tattoo on his face. "That's Stutter." His finger swings toward a shorter, stockier man with chest muscles bulging from his soiled wife-beater. "And that skinny guy is Gordo." Jax laughs at the third man, who can't weigh more than a hundred and thirty pounds soaking wet. He looks barely old enough to drive, let alone be seated at that table, but he bristles with bravado when he catches me starting at him.

"Figueroa is asleep in the bunk room, through there." Jaxon jerks his chin to the left, where a dim hallway extends into darkness beyond my line of sight. "There are only four berths, so we sleep in shifts. 'Cept me, of course. I get my own room.

Captain's quarters. My perk for organizing this little expedition."

The rest of the crew look considerably less thrilled by this setup than Jaxon. In fact, they look borderline homicidal as they stare from me to my brother and back again in terse silence.

"Who the fuck is he?" Lopez asks, setting down his cards.

"Yeah," Gordo hisses. "What is it, bring a narc to work day?"

Jaxon rolls his eyes. "He's not a narc."

"He dresses like one." Gordo looks me up and down. I barely breathe as his eyes pass over the top button of my shirt.

Don't flinch.

Don't shift.

Don't fidget.

I fix my face in a *don't-fuck-with-me* mask, firing it right back at Gordo. His cheeks are pockmarked with acne. I'd guess he's no more than seventeen — and aching to prove himself a real man. He'd probably shoot me just for the street-cred.

"Where do you shop?" I ask him, smirking. "BabyGAP?"

Jax snorts in amusement.

Gordo slams his fist on the table. The handgun is only inches from his fingertips. "Say that again, asshole. See what happens."

"Gordo, chill." Jaxon doesn't even look at the gangly teen. His focus is on Lopez. The large man has barely spoken, but his lethal expression is communicating his thoughts quite clearly. "He's my kid brother, all right? He's here to learn the tricks of the trade."

"The fuck he is," Lopez mutters. His eyes cut to me like knives. "We already have a full crew."

"We can always use another set of hands and you know it," Jaxon snaps. "Cut him some slack."

"Cut him some slack? Are you fucking kidding me, Reyes?" Lopez's voice rises with each word, as does his anger. "We have a full hold to unload before dawn. It's not the time to stroll in here with a stranger who'll fuck up our plans."

"Like I said," Jax says tightly. "He's not a stranger."

"He's a s-s-stranger to us," Stutter points out, revealing the source of his nickname. "I'm w-w-with Lopez. I s-s-say we g-g-get rid of him. Now."

Any warmth Jaxon's expression once contained is gone in a heartbeat. "I don't care what you *s-s-s-say*, Stutter," he mocks. "I'm in charge here. I make the rules. If I say he stays, he stays."

Lopez stands with a sudden violence that makes the whole table jump. Cards and chips scatter across the surface. I hope like hell the tiny button-camera is capturing the fact that he's got a very large gun holstered to his side. "Getting real tired of you pulling rank on me, Reyes. I don't know whose dick you sucked to get where you are and I don't give a shit. Far as I'm concerned, we were operating just fine on land before you showed up and dragged our operation out to sea. Now, instead of sitting on my ass in my apartment with my old lady, I spend half my days stuck on this rust bucket in the middle of the goddamn ocean, hurling over the side."

"Try some Dramamine," Jaxon suggests snidely. "And save me your whining. This is the job. You don't like it, then leave. I'll be happy to tell Philippe you were too chickenshit to handle it."

Whoever Philippe is clearly has some serious pull, because all three men at the table go slightly pale at just the mention of his name.

"No?" Jaxon asks smugly. "I didn't think so."

He seems to think he's snuffed out the spark of rebellion, but I'm less optimistic. I feel like I'm standing in a room filled with gunpowder, holding a lit match. Lopez is looking at my brother with such unconcealed hatred, I know he's just itching to wrap those beefy hands around his throat and squeeze. I can't see either Stutter or Gordo stepping in to stop him.

I wonder if my brother realizes just how tenuous his authority is. How close these guys are to flipping on him. I swallow hard, trying to clear the lump of nerves lodged in my throat. Trying to remember what Stanhope and Pomroy told me, back in the van.

Just hang in there until we get verbal confirmation.

As soon as we have enough evidence, we'll move in.

How much is enough?

Jaxon mentioned moving product, but only in the loosest of terms. Nothing specific. I doubt 'Stutter' and 'Gordo' are given names, easily searched in a database of criminals with open arrest warrants. All I really know so far is that there are six men on board and at least as many weapons.

I need more.

Solid confirmation.

Enough to shut this down for good.

"Look, I'm not here to cause problems," I tell the men, trying to keep my voice level. Every set of eyes flies to my face. It's hard not to turn and bolt for safety.

"Why are you here, then?" Lopez asks.

"My brother told me this new gig you guys are running is a gold mine." I shrug. "I want in."

"Your brother has a big mouth." His eyes slide to Jaxon. "Might get him in trouble."

Jax stiffens beside me. "Watch it, Lopez."

"You watch it, Reyes."

"This is my crew. You don't like it, you're welcome to leave. Go back to selling dime bags of black tar on street corners — we'll be here moving bricks, surrounded by stacks of money, making the Kings so rich no one can touch us."

"Stop running your mouth about our business," Lopez roars, putting a hand on his holster. "This kid isn't a King—"

"He will be," Jaxon shouts, shooting me a look. "And he's family. I trust him."

"*I* don't trust him." Lopez strides forward, standing nose to nose with Jaxon. "And I don't trust you. Not anymore."

"What are you saying, Lopez?" Jaxon's hand moves subtly toward the small of his back, where the base of a handgun juts from the waistband of his jeans. I inch backward, certain I'm about to be caught in the middle of a shootout.

Where the hell is the DEA?

They must have enough evidence to move in by now.

I try to think of something I can say to diffuse the tension in the room, to prevent the powder-keg of drug-fueled testosterone from exploding. Anything I say right now feels highly flammable. As liable to trigger an explosion as it is to prevent one.

"Look, Jax, I didn't come here to cause you problems," I murmur in what I hope is a diplomatic tone. "If it's this big a deal for me to be here, I'll just go—"

Lopez looks at me. "You're not going anywhere, kid. No one is going anywhere."

Fuck.

What was my extraction code, again?

Something about high tide...

My brain is a mess of static; my limbs feel stiff as plaster. In the myriad scenarios I ran with the DEA, this — Jaxon's crew pulling a mutiny — was not one of them.

I can sense things going south rapidly. It's only a matter of time before bullets start flying. I have no plans to be here, when that happens.

"Don't threaten my little brother!" Jax's fingers curl around his gun. "You're out of line, Lopez."

"What the hell is going on out here?" The question precedes the arrival of another man from the sleeping berths. Everyone turns to watch as the door swings open and he emerges, rubbing his eyes and yawning. His face is full of ill-temper. "I was trying to sleep! Who could rest with all this fucking racket—"

I use the momentary distraction of his arrival to inch backwards, toward the exit. Under my breath, I murmur the catchphrase I memorized this afternoon. The one that Pomroy and Stanhope promised would deliver salvation within ninety seconds.

"I think it's almost high tide."

I speak so lowly, I'm sure no one else can hear it over the volley of shouts firing back and forth across the room; so lowly, I'm worried the microphone embedded in my shirt can't pick it up, either.

I don't care.

I'm not waiting.

I'm getting the fuck out of here.

I take another step backward, toward the door — and hit a wall. Except it's not a wall at all.

Walls don't breathe.

I'd forgotten all about Cisco, the guard up on the bow.

He's not on the bow, anymore. He's standing directly behind me. Close enough to hear my murmured extraction code. Close enough to notice me edging toward the door unnoticed.

When I realize my fatal mistake, I don't even have time to bolt for the exit — his arm is already banding around my neck, his full strength compressing my windpipe.

"What did you just say, kid?"

I choke out an unintelligible gasp.

The rest of the room falls silent as they all turn to look. Jaxon's eyes go wide as he sees me in Cisco's grip.

"Let him go," he snaps, taking a step toward us. Drawing his gun. "I mean it, Cisco."

"He was muttering something under his breath!" Cisco yells over my shoulder. "Did anyone check him for a wire?"

"No." Lopez stalks toward us, murder in his eyes. "Let's do that."

Jaxon's expression darkens. "Don't be ridicul—"

He never finishes the word.

Because, in that moment, the loudest bang I've ever heard shakes the ship and the entire cabin explodes around us into a shower of debris. The air is no longer air — it is shards of glass, splinters of wood, scraps of metal. Every portal window shatters simultaneously, every overhead hatch rips clean of its hinges.

I drop to the floor as gas canisters fly through a gaping hole in the roof, spilling noxious fumes as they roll across the cabin floor. It's instantly pitch dark. I cough against the burn in my throat, shielding my head as I hear the sound of gunfire behind me. The ceiling rattles as boots pound up the metal gangplank, a prelude to a fleet of arriving agents.

Unable to see more than two inches in front of my face thanks to the smoke-bombs, I crawl blindly in what I hope is the direction of the exit. I drag my body over broken glass, barely feeling the pain as I scramble toward air and light and safety. I almost make it, too. My hands hit the track of the sliding glass door that leads outside. I can practically taste freedom on my tongue.

Until a massive hand curls around my ankle and drags me back, into the darkness. Until two hands lock around my throat and begin to squeeze and squeeze and squeeze, so hard I think my neck will snap.

I struggle, but it's no use.

He's too big.

Too strong.

I can't get away.

Can't move.

Can't breathe.

My vision clouds over with stars. The stars turn black, spreading from my peripherals inward, darkening my entire visual field. The last thing I see before I lose consciousness is Lopez, looming over me like a demon straight from hell, vengeance burning in his eyes.

"You did this," he hisses, squeezing even harder.

The last bit of fight leaves my body.

And then... the world goes dark.

THIRTY-THREE

josephine

I USE MY BEST PENMANSHIP, carefully inking each word on the thick, creamy stationary my parents' secretary purchased for my sixteenth birthday.

> Blair and Vincent,
>
> I am your daughter.
>
> Your child.
>
> Your only offspring.
>
> I have spent my entire life — every minute of every day for nearly twenty years — trying to win your love.
>
> When I realized that was an impossibility, I downshifted my expectations. I thought, perhaps, if I worked hard enough, if I achieved academic success, if I won every contest, if I never stepped a toe out of line... I might one day win your affection. Your approval. At the very least, your grudging pride in all I have accomplished.
>
> I see now, the flaw in my plan; the grave miscalculation under which I have been operating.

There is no use trying to win the hearts of people who do not possess them.

You cannot love me — you do not have the capacity for it. You look at me and see another corporate asset, an inanimate acquisition you can play to your advantage in the business world.

I forgive you for that.

After all, you cannot change who you are.

But neither can I.

I will no longer attempt to mold myself into a shape you find acceptable. I will no longer chase after anything you have to offer. I will no longer be made to feel like a disappointment.

The truth is?

You two are the disappointment.

You have let me down, not the other way around. You have failed, at every turn, to live up to any expectations I possessed for what a mother and father should be. For how they should raise a child. For how they should build a family.

From this moment on, I am not your daughter.

Not your child.

Not your offspring.

From this moment on...

We are not family.

But then... we never really were.

Were we?

I wish you success in your future endeavors at VALENT.

We all know, that's what you truly care about, anyway.

Best,

Josephine

I stamp it with international postage pilfered from my father's office, address it, drive it straight to the post-office, and drop it in the slot before I have a chance to change my mind.

It is the only farewell my parents will ever receive from me. The only goodbye they will ever hear — not from my lips, but from the tip of my pen.

A letter feels like a fitting end. After all, it was a letter that started this. A letter that broke us. I can only hope, when they receive it, they feel half as much pain as I did when I read the one they forced Archer to write me last summer.

More likely, they'll simply file it away in a folder of other corporate grievances, to be dealt with by an underling at a later date — assuming they even bother to read it at all. There's a high probability they'll toss it straight into the bin without digesting a single word or sentiment. But that doesn't matter.

That's not why I wrote it.

Taking a deep breath, I tighten my hands around the steering wheel and pull away from the post office. My nerves mount as I make the winding drive from downtown Manchester across the town line into Gloucester. Now that I've cut ties with my parents... cut ties with my past...

There's only one more thing to do before I leave this life behind. One more person I need to see before I walk away for good.

The only person who really matters.

My hand reaches up to clasp my necklace as I turn toward the harbor.

———

I stand in the night, knocking on his door like a crazy person.

"Archer! Archer, are you home? It's me," I yell through the wood. "It's Jo. I need... I need to talk to you. Please, if you're there..."

My heart is in my throat.

My hands are shaking.

My knees are quaking.

I'm here.

I'm ready.

Ready to take the plunge.

Ready to tell him how I feel.

I love you.

Let's make this work.

I don't know where I'm going, I don't even know where I'm sleeping come tomorrow... but it doesn't matter. So long as we're together.

"Archer?"

There is no answer.

Not after five minutes.

Not after ten or twenty or thirty.

No matter how loud I pound, he does not come. No matter how many minutes I stand there waiting, my skin growing clammy with cold, he does not appear.

When my hand is beginning to ache and my courage is beginning to falter, I force myself to stop. To admit what I've known for quite a while, now.

Archer isn't here. Or, if he is...

He doesn't want to see me.

My smarting fists drop to my sides.

My leaden legs carry me off his porch, down the steps, onto the sidewalk.

Back to my car.

Back to Cormorant House, to pack what few belongings I

will take with me when I leave this town behind for the second time in a matter of hours.

I know in my gut, if I don't track him down before I leave... it will truly be over. Our second chance will evaporate on the wind, a fleeting promise gone before fulfillment.

Maybe it's bad timing.

Maybe it's bad luck.

Or maybe...

We're just not meant to be.

THIRTY-FOUR

archer

WHEN I SNAP BACK into consciousness, I'm lying on a medical gurney with strangers crowded around me. The patches on their uniform sleeves say EMERGENCY MEDICAL TECHNICIAN. Their faces flash blue-red-blue-red in the night. They're wheeling me across the parking lot, to a waiting ambulance parked at the edge of the harbor.

"Whoa there!" The female EMT pushes firmly against my shoulders when I attempt to sit up. "Sir, calm down!"

"What happened?" My voice is croaky; my throat burns with pain, my injured vocal cords protesting at each syllable.

"You're okay. You briefly lost consciousness. You're going to be just fine, but we need you to stay still—"

It comes back in a flash.

Lopez.

Hands around my neck.

Squeezing the life out of me.

Sending me into the dark.

What happened after he knocked me out?

Was the raid successful?

Did they arrest everyone?

I crane my neck to either side, trying to get a look at the action unfolding all around me. I hear a cacophony of voices and sirens, but I can't make out any details from this angle.

"Sir, I really must ask you to lay back down. We haven't finished evaluating you—"

"I'm fine." I push out of her hold and sit up. She backs off with her hands up, muttering something about not getting paid nearly enough to deal with impossible patients who won't let her do her goddamn job. My visual field dances a bit but clears after a few hard blinks. Besides the passing dizziness and bruised throat, I feel totally normal.

Well, almost normal.

When I swing my legs over the side of the stretcher and stand, I sway a bit on my feet.

My eyes scan the parking lot, seeking any point of familiarity in the chaos. Uniformed agents swarm the docks like a hive of agitated bees. A fleet of unmarked black SUVs fill the lot usually reserved for rusty bait-trucks and flat-bottomed dinghies. I spot Agent Stanhope hauling a highly combative Gordo toward a waiting van. There are handcuffs on his wrists. He's cursing like a sailor, struggling like a rabid dog on a leash. Stanhope looks like she's enjoying herself — her step is practically jaunty as she forces him into the backseat of an armored DEA cruiser and slams the door shut behind him.

Pomroy looks somewhat less enthused as he and two other agents attempt to get Stutter into the back of a second vehicle.

I make my way in their direction, winding a path around several officers chattering into radios, bypassing crime scene analysts carrying sealed evidence bags in the direction of the trawler. I've never seen so many law enforcement personnel in one place. Coast Guard, DEA, Gloucester PD, State Police. Even a few firefighters are on the scene, milling about with the EMT crew.

"Archer." Pomroy's hand comes down on my shoulder and squeezes. "You okay? I thought you were headed to the hospital."

"I'm fine."

"You sure? You were out cold when SWAT pulled you out of there. Maybe you should get checked over—"

"I said I'm fine." I hold the agent's eyes, trying to read him. He seems to be avoiding my gaze. "What happened? Is it over?"

"You did great, kid." Stanhope steps up to Pomroy's side. She's smiling. "We got 'em. Hold was chock-full of heroin and meth. Biggest drug bust in Massachusetts state history. At least three tons, maybe four. It'll take days to measure it all. The crime scene guys nearly blew a gasket when they got a look inside." Her grin gets even wider. "Your brother's crew is going away for a long time. Lopez, Cisco, and Figueroa already have pretty long records. We're running background checks on the ones they call Gordo and Stutter. If they aren't already in the system, they will be after this."

"And my brother?"

Both agents are noticeably silent. The grin on Stanhope's face fades a bit.

"About that..." she hedges. "There's a tiny fly in the ointment of our otherwise spectacular success."

"We had eyes on every member of the crew. But when the smoke bombs went off inside the trawler..." Pomroy trials off. Guilt twists his features. "It was impossible to maintain a clear visual. We lost sight of your brother in the chaos."

I look from him to his partner and back again. Stanhope is no longer smiling. She looks downright contrite. Neither of them can seem to bring themselves to say it. But they don't have to — I already know.

Jaxon escaped.

"No," I hiss, voice vibrating with anger. "*No.* Do not tell me he got away from you."

"Kid, relax. He won't get far."

"How the *fuck* did you lose him?" I explode. "You told me — you promised me — you'd get him. That's the whole reason I agreed to this plan in the first place. And now you're telling me you let him get away?"

"We never promised. We don't make promises in this business." Pomroy sighs deeply, running a hand through his hair. "I'm sorry, Archer. Truly."

"*Sorry* isn't going to fix this, is it?"

"Watch your mouth. Pomroy is right — we never promised you a damn thing. No operation is perfect. No raid ever goes off without a hitch. But make no mistake, we will apprehend your brother eventually."

"That's such a comfort," I snap sarcastically. "Thanks. It's so great to know *eventually* I'll be able to live my life in peace. It's such a relief to know *eventually* he'll be behind bars, unable to terrorize the people I love."

Stanhope's eyes narrow to slits. "We've got the entire area surrounded. His whole crew is in custody. He has nowhere to turn."

"That's what you said about the trawler," I growl. "And that clearly didn't turn out the way you expected."

"Kid—"

"I'm not a kid. Stop trying to placate me. I want to know how the fuck you managed to let my brother slip out of your grasp."

"With a sting operation, there are always a lot of moving parts. By the time you called in your extraction code, we were already in motion. Our agents began closing in the moment we had verbal confirmation of the drugs onboard. We were poised for a perfect strike. But when you said that code... emergency extraction trumps everything. Wires got crossed in the chaos. A few agents moved before they were meant to. As a result, one exit point at the stern was left unmanned for approximately two minutes." She sighs. "Our best guess is, during that short interval, your brother jumped from the trawler into the water and swam off."

"No one saw where he went?"

"It's dark. The harbor is pitch black." Pomroy stares at his shoes. "It wouldn't take more than a few strokes to be completely out of our scopes."

I'm so angry, I don't trust myself to speak.

"We're going to find him," Stanhope repeats. "The Coast Guard has a firm eye on the coastline. State Police have barricades set up all along the harbor perimeter. I wouldn't be surprised if we get a radio call any minute now, confirming he's in custody."

"And if they don't catch him tonight? What am I supposed to do?"

"Lay low. Let us do our jobs. He won't get far on foot."

I glare at Stanhope, then Pomroy. "He's going to come after me. You realize that, don't you? He knows I betrayed him. He knows I'm the reason his operation fell apart. He's going to take revenge."

"That's not going to happen, kid."

But I'm not listening to their assurances, anymore. Because, even as they make more hollow promises about bringing my brother to justice... a memory is unfurling across my mind with startling clarity. I can see the menace in Jaxon's eyes; hear the scathing vow he uttered.

You think you have nothing to lose. You think you're untouchable. But if you breathe a word about my business to anyone, you won't be the one who suffers. I promise your precious Josephine will pay the price.

"I need a ride," I say abruptly, cutting off Stanhope mid-speech. "Now."

She blinks at me, startled. "What do I look like to you, a taxi service?"

"Where do you need to go, Archer?" Pomroy asks quietly. "I'll take you."

I glance at him and give a shallow nod of thanks. "The Valentine family estate, in Manchester. If my brother manages to elude you... I guarantee that's where he'll go next."

"Why there?"

"Because if he wants to hurt me..." I swallow roughly. "The best way to do that is to hurt *her*."

———

It's nearly midnight when Pomroy leaves me at the ornate wrought iron front gates with strict instructions to keep my phone on and contact him if there's any sign of my brother. He taps the steering wheel restlessly as I unbuckle my seatbelt, eager to get back to the manhunt at the docks.

When we bring him in, you'll be the first to know, he promised hurriedly, before racing off into the night. *Don't worry. You did great getting us that confession— but your part in this is over.*

It was clear from his overly soothing tone that he only brought me to Cormorant House to mollify me. My hunch means nothing to them.

Why trust the gut-instinct of a nineteen-year-old kid when you have the full force of federal law enforcement at your disposal?

The DEA is confident they'll capture Jaxon within hours. They don't think he'd be stupid enough to resurface — certainly not to seek revenge. They think I'm nuts for even suggesting that instead of running for cover, putting as many miles as possible between himself and the North Shore... he'd dare to show his face in front of the brother who betrayed him.

But they don't know Jaxon.

Not the way I do.

They don't know how his brain works. They didn't see the flash of unadulterated hatred that filled his eyes the moment before that first smoke-bomb went off, as he realized I'd betrayed him.

He will come for me.

I know it in my bones.

I punch in the front gate code, praying it hasn't changed since last summer. There's a moment of silence, followed by a low clanking sound as the gates swing inward. I walk up the circular driveway, my footsteps crunching on the imported pea stone as I make my way to the house.

It's late. All the lights are off. No doubt, Jo is fast asleep inside. Probably curled up beside her boyfriend.

I don't like it — the thought sets my teeth on edge — but so long as she's safe, I'll deal with it. I don't intend to tell her I'm here. Not now, not in the middle of the night. I'll just keep watch until dawn, an invisible layer of protection in case my brother really is dumb enough to show his face here. The chance I'm right — however slim — is still too big a risk to ignore.

I forget sometimes that this was his home, too. Before he went to prison, Jaxon lived on this sprawling property. Or, more specifically, in the staff quarters tucked away in the back thicket of trees. Gull Cottage — a single-story, shingled building we shared with Ma and Pa. I doubt he'd come back here now, but it's worth checking.

I divert down the side path that leads away from the main house toward the cottage. It's strange to be back here, but I can't deny, there's a certain morbid curiosity in my veins. Each footstep I walk closer to the place where I spent my childhood makes my pulse pound faster.

On this side of the estate, the lawn is slightly overgrown, the hedges trimmed with a rushed sloppiness my father never would've allowed, if he were still in charge of the grounds. I wonder who Blair and Vincent got to replace him. I wonder if they even hesitated as they dismissed a man who'd cared for their precious Cormorant House with meticulous precision for more than two decades.

It was all for the best, in the end. Pa sounded happier than I've ever heard him when we spoke on the phone yesterday. He has a house of his own to care for now — one he and Ma have made into a home on a small island off the coast of their native Puerto Rico.

I could hear the sound of waves crashing in the background as we chatted, tropical birds singing high-pitched songs from the trees overhead, the creak of a hammock strung up between two palms.

There are more wild horses on Vieques than there are people. They run through the yard like chickens, grazing on the herb garden, driving your mother crazy, Pa told me, a grin audible in his voice. *You'll love it. When are you coming to visit, mijo?*

Soon, I'd assured him. *Maybe I'll try out fishing in some warmer waters.*

He'd laughed, launching into a vivid description of the local catch. Long-billed marlins and colorful mahi-mahi; massive blackfin tuna and razor-mouthed barracuda.

We'll catch them all, when you visit.

Okay, Pa. It's a deal.

Some of his exuberance faded as we eventually circled around to the real reason behind my phone call. He was sad — but not entirely surprised — to hear that Jaxon has once again landed himself in trouble; that he'll most likely be heading back to prison — this time, for far longer than two years.

Before we hung up, Pa promised to share the news with Ma as gently as possible. He always does his best to spare her whatever pain he can.

Be safe, Archer. Remember, you are loved. Even if we're far away, we are always with you.

It's amazing — even through a phone, from thousands of miles away, Flora and Miguel Reyes' love shines so brightly, it could blind you. Their love for me, but also their love for one another. When I hear how happy they are in this new life they've built, it fills me with hope. Hope that love really is enough to make a relationship work.

Despite the obstacles.

Despite the whole world stacked against you.

Despite setbacks and hardships and struggles.

Love is enough.

You can watch the ground give way to darkness and defeat.... You can stand in the rubble of your old life... and you can survive it. So long as you have someone standing there beside you, picking a path forward through the ruins.

I clear the final stretch of woods and step off the path. Gull Cottage sits quietly in the clearing, its windows shuttered tight against the night, its screen porch latched closed. The sight of it hits me like a punch to the stomach. There are so many memories here. The air feels thick with them. Ghostly visions dance at the corners of my vision — Jax, Jo, and me as little kids, sprinting across the grass with bare feet, a race to the cove.

Last one in the water is a rotten egg!

Three bikes toppled over in the dirt. Three sets of muddy sneakers, left to dry on the front steps. Three colorful popsicles, half-melted in the sun.

I wish I could go back. Take those three innocent kids by the hand and steer them down a different path. One with an easier ending.

But if I've learned anything this past year...

You can't go back.

You can't change the past.

And you can't let who you used to be dictate who you're destined to become.

josephine

I CAN'T SLEEP.

I pace my bedroom, a ping-pong ball of energy flying frantically from one side to the other. There's nothing left to do. My suitcases are packed, stuffed with some clothes, my sketchbook, my laptop, and enough toiletries to get by for the next week or so. A printed copy of my reservation sits on the bed, beside my wallet — a short-term apartment rental in Rhode Island, not far from the Brown campus. Nothing fancy, but it'll suffice until I can find something more permanent. Or, until the Student Housing office decides to answer my emails.

Tomorrow afternoon, I'll take a train down to Providence — a jolting, three hour journey on the Commuter Rail. Not quite the same experience as cruising the backroads in the Porsche Cabriolet. My father's hunter green convertible — a car I've come to think of as my own, after so many hours spent driving it — is the only thing I'll miss, around here.

Or...

Almost the only thing.

My feet carry me from my bedroom almost on auto-pilot. I walk through the empty house — the furniture eerily draped

with white sheets, like a haunted mansion in a ghost story —
tugged by an instinct I do not question.

Outside, the night is cooler than expected. I shiver and
wrap my sweater tighter around my pajamas as I make my way
down to the boathouse. Moonlight bathes the grass, turning
the world to silver. I follow the sound of waves crashing in the
cove, a rhythm embedded deeply in my heart.

With each step, I try to memorize the sound. Sleeping
without the metronomic crashing of the ocean will take some
getting used to. When I first arrived in Geneva last summer, it
took weeks before my ears acclimated to the quiet.

Rhode Island is on the Atlantic, I remind myself. *Brown is just
a short drive from the ocean. And there's a university sailing team
you can join, when you're ready to take up the tiller again.*

Since I lost Cupid in the storm on July 4th, I haven't stepped
foot on a sailboat. The wounds from that day are still fresh. But
I know I'll sail again, someday. Me and the ocean — we are a
lifelong love affair. One pesky little near-drowning incident
isn't enough to change that.

The empty docks are a sad sight. I turn my back to them
and head for the boathouse instead. This is what I came for —
this is the last farewell I need to say before I leave this place for
good.

Our spot.

If I can't say goodbye to Archer in person, I'll say goodbye
to the place that most reminds me of him. I'll sit on the rafters
where we watched so many sunsets, trace the initials carved
into the wood wall, and whisper all the things I wish I'd had a
chance to tell him.

Things like, *I'm sorry.*

Things like, *I love you.*

Things like, *I can live without you...but I don't want to,
anymore.*

Inside the boathouse, my father's navy blue picnic boat rocks quietly in her berth. As I climb the ladder up into the rafters, I struggle to keep the memories of prom night at bay. They claw at me insistently, demanding my attention.

Archer and me. Skin to skin, heart to heart. Hands tugging at shirt-hems, fingers fumbling for buttons. A sting of pain. A slow-build of pleasure.

If I'd known that night was the only one I'd ever share with him, I would've never closed my eyes. I wouldn't have wasted a single second on sleep. I would've held him so close, nothing — no one — could ever pull us apart again.

I grip the rungs tighter as I reach the top, moving carefully as I haul myself through the gap in the floorboards. I maneuver slowly around the low-ceilinged space, picking a pathway through the boxes. Cursing lowly as I stub my toe on Miguel's old toolbox, I flip the switch on a small camping lantern. It emits a dim glow, lighting the rafters in shades of dusky orange.

Shaking the dust from one of the wool blankets, I spread it across the floorboards and settle atop it. It smells familiar — the faint scent of leather and fresh cut grass clinging to it, conjuring images of a boy with hazel eyes and dark hair. I burrow deeper into the fabric, arms curled around my knees, eyes fixed on the lapping waters of the cove below. The moon's reflection shines like a spotlight on the surface.

In the dark, my fingers creep to the wall, tracing the gouges like Braille. Over and over and over again.

AR + JV

4EVA

———

I must've nodded off, because I wake with a start to the sound of footsteps coming from below.

Someone is inside the boathouse.

For a second, I think it must be the maintenance man. I quickly dismiss the idea — it's still dark outside. Nowhere near dawn. I've been asleep mere minutes, not hours. Whoever it is, they aren't here to service the Hinckley. Worse, they've undoubtedly seen the light from my lantern. It's too late to hide.

Why didn't I bring my damn cellphone?

The sound of footsteps is replaced by the groan of the ladder as the intruder climbs slowly up the rungs, into the lofted space. I look around, searching frantically for some kind of weapon. My hands land on the old toolbox, plucking a rusty hammer from the depths. I cling to it, wishing my palms weren't so sweaty.

There's no place to hide. I duck my body behind a stack of boxes, partially shielded from view. My eyes are locked on the shadowy gap in the floorboards, straining to make out details. The light from the lantern barely reaches back there. When the top of a head appears, I suck in a sharp breath, steady my shoulders, and call out to the stranger.

"Stop right there! I have a weapon and I will use it!"

The head stops moving.

For a moment, there's only silence. But then, in a voice choked with barely contained laughter, the intruder calls back to me.

"Don't shoot. I come in peace. And, if memory serves, you're a lousy shot. Remember the paintball incident of sophomore year?"

The hammer slips from my grip, falling to the floorboards with a thud. I very nearly fall down after it.

"Archer?"

He pulls his long limbs up into the loft, his grin flashing brightly in the dim light. I can't think as he makes his way to me, moving methodically around stacks of boxes and haphazardly piled furniture. His eyes are locked on mine, pinning me in place. I don't dare blink, don't dare breathe, as he comes to a stop before me.

"Hey, Jo." His voice is whisper-soft. "What are you doing up here?"

I blink stupidly at him. "What am I doing up here? What are *you* doing up here?"

"I saw you walking down the lawn about twenty minutes ago. When you didn't walk back, I figured I'd check on you."

"I fell asleep..."

"I suspected as much."

"But that doesn't explain why you're here — at Cormorant House, I mean." My brows furrow in sudden agitation. "I've been looking for you!"

His mouth parts in surprise. "You were looking for me?"

"Yes! I went to your apartment. I knocked for ages."

"When?"

"Yesterday! I thought..."

"Thought what?" he murmurs when I trail off.

I thought you didn't want to see me.

I thought I wouldn't get to say goodbye.

I swallow hard. "It doesn't matter! The point is, I was looking for you. And you're telling me you were right here this whole time?!"

"Not the whole time. I only got here about an hour ago."

"You came here in the middle of the night?"

"Yeah."

He's staring at me with such intent focus, it steals my breath. His face is distractingly close. I can't think straight with his mouth mere inches from mine. I try to step back, but there's nowhere to go in the tiny space.

Why is he here?

Why now?

"So..." I whisper breathily. "You just thought we'd have a quick chat at two in the morning?"

He laughs, but can't quite disguise the strain in his voice. "Afraid not. I'm just here to keep an eye out in case my brother shows up."

"Why would Jaxon come here?"

"He's on the run. The DEA is hunting him down. That's the reason I wasn't home last night... there was a raid at the docks. Jaxon and his crew have been trafficking drugs through Gloucester Harbor. I helped the agents get enough evidence to shut it down. They arrested everyone — Jaxon's whole crew. But he somehow slipped away during the chaos."

My eyes have gone wide. I can feel them, saucer-like on my face, staring at him. "You helped the DEA conduct a drug raid?"

He nods.

"That's so dangerous!" I smack him on the arm."What were you thinking?"

"I was thinking it's about damn time someone put a stop to my brother."

"What if you'd been hurt? What if—"

"I'm fine!"

"But—" I splutter into silence as he reaches out and takes my hand. His callused palm scrapes lightly against mine as its enveloped in his strong grip. I bite back an involuntary gasp as the feel of his touch radiates through me, moving from my fingers up my forearm, straight into my chest, where my heart is pounding a mad tattoo.

"Jo." His hand tightens — strong and sure, steadying me instantly. "I'm okay. Really."

"Okay," I breathe, barely trusting my own voice. "Okay."

"Why did you come looking for me yesterday?"

The question catches me off guard; I don't have an answer at the ready. "I wanted to tell you..." I struggle for the right words. "I'm leaving."

"Oh." He stiffens. Something like defeat flashes in his eyes. "You're going back to Geneva, then. You're going back with him."

"No!" I tighten my grip when he starts to pull his hand from mine. "No, Archer. I'm not. I'm just leaving Cormorant House. Or...Technically, I'm being forced to leave. My parents are changing the access codes tomorrow."

His brows lift. "What? Why?"

"When I left your apartment the other day... I was over-whelmed. I was shocked. I was sad. I was angry. But most of all, I was just... *Done*. Finished. Finished with this life. Finished with being my parents' puppet. Finished with living under their control. Finished letting them dictate who I am — and who I love."

Archer inhales sharply, but doesn't interrupt.

"I drove to Providence. Met with my academic advisor. I'm not going back to Switzerland. I'm officially enrolling at Brown for the fall semester." My lips twist. "Of course, I'll have a mountain of student loans and probably spend the next decade paying them back. The bank will be my new puppet-master. But it'll be worth it. Because it will be my choice. Because I'll be living on no one's terms except my own, for the first time in my life."

His gaze is soft. Warm. Full of pride. "That's amazing, Jo."

"Thank you." I smile wryly. "Blair and Vincent felt differ-ently, as you can imagine. They're furious I'm not going back to work at VALENT. They cut me off. I think they're under the impression that I won't make it without their money and connections. But I'm pretty damn determined to prove them wrong." I shrug my shoulders. "I'd rather be all alone, living off microwavable ramen noodles in a crappy apartment than trapped in a life without meaning surrounded by fancy furniture and people who don't understand me. Who don't love me — not for who I really am."

Archer doesn't say anything for a long moment. But then, he lifts our interlocked hands, examining them in the low light. After a few seconds, I realize he's searching for an engagement ring on my fourth finger. When he finds it bare, I hear him inhale sharply. His eyes drift back to mine; I see a question smoldering in their depths.

"I gave it back," I whisper. "The ring."

Archer's jaw tightens. I see a muscle leap in his cheek. "Why?"

"I couldn't marry him." I swallow hard. "Not when..."

"When what, Jo?"

I reach up to cup his face with my free hand. He leans his cheek into my touch, his eyes half-closing on a sigh. "Not when I'm in love with someone else."

His arms come around me, hauling me against his chest. He bends, catching my mouth with his as we sink down onto our knees. The wool blanket is scratchy-soft beneath us. His lips crash down against mine in a kiss that makes the whole world spin, a kaleidoscope of color around me. I tremble in his arms as he slides his hands beneath the back of my sweater, callused palms skimming up my spine.

My hands are conducting an exploration of their own — pushing at the bottom hem of his white t-shirt, tracing the defined indentations of his abdominal muscles. His stomach contracts as he sucks in a sharp breath when my fingers dance up the line of hair that leads from his naval down toward the button of his jeans.

Our mouths break apart only long enough to strip off our clothing. I gulp in air as he tosses my thin pink pajama top across the loft. He pants as I pull his t-shirt up over his head. When his eyes return to mine, scanning up and down my naked torso, they're full of fire. The same fire that ignites in my core when he reaches out to palm my breasts in his hands. The sensation of rough callus against sensitive nipple knifes through me so sharply, I have to swallow down a moan.

"Do you know how often I think about this skin?" he whispers against my lips, kissing me deeply once more. "So soft. So delicate."

His bare chest presses against mine, warm and strong. His hands slide beneath the drawstring waist of my sleep shorts, cupping my ass firmly, pulling me flush against him.

"I'm not so delicate," I whisper back, leaning into him.

"You are." His teeth sink into my bottom lip, tugging gently. It's excruciatingly erotic. I nearly mewl into his mouth. "I'm almost afraid to touch you. Like... I might break you."

"You won't break me," I promise as I reach for his zipper. I can feel the steely length of him, pressed against the confines of his jeans, begging for release. "But Archer?"

"Yeah, Jo?" he asks in a husky voice.

"Even if you did break me, I don't think I'd mind."

I push at the elastic band of his underwear until they fall down around his knees. His cock springs free, hard and ready. A breath hisses from between his clenched teeth as I begin to stroke him, marveling at the strangely intoxicating mix of velvet skin and steely desire.

I have no idea what I'm doing, no real experience to draw on, so I follow my best instincts — closing my hand around his shaft, pumping gently up and down. His grunt of appreciation tells me I'm doing something right. I increase my speed, staring into his face the entire time. Watching as my touch slowly drives him wild. His eyes are slits of desire, locked on mine. He's almost shuddering with it.

When his hand moves between my legs, cupping the most sensitive part of me, it's my turn to shudder. His fingers slide through the wet evidence of my desire and push into my core, filling me in a way I've been longing to be filled for so long, it's hard to fathom.

Our mouths meet again, more frantic, more ravenous than before, devouring each other as our hands work in tandem, bringing our passion to the precipice. The ache between my legs is growing unbearable. I need to be sated, filled by something far more substantial than his fingers.

We tumble to the floor, Archer coming down hard atop me. His weight flattens me completely, but I don't care. My bones have turned to liquid gold, molten with longing. When he pulls his lips from mine and looks down at me, his eyes are full of such stark desperation, I know I'm not the only one on the brink of combustion.

"I wasn't expecting this," he says breathlessly. "I didn't... I don't have a condom."

I shake my head. "It doesn't matter. I'm on the pill."

He looks at me for a long time. "I haven't been with anyone else. Not since last summer. Not since we were together."

"Neither have I," I whisper.

His mouth slams onto mine again, a kiss of so much passion, it almost feels like a possession. Like I'm being claimed, owned, marked as his. With any other man, I might mind. I might protest. I might refute. But this is Archer. There's no lie in his kiss — no refuting the truth of it.

I am his.

I have always been his.

I watch him through slitted eyes as he shoves the rest of the way out of his jeans and underwear. My hips lift eagerly as he hooks his hands in the fabric of my pajama shorts and strips them off me.

"God, Jo. You're so fucking beautiful. Do you know that?" He kisses his way down my stomach, a trail of adoration that makes me squirm against the wool blanket. "I could stare at you for the rest of my life, it wouldn't be long enough. And when I touch you... it's like an addiction. The more I get, the more I want. I don't think I'll ever be satisfied."

"There are worse addictions," I murmur, pulling him back up my body, so our faces are level. "Don't you think?"

His mouth returns to mine, kissing me hungrily as he settles between my legs. I revel in the sensation of his weight on me; at the press of his shaft, poised at the apex of my thighs.

I need him inside me, now. I need us to be joined as one again. Together in the most intimate way. I've needed it for a year — every minute of every day since we parted last summer. Every second since he walked out of my life and left me a hollow shell.

"Archer," I beg, winding my legs around his hips. My hands slide across the broad planes of his back, where muscles ripple. "Make love to me. Please."

We both cry out as he pushes inside me. I tense. It's a tight fit — for a moment, I brace myself for the initial pain I felt the first time we did this. But the pain never comes. Instead, a wave of pleasure sweeps through me — a ripple of need that builds and builds with each thrust, cresting into a tsunami that sweeps through my entire body. A relentless tide.

"There are no words for what you make me feel, Josephine." He grunts out the statement, each word timed to another thrust. "You're mine. You've always been mine."

"*Archer!*" I cry, lost in a current of rapture.

"Say it."

"I'm yours," I gasp. He's so deep, it's making me delirious.

369

"I've always been yours." My fingertips dig into his shoulders. "And you're mine."

"Damn right, baby." His tongue strokes mine, a brutal kiss that steals my breath. "I'm yours. Now. Then. Always."

Our mouths connect and, this time, refuse to break apart. There are no more words to exchange, no more thoughts to share. We are beyond that, now. I can only cling to him as he fucks me harder, deeper, his hips moving faster and faster. Driving me beyond the point of logical thought, to a place of pure sensation.

Him.

Me.

Our spot.

Skin on skin.

Heart to heart.

Our hands lock together, flat on the floorboards above my head. Our gazes are magnets, never shifting as we both ride the wave all the way down to the depths.

Drowning in one another.

Never wanting to resurface.

I cry out his name as the orgasm shatters through me, sending me crashing. And I hear mine on his lips, an exultant shout of release, as he spills his passion into me with desperate pumps.

I love this man.

Beyond thought.

Beyond sense.

Beyond reason.

And as I hold him close, breathing hard from the efforts of our lovemaking, my head still awhirl with aftershocks of desire, I only have one thought.

He is mine, surely as I am his.

I will never let him go.

———

After, we lay in the darkness — a tangle of naked limbs sprawled across the wool blanket. Dawn is breaking in the distance, the first rays of the day lightening the horizon. We do not move. We stay exactly as we are, breathing each other in. Savoring the moment.

"Sleep," he murmurs, kissing the crown of my head. "You must be tired."

"I... I'm scared to fall asleep."

"Why?"

"The last time we did this..." I press my eyes closed at the memory of prom night. The ache in my heart when I awoke that day alone. "You were gone."

His arms tighten around me, holding me firmly against his chest. His mouth presses harder against my hair. "I'm not going anywhere, Jo. I'm not going anywhere ever again."

"You promise?"

"I promise." His body shudders beneath me as he inhales. "And I'm sorry. You'll never know how sorry I am, about that day. If I could take that memory away, I would. If I could go back and change things..."

I tilt my head to catch his eyes. "I know. And you don't have to be sorry. I forgive you."

His lips brush mine gently — a kiss so sweet and so soft, tears fill my eyes. "Thank you. You have no idea how much I needed to hear that."

We're quiet for a few moments. I trace patterns on the bare skin of his chest, mimicking the carved letters on the wall.

AR + JV

4EVA

He chuckles sleepily, his lips curved in amusement. "That's right. 4EVA. *Forever.* Knew it even back then."

I snuggle closer. If I could burrow under his skin and disappear, I would do it. I appease myself with listening to his heartbeat instead, each steady thump a reminder that he's really here. Holding me. Loving me.

Mine.

"Archer?"

"Mmm?" He sounds drowsy. His eyes are closed.

"Can I ask you something?"

"Anything."

"You said Jaxon is on the run..."

"Mmm."

"And you came here because..."

"He knows I betrayed him," he murmurs. His voice is thick with sleep, teetering on the edge of consciousness. "He'll lash out at me however he can."

"Right..." My mind turns over the details, trying to make sense of this unexpected turn of events. "But... why would he come *here*, of all places? If he was hunting you down, wouldn't he go to your apartment? Or your boat?"

"Because he knows..." He pauses carefully. His eyes sliver open, staring up at the rafter ceiling. When he speaks, it's with such quiet conviction, such stalwart purpose, there's no denying the truth in his words. "I love you, Jo. More than anything. He could trash my apartment, he could sink my boat. I'd recover. But if he ever hurt you, I wouldn't survive it. If he took you from me..." His arms are so tight around me, I can barely breathe.

I don't care. I hug him back, just as hard.

"I don't want to live in a world without you, Josephine Valentine. Even when we weren't together... the only thing that kept me going was the thought of you out there somewhere, lighting up the room — lighting up the damn world — with your smile." His chest expands and contracts, a rattling breath.

"Even when I'd lost everything else... you were my reason to carry on. To keep breathing. To keep hoping that, someday, things might get better. I meant it when I said you were my dream. My hope. My whole heart."

For a moment, I can't say anything at all. A tear drips down my cheek — I watch it pool on his skin. I trail my fingertip through it, tracing the shape of a heart. My voice comes out thick with emotion as I lay my head against his ribcage and close my eyes.

"Archer?"

"Yeah, Jo?"

"I love you too."

archer

THE SMELL of smoke wakes me.

My eyes snap open. It takes a few seconds to shake off my confusion; to remember where I am. The naked girl in my arms is a pretty big clue. We're in our spot in the old stone boathouse, bodies curled together beneath a scratchy wool blanket. I smile at the memory of last night.

The smile flattens as another wave of smoke — astringent and bitter on the wind — hits my nostrils. Something is burning. Something far bigger than a beach bonfire or a backyard BBQ grill. The smell is so strong, for a terrifying heartbeat I think it might be up here with us, in the wooden rafters. When I look out over the water, I see a massive black plume drifting across the cove, noxious and roiling against the pale morning sky.

"Jo," I murmur, shaking her gently. "*Jo!*"

Her dark lashes fan across her cheeks, fluttering as she stirs awake. "Archer?"

"Jo, wake up." I glance around for my clothes. My jeans are slung over a nearby nightstand. My t-shirt is wadded in a ball beside an old toolbox. "We have to get out of here. There's a fire."

"A fire?" She sits up, abruptly awake. Her hair falls around her shoulders in messy waves. She holds the blanket against her bare chest, staring at me with worry. "What do you mean, a fire?"

"Don't you smell that?"

She inhales deeply. I watch her eyes widen. "Oh, god. Wait — *listen!*"

I pause, jeans frozen halfway up my hips. My ears strain for a moment before I hear it. There's a dull roar in the air. The searing, steady crackle of a massive flame.

It's close.

Very close.

Fear grips me as I meet Jo's eyes. I see the same terror reflected back at me.

"Hurry," I order, tossing over her pajamas and sweater. "Put these on. We'll go see what's happening."

We dress in haste, then scramble down the ladder as quickly as possible. When we emerge from the boathouse, into the daylight, the sight that greets us is so shocking, we both stop short.

Cormorant House is engulfed in fire.

Flames lick at the windows, dance across the roof shingles. The whole structure is ablaze, from the terrace all the way to the upper turrets. It's hard to believe a fire could spread so fast, could burn so hot. I've never seen anything like it. Even here, halfway down the lawn, it's hot as a furnace. Heat billows at us, like standing in front of a thousand-degree oven.

"Oh my god," Jo whispers. "Oh my *god.*"

I grab her hand and interlock our fingers together. "It's okay," I tell her, though the statement feels laughably far from the truth. "You're okay. There's no one inside, right?"

"No." She shakes her head. "Thank God I went to the boathouse..."

We glance at one another, then at her bedroom window. The glass pane has shattered. Her curtains are burning. Inside, the inferno rages visibly, spreading across her bed, up the wall panels.

If she'd been inside...

She'd be dead.

No one could survive that.

No one.

Jo's eyes never shift from her bedroom window. I know she's thinking the same thoughts.

"Here," I say to distract her, reaching into my pocket and pulling out my cellphone. I press it into her palm. "We'll call 911. They'll send over the fire department. Maybe something can be salvaged..."

It's a lie. We both know it's a lie. Even if the fire department manages to subdue this blaze, there will be nothing left but waterlogged wreckage when they're finished. But Jo curls her fingers around the phone anyway and begins to dial.

"Drop the phone," a disembodied voice says from our left. "Now."

We both whip toward the sound, just in time to watch Jaxon step from the tree-line. He reeks of gasoline — my first indication that this inferno was no electrical fluke. His fingers are black with ash... and curled around a handgun.

He lifts it, aiming straight for Jo.

My heart stops.

"I said," Jax mutters lowly. "Drop the fucking cellphone."

She lets it tumble from her fingers, landing in the grass with a dull thump. I step in front of her, so she's shielded by my body. Jaxon watches me with unmasked amusement. He can see clearly that I'm scared. He's enjoying it.

"What are you doing here, Jaxon?"

"Isn't it obvious?" He laughs. There's an unhinged edge to it — the sound of a man at the end of his rope, watching it fray a bit more with each passing moment. "Don't say I didn't warn you, brother. I told you what would happen if you betrayed me. I told you I'd come after her."

"This has nothing to do with her. This is about you and me."

"This stopped being about you and me when you brought in the fucking DEA. After all I did for you — all I offered you. You chose to turn your back on me. For what? For *her*?" He spits on the ground. "She's not worth it."

"So what are you going to do, Jax? You're going to kill me? Shoot me dead, right here?"

"Maybe." He cocks the gun higher, so it's pointed straight at my chest. "It's no more than you deserve. Maybe I'll kill the both of you. If the bitch had been in her bed, like she was supposed to, she'd already be a pile of ash."

I nearly lunge for him — only the gun aimed at my chest keeps my knees locked and my feet still. My self-control is dangling by a thread. Rage flares through me, deadly as the fire raging only feet away.

Behind me, I can feel Jo shaking violently. Her hands press against the upper planes of my back, her forehead digs into my spine. I wish there was something I could do to comfort her. Mostly, I wish there was some way to get her out of here — away from the fire, away from Jaxon. Somewhere safe, where he can't touch her.

If the DEA had only listened to me last night, we wouldn't be in this fucking predicament. They're off searching the harbor for Jaxon, running around in circles like chickens with their heads cut off.

Useless.

Again.

My mind whirls, making calculations, weighing pros and cons rapid-fire. If I can retreat a few steps, get close enough to the boathouse door... maybe I can distract him long enough for Jo to make a run for it.

She could get to safety.

And I...

I don't think too hard about what will happen to me.

"You think killing me is going to fix this mess you've made, Jax?" I step backward, making sure to shield Jo as I do. She moves with me, shuffling backward across the grass. "You think getting revenge on me is somehow going to erase everything you've done?"

He glares at me, his jaw clenched tight.

"You hear those sirens?" I ask. They're still distant, but coming closer. Someone — maybe a neighbor — must've called the fire department. "You'd better make up your mind, Jax. Kill me if you want. But let Josephine go."

"No!" she cries, her voice muffled by my t-shirt.

"I don't think you want to kill me," I tell him bluntly, taking another step backward. "I think you just want to make me as miserable as you are. Your insides are so toxic, so full of poison, the only way to feel better is by spreading it to everyone around you."

"Shut up!" he snarls.

"You think Ma and Pa will understand? That they'll forgive you?" I shake my head, laughing. Taking another careful step. Jo's fingertips dig into my shoulder blades, trying to send me some kind of message through the fabric. "They'll disown you. You'll be dead to them, along with me. They'll lose both sons. Is that what you want?"

"They've already disowned me!"

"That's not true. Our parents love you, Jax." Another step. Under my feet, I feel stone instead of grass. I don't dare look, but I know we're only a handful of feet from the door. "Even now, after everything, they'll find a way to forgive you. To love you. But if you kill me? If you kill Jo? What do you think will happen?"

His jaw tightens even more. He looks away for a moment, considering my words. I use the momentary distraction to shove Jo, hard, toward the boathouse. She bolts for the door. She's nearly there when Jaxon screams, "*STOP!*"

He's pointing the gun at me again, advancing on us. Jo is frozen at my side, clear in the line of fire. I vault in front of her, flattening her back against the stone wall of the boathouse. I hear her gasp as the breath leaves her lungs in a whoosh of air.

There's fury on Jaxon's face as he closes the gap between us. I see my death in his eyes, my gruesome fate playing out on the pinpricks of his pupils like a tiny projector screen.

He's going to kill me.

He's really going to kill me.

"Jo," I say.

One word.

The only word I have time to say.

I hope it's enough.

I hope she knows what it means.

I love you.

I love you.

I love you.

Jaxon takes aim.

His trigger-finger tightens.

I close my eyes.

———

The sharp flash-bang of gunfire never comes. Instead, there's a dull sort of boom. When my eyes snap back open, Jaxon is lying on the grass in an unconscious heap of limbs. Standing over him is none other than Tommy Mahoney. He's holding a wrench in one hand — which I presume he's just used to bludgeon my brother — and Jaxon's gun in the other. His toolbox sits by his feet.

"T-*Tommy*?" I stutter in disbelief.

I've never been so shocked to see someone in my life.

"Hey, kid." His eyes flicker to Jaxon for a moment. "Assuming this is the brother I've heard so much about."

I can't form words. My brain seems to have short-circuited. The sirens are getting louder; the fire department will be here any moment.

Josephine plants her hands on my back and shoves her way to freedom. "God, you nearly flattened me," she gasps, stepping out onto the grass. "I couldn't breathe back there!"

"Next time I'm shielding you from gunfire, I'll try to keep that in mind."

She's glaring fiercely. "Next time? There will be no next time! Unless I decide to kill you myself! What did you think you were doing, offering yourself up as a sacrifice? Trading your life for mine?" She smacks me on the arm. Beneath the thin veil of anger, I can see how scared she is — her whole body is trembling like a leaf in a gale. "You said you weren't going to leave me! You promised!"

I reach for her, trying to pull her into my arms. I know as soon as I do, this facade of anger will crumble.

She dodges, still glaring at me. A petite blonde ball of pure fury. "Don't you get it? You can't leave. I just got you back."

"Jo..."

"You're not allowed to die, Archer Reyes! You're not allowed to be the hero! Do you hear me?"

"I hear you, Jo."

"That means no more bargaining with bad guys. No more

acting like your life isn't worth anything. No more hurling yourself in front of guns." Her finger jabs into my chest with each new demand. "Swear to me!"

"Okay! Okay. I swear!"

She nods, satisfied.

Behind us, there's a low chuckle from Tommy.

Peering around me, Jo smiles at him like they're old friends. "Oh. Hey, Mr. Mahoney. Good to see you again."

"Again?" I glance back and forth between the two of them. "You two know each other?"

"He's the boat maintenance man," Jo says, like it should've been obvious. She hooks her arm through mine, so our elbows lock together, and cranes her neck to grin up at me. "He's been coming here every week, all summer long."

I eye my old boss. "And you never told me."

Tommy looks beyond pleased with himself. Beyond that, he looks undeniably proud. His eyes move back and forth between me and Jo, glinting with emotions I know he'll never say aloud. "Told you, kid — every Superman needs a Lois Lane to keep him in line. Glad you've finally found yours."

I shake my head, not sure whether to laugh or scowl.

Jo's brows lift, but she doesn't comment. "Lucky you were here today," she tells him, coughing lightly. The smoke is still thick in the air, blowing toward us in relentless black puffs. "Thank you. You saved us."

"I saw the fire through the trees when I pulled up out front. I got worried — no one was answering the intercom. So I called it into the station, then..." He shrugs sheepishly. "Rammed down your gate with my truck. Hope that's not a problem."

Jo laughs. "Not at all."

He nods. "The front of the house was fully engulfed, so I came around the back..." His gaze moves to mine. "That's when I spotted you down here with your brother. Didn't look like a warm and fuzzy family reunion — at least, not to my old eyes. Thought you might need a bit of backup."

I glance down at Jaxon's unconscious form. "You thought right."

Tommy pauses a long beat. His expression grows misty with memories. "I'm just glad I got here in time. When I was younger... there was a fire at my house. I lost everything. My entire family, gone in a blink."

I gently detach my arm from Jo's and walk toward him. His hands are occupied, still holding the gun and the wrench, but that actually works in my favor. He can't do a damn thing to avoid it when I step forward and embrace him tightly.

"You have a family now, Tommy. We're family."

He doesn't say anything, but that's okay. He doesn't have to. A gruff grunt escapes his mouth, followed by a muttered, "All right, all right, don't make a fuss."

I grin as I step back.

Jo's hand creeps into mine. "The fire department is here."

I glance up the slope of lawn. Sure enough, uniformed men are running around Cormorant House, doing their damndest to battle the flames. I doubt they'll try for long — it's a lost cause.

"Waste of water," I murmur. My eyes find Jo's. "I'm sorry. I know it's your home."

"That place was never my home. Let it burn. I won't miss it."

"Jo..."

"*You're* my home," she says simply. "You're enough."

I wrap my arm around her shoulders and press my mouth to hers.

"Well, well, well," a smug voice calls, arriving on the scene. "It's about damn time!"

I groan as I pull my mouth from Jo's. Chris Tomlinson is jogging down the lawn, grinning like a crazy person. He whistles wolfishly. "You two crazy kids finally admit you're ga-ga for one another?"

I roll my eyes. "Tomlinson, can you please focus?"

"Oh, I am." He waggles his eyebrows.

Jo snorts softly. "I think he meant focus on the arrest, Chris."

At Tommy's feet, Jaxon is coming to. He moans pathetically, reaching up to rub his temple. There's a massive red welt forming there — Tommy really clocked him.

"Should I hit him again?" Tommy asks.

"That won't be necessary," Chris says cheerfully, pulling out a set of handcuffs. "I can see the headlines now: *MBTS Officer Chris Tomlinson cracks drug case after failed DEA manhunt.* If this doesn't get me off desk-duty, nothing will..."

Tomlinson takes my brother into custody, dragging his sorry form up the lawn with the help of two other MBTS officers. Tommy follows, giving a statement to one of the policemen.

Jo and I stand together by the boathouse, watching Cormorant House disappear. Beams crumble, falling to the ground in an eruption of embers. Vintage furniture, draped in flammable sheets, goes up like kindling. Heavy draperies, doused with Jaxon's gasoline, spread the flames from floor to ceiling, leaving no inch spared.

Soon, there will be nothing left.

"A world without the Valentine estate," I murmur, watching the ceiling collapse. "It's the end of an era."

"No," Jo whispers. "Not the end."

I look down at her. My lips skim hers, the whisper of a kiss. "You're right. It's the start of something better."

She pushes up onto her tiptoes, deepening the kiss. Sliding

her arms around my neck. I close my eyes and hold her close, shutting out the rest of the world. With each passing moment our mouths move together, a bit more of the past burns away. All the darkness, all the damage. I feel it lift, rising off my shoulders and into the sky, drifting away on clouds of smoke.

Leaving space for light.

For love.

For life.

Our life.

The one we begin to build in this moment, on the fire-razed ground of everything we have endured. A future full of promise, instead of pain. I don't know what that future will look like. But I know, so long as I have Josephine by my side, it will be well worth the struggle it took to earn it.

"Let's go," I tell her softly. "Let's get out of here."

She doesn't ask where we're going. She merely smiles at me — a smile of so much sunshine, it makes me smile back — and laces her hand with mine. So tight, it makes my finger bones crunch.

"Together?"

"Together."

epilogue

SIX MONTHS LATER

THE SAND IS hot beneath my bare feet. A light, tropical breeze stirs the hair around my face as I stare out over the crashing turquoise waves.

I'm going to miss this.

Two tan arms wrap around my midsection without warning. I'm pulled back against a warm chest. Archer's deep voice rumbles in my ear as he bends his head to nuzzle my neck.

"You ready to go back to cold New England?"

"Not at all." I sigh. "But spring semester starts on Monday."

We've spent my winter break here, on the sun-kissed beaches of Vieques. Riding horses with Miguel, cooking delicious meals with Flora. Laughing and loving each other far

385

from the snowdrifts of Rhode Island. The frigid waves of Narraganset Bay seem a world away, as we stand here on the precipice of the Caribbean, our toes in the sand, warm sea-foam frothing around our ankles.

"We'll come back next winter," Archer promises. His chin hooks over my shoulder. "Maybe we'll bring Tommy. He's going out of his mind with boredom, now that he's retired. The man joined a bowling league for god's sake."

A laugh tinkles from my lips. "We should invite him. I'd pay good money just to see that stubborn old fart in a Hawaiian shirt and shorts."

"That would be quite a sight."

I turn in his arms, looping my wrists over his shoulders so we are face to face. His eyes scan down my body with appreciation, lingering on every curve beneath my bright yellow bikini.

"Don't you look at me like that, Archer Reyes."

"Like what?"

"Like you're planning to eat me alive."

His grin is wolfish. I have no more than a second to brace myself when he drops suddenly, ducks his shoulder into my stomach, and hitches me up over his shoulder.

"Hey!" I protest, spanking his butt. I can barely get the word out over my laughter.

He runs headlong into the waves. They crash around us, a warm embrace, as we fall into them in a tangle of limbs. When our heads break the surface, I wind my legs around his waist and bring my lips to his in a lingering kiss that sets a fire inside me.

"Remind me again why we have to leave?" I whisper.

"You can't miss your classes."

"Right. Classes." I bump my nose into his. "Plus, you have your new coaching gig."

Archer smiles. "As soon as the diamond is thawed, we'll start spring training."

He doesn't talk about it much, but I can tell he's thrilled by this new venture. Last fall, at the urging of Chris Tomlinson, Archer called his old coach at Exeter Academy to ask if he knew of any coaching opportunities. His tee-ball camp was over, and he wanted to find a way to keep baseball in his life.

Coach Hamm offered him a position as assistant coach on the spot — one Archer gladly filled all autumn, while I was away in Providence. It was a perfect fit for him. The long practices kept him busy while I was in classes during the week; the games occupied him on the rare weekends I wasn't able to make it home. He did such a great job as assistant coach, he's been put in charge of the entire JV team this spring.

It doesn't pay much. Archer still heads out most mornings to check his traps on my namesake, The Josephine. Lobsters keep the lights on and the rent for our new apartment — a modern loft overlooking Gloucester Harbor, a stone's throw from the docks and a four minute walk to Tommy's place — covered each month. But Archer doesn't coach for the stipend. He coaches because he loves the game.

Baseball is a part of him. It's in his soul. And getting out on that field again has brought so much light back into his eyes, sometimes it nearly blinds me.

It hasn't been all sunshine, of course. After Jaxon's arrest, after the fire, we had some dark days. It's not easy to shake off the past and start anew. We had so much baggage to unpack.

His brother.

My parents.

Our year of distance.

But with him by my side, I have no doubt we're going to make it. There's no question in my mind. We were broken, once, so badly I feared we could never be rebuilt. But the damage only made us stronger.

At my neck, the fisherman's knot necklace catches the sun, glinting gold.

True love does not break.

It only strengthens.

And so will we.

I stare into Archer's face. A face I know as well as my own in the mirror. I could trace its lines by heart. I could draw it in total darkness. It is the face of the man I love. The face of my best friend. The face of my oldest confidant. The face of my lover. The face of my someday-husband.

One day, we will build a family together — one with children and a house and maybe a dog. There will be too much laundry and a stack of dishes in the sink. Baseball cleats of many sizes will line the mudroom. It will be loud and messy and chaotic.

And I can't wait for it.

But until then — until we're ready — I will be content with what we have.

This.

Us.

This moment.

This man.

Together, in the sun.

Forever.

THE END

playlist

1. **The Medicine** — Sam DeRosa
2. **Love You From A Distance** — Ashley Kutcher
3. **Dancing With Your Ghost** — Sasha Alex Sloan
4. **If I'm Being Honest** — Anna Clendening
5. **Swollen** — Francisco Martin
6. **A Little Bit Yours** — JP Saxe
7. **Kids Again** — Sam Smith
8. **Friend** — Gracie Abrams
9. **You Broke Me First** — Tate McRae
10. **Words Ain't Enough** — Tessa Violet
11. **Motion Sickness** — Phoebe Bridgers
12. **Lonely** — Friend In Law
13. **Don't You Worry** — Oh Wonder
14. **Remember That Night** — Sara Kays
15. **Is It Just Me?** — Emily Burns
16. **Liability** — Lorde
17. **Renegade (feat. Taylor Swift)** — Big Red Machine
18. **Out of This Car** — Emily Weisband
19. **Rich Boy** — Sara Kays
20. **Till Forever Falls Apart** — Ashe & FINNEAS

about the author

JULIE JOHNSON is a Boston
native suffering from an extreme
case of Peter Pan Syndrome.
When she's not writing, Julie can
most often be found adding
stamps to her passport, drinking
too much coffee, striving to

conquer her Netflix queue, and Instagramming pictures of her
dog. (Follow her: @author_julie)

She published her debut novel LIKE GRAVITY in August
2013, just before her senior year of college, and she's never
looked back. Since, she has published more than a dozen other
novels, including the bestselling BOSTON LOVE STORY series,
THE GIRL DUET, and THE FADED DUET. Her books have
appeared on Kindle and iTunes Bestseller lists around the
world, as well as in AdWeek, Publishers Weekly, and USA
Today.

You can find Julie on Facebook or contact her on her
website www.juliejohnsonbooks.com. Sometimes, when she
can figure out how Twitter works, she tweets from @Author-
Julie. For major book news and updates, subscribe to Julie's
newsletter: http://eepurl.com/bnWtHH

———

Connect with Julie:
www.juliejohnsonbooks.com
juliejohnsonbooks@gmail.com

also by julie johnson